THE NINE ROAMERS
BOOK 1

THE SYLVAN SWORD

THE NINE ROAMERS BOOK 1

THE SYLVAN SWORD

N. Gabanski

The Nine Roamers and the Sylvan Sword

Copyright © 2020 N. Gabanski

Content Editor: Katie Schmeisser
Copy Editor: Anita Gibson
Cover Art: A. Gabanski
Editor-in-Chief: Kristi King-Morgan
Formatting: Kristi King-Morgan
Assistant Editor: Maddy Drake

ISBN- 978-1-947381-39-1

www.dreamingbigpublications.com

I dedicate this novel to my late father, Gilbert. You may not have said that you were proud of me, dad; only finding out after your passing, that you were. I know you're smiling down on me, wherever you are, old man. I finally did it.

PROLOGUE

Ivory cloak rustling in the wind, the tall woman padded along the streets of Sraztari. Peasants and merchants alike bustled about, tending to their own business. None of them saw the mysterious woman walking by, for she was a witch and her spell rendered her invisible to all. As she strode along her path, some unseen force shoved others out of her way. Confused protests clamored behind the smirking woman; her face obscured by the cowl of her hood. Before her loomed Castle Sraztari, the king's great hall and hearth. Approaching the towering walls of the keep, she murmured another spell.

"Thaero minochamli temfyra."

Seemingly of its own volition, the drawbridge lowered itself on thick clanking chains. Much to the witch's amusement, the guards stationed on the wall were sent into a frenzy as they tried to raise the bridge, struggling at the unyielding cranks. Silent as an owl in flight, she crossed under the portcullis and made her way for the keep proper, swinging the wide doors open with a sweep of her arms. As she entered the castle, her enchantments faded, and the guards hurriedly cranked the drawbridge shut as the doors closed behind her.

Now the witch glided down wide hallways, her bare feet stepping lightly along the carpeted floor. Entering the throne room, she wasn't completely disappointed to find it devoid of royalty, but the few servants and lower-ranked officials present were more than helpful. Delving into their minds, the witch quickly gleaned the king's location.

"In your Great Hall with talks of war, are we?" she chuckled softly, quickly leaving the throne room to head deeper into the castle.

The dark-haired witch soon found herself before a pair of thick oaken doors, guarded by four sentries. Flicking a few pale fingers, the doors unbolted and opened of their own accord, swinging inward on oiled hinges. It took but a moment for the king and his Council to notice the portals had opened to disrupt their meeting.

"Who dares!?" the king growled, rising from his seat at the high table.

At the far end of the hall, the witch stepped through, passing unseen by the confounded guards. She reached up to lower her white hood, lifting her spell of invisibility and let out a rich laugh.

"Who dares indeed, King Malder!"

"Alura!" he snarled. "To what displeasure do I owe this unwelcome visit?"

"Oh?" she mock-pouted, gliding to the Council's wide table. "I cannot simply call on my neighbor? And I came bearing good tidings."

"Bah! The only good tidings you bring are good for yourself. Begone, witch!"

Alura stopped, a mere few meters from the king. A wicked grin slowly spread across her pale lips and so very suddenly, she was standing atop the table, leaning down at Malder, their faces no more than a handspan apart.

"Mind your manners, foolish Human," she chuckled as cries of fear and alarm rose up from the older men.

Malder was the only one who did not flinch from the witch's inhuman speed.

"Speak if you must then, but leave all the same when you've finished," he spat, folding his burly arms as he glowered up at her.

"My, my, you are a bold one," the witch snickered, turning to pace about the table, her feet sending parchments and goblets tumbling to the floor. "I have discovered an ancient elvish legend. Their ancestors were given weapons of unimaginable power: five Elemental Swords. Imagine if you had one of those in your possession, Malder."

"Even if we knew where they were, there would be no way of retrieving them. I do not have time for chasing fairy tales when I have a war to prepare for."

"Ahh, but I know where one of these Swords rests. And I know just the band of warriors to get it."

"Pray tell," the king sneered, his voice dripping with sarcasm.

"The Roamers," Alura grinned, turning to face him once again.

"There's no way-"

"Leave that to me," she quickly cut him off, raising a hand for silence. "You worry about getting your army ready for King Jamiel's onslaught."

With that, the witch gracefully stepped off the polished table and drifted lightly to the floor. Once her feet touched down, she made her way out of the Great Hall, the guards not daring to cross her. As she passed through the doors, Alura pulled her hood over her raven-black hair and vanished from sight before their very eyes. Tiredly, the king slid back into his chair, all tension leaving his body at once.

"Do you really think she intends to aid us with this so-called Elemental Sword?" Halfen, a younger advisor, inquired in the wake of the witch's presence.

"Of course not," the king sighed. "This can only bode ill for us all."

CHAPTER 1

In her castle on the Barren Plains, Alura sat before the crystalline mirror in her bedchambers. Looking upon herself, the vain woman admired her beauteous form.

Alura's glossy black hair tumbled down in gentle waves, reaching her upper back. Her flesh was smooth and pale, almost deathly so, and her body was slim and tall, standing just under two meters in height. The curves of her ample breasts and hips only added to her elegant and graceful form. A simple sleeveless white dress fell to her ankles, not a stain marring the flawless fabric. Alura turned her head to better see every angle of her slender cheeks and full lips.

Her mouth parting in a grin to reveal white teeth, the witch began to chant softly in the Archaic language. *"Thaero evimre setdi argeoarna."*

Her reflection swirled away and was replaced by the wide landscapes of Ath're.

"Where have you hidden yourselves away?"

Some of them were easy to find while one or two proved more difficult, but no matter to the witch. She found most of the exiled Roamers, and she knew just who to visit first. Rising from her soft bed, her snowy dress shimmering in the pale sunlight, Alura walked to a wide window. Through the clear panes she could see for leagues and leagues, the desolate gray landscape stretching as far as the eye could see. Chuckling at memories long since passed of a kingdom that once was, Alura snapped her fingers, the sound echoing sharply. Soon enough, there came a knock on her door.

"Come."

The entrance swung open without a sound and a barrel-chested man entered.

"My Mistress Alura," he said, kneeling before her.

"Rise, Sivart. I have an important task for you."

The dark-haired Human stood, awaiting her command.

Sivart only stood a meter and a half tall so he had to look up to meet the witch's gaze. What he lacked in height, though, Sivart made up for with trunk-like limbs and a bulky frame of muscle. His wiry hair rested in unkempt coils atop his head, thick and matted. The Human's olive-toned skin was lined with scars from numerous fights and battles, and some still from torture. Upon his torso he wore a ragged brown linen shirt, though whether the clothing was that color from dye, or blood and dirt, it was hard to say. Over that he wore a crude jacket of stitched leather and black leggings. Heavy boots covered his feet, a knife hilt protruding from the left one. Upon his belt hung a throwing axe in a leather loop on his right hip.

"Gather twenty of my Huirds and fly over to Wyst'hin."

When nothing more was forthcoming, Sivart shifted his feet uneasily. He'd learned in his early years of servitude not to question her. His plain brown eyes studied her green orbs and dared to say, "Is that all, Mistress?"

She smiled warmly, her eyes shifting to a light hazel. "Camp within one league of the city along the north. There you will wait until the Roamers arrive."

Sivart's dark eyes widened in surprise. "The Roamers?"

"Yes, dear Sivart. I shall be back to check on you. If you are not encamped when I do," her eyes hardened to icy blue. It was all the warning Sivart needed. He gave a quick nod and kneeled before her again.

"Good."

With that, she turned and waved a hand, one of the wide window doors gliding open. Stepping up to the ledge, she turned her gaze back to Sivart once more, a wicked grin flashing across her visage before she stepped off the ledge and fell from her tower, her dress and hair whipping in the wind. In her mad descent, white light shone upon the witch's back and massive feathered wings sprouted forth. One powerful flap sent Alura soaring high into the clouded sky, propelling her far from her castle.

Sivart watched his Mistress for but a moment before turning and heading down to his quarters. Within the simple dwelling, he took up his broadsword and buckled it to his belt. Slinging a small pack over his shoulder, filled with his bedroll and some foodstuffs, the Human drew a deep breath before stepping down the winding stairs. Reaching the main floor of the castle, Sivart continued down several hallways, passing multiple servants as he went. Every single one of them stopped and bowed their heads to the man as he strode past. Coming to a wide and heavy door within the vacant throne room, Sivart turned the heavy iron ring-handle and gave a hard tug. The entrance to the dungeons cranked open with a horrendous groan. Foul air immediately wafted up to greet his senses, nearly causing the Human to step away. Flaring his nostrils in disgust, the witch's henchman steeled his nerves and began his descent.

He had not taken two steps and already he was breathing through his mouth, and the low light made it difficult to find secure footing on the damp steps. No matter how many times Sivart went down there, or worse yet, was dragged down those stony stairs, he never got used to the smell of excrement, nor hearing the screams of the imprisoned and the damned. As if on cue, a shriek howled up the stairs, causing the seasoned warrior to flinch. Torches lined the walls, ever burning in their sconces, sending eerie flickering shadows dancing across the stony floor, some moving of their own volition when Sivart glanced out the corner of his eye. Upon reaching the landing, his boots echoed heavy footfalls as he passed by several iron-barred cells, some containing emaciated occupants or others still who had suffered from the witch's hands directly. One of Alura's favorite pastimes was torturing those who had crossed her. Hurrying along, Sivart passed one of the Dungeon Keepers, the giant brute of a man spitting at his feet in greeting. Sivart halted, slapping a large hand on the man's toned chest and glowered up at him, demanding respect. The leather-clad torturer paused and gave a slight nod, bowing his head in deference and moved on.

Once he'd crossed the main corridor of the dungeons, Sivart came before a huge ironbound door with no handle or keyhole upon it. Placing his right hand, fingers splayed, upon the surface, the magically sealed door reacted to his touch. With a hiss of pain, Sivart hurriedly withdrew his hand, the skin smoking from the heat. The imprint of his fingers and palm remained, glowing faintly in the gloom before the door cracked open. Swinging inward, iron grating against the stony floor, the shrieking metal reverberated through the dungeons and into the abyssal maw before him. Doing his best not to inhale the stench of rotting flesh and bird-filth, Sivart stepped through the portal, the thick door sealing shut behind him. Before the Human was a vast cavern, well-lit from wide shafts of sunlight through several grated openings in the roof. From the light, Sivart could make out several pillars of stone, reaching up to the wide cavernous ceiling. Upon those pillars, resting on wooden beams driven through the rock, dwelt the Huirds.

They were creations of the witch, a perversion of nature. Humanoid in nature, but covered in feathers, their limbs ending in talon-like appendages, with great wings resting on their backs. Their heads were more akin to a hawk's than anything, with a great hooked beak for a mouth and wide eyes filled with malice. Their plumage ranged from black and brown to a dark, disgusting green. Usually, the air was filled with their guttural cawing and squawking, but upon Sivart's entry, they fell quiet, their black glinting eyes boring into the Human.

"Alura has ordered twenty of you to come with me!" he commanded, speaking firmly.

10

Sivart's voice echoed and bounced off the stony walls, his speech distorting before fading away. After an eternal minute passed, several of the perverted creatures spread their wings and glided down to stand before him. Slowly but surely, twenty of the abominations gathered around and stood awaiting further orders. Taking a deep breath through the mouth, Sivart made his way to the other side of the cavern. Bloody pulp and yellow excrement squelched and gurgled under his boots while the sounds of talons scraping against stone echoed shrilly through the air.

Finally, Sivart reached the far side entrance, a thick slab of stone with thicker chains to hold it shut. Wrapping his callused hands about a giant lever, he pulled it down with a grunt. Hidden gears and winches cranked and creaked as the stone slab lowered like a drawbridge, casting wide rays of sunlight into the wide chamber. The fresh air filled Sivart's lungs, bringing a wave of great relief to the Human. He hurriedly strode out of the Huirds' cavern, the company of creatures stepping after him. Once they were all out in the open, the drawbridge shut of its own volition, slamming shut with a dull *boom*.

"We fly east," Sivart ordered, turning to face the bird-like creatures.

The Huirds nodded, two of them coming forward to take hold of Sivart's torso and legs. They leapt into the air, their massive wings carrying them up high with ease, the rest of the flock following. Soon they were above the clouds and heading for Wyst'hin.

*****

The Fire Elf stood in the center of the cave; sword drawn. Behind him, the storm pounded the Igneous Plains; cursed water splattering into the entrance of his dwelling. He stayed well back from the opening, his longsword in hand as he slowly shifted his bare feet, blade swinging gently. He brought the weapon up, gripping the hilt in both hands and for a moment, he stood still, the only sound was thrumming rain. Slowly, he slid his feet along the black rock, the edge of his sword singing through the air. Over his head, then down to the left, a cut across to the right, and thrust. Faster and faster he swung his blade, cutting down invisible enemies all around.

He stood just under two meters in height, his body lean and sinewy. His clothing was black, rough, and ragged, the edges of his trousers frayed and tattered at the knees. His shirt sported gaping holes and one of the sleeves was nearly gone. Through the rips of his clothing, scars could be seen, all earned in battle. His face was angular with short-cropped messy black hair upon his head. A long scar ran from his forehead through his right eye down to his cheek, but his yellow eyes were clear and fierce as ever.

As the elf went through his exercises, another sound could be heard over the rain, causing him to glance over his shoulder to the dark expanse outside. Setting his sword down, the Fire Elf took up his longbow and nocked an arrow to the string. Heavy wingbeats were drawing nearer, and then something landed just beyond the cave. With a *twang,* the arrow flew from his bow, but no cry of pain sounded. Shortly after, a tall woman clad in a white dress strode in, holding the arrow in her hand.

"120 years and your manners have not improved."

The witch folded her wings and tossed the metal arrow to the ground, making a loud clatter. The elf merely stared at her as she willed herself to dry, steam rising in fumes off her hair and clothing.

"So," she said, placing her hands on her hips, "are you going to even grace me with a proper greeting, Nihak?"

He regarded Alura for a moment longer, old anger simmering in his eyes. She smirked at his temper.

"What do you want?" he finally said.

"Jamiel will make war on Malder."

The Fire Elf showed neither surprise nor concern. "You found me and came all the way across Greenearth just to give me this news?"

Alura gave a clear laugh, her voice echoing above the pounding rain. "I think you know I came for more than that small reason."

"Whatever your reasoning or motives, I want none of it. You'll get no use out of me!"

The pale witch grinned at that, stepping towards him. Nihak grabbed another arrow, notching it and drawing the string back in a mere second. Alura held her left hand outstretched, fingers splayed, holding the arrow in place. Though the elf had released, the arrow hung there, quivering in midair. His knuckles whitened from gripping the bow so tight, until Alura wrenched it from his grasp with her magic. Not once did she break her stride as she approached the Fire Elf.

"Your weapons won't harm me. I've grown stronger since we last talked, my dear Nihak." She threw the bow and arrow down as the elf backpedaled, stumbling over the uneven floor of the cavern. Before he fell, she caught him in midair, her right hand clenched as if she were physically holding him up. Fire glinted in his eyes as she stood over him, bringing her first two fingers up to his brow, her harsh eyes closed. It didn't take long for the witch to overcome Nihak's mental defenses as she invaded his mind.

The elf growled in pain; his eyes shut tight. Only a moment passed before Alura released her hold, letting him fall to the stones, unconscious. She looked down at the young elf, allowing a cold sneer to show.

"I will always have use for you, foolish Nihak."

*****

When he woke, the storm was over, and the fierce sun had heated the land, so no water remained. Groaning, the Fire Elf rose on stiff legs, head in his hands. Bending and twisting, loud cracks and crunches emitted from his back and shoulders. Sighing, Nihak snapped his head to the right, his neck popping loudly in protest. Once the kinks in his back were gone, he flexed his shoulders and returned his fallen arrows to his quiver. The elf grimaced in pain as brief images of Greenearth's landscapes flashed through his mind.

He saw himself standing on the Igneous Plains, his vision blurred and faded. Then with a rush, he found himself hurtling through forests, plains, and cities until so very suddenly, Nihak came to a halt before the Duriviel Forest. In his vision, he paused for but a minute before rushing within the barred woods. He suddenly stopped in a clearing and saw before him a broadsword with a green blade. The Sword had been driven half its length into the trunk of a massive and once-proud willow tree. Just as suddenly as he had arrived, Nihak felt himself being flung backwards through the land until he found himself in his own body again.

Groaning in pain, he fell to his knees, holding his head again. "Damn it!" After the pulsing pain finally passed, the Fire Elf slowly rose to his full height with new purpose. It was time to wander the Wildlands again, for he had spent too long in this cave! Taking up his quiver of arrows, the Roamer slung it over his right shoulder. His longsword he sheathed and belted to his left hip. Holding his right arm aloft, a small flame lit upon his palm to better light the way as he moved to the back of the cave. Tucked behind a few stones, Nihak came upon his other sword and old pack. The rough-clothed sack he stuffed with dry meat, bandages, and his bedroll. Once full, it was slung over his right shoulder, so it rested under his quiver. The other sword was a falchion, wrapped in a simple leather sheath. The elf tied it to his back, the plain black hilt accessible over his left shoulder. Briefly gripping the hilt of his knife, kept always on his right hip, Nihak rose to his feet. With most of his gear ready, Nihak headed towards the mouth of the cave. Lastly, the elf took up his black longbow and left without a second glance back.

If he was going to journey across Greenearth, he'd need the rest of the Roamers; fortunately, one of them was very close. The fierce sun beat down on the short-haired elf as he turned and headed east, towards the Twelve Volcanoes. *Seilnurig'Feriar-Magryem*, the Holy Fire-Mountains. They loomed in the distance, their shadows reaching far across the blackened plains.

He shook his head at the name, for never did he think he'd have to return to his homeland. Sighing, the Fire Elf glanced up at the rising sun to see it was only just rising above the peaks. Living in a cave on the Igneous Plains was the outskirts of the Firelands, the wasteland of the barren place. There was nothing but uneven, black rock, some surfaces flat and rippled; others jagged and broken. Every so often, caves could be found but they were few and far in between. As the sun rose higher, so too the heat rose with it. All too soon, scorching heat wafted and waved off the Igneous Plains, turning it into a scalding desert. However, the burning rocks had no effect on Nihak's callused feet, nor did he feel parched as his long legs carried him in easy strides over the desolate ground. There was almost no life out here save for a few indigenous species of reptile and haznmua, a kind of long-toothed, horse-like creature. As if on cue, a low hiss drew Nihak's attention to a wide crevice not four meters away. He came to an abrupt stop and looked to the dark hole, waiting. The low hissing continued, growing louder and louder until suddenly a thick-bodied, red-scaled lizard shot from the crevice. It was a tremak, a powerful, muscled reptile, as big as an elf and twice as long; thick legs propelled it from its hole, with a wide gaping snout lined with serrated teeth. A long, barbed tongue slithered out its mouth, thick saliva flying from its deadly maw.

A flash of steel glinted in the hot sun and the creature fell to the ground in two, its head landing a meter from where Nihak stood. His longsword dripped black blood, the drops sizzling as they hit the ground. The elf ripped off a piece of his ragged shirt, wiped his blade clean, and returned it to its leather sheath.

Quickly, he glanced about, scanning the surrounding empty lands, for it wouldn't remain empty for long. The elf didn't forget to glance skyward too, making sure nothing was watching. Muttering a quick prayer to Seylivonia as he pulled his knife from his belt, Nihak crouched down. His knife sliced through the tremak's tough hide with ease as the ebon rockscape sizzled and sputtered when the hot blood and guts spilled out. Wrinkling his nose at the foul smell, the elf took what meat he could carry. Returning his knife to its sheath, he picked up his fallen bow and fled from the roasting corpse. His legs carried him swiftly over the ground in long strides, but such quick movements could attract attention. However, with a free meal lying about, the Fire Elf would not likely be taken as prey.

Hopefully.

Glancing over his shoulder, Nihak could see black creatures appearing in the distance, running fast towards the tremak kill. Blowing a sigh of relief, the Fire Elf lessened his pace but did not stop. The *Feria'Setasr*, the Fire-Eaters, were feared by even the fiercest Fire Elves. As he walked, he pulled out some of the fresh meat and roasted it in his hands. It didn't take long to cook, and soon the elf was biting into the lizard's thigh, the tang of iron all too familiar in his mouth. Shrugging, he ate the tough flesh, the crunch of burnt muscle sounding loud in his pointed ears. Soon finished with the meal, he threw the bone far from his path.

As he walked on, Nihak constantly scanned his surroundings. If the *Feria'Setasr* found him, he would have no choice but to fight. Much to his fear and chagrin, a bone-chilling screech split the air as the thought crossed his mind. Directing his gaze skyward, the elf's sharp eyes made out one of the foul creatures flying towards him, folding its black leathery wings in for a swift dive. Growling, Nihak threw his bow down once more and drew his longsword from his hip. The Fire-Eater was closing in at tremendous speed, the wind whistling sharply around it. As the monster neared the ground, it flared its wings and brought its powerful hind legs up. Nihak saw the black glint of the creature's sickle-claws in the hot sun as time seemed to slow for the Fire Elf. As death drew nearer, Nihak raised his sword above his head, then spun to the left. As he moved out of the Fire-Eater's path, his sword swung and bit through the creature, splashing sickly yellow blood over the ground. The *Feria'Setasr* tumbled to the rocky terrain, shrieking in pain as its right leg and wing were severed. Nihak turned and dropped his stained sword, bringing his bow to his hands with a swift flick of his foot. Even with only one leg and wing left, the Fire-Eater was furiously dragging itself towards him, hate glowing in its abyssal crimson eyes. The beast's crest flared out, three blood-red feathers standing erect atop its narrow head. Nihak glared back, matching its hate and anger as he set his feet, pulling an arrow from his quiver. Notching it, he ran his callused fingers along the blood-red fletchings, then drew back, aiming down the shaft. The Fire-Eater opened wide its maw and split the air with another screech, its serrated teeth glistening with rotten drool.

With a singing *twang*, the arrow flew from his bow and buried itself deep into the creature's chest. It gave an angry shriek and clawed towards him faster, but Nihak merely notched another arrow and let fly again. Twice more, he loosed arrows into the foul creature, its strength waning rapidly. Its breathing quickly became shallow and pained, rasping desperately as a fifth arrow hissed through the air, piercing its scaly hide and burying itself to the fletchings. The

Feria'Setasr breathed its last ragged breath and was finally still, the glint of hate leaving the pupil-less eyes. Breathing a deep sigh of relief, Nihak slung his bow over his shoulder and knelt to take up his sword again. Stepping up to the carcass, the Fire Elf flipped the blade about to a reverse-grip and drove his weapon clean through its skull with a sickening *crunch!* Leaving his sword embedded, he quickly collected his arrows, straining as they cracked and split scale and bone. Wiping the stinking blood off the shafts, the Roamer returned them to his quiver and glanced around. When nothing presented itself on land or air, he pulled his sword free, cleaning it as well before sheathing it. Once more, he took off at a run, putting as much distance as he could between him and ravenous beasts.

The more he ran, the closer he came to the volcanoes. As his long legs carried him over the uneven ground, Nihak found himself praying that Ejen and his clan didn't occupy *SeilnurigNaelka*, the Holy Flame. It was the tallest fiery peak and resided in the very heart of their land. Fortunately, the Redfire Clan's permanent dwelling was nearer the outer ring of volatile mountains. As he drew closer, the volcanoes rumbled and shook the ground. Off to the far right, Nihak spied one of the mountains as it shuddered and quaked, thick black smoke spewing from its wide maw.

"Home foul home," he muttered, turning away from that peak and heading towards the neighboring volcanoes.

Ejen's home wasn't too much further now. And fortunately for the lone Fire Elf, no hunting parties or the odd patrol was out at this time. As he approached, the sun sank lower and lower in the sky, the red orb setting the land awash in dark hues of fire, making him shudder. Nihak hurried on, not wanting to be caught out in the open at night. He didn't want to risk lighting a flame to show the way either. That would just be begging the creatures of the Ashlands to attack him. As he strained to see in the fading light, he knew Ejen was in one of the caves at the base of the black mountain. The only question was, which one?

Coming to the wide base of the formidable slopes, Nihak craned his head back to see its wide maw alighting the night with an angry glow of magma churning and bubbling deep inside. Every now and then, it would spew new clouds of noxious fumes into the nightly air. Running his hand along the stones, Nihak walked near the side of the volcano, feeling for openings. When his hand fell away into nothingness, the elf stopped and listened intently. With each cave, he could hear nothing within; nothing that showed signs of life. As the night deepened, his worry grew; not that Fire-Eaters ventured to their very dwellings but being exposed at night with no fire to light the way was nerve-wracking for the elf. Finally, he found a wide cave with the faintest of light flickering at the back.

Stepping inside quickly, Nihak felt his way as he walked slowly deeper, sliding his tough feet along the rocky ground. His hands spread out, feeling for any walls or low-hanging ceilings, he soon found the cave curving gently to the left. His eyes having adjusted to the dimly lit dwelling, Nihak glanced back to find he could no longer see the starlit sky from the entrance. Sighing in relief, he summoned a flame to the palm of his right hand and held it high.

"Much better," he whispered.

"It is quite," came a reply from the depths of the cave.

Nihak grinned and strode to the back of the cave, turning another bend to see a lone elf sitting before a small fire, the flames dancing on the bare rock floor. "Twenty years, old friend," he said, looking up at Nihak.

The Fire Elf smiled, tossed his flame into Ejen's fire on the floor, and sat cross-legged across from his friend.

Ejen'Feriar-Akroa was taller than Nihak by half a head. His hair was an ashen gray, falling down his forehead and covering his pointed ears. Twin scars ran jaggedly across his left cheek. His eyes were a darker shade of yellow, but just as fierce. His face, too, was angular with high cheekbones. The older Fire Elf's clothing was a reddish hue, spotted with dull patches of gray. Like his companion, his clothing was ragged and dirty, battle scars visible through the holes and tears. And just like Nihak, his feet were bare and callused.

The two regarded each other in silence for many minutes, the only sound was the crackling fire between them. Shadows of flames danced upon their faces and the walls around them. Nihak shifted his legs a little for a more comfortable position when finally, Ejen spoke, "What brings you back here, Nihak?"

"It was worth the risk to seek you out."

"You would not have made the risk for a simple visit," Ejen mused, rubbing his chin. "So, what brought you back to the Homeland?"

Nihak leaned forward, as if speaking too loudly would awaken the whole Fire Elf race. "I know where the Sylvan Sword is."

Ejen blinked in surprise, then sighed and rose on scarred legs. "Even if we could get it, what would you do with it? Even your absurd belief in the Forest Goddess won't allow you to touch that Sword."

"It won't be for us to use."

"Oh?" Ejen cocked an eyebrow. "Who would use it then?"

"King Malder."

Ejen blinked in surprise again at the simple answer. "King Malder?" he echoed.

"The kings will march to war again."

"How do you know this?" came Ejen's sharp response.

Nihak hesitated. "The witch found me."

Ejen's glare turned to concern. "Nihak…"

"I know! I was careful though. She did not lay any spells on me."

The taller elf stepped through the fire and lifted his friend to his feet. He turned Nihak's face this way and that, his dark eyes searching. No markings could be found, and his eyes showed no glassy or hazed look. Satisfied, Ejen pushed him back to arms' length. "Very well. What will we do?"

A grin played at the corners of Nihak's mouth. "The blade is hidden in the Duriviel Forest."

The older elf gave a dark chuckle. "That's across Greenearth. The itch in my feet was becoming unbearable. It will be good to wander the Wildlands once more!"

The Fire Elves clasped their right hands together, both grinning and chuckling. "Aye!" Nihak exclaimed.

Staying up long into the night, the brothers-in-arms shared tales of their time in exile before drifting off to sleep, but all too quickly, it seemed the rest of the night flew swiftly by.

The younger elf awoke early, the cave nearly the color of pitch. Lighting a small fire on his palm, he stood up and stretched, rotating his shoulders and neck to ease out the stiffness. He had laid his weapons near a wall along with Ejen's the night before. There was no reason to have them on his person right now, save his knife. Yawning quietly, Nihak headed to the mouth of the cave, where he extinguished his light and stared out at the dark expanse before him. The cold stars shone brightly in the pre-dawn sky and a rare sight it was indeed, for the skies were seldom clear over the volcanos. A stiff breeze was blowing from the West, causing the Fire Elf to close his eyes and let the air wash over him for many long minutes.

Upon opening his eyes, Nihak watched the sky begin to turn faint hues of red and yellow, the stars fading away. He'd have to wake Ejen, which was a task unto itself, for that elf never was an early riser.

Unless there was a fight to be had, he chuckled at the thought.

Lighting his palm once more, he strode to the back of the cave, dark shadows dancing on the walls from his tiny flame.

"Ejen?" He found his companion lying on his side, his back to him. "Ejen arise!"

No response.

"Ejen!" the elf said as loud as he dared, not wanting to alert unwanted ears outside. He gave a sigh when his companion did not move.

"Just like on the hunts. You won't wake unless you need to."

The younger Fire Elf dared not approach the sleeping Ejen. Looking about, he found a loose stone and scooped it up. "Well... you leave me no choice."

Drawing his arm back, Nihak threw the stone, hitting his friend square in the back. The reaction was instantaneous: Ejen whirled around, a knife flashing in his hand. In his other hand red flames roared to life, lighting the cave walls around him. His eyes shone brightly as he leapt to his feet, ready to strike. When no threat was apparent, his fierce gaze turned to Nihak.

"You woke me."

"Aye. We have a long way to journey, and I wish for us to leave early."

Growling and grumbling, Ejen extinguished the flames and returned his knife to his belt. Tilting his head to the side, the older elf's neck crackled loudly as he gave a satisfied grunt. Stepping lightly to their weapons, Ejen bent down and took up his sickle-sword, belting the simple black sheath to his left hip. His war scythe, a polearm with a curved blade and crossbars, leaned against the rock wall. Before he grabbed the formidable weapon, he packed his bedroll and foodstuffs, and slung it over his back.

"Ready," he stated, picking his scythe off the wall.

Nihak quickly and expertly belted on his swords and slung on his quiver and pack, while his bow he carried in his left hand. The elves walked out of the cave and into the shadows of the mountains, the sun still hidden at their backs. Ejen rolled his shoulders, his muscles protesting loudly before resting his war scythe across the back of his neck. Once clear of the cave, Ejen spat on the cold stony ground, his saliva casting a small light, the tiniest flame burning in the spit. Nihak shuddered at the feeling of the cold rocks beneath his feet, but soon enough, they reached the light of the sun. The feeling of warm stone was a welcome relief for the Fire Elves.

"Who's still left out there?"

Nihak glanced at his companion. "You don't remember?"

The taller elf shrugged. "It's been nearly twenty years, brother. The Roamers are a distant memory to me. Almost a dream."

He nodded a little. "What kept you from going mad, Ejen?"

"Staying at the base of my Clan's home helped."

Nihak could only nod. "All I could think of was the Roamers. Of what we did. Of freedom to have the road beneath our feet."

"Seems thinking like that drove you into a deeper frenzy than usual. Why did you stay in that cave all those years?"

"Where else could I have gone, Ejen?"

"What about the Selveryn Forest?"

"I was weak and wounded and we were running for our lives. Both armies were after us. There was no way for me to get back to that forest."

"Then why didn't you go back after you were healed?"

Silence followed that question as Nihak looked away to the north, jagged mountains rising taller than the Volcanoes in the far distance. What lay beyond those Nameless peaks, they did not know and were not meant to know.

At length, Ejen decided not to press his friend on the matter. As they walked, the rising sun turned the land into a scalding anvil. They welcomed the mounting heat, feeling it coursing up through their feet and down through their heads. Finally, Nihak spoke, "I wasn't ready to go back on the road. And no one should travel alone." He laid a reassuring hand on Ejen's shoulder for a moment as they walked.

"You always had wanderlust more than I, Nihak. But I'm glad to accompany my brother on these journeys." The elf gave a slight grin, adjusting his grip on the scythe to use it as a walking staff. They walked in silence for hours after that. As the sun rose higher and higher in the grey sky, they kept up their habits of constantly scanning their surroundings. Every now and then, a pack of *Feria'Setasr* ran by in the distance. Nihak and Ejen's hands tightened on their weapons, muscles tense whenever they saw them, but it was the ones on the wing they really had to worry about. As they walked, they ate from their packs, chewing on tough dried meat.

"Where's our first stop on this road?"

"Wyst'hin."

"That massive city? Who would be there?"

"Danira. Maybe Aen and Myles. Not sure where Rom and Jolek are. I'm not sure who else survived."

"Only seven? Not much from near a hundred."

"Aye," Nihak nodded slowly.

"Well, Wyst'hin is at least a week of walking from here."

"Right," he glanced sidelong at Ejen. "How are your skills with that war scythe? Intact, I hope."

The taller elf met Nihak's grin. "As I hope your skill with the sword is too."

By this time, the sun was beginning its rapid descent to the horizon before them. Fortunately for them, Nihak's cave came into view.

"Welcome to my humble abode."

"Your sarcasm has been sorely missed," Ejen chuckled.

Nihak extended his left arm and cast a ball of fire onto the stone floor as they stepped inside, spreading light in the black cave. He felt much safer with Ejen so he could afford to risk the light this time. Things finally seemed to be turning out for the better. The Roamers would wander again.

CHAPTER 2

It was still dark out with veiled stars when Nihak snapped wide awake. Straining his sensitive ears, a soft scratching could be heard beyond the cave. Sitting up slowly, he drew his knife as Ejen rose to his feet, sickle-sword in hand. They shared a glance, both seasoned warriors knowing what was approaching their dwelling. The scratching and scuffling was growing louder, accompanied by low hissing and soft screeches. Returning the knife to his belt, the younger Fire Elf took up his bow and knelt beside his quiver. Swiftly, he notched an arrow and drew the string taut while Ejen set his feet, a grin slowly spreading across his face. Nihak felt the same insane grin appear across his visage; it was the smirk of battle lust for all Fire Elves. Though it was nearing dawn, the light was too dim for their eyes, so fire alighted upon the taller elf's left hand and he cast it towards the mouth of the cave. With an upward flick of the wrist, Ejen commanded the fire to grow and spread, lighting up the entire entrance. The Fire-Eaters' eyes blazed from the light, shrieking in surprise. Nihak let fly, sending arrow after arrow slicing through the air. One of the five creatures fell with six arrows through its neck and skull. The others charged forward, only to be met by Ejen.

His sickle-sword flashed in the dancing wild light and a Fire-Eater fell, its head rolling along the floor, jaws still snapping. Another dropped at the elf's feet, its head riddled with arrows. Seeming of its own accord, Ejen's knife flew to his hand to pierce slashing claws. With the creature's attack halted, the Fire Elf hooked his curved blade deep into its serpentine neck. The monster gave a gurgling screech as it was kicked against the wall, left to drown in its own putrid blood. As that one died, the last creature leapt upon Ejen, pinning him to the ground. Hot saliva splattered the elf's face as the Fire-Eater shrieked, opening wide its maw for the killer-blow when suddenly a longsword stabbed through the creature's flank. With ease, Nihak lifted the screeching monster up by his blade and slammed it against the wall as it struggled and flailed, loosing horrid scream after scream. The splitting shrieks were brought to a swift end when Ejen sliced the upper half of its head off, leaving its tongue and lower jaw to flop uselessly on its neck. Nihak ripped free his sword, letting the body fall as he wiped his weapon clean.

"How close is the dawn?"

Ejen stepped outside for a moment to better glimpse the reddening sky. "The sun's first rays are hidden behind the mountains."

"That's early enough. We can't stay here any longer," Nihak grunted, pulling his arrows from the smelly carcasses. The Fire Elves hastily finished cleaning their arrows and blades, then left the cave at a dead run. Leaping over jagged rock and across shallow chasms, they dared not stop running until the sun peeked over the mountains. With the coming of day, it was no longer safe again to move swiftly, lest more *Feria'Setasr* saw them. Slowing to a walk, they kept a steady pace, not even winded by their morning run. As the Roamers strode along, a hot dry wind began to blow from the North. Nihak turned his gaze to the right to see black clouds in the far distance.

"Damn."

"Too bad Aen isn't here now!" Ejen laughed, following Nihak's gaze. "That old bastard could do something to divert the storm."

"If only."

Nihak began to sprint again, his eyes ever on the lookout for unwanted attention. Ejen followed suit and took off after his friend.

"I would say we have the rest of the day to find a cave before that storm hits us!"

The younger elf did not respond. He didn't want to think about the possibility of not finding shelter. He didn't want to think about the fate that awaited them if the rains came. So, they ran, their tough feet scraping against the rough black rock. They breathed deep, feeling the coming storm, slowly sapping their energy. There was no time to stop for rest and food, so they ate on the move, trying to replenish what strength they lost. As the ground flew beneath their feet, more Fire-Eaters noticed their swift passage and gave chase.

"Of course. No fun to be had if they didn't pursue their prey!" Nihak shouted, drawing his falchion from his back.

Ejen merely chuckled, readying his war scythe. Four *Feria'Setasr* were behind them, quickly gaining ground while two more flanked them, screeching and roaring. The nearest one leapt at the elves and was immediately cut down by Ejen's long-reaching blade. Another one of the flanking monsters lunged, only to meet the enchanted edge of Nihak's sword. Though it only sustained a gash to its chest, the Fire-Eater fell to the ground dead. Suddenly, a booming crack of approaching thunder brought the vicious creatures to a halt. Snarling and growling, they spread their wings and took flight, leaving the elves behind.

"I'd rather deal with them than the storm."

"Not sure which is worse," Nihak replied, sheathing his falchion as they continued running. It had taken most of the day, but the black clouds were directly overhead now. Nervously Ejen and Nihak glanced skyward as they continued their desperate run. Thunder boomed overhead every now and then, making them shake as they kept up their search for shelter.

Then, the rain began to fall.

Ejen grunted in pain as he felt a fat drop of water hit his arm. The spot sizzled softly, leaving an angry burn. Nihak gave a sigh of relief as he looked ahead, spotting their salvation. "There's a cave!"

The elves hurried to it as the raindrops began to fall in abundance. Splatters of the cursed water struck them, leaving red marks on their bodies. As they climbed down into the cave, a wide hole in the ground, the clouds split open and a torrent of rain smashed into the earth, lightning flashing across the black sky.

"Are you all right, Ejen?"

The taller elf lit a fire on his palm and inspected his wounds. "Not too bad. It could have been worse."

Nihak fared no better than his companion. Together they moved deeper into the cave, away from the splashing and gathering water. However, it soon became clear it was impossible to escape the rain as rivulets began to run down the slanted cave floor. Flames lit on their hands, the pair moved further down, seeking a dryer place.

"The sooner this wretched storm ends, the better."

Ejen sniffed the air, his nose wrinkling at the faint odor of decay. "The sooner we find out we're alone in here, the better." He formed his fire into a sphere and tossed it farther down the cave. Old bones and rotten, ripped flesh could be seen from the dancing light.

A Fire-Eater hole.

"Tawschei," both elves swore at once.

Falchion and sickle-sword flashed in the faint light as they cautiously stepped deeper into the cave, bones crunching beneath their feet. All the while, the rivulets of water ran past them down the sloping stone floor, mixing with old blood and rotted flesh. Elf skulls could be seen among the remains, making the Roamers cringe inwardly. The rough walls of the cave were growing narrow and tight and so the light from their fires spread, filling more cracks and crevices. The further down they went, the more the water collected in puddles and soon they stopped when they came to a growing pool's edge, the tiny streams of rain slowly filling the cave.

"Let us hope this hole is deep enough to hold enough rain without entirely flooding," Ejen remarked, sighing as he tucked his curved sword away.

It was obvious this den had been abandoned. Fire-Eaters were not allergic to water like the Fire Elves were, but they hated it, nonetheless. Which left a disturbing question for the trapped elves: did the *Feria'Setasr* abandon this cave because it flooded, or did they simply not make it back to shelter from the storm?

Nihak slid his falchion back in its leather sheath and followed his companion back the way they came; the water flowing along the floor was a constant reminder to them that they may possibly die in this wretched place. Climbing up the angled stony ground, the elves came back to the widest section of the cave and sat, shifting every so often to regain their comfort against the rough rocks. Lighting fires on the walls where they could, they were certainly careful not to cast the flames where they would touch water. Any thoughts of sleeping this night had long since been forgotten; Nihak in particular kept glancing down the cave shaft, wondering when they'd see the water rising. While his eyes kept flitting about, Ejen sat with his back resting against the curved wall, his head bowed, and his arms folded across his chest. The taller Elf wasn't showing it, but he was very tense. They both were, and there was no point in talking about it either. Not in such a charged atmosphere. As the moisture in the air grew, the elves had to conserve their breathing, keeping flames near their mouths so they didn't inhale the toxic dampness.

Outside, thunder rumbled across the sky and lighting flashed, lighting up the dark land. The hours of the night passed slowly, but much to the elves' relief, the rain began to lessen until it was nothing but a light drizzle. Finally, the water stopped streaming into their shelter, and they had yet to see the lapping pool below rising to where they sat.

"Thank Seylivonia," Nihak breathed, spreading more fires around the cave.

Ejen ignored the blasphemous statement and stood up, rubbing his arms gently. "Are you strong enough to ward off the mist?"

Nihak glanced up at his friend. "I think so. Maybe you create a shield while I make the ground safe to tread upon?"

Ejen merely nodded. "Then let us leave. The creatures of the Ashlands shouldn't bother us."

Nihak rose to his feet and stretched out his stiff back with a groan. Once he was ready, Ejen raised one arm high, his palm facing skyward. A thin line of fire spread from his hand and enveloped them, shielding them from the misting rain. Nihak lowered the palms of his hands towards the black rough and ragged ground, bursts of fire whooshing down to dry the jagged stone. As they left the cave, steam angrily hissed into the air as the mist hit Ejen's shield, but no harm came to the elves. They found comfort as the ground was pleasantly warmed, ensuring their feet were not burned by water.

Dawn was approaching swiftly, though they could not see any light beyond the grey sky. Eventually the mist also ceased and both elves could dry the ground to safely walk upon. Neither did they have to worry about any attacks, for not even a single creature made itself known to them, making their journey that much safer and easier.

"I don't think I shall ever return here once we leave."

"And go where?" Ejen asked, turning to look upon his kin. "Your precious forest?"

Nihak ignored the venomous tone. "Yes, I will. Unlike you, I find the Selveryn Forest beautiful and majestic."

"Nothing is as majestic as the raw power of Ignicendir!"

"Ejen…" the elf sighed. "I will not have this debate with you again."

Ejen replied with his own sigh. "Very well. I just can't understand why you have such love for such weak creations."

The elves continued to walk in silence, the dark sky slowly clearing. As the sun shone through, bright and strong, the wet stones slowly dried and they no longer needed to spread their fire. Now, so very far from the Volcanoes, the igneous stones began to lessen and sift into loose rock and black soil. The volcanic mountains were nothing but distant peaks, piercing up into the black clouds above, while gray clouds drifted lazily in a sea of blue over the Fire Elves.

"It's been a long time since I've seen the blue sky."

Nihak stared upward, his yellow eyes glistening in the light. Ejen kept his gaze level, casting his eyes about only to see patches of pale grass sprouting among the dark soil. He blanched in disgust, wiping his earth-stained soles on his calves.

"How many days before we reach Wyst'hin?" He paused, looking over at his fixated comrade. "Nihak!" he grabbed the elf's shoulder, snapping him out of his trance.

He looked sharply at Ejen, blinking a few times. "Sorry you were asking something?"

"Yea." He repeated his question.

"Ah. Five days, and there's a forest between us and that city. Not to mention skirting the Glaysher Mountains."

The Fire Elves looked off to the far distant West. Sure enough, white-capped peaks stood sharply in the distance.

"Aye, the city rests in the lee of that range. I do not wish to venture up those mountainsides and risk snow and ice burns." Ejen visibly shuddered at the thought.

"Nor I," Nihak agreed, feeling a chill run up his spine as well.

As the elves continued westward, the volcanic rock and stone soon fell away to short grassy plains, swept by the gentle spring breeze. A small tree line sat less than a league away, the leaves swaying softly in the wind. Ejen gave a grunt of disgust.

"Never shall I get used to seeing trees," he muttered.

Nihak stared at him. "You didn't have to come with me, all those years ago."

"And stay while Sania murdered her way to dominion over the clans?" The elf shrugged. "I would rather be exiled than die by her hand."

"And now?"

"I can't let you go out on your own. You'll get killed. Remember how many times I've saved your life?"

"Eight times was it?"

"Try twelve, little spark."

Nihak glowered at the childish name. "Do not call me that."

"Why?" Ejen playfully twirled his war scythe expertly in his hands, the gesture carrying the reminder of how fast and deadly he was. "You can't best me in combat, Nihak. You never could."

"No, but my bow has greater reach than your scythe."

Ejen turned a sharp glare on his young friend. "Fighting with a bow is cowardly and low of any Fire Elf."

Nihak merely grinned back, knowing the nerve he struck with Ejen. Their culture frowned upon such means of combat, for Fire Elves prided themselves at their prowess with blades and close-quarters fighting. Only five elves before Nihak had taken up the bow as their choice of weapon throughout their people's history. Not that he was helpless with a sword though. This was not the first time they postured and tested each other's nerves with who was the better warrior.

They also already knew the outcome should such a fight occur.

Oddly enough, the elves found themselves thinking back to their youth, when all young Fire Elves learned how to fight. It was the only time all the clans came together without total desire for bloodshed. That was how they had first formed their friendship, despite coming from different clans.

The small forest before them drew closer as they thought back on the rigorous training, the harsh sparring, and the unforgiving ways of battle ingrained in their minds and bodies. A cool breeze swept up, brushing through their short-cropped hair and shaking the gentle leaves.

"Does that not feel good?" Nihak asked, closing his eyes. He held his arms out wide to better enjoy the caressing wind.

"Any wind that feeds my fire is a good wind."

The younger elf could only sigh and grin at his friend's zealous nature. He glanced up at the lowering sun, clouds gathering in the coming dusk. "Perhaps we should stop and make camp." His stomach gave a rumble, accentuating his point.

Ejen merely grunted and sat where he stood, the trees now only meters away. "Let's eat and then sleep. I'll not make camp in those woods."

"Why? You afraid the trees will bite?"

"No. But my war scythe will bite you."

Nihak scoffed but said nothing more, folding his legs as he sat down. Reaching into his simple pack, he pulled out some dry meat and tossed it to Ejen, who bit into the tough food hungrily.

"Tremak leg," he noted, a sour look twisting his mouth.

"Aye," Nihak replied, biting into his own meal. The two ate in silence, save for the occasional grunt as they ripped the fibrous meat apart with their teeth.

"Once we're to the city, what then?" Ejen asked after he finished his meal.

"We find Danira, Aen, and Myles, then we'll start journeying west. Jolek and Rom will be on the Ir'Afa Plains. Where else would Earth Elves be?"

Ejen nodded and extended a finger, a tiny ball of fire leaping from his fingertip to alight upon the ground. With a flick of the wrist, the flames grew bigger to form a proper campfire as the sun slowly set.

"Will you take first watch, or shall I?"

Ejen merely shrugged. "It's all the same to me. I'll stay up first. See you when the moon is at her highest."

The younger elf gave a nod and unrolled his simple bedding and curled up, keeping his swords and bow close. "Good night, Ejen."

CHAPTER 3

The image of the Fire Elves began to distort and shift, the smoke from their fire swirling unnaturally until they were obscured from sight. Waving her hand over the surface of the mirror, the witch cleared the haze to leave only her reflection. Taking a moment to admire herself, she rose from her seat and strode towards the window to lean upon the sill. Alura gazed out over the gray, dead plains surrounding her castle, a starless, moonless sky hanging over her domain.

"What a beautiful night. Such a shame I have to spend it running errands."

With that said, the witch slid her cloak over her delicate frame and vanished from her chambers in a blinding flash of white light. Far off to the East, in the small town of Cendril, Alura appeared in another flash of light. Glancing around, she sighed and stepped forward, having teleported to a deserted alleyway. The witch strode forth, not bothering with invisibility; the tall woman turned onto a street, walking among the few people still out and about. She relished in the outcries of the hapless fools as they were forced from her path by her magic. Some of the passerby, though, gasped and hurried well out of the witch's way, clearly recognizing her.

Chuckling, she turned down another street and made her way down the cobbled path, bare feet making not a sound. Pausing near the stables, the witch glanced about. "I know you're around here somewhere."

"Closer than you think. Too close for my liking," came a voice behind her.

Alura turned and stared at the woman who had spoken. "And whose fault is that?"

Gesturing for her to follow, the witch entered the stable, passing several horses before coming to an empty stall where they would not be bothered. "As I recall, it was you, Sarra McKeer, who let me get too close."

Sarra stood a meter and a half tall, with long red hair falling past her shoulders in gentle waves. Her skin was light and smooth; her eyes a deep sea blue tone. Sarra's clothing was comprised of black boots, brown leggings, and a sleeveless gray shirt. The only armor the woman wore was a leather cuirass and black leather bracers. Over her shoulders, laid a cloak the color of a moonlit night, points of silvery thread like the stars spread over the heavy fabric. Hanging in a loop from the right side of her belt was a war hammer, while on the left side was a sheathed falx. Behind her waist, tucked parallel with the ground, sat a broad knife in a plain brown sheath.

The women stared each other down, neither saying a word.

"What brings you to Cendril?" Sarra finally asked.

Alura smiled at the nervousness in her light voice. "Perhaps you have heard the talks of war?"

She shook her head quickly, much to the witch's amusement. "Don't lie to me, girl." Alura stepped forward, the younger woman backpedaling until she was pressed against the stable wall. Not a handspan of space was between them as the witch towered over the young Human. Her eyes slowly faded to gray, the green tint bleeding from her irises, causing Sarra to gulp in fear.

"Why are you still so armed? It's as if the Roamers still walked the wilds of Greenearth."

Alura smiled knowingly, glancing down at her boots. "Your feet itch, do they not? That insatiable wanderlust," she chuckled as Sarra stared up at the witch. "Well?" she asked when no answer was forthcoming.

Still Sarra did not speak, fear shining brightly in her eyes. The pale sorceress gave a sigh and pressed a single finger into the center of Sarra's chest, making her cringe and writhe in pain. Alura pressed harder, pinning her to the wall as the burning in her chest intensified. "Answer me, dear Sarra."

"I provide protection for wagon caravans!" she cried in pain, tears streaming down her fair cheeks. The woman sobbed harshly, her knees giving out as she slid to the dirty hay-covered floor. "P-please stop!"

Alura left the tip of her finger pressed to McKeer's chest a moment longer before pulling her hand away, leaving the woman to curl up in agony. The snowy witch stared down at her, empty pity flashing for the faintest of moments in her steely eyes. After a few moments, she brought her hand up to her waist, palm up and curled her fingers once. Sarra was lifted into the air by her magic and turned so she was set on her feet. "That's enough crying, girl. You know I didn't come to you for worthless banter and amusement. I'm here with news."

Sarra merely nodded, tears still glistening in her blue eyes. She held a hand over her chest, breathing heavily as she recovered from the torture.

"The Roamers have begun to wander again and eventually they will pass through Cendril. It would be wise if you go with them. I'm sure at least one of them will remember you, Human though you may be." Alura snickered at that, enjoying Sarra's pathetic frown.

After a span of silence, she wiped her tears away and met Alura's gaze, "When do they arrive?"

"Before the month is out if all goes well. I wouldn't take on any more jobs either. Wouldn't want to risk not seeing them, now would we?" the witch replied, giving a devilish grin as she held out her finger again.

Sarra flinched back nonetheless, much to Alura's delight. She gave a dark chuckle and turned to leave. "I'll check in on you every now and then dear girl." She gave a wave without looking back and left the stable. Once outside, the witch disappeared in a flash of white light and was gone back to her castle.

*****

Metallic singing hummed through the air as the scythe blade felled saplings and brush alike. Nihak walked behind, frowning while his comrade grunted and cursed as he cleared a trail for them. The Fire Elves had been tramping through the small forest for only a day, and already Ejen was grumbling and complaining. While Nihak did not like that his friend was cutting them a path, he much preferred this over fire any day. It had taken great convincing to keep Ejen from just burning down the whole forest.

Sighing from exertion, the older elf stood back and leaned upon his war scythe. "You know, we could move faster if you helped cut this filth down."

"You know why I won't do that. Let us just pass through this place and leave it as we found it."

"I swear you were born to the wrong race."

"I'm fully aware," Nihak replied. He gave a slight shrug under Ejen's fierce gaze, knowing he would lose the argument. Without another word, the young Fire Elf pulled his longsword from its sheath and started hacking a path out for them.

"If you use your falchion, you'll make better headway."

Nihak stopped, lowering his sword so the tip rested in the dirt, and turned to look back at Ejen. "The curse on Sudden Death does not work with flora. Only flesh and blood are affected."

"Even so, falchions are renowned for hacking and cleaving. It would suit our needs better than your longsword."

As much as Nihak wanted to argue with his counterpart, what he said bore truth. Still, the young elf hated wielding that damned weapon. Sighing, Nihak reluctantly sheathed his longsword and drew

Sudden Death from his back. The single-edged sword chopped with ease through the vegetation, quickly making travel easier once more. Indeed, the falchion even seemed to slice through the forest faster and cleaner than Ejen's war scythe. As they walked, the sun climbed higher into the sky, the songs of birds and buzz of insects a constant noise in their sensitive ears. Soon enough though, a new sound made itself known: loud rumbling emanating from the elves' stomachs.

"I'm starving. No more of that lizard flesh! I need fresh meat," Ejen grumbled.

No sooner had he said it, then a startled deer sprang from the brush nearby, making a swift getaway from the Roamers. Their yellow eyes gazed after it, both hungry as fiery saliva gathered in their mouths.

"Give me your sword. I'll keep clearing brush while you get us food."

"Use your scythe," Nihak scoffed, returning his cursed weapon to its sheath.

Grumbling, the older elf began swinging away with his long-reaching weapon. As he continued forward, Nihak unslung his bow, notching an arrow to the string. Crouching down near the deer's tracks to better examine them, he surveyed the trail. "Keep moving until dark. I'll find you easy enough if you stay in a straight line westward."

Ejen paused long enough to grunt in agreement, then turned back to the task at hand. When no further reply was forthcoming, he glanced back once more only to find that Nihak was already gone, as silent as a Forest Elf. Rolling his eyes, Ejen resumed felling brush, leaving his companion to the hunt.

The nimble creature had long since left his sight; nothing the Fire Elf couldn't track. He moved at an easy pace, his bow held lightly in his callused hands, arrow tip pointed down.

Fire Elves were typically swordsmen and scythe wielders, with only one elf in every few generations ever becoming archers. Made from the feathers of Fire-Eaters and obsidiron from the heart of the volcanoes, Nihak's black arrows were near-indestructible and lightweight. Obsidiron was hard to work and trickier to craft, so the tips carried no edge. They were merely honed points on the shafts. These arrows did not cut, rip, or tear through flesh, so the elf's accuracy needed to be flawless.

The deer's tracks were starting to slow down, its leaps and bounds turning to a walk. Nihak glanced up, gauging the time from the lowering sun, sensing his prey was close now. His bare feet made not a sound on the leaves and twigs as he slowly moved in a crouching pace. The archer inhaled softly, giving pause; he could practically smell the beast now. It wasn't much longer before he could see his quarry grazing lightly, white tail flicking away flies and mosquitoes. Setting a knee to the ground, Nihak slowly raised his bow, tilting it horizontal. With practiced movement, he drew the string back, sinewy muscles bulging. Inhaling deeply, he took aim, holding the 300-pound draw-weight with ease. Pausing in its feeding, the deer moved to look around, but never saw the Fire Elf hidden in the brush. Finding his mark, he exhaled and let go, a loud *twang* sent the arrow whistling through the air. At twenty-seven meters, the missile struck the deer just above its forelegs and passed clean through the beast, *thudding* into a tree nine meters behind the fallen creature.

Slowly he rose and retrieved his arrow, returning the black shaft to his quiver. Once that was done, Nihak approached the fallen animal and knelt before his prey. Reverently, he laid his bow upon the leaf-littered ground and rested his left hand atop its still chest, bowing his head.

"I'm sorry for killing you, noble runner. Your spirit goes with Seylivonia, to run free in Her Forest of Eternity. Go now and rest," the elf prayed in Forelvish, his words soft and song-like.

In the gathering gloom of evening, Nihak let a moment of silence pass before pulling his knife from his belt. Shifting onto his knees, the Fire Elf lifted the creature's hind leg and deftly slid the edge along its belly. Despite the length of the blade being 23 centimeters, Nihak was more than skilled enough to gut the deer without rupturing the bowels or stomach. Sliding a hand inside the deer's chest cavity, the elf cut the larynx and yanked the guts out in one go, blood spilling over the leaf-litter to splatter his knees. Leaving the mess of organs in a bloody pile, Nihak cleaned his knife, sheathed it, then took up his bow and began dragging the deer after him.

It was nearly dusk by the time Nihak found their camp. Ejen already had a roaring fire with a spit ready for roasting venison. The Fire Elf hauled the kill over and began carving slabs of meat off the flanks and torso. Passing the bloody flesh to Ejen, the older elf skewered them over the fire and soon the sound of sizzling meat filled their camp.

"What took you so long?"

"If you were out here by yourself, you would not last a week."

"I'd have managed, I assure you," Ejen retorted. "I don't need a bow to hunt."

"Just remember that out here, the prey runs *away*, not *toward* you."

"Where's the fun in that?"

Nihak merely rolled his eyes and turned the spit so the meat cooked evenly. "You know nothing of hunting outside the Ashlands. Just admit it."

"I don't need to."

"Of course not," Nihak replied, taking the cooked meat and handing Ejen his portion of food.

The elves ripped into their meals with gusto, hungrily devouring the blackened venison. As they feasted, the sun sank past the trees until it was gone from sight, the great fire becoming their only light. Once they had finished, they cut up more meat and threw that on the spit too, such was their appetite.

"We should reach Wyst'hin in a few days."

"I can't say I'm looking forward to seeing Humans again," Ejen remarked, biting into his second helping.

"Nor I," Nihak agreed.

Finishing their hearty meal, they cut up the rest of the meat from the carcass, wrapping it in a spare blanket. As the dancing flames cast wavering shadows, Nihak took the remnants of the deer and dragged it far from their camp, well beyond the light of the fire.

"I'll take watch tonight. Sleep, Ejen."

"Wake me if you need me."

With that, the Fire Elf rolled over onto his side and curled up on his bedroll. Nihak stared deeper into the flames, the sounds of the night echoing in his pointed ears. Soon the moon rose and the stars glimmered and winked overhead. Crickets chirped in an ever-growing chorus and the nightbirds sang their mournful songs. A sudden twig snapping beyond the fire's light had the elf's bow in hand, arrow notched and drawn back. In the dark, he could barely make out the shape of a small wolf, staring back with green eyes glowing softly in the night.

Shaking his head slightly, Nihak eased the string so it was no longer taut and returned the arrow to his quiver. The wolf stared for a moment longer before turning about and loped back into the woods, melding into the darkness. Turning back to the fire, Nihak added more flames, rekindling its dying light. Ejen rolled over in his sleep, fiery drool running down his chin. Tiny flames danced on his face, much to Nihak's amusement, glad to have the older Fire Elf with him. Though he got on Nihak's nerves at times, but then, he drove Ejen mad too more often than not. Even so, they both respected each other as warriors and would always watch the other's back.

As the night deepened, he brought his knees close to his chest, the cold setting in. He knew there wasn't any immediate danger but growing up in the Volcanoes had made him always alert. Spending years wandering the Wildlands of Greenearth had only heightened his senses and skills. Indeed, it felt strange to be back on the road again instead of being stuck in a cave for years on end.

"Maybe more Roamers will be out there. Maybe more survived the war."

His mutterings made Ejen stir, but not wake. As the fire began to die again, Nihak regrew the flames. With his turn on watch coming to an end, Nihak wasn't looking forward to waking Ejen. Shrugging, he opened their bundle of venison and pulled out a piece of meat. Using his knife to cut away the cloth, he tossed the slab into the fire for cooking.

The aroma of roasting meat soon filled the air once more. As his meal finished frying, the moon set and the sun soon peeked over the horizon, filling the black sky with golden hues. As the light grew, Nihak saw Ejen's nose twitching, then his eyes snapped open.

"Food."

Chuckling, Nihak cut open another slab of meat from its cloth and tossed it to the elf. Ejen easily caught it and tossed it into the flames.

"Did you stay up all night?" He wondered, rubbing his eyes as he sat up, stretching his arms out.

A soft panting could be heard behind him. The elf turned, sickle-sword in hand to find the same wolf staring at him, not three meters away. Ejen growled and hopped to his feet, ready to fight. Nihak stood as well and laid a calming hand on his friend's shoulder.

"Lower your weapon. He will not attack us."

"How do you know it won't?" Ejen glowered at the wolf, the beast still eyeing him coolly.

"If the wolf was hostile, he would have attacked already," Nihak replied, sitting down. "Come, sit and eat."

"I'll not turn my back on that creature."

"The wolf is not a tremak or a Fire-Eater. Relax and eat your breakfast. Your meat is turning charred."

As Nihak plucked the overcooked meal out of the flames and crunched into burnt food, Ejen grudgingly sat down, curved sword laid across his lap. The wolf mimicked him, tongue hanging from its jaws as the rest of the pack appeared among the trees. Eating in silence, the elves helped themselves to a second portion before Ejen extinguished the flames with a clench of his fist.

"Let's move out. We should make the city a day earlier if we run."

"Fine by me," Ejen remarked, gnawing on a bone.

Nihak cut open the last of the meat from their cloth wrappings and tossed it the ground, prompting a few wolves to hurry forward and hungrily snap up the meat. The elf grinned and headed off after his friend as the sun cleared the tops of the trees. Nothing of significance happened to the pair of Roamers as they made their way through the woodland, save for Ejen's occasional grumbling. Indeed, it took the Fire Elves the better part of three days' walking before they finally stepped past the last tree of the small forest.

"Finally, we're out of those woods," Ejen allowed a sigh of relief to escape his mouth.

"You'll be begging to be in the forests again as soon as we reach Wyst'hin."

As he said it, the city came into their view, far off in the distance. An icy mountain range, its peaks numbering four, stood in crescent formation, as if sheltering the city.

"City or forest, I pray to Ignicendir we never venture into those mountains," Ejen remarked, drawing a nod of agreement from his companion.

Gray clouds flew overhead, carried by the strengthening winds. The short grassy plains rolled in waves, tickling the Fire Elves' callused feet.

"Do you feel free out here?" Nihak wondered at length.

Ejen swung his war scythe up to rest across his shoulders, letting the question fly away and leaving Nihak to not press the matter any further. As the day went on, Wyst'hin drew nearer, its domed library standing proudly in the heart of the city; though they still had another day of walking before they reached the gates. As the city slowly grew bigger, anticipation and nervousness rippled through Nihak. The Glaysher Mountains began to tower over them, casting long shadows over the walled city.

Off in the far distance, Sivart and his horde of Huirds watched them approaching. He laid a hand on his chest and spoke. "Mistress, the Roamers are here now."

CHAPTER 4

The massive gates slammed shut with a rumbling *boom*. Bows were drawn taut, swords unsheathed, and spears lowered for attack. Five guards stood before Ejen and Nihak, four behind, and ten had weapons trained on them from atop the city wall. Both elves gave a sigh and waited.

"State your names and business!" the middle guard shouted. The markings on his armor suggested he was a captain or some high-ranking officer.

The elves shared a glance before Nihak stepped forward, prompting the archers to draw their bows tighter.

"I am Nihak, exile of the Fire Elves. This is Ejen'Feriar-Akroa of the Redfire Clan. We are merely journeying across Greenearth and we have stopped at your city for supplies and to find friends. May we enter?"

"Fire Elves?" the captain repeated. "Fire Elves?! The last time your kind were wandering the Wildlands, it was during the Great Kings' War. You're Roamers!"

"Utduan'Osiem tetardan mataborum kesne," Ejen muttered in Firelvish.

"What did he say?" the captain snapped, glowering at him.

Nihak raised a hand to signal quiet. "Sir, my friend merely stated that you are most observant. Now, may we pass through these gates?"

The broad Human glared at them, eyeing their weapons. As they waited, Ejen shifted his weight to lean upon his scythe, he and Nihak staring back unblinking. Many long minutes of uncomfortable silence passed before the younger elf finally spoke again.

"What is your name, sir?"

"I am Captain Henlow. And you will not step past these gates without my approval."

"Very well, Captain Henlow. If you were smart enough to figure out who we are, then you're smart enough to know what Roamers are capable of. One of two things can happen. You either let us through, or we fight our way through. Either way, we're entering this city. Our quest cannot go on otherwise."

"Is that a threat?" Henlow bellowed.

"It will be if you make the wrong choice."

The older Human growled, baring his yellowing teeth as he stomped up to Nihak. They stared each other down, neither moving before the captain spoke.

"You may enter my city."

The Fire Elf nodded, taking a step forward before the captain slapped a meaty hand against Nihak's chest. "But you will surrender your weapons until you leave!"

Stepping back, the Roamer nodded to Ejen. Two guards sheathed their swords and stepped forward while the rest kept their weapons trained on the elves. Grudgingly, Ejen handed over his war scythe while Nihak unslung his quiver. Once the guards had those in hand, the elves unbelted their swords as well. After they'd turned over their weapons, Captain Henlow looked them over.

"Your knives," he growled, eyeing the long blades on their hips.

With an angry sigh, they unbelted those as well and handed them over. Once that was done, the captain gave a curt nod and stepped aside, waving for the guards to stand down.

"Now you may enter. If you two cause any trouble, you will face imprisonment, or even death. When you wish to leave, your weapons will be here."

"Thank you," Nihak replied, venom in his tone.

The gates were pulled open with a rumbling *creak* and the Fire Elves strode into the city. In the dying light of the sun, they walked down the main cobbled road, lines of shops, inns, and stalls on both sides. The outer districts of the city were occupied by the marketplaces, while the inner city was where the scholarly folk dwelt, along with the squat fortress, belittled by the massive library beside it. With the coming of twilight, what few people still out were leaving the streets to head home for the night. Everywhere the elves looked, they found shops closing. The only establishments still open were taverns and inns, filled with dirty light and the sound of men at drink. As the Roamers wandered the streets, turning down different paths at random, passerby stopped and stared with fear and hatred in their eyes. Ejen glanced around, clearly on edge as he repeatedly clenched his fists. The city guard may as well have stripped them of their clothes too for how vulnerable he felt.

"Well, we're here now. Where is she?"

"I remember Danira saying she might open an herbal shop or some sort. We just need to look for one."

Ejen rolled his eyes. "Aye. That will lessen our search. Shall we ask for directions? I'm sure the townspeople would be overjoyed to assist a pair of ragged elves!"

Nihak ignored the biting sarcasm and kept looking, his eyes constantly scanning the various signs and names of the shops. In his searching, he glanced upon a mother and her child passing by. The older woman hurriedly crossed to the other side of the street while the child pointed at the elves.

"Don't look at them!" she whispered.

Her hushed tone was still heard by their sharp ears.

"Do you think they know who we are?" Ejen asked in Firelvish.

"Aye, or they've never seen Fire Elves before," Nihak replied in turn.

As they walked, dusk faded to night and the only light to be had came from the taverns and inns. A loud ruckus sounded from one such place before a man was thrown through one of the windows with a sharp report of shattering glass. He rolled a few meters amidst broken shards before slowly getting up and staggering back inside, only to be hurled through the same window.

"Aen always favored the bottle. Perhaps he's in there?" Ejen wondered, drawing a shrug from his counterpart.

A blast of wind shattered the remaining windows, throwing several men out onto the street. They lay groaning on the cobbles before struggling to stand amongst the debris. The elves shared a glance before saying in unison, "Aye, that's him."

Stepping over groaning drunkards, broken glass and splinters of wood crunching underfoot, Nihak pushed the door open. They entered, pausing and blinking as the smoky air hit their eyes.

Ejen inhaled deeply, "*Tawschei* these Humans smoke more than our Chieftains."

Nihak nodded and scanned the room. Tables and chairs had been flipped over, along with many pressed against the far wall under the broken windows. A few other men lay about on the floor in puddles of spilt mead and ale, some unconscious and others groggily sitting up. As the elves moved into the wrecked place, Ejen casually kicked one man in the face, knocking him out cold. The Roamers stepped around a few split tables and fragmented chairs until they reached the counter where one lone man sat, hunched over his mug of ale. Beside him, a gnarled staff of black oak leaned within easy reach. Nihak and Ejen pulled tall stools out from under the counter and sat on either side of the aging man.

"Who pissed in your drink this time?" the taller elf inquired.

"Only everyone in this tavern," was the reply, followed by a sip of ale.

"Or was," Nihak pointed out, glancing back at the mess.

Aen Marlfen's face was weathered and aged. His hair was no longer black but peppered with gray. A messy mane fell past his ears while his thick beard was nearly down to his chest. Unlike his face though, his grayish blue eyes carried a sharp edge, shining clear and bright. In truth, Aen was no old Human, for Wind Elf blood flowed through his veins. The Elvan, or half-elf, was well into his second century, though he looked to be in his fifties, standing over a meter and a half tall, still sturdy and strong. His attire was a gray weathered and ragged cloak, a thick dark robe, and matching pants. Equally ragged were his boots, the ancient leather full of holes.

"Were they too noisy for your old ears?" Ejen asked, taking the mug from him.

Aen watched with a twitching eye as the Fire Elf spat into the drink, lighting the ale aflame. He downed it in one go and slid the empty mug across the worn and scratched counter.

"Tharm!" Aen called.

A balding man poked his head out from the other side of the counter, shaking. "Yes sir?"

"Another mug of ale, if you please," he said, producing several gold coins from a pouch on his belt.

Sliding them across the counter, the money promptly disappeared into the short owner's pouch. "If you didn't keep paying for the damages caused to my tavern, I'd have you thrown out. If only my hair would grow back." He looked at Nihak and pointed at his dirt-covered head. "Twenty years ago, I had a full head of hair. Then this half-elf moves in and look at me!"

Nihak slid back a little in his seat, an eyebrow raised. He didn't know which was more surprising: the fact that Tharm didn't seem aware he was talking to a Fire Elf, or that Aen had made him lose all his hair.

"Be silent, old man. Get my old comrades a drink too."

Tharm nodded and poured out two more mugs of ale and slid them to Ejen and Nihak.

"So," Aen chuckled, sipping his drink, "it's been twenty bitter winters since I saw you two last. What's brought you from your fiery homeland?"

"Have you heard the talk of war?" Nihak asked.

"Aye I have. Though I can't say I'm concerned over this one. We're not exactly out there getting caught between armies."

"Well that's why we're here, Aen," he said as the Elvan took a long swig. "We're going to take part in this war and we're going to do it with the Sylvan Sword."

Aen's eyes snapped open as he spewed half his drink against the far wall, spraying Tharm in the process. Ejen burst out laughing as the Elvan coughed and spluttered, ale dripping down his salt-and-peppered beard.

"The Sylvan Sword? Have you gone mad, Nihak?" he demanded, coughing more.

"I'm serious, Aen. We'll get the Sword and aid King Malder."

The old half-breed finally managed to inhale deeply, his coughing subsiding. "By Vuntales, we've not even set foot on the road yet and you're already trying to kill me!" He coughed again then gulped the rest of his drink before anything else was said. Slamming the empty mug down, he shook his head and narrowed his eyes.

"And since when did you ever pick sides? When, in all the years I've known you, have you ever considered fighting alongside a Human King?"

"It's because the witch put this idea in his head," Ejen stated, drawing Aen's sharp gaze. It was quickly turned back to Nihak.

The younger elf held the Elvan's gaze coolly, unblinking under the stern glare.

"Lad…" he sighed, shaking his head.

"Aye, that was my reaction too when he told me," Ejen remarked, sipping his ale. "But there's no haze in his eyes or any sign that he's under a spell."

"Well, Danira's the one who'd be able to know for sure."

"Where is she?" Nihak asked, taking a drink.

"Near the center of the city. She's been running a quaint medicine shop for nearly fifteen years now."

Nihak smiled. "She did what she dreamt of."

"Aye. And she and I aren't the only Roamers in this city."

"Aye?" Ejen wondered aloud, taking another long sip.

"Myles is here too."

Ejen spewed fiery ale across the counter in surprise, alighting the far wall in flames. Nihak laughed so hard he fell from his seat as Tharm frantically tried to put the fires out, shouting and cursing the day Aen set foot in his tavern. The Elvan calmly took up his staff and flicked it towards the flames. A visible veil of wind drifted through the air towards the wall, blanketing the tongues of fire. Twirling his staff in a tight circle, a funnel formed from the wall to the Elvan's mouth, upon which he inhaled unnaturally deeply. The very air within the confined fire was sucked out, smothering the flames until there was nothing but a blackened, charred wall, gently smoking. Aen sat back, waving his staff to disperse the wind, causing a light gust to blow over them. The short Human slowly turned to face the three Roamers, one of his eyebrows singed. "Please get out and never come back."

Aen nodded and the Fire Elves finished their drinks before rising from their seats. Turning about, the Elvan picked his way through the debris and groaning men, the elves right behind him.

41

"The hour is late. Danira will be asleep in her quarters above her shop, sensible woman, she is. As for Myles, I've not the faintest idea where that slippery Ice Dwarf is. No doubt bouncing his way around the foot of the Glayshers."

The elves shuddered at mention of the name; it didn't go unnoticed though the Elvan had his back to them. "Not to worry lads. You'll not venture there. If the Odd Dwarf is in his homeland, I shall retrieve him."

"Let us hope he isn't. I do not wish to dwell long in this city."

"Aye," Nihak agreed as they walked down the darkened street. They passed by the occasional tavern, the sound of laughter and drunken shouting still heard within, the lights casting yellowed shadows on the cobbled street.

"How much further?"

"Patience, lad," Aen stated, grinning at Nihak's quiet grunt. "She lives more toward the scholarly section of town near the citadel."

The sound of heavy boots could be heard approaching, stamping from a side-street on the right. Hands reaching for weapons no longer there, the Fire Elves grew tense. Aen however remained at ease, leaning on his staff. Torchlight came into view first, then two men. They wore red jerkins emblazoned with an open-winged falcon wreathed in white fire. The guards approached them, hailing, "Who goes there?"

"Just an old man and two unruly elves."

Nihak and Ejen stared at the Elvan. "Are you trying to get us arrested?"

The guards stopped before them, one of them resting a hand on the hilt of his broadsword.

"Who are you three? Do you live in this section? Highly unlikely, given your appearance," the torchbearer remarked, waving the flames too close to Nihak's face.

The elf scowled and blew on the torch. Much to the guard's surprise, it went out like a candle.

"By the fiery depths of the Abyss?!" he bellowed in confusion, quickly backing away from the smirking Roamer.

"Are you a Fire Elf?" the other demanded, drawing his sword with a sharp *hiss* of steel.

The blade gleamed sharply in the moonlight, leaving the seasoned warriors unafraid. Aen casually extended his staff to tap against the sword, pushing the tip away from Nihak. "At ease boy. They're my companions and I'm just giving them a nightly tour of the city."

"Your companions are Fire Elves," the torchbearer growled, striking his flint and tinder for light.

"Very observant of you!" Nihak snapped, lighting fire of his own on his right palm.

Aen quickly turned and sent a sharp gust of his breath to snuff out the flames, leaving the elf's hand smoking. A warning shake of his head was enough for Nihak to stay his hands and hold his tongue.

"These are the Fire Elves Captain Henlow warned us about?" the other guard wondered as the torch was relit.

They held the dancing flames aloft to better examine Nihak and Ejen more closely, finally noticing the pointed ears and the yellow glimmer in their eyes. Aen cleared his throat loudly, drawing their attention away from the Fire Elves.

"Unless you are going to arrest them, may we please move along?"

The guards looked at each other for a moment. Slowly, the sword was sheathed. "Very well. We advise you get off the streets soon though."

"Easy enough. Thank you good sirs for keeping the streets safe at night," Aen said, shoving them out of the way with his staff, much to their protests.

As the guards moved on with their patrol, Aen and the elves went off in the opposite direction, eager to put distance between them and the nightly watch. Before they were completely out of sight, Ejen looked over his shoulder and flicked a finger. The torch went out once again, followed by the guards' bellowing curses ringing loudly in the night, accompanied by Ejen and Nihak's snickering. It wasn't much further along the street before Aen led them to Danira's tiny shop. The elves lit fires on their palms and held the lights high to better see.

Her store was indeed quaint, the red-painted walls cracked and faded. An old wooden sign swung gently in a light breeze, the words *"Luerhennai esu Lasemdiaghnan"* in broad, sharp curving strokes. Beneath them read in the Common Tongue "Herbs and Medicines". Nihak smiled as he read the sign. "She used Forelvish," he chuckled.

"Aye, she remembered what you taught her. I'm sure she left the backdoor open for Myles."

With that said, the Elvan turned down a dark alleyway and led the elves to the back where he tapped upon the door with his staff. They heard a soft *click* and the door swung open on oiled hinges. Aen stepped over the threshold, gesturing for Nihak and Ejen to follow. They stepped inside, looking about as their eyes tried to adjust to the darkness. Ejen added more fuel to the fire dancing on his hand, only to have it promptly blown out by Aen.

"No fires in here, if you please. Much of her goods are dry and burn easily."

Nihak closed his fist, extinguishing the fire on his palm, leaving them in total blackness within the shop.

"Then how will we find our way around in here? Our eyesight is not so good in the dark," Ejen stated, feeling around against a wall. A barbed vine stuck him, drawing a violent Firelvish curse from the elf. Aen hurriedly clamped a hand over his mouth, though that did nothing to halt the steady stream of profanity.

Nihak lit a tentative light on his finger, the single flame waving back and forth ever so gently. The tiny light added to the glow coming from Ejen's blood, orange flame merging with reddish hues. Ejen's wrist had a deep cut, the fiery blood running down his arm in rivulets. Nihak quickly ripped a piece of his ragged shirt off and pressed it to Ejen's wound, stopping the bleeding.

"Well," Aen sighed, slowly taking his weathered hand from Ejen's mouth, "I guess we have to wake Danira now. That vine was most likely poisonous."

They all stopped and looked at each other in the dim light. Nihak rapidly waved his finger, putting the light out.

"Not I!" he whispered loudly.

Ejen quickly followed suit, overlapping Aen's voice, beating him by a second. The Elvan sighed angrily. "I will pour water on you both while you sleep!" He shuffled forward, trying to make his way through the shop in the dark. There was a loud *bump* followed by a louder *clatter* of breaking glass.

"Oh, son of a whore!" he bellowed.

A light shone from the top of the stairs off to their left and the sound of footsteps above could be heard, drawing their gaze upwards.

"Now you've done it," Ejen muttered.

"I'll blow all the hot air out of you!" Aen growled.

"Not before I slip drulsem leaves into your food," came a soft voice from the top of the stairs. All three looked up to the figure silhouetted by soft lantern light. "It helps speed up digestion and soothe the bowels, but too much and well," she chuckled, padding down the steps, "let's just say your insides will be empty and your arse will be burning for days."

Danira Shoren was a short Human, just barely coming up to a meter and a half in height. Her hair was black and short, falling halfway down her neck. Equally dark were her eyes. The woman's flesh was olive-toned, smooth and flawless; her face just as soft with round cheeks and a button nose. At the moment, she wore a long gray nightgown, her bare feet sliding softly along the wooden planked floor. As she came to the landing, the witch whispered a spell, waving a callused hand through the air; the lanterns scattered about the rafters suddenly became aglow with warm candlelight.

"Danira, I see you haven't aged a day," Nihak remarked, smiling as she sat down at a table.

"Yes well, having a store of near-limitless herbs and plants, I don't need magic to keep myself young," she replied.

"Nothing could change your height though."

"Aen, remind me to slap him later."

"Get in line, Danira," the Elvan muttered, taking a seat as he pulled a long-stemmed pipe from his robe.

"Now, why did you make such a noise and wake me, boys?"

Ejen held up his bandaged wrist. "I got stuck by one of your disgusting plants."

Aen gestured to the creeping vines growing along the back wall, the spines as long as fingers. The witch rose to her feet to examine the plant.

"This is *Lirami'Fenlai unavnif* or by the Common Tongue, Wolf's Tooth vine."

"How long do I have to live before the poison takes effect?"

She cast a peculiar glance his way before chuckling. "Oh, this isn't a toxic plant. Wolf's Tooth is usually used for sewing needles. The vine itself has very little qualities beyond durable thorns and nutritious leaves. I use them for tea on occasion. Though the aftertaste can be bitter. Whatever gave you the idea it was poisonous?"

"An old fool," Ejen stated, glaring at Aen.

The half-elf merely rolled his eyes and struck his flint and tinder together, lighting the weed in his pipe. Leaning back in his seat, Aen took a long drag on the stem and blew a plume of bluish smoke from his mouth.

"Aen, if you're smoking Illu Leaf," she cast a stern glare on the Elvan, who shrank back. Her gaze softened with a devilish smile. "You better share it."

He chuckled a little, taking a quick puff before he handed the witch a small, folded leather parcel. Danira came back to her chair, pulled out a short-stemmed ivory pipe, and tapped some of the crumbled weed into the bowl. Whispering the spell for fire, a single flame lit upon her finger. Leaning back, she inhaled deeply, blowing a perfect smoke-ring as she exhaled. "So here we are, in the wee hours before the dawn, enjoying a good bit of weed. If I close my eyes, I can imagine us out in the Wildlands. Which brings me to the question of why are you two here," Danira remarked, staring at the Fire Elves.

"We're going for the Sylvan Sword," Nihak stated.

Danira's thin black eyebrows slowly rose. "One of the Elemental Swords? Why ever would the Roamers do such a thing?"

"You've heard the talks of war between Malder and Jamiel. We all know Malder has not the strength he once had. He'll need all the help he can get."

"And you think the Forest Blade will even the odds? That and us at the head of the king's army?"

"Perhaps. Right now, I'm just focused on *getting* the Sword first."

Danira inhaled deeply, blowing twin streams of bluish smoke from her nose. The clouds formed into tiny horses that reared on their hind legs and galloped through the air, smoke wisping off in trails behind them as they circled the others' heads.

"Well, as much as I've grown to love the steady life of a shopkeeper and benign witch, I must admit I've felt a familiar old itch in my feet. The wanderlust never truly goes away." She blew another smoke ring and rose to her feet. "The dawn is but a few hours away. I shall do the reasonable thing."

"And that's get dressed and pack for the long road ahead?" Nihak asked, smiling.

"Dear me, no. I'm going back to sleep and enjoy my last night in a feather bed. You three can sleep down here. I've a spare bed in the backroom here when Myles is around, so one of you can have it. I'm sure the floor is still more comfortable than the rocky road too. Good night," she said, giving a close-lipped smile and tapping out the remnants of weed from her pipe. They stared at her as she stepped back up the stairs, listened as her bedroom door softly closed, and then watched the light winking out, leaving the upper floor completely dark.

Aen stared at the elves as they stared back at him. Slowly, they rose together and made their way through the backroom, searching for the bed. It didn't take them too long, finding it tucked away in a far corner, hidden by lush flowered leaves. The Roamers stood not three meters from the prized cushion, slowly turning their gazes upon each other. Indeed, it was only big enough for one person, and none of them were about to share! Hurriedly they shuffled forward, trying to stay as quiet as possible in their race for relative comfort. Aen got there first, but before he could claim the bedding, Ejen grabbed his cloak and yanked him back. As the Elvan was pulled back, he tripped the older Fire Elf, only succeeding in knocking them both off their feet to land in a heap. Taking the opportunity, Nihak came from behind the fallen pair, moving to step over them, but Aen was quick to grab his ankle and pull him down too. The three cursed and swore in hushed tones as they struggled to rise above each other. Ejen was able to clamber to his feet but Aen grabbed the front of his shirt and blew out the remnants of weed from his pipe. The hot ashes flew in a cindered flurry into Ejen's face, drawing a hushed cry of irritation from him. He fell out of the pile onto his back, trying to rub the ashes out of his eyes. While Aen was busy with Ejen, Nihak rose to his feet, reaching for the bed. His fingertips were but a few centimeters from the edge when Aen's staff rushed up, taking the elf between his legs.

Freezing in place, his eyes clenched shut as he gave a muffled groan, slowly toppling to his side. Panting slightly, the Elvan stood, chuckling as he dusted himself off and softly slapped a hand on the wide cushion.

"To the victor goes a decent night's sleep."

With that, he took his cloak off and laid it over the bed for extra comfort. Before he took his sleep, the Elvan pulled out their simple bedrolls, tossing them over the sprawled elves, and bade them a good night.

Neither gave a coherent response beyond a groan of pain.

*****

Danira awoke from her soft bed, the warm rays of the sun laying across her waist. Smiling, she threw back the blankets and idled down the stairs, making her way to the backroom.

It was a wide room, filled with tables of assorted plants, potted or hanging. From the stairway off to the far left was the spare bed. Straight ahead in another corner was an alcove for a fireplace. Next to that was a small metal cabinet, while above hung various pots and pans and other kitchen tools. Nearer the foot of the stairs were more cabinets, a wide shelf, and a table set against the wall.

As the witch came to the foot of the stairs, she found the Fire Elves curled up under their bedrolls instead of on them and a short, beardless dwarf lying atop the snoring Elvan. Chuckling, she padded over to the fireplace and threw some logs in. Murmuring the incantation, *"Evnecite mieh pame Anfais"* she summoned fire to her hand and tossed the flames onto the wood, starting her cookfire. Next, she pulled a wide iron skillet down from above and rested it upon a metal grate over the fire. Leaving the pan, the sorceress shifted over to open the metal cabinet, frosty air hissing out. Reaching in, Danira retrieved several sides of bacon and eggs. One by one, she cracked them open and dropped the yolks into the skillet, laying the bacon alongside. The thick meat instantly began to sizzle and crackle, sending a delicious aroma into the air. Taking up a wide, flat wooden trowel, repurposed for cooking, she flipped the eggs and bacon. Once they were fried to her satisfaction, Danira lifted the skillet from the fire and took down five plates from the shelf. Expertly laying them out on the table, she waited for her friends to wake. Time barely passed as the scent of a hot meal wafted over the sleeping Roamers, beckoning them to rise. Slowly but surely, the Fire Elves crawled out from under their bedrolls, groaning from faded pain and stiff joints. Rubbing the sleep from their eyes, Nihak and Ejen managed to stand up and shambled toward the table, sniffing deeply.

Ejen grumbled something, but Danira found it hard to decipher. With the way he held his hands out, she could only assume he was hungry. Or angry. Perhaps both. Shrugging with a smile, she handed him a plate and slid on three eggs and two pieces of bacon, the food still sizzling. The Fire Elf shuffled stiffly over to a chair and plopped down, eating the eggs with his bare hand. Yolk dribbled down his chin and between his fingers as he shoveled the delicious meal into his hungry maw. Nihak took his plate, received the same amount, and joined him shortly, devouring the bacon hungrily. As they wolfed their food down, there came a loud *creak* from the bed, followed by a louder *thump*. Aen bellowed a loud curse as he sat up from the floor, rubbing his head. The elves and witch didn't need to look to know who was approaching; the sound of running feet towards the table was more than enough.

Standing before Danira, his rough hands held out for his breakfast, was Myles. Myles Beseru-Meseru was an Ice Dwarf, also commonly known as an Odd Dwarf. Not one, in the entire history of their race, did they ever grow past the height of one meter. Neither were they known for their beards, instead having hairless, boyish faces. Myles' eyes sparkled with the light of innocence, as blue as a glacial lake. His short black hair was a complete mess and no comb or brush in the world could tame it. While he was stocky and broad-shouldered, and though he looked like a child, he had no shortage of strength. The dwarf had a near-infinite supply of energy too, and the way he used that energy was how the dwarves had earned the nickname of "odd". His usual attire was black worn boots, gray pants, a mottled white and gray tunic, and blue hooded-cloak.

The witch gave a slight chuckle, her white teeth showing in a hearty smile as she handed him his platter, followed by the eggs and bacon. Aen stumbled in last, holding his side as he leaned heavily on his staff.

"Little shite used my body to launch himself off the bed," he grunted, accepting his breakfast and sitting at the now-crowded table. Danira slid the last of the food onto her own plate and came to sit at the table.

"We seem to have a problem with the number of seats," she remarked, staring at each Roamer in turn.

Myles grinned, his left front tooth missing, and hopped out of his chair and onto Aen's lap, much to the Elvan's aggravation. He grunted in surprise and shoved the Odd Dwarf off his lap, sending him tumbling to the floor. Myles expertly hung onto his dish as he fell, even keeping all the food on as well, much to Aen's amazement.

"Pain in the arse!" He muttered, ripping into his bacon. "Where were you last night anyway?"

"I could ask you the same thing," Myles replied, his voice higher pitched like a boy.

"It matters not where you two were," Danira stated, sitting in Myles' vacated chair. She ate quietly, while the Fire Elves finished up their meal. Aen paused midway through his, reaching into a small pocket on the inside of his robe to produce a tall bottle of cider.

"Why I agreed to enchant your pockets, I'll never know," Danira remarked wryly as the bottle was uncorked.

"You've no idea, woman," he replied, taking a swig.

"Here," Ejen said, reaching across the table, "let's have some of that."

Aen held it close like it was his first-born. "No. You'll set the whole bloody thing on fire and waste it!"

"Well it won't be wasted on us," the elf replied without missing a beat.

Shaking her head in amusement, Danira rose to her feet and stepped over to one of the cabinets. She quickly returned with two tankards and handed them to the elves. "Aen, be a good friend and share with them."

The half-breed looked from his drink to the Fire Elves, then back again before sighing and filling the tankards halfway. He took another swig, stoppered the bottle, and stuffed it back into his robe.

Danira finished her meal and rose once more, stretching her arms out. "Well boys, allow me to get dressed and pack up my shop and we'll be on the road once more."

The others finished eating and drinking while she headed back up the stairs. As soon as her bedroom door could be heard closing, Myles hopped to his feet with a grin.

"I'll pack too!" he declared, rushing to the other side of the backroom. Underneath the bed lay a single-bladed battle axe with the likeness of frost patterned on the broad blade. A baldric with a single dagger lay sheathed next to it. The Odd Dwarf slung it over his torso, from his right shoulder to his left hip with the dagger resting comfortably over his chest. There were two loops of leather, one located behind his shoulder while the other was at the center of his back. Myles slid the shaft of his axe through the loops and hurried back to the other Roamers. "Ready!"

While they talked and told Myles of their plans, Danira prepared. She slipped out of her nightgown and pulled on brown leggings, a blue shirt, one of the long sleeves missing at the elbow, and knee-high travel boots; they were so worn and weathered they had turned grey. She threw a black cloak over her shoulders and tied her hair back into a short ponytail. Next, she grabbed a leather pack, large and empty.

Her bedroll went in, followed by several changes of clothing, a sewing kit, and a spare pair of boots. That done, she walked back downstairs to find Myles and Ejen arm-wrestling on the table. So far, the two seemed evenly matched as Danira went into the kitchen and opened a different flap on her bag. Into this one she dumped her pots, pans, spoons, knives, plates, and other tools needed for cooking. Next came her stores of food, all going into the pack, though it retained its initial size, as if only a few items rested within.

As the witch finished emptying her kitchen, her gaze was drawn to the table as Myles' arm was slammed down with force onto the wooden surface, followed by Ejen's jubilant cry, "Fire always beats ice!"

Rolling her eyes, Danira headed into the main room of her shop and opened the largest section of her pack. Weaving her fingers through the air, chanting softly, *"Suno'bryum onterpalfe iteka malcere'pesune"* the vines, roots, shrubs, bushes, and flowers all began to shrink in size. As the potted plants all hovered into the air, leaving only dirtied empty tables, Danira produced a plethora of glass jars from her bag. Every single plant in her shop, from the backroom too, went into their own jar, sealed by a wooden cap. One by one they all floated down into the open maw of her bottomless pack until there was nothing left in her store. Sealing her bag shut with a satisfied smile, the witch gathered her quills, parchments, inkwells, and money from her desk and deposited them into an outer pouch sewn to the side of her pack. Upon returning to the backroom, she found Aen blowing smoke rings while the elves and dwarf competed for who could shoot through more wispy hoops.

There were scorch marks and melting icicles stuck along the walls and ceiling everywhere.

"Ahem," she cleared her throat curtly.

All four immediately stopped and stared at her. Shouldering her heavy pack, Danira grinned at them. "Shall we, boys?"

Myles vaulted over the table, only to snag his boot on the edge, sending him tumbling headfirst to the floor. The energetic Odd Dwarf rolled once and smoothly hopped to his feet with a boyish grin. Aen snuffed out his pipe, tucked it away, and rose on crackling limbs. "A good sign," he muttered with a wry chuckle and leaned on his staff. The Fire Elves stood as well, more than eager to go.

"You packed enough?" Ejen remarked, eyeing Danira's bag.

"Just everything I own, save for the shop itself and furniture. I mean, I could *fit* some of the chairs and maybe the desk, but that might strain the dimensional spell just a bit."

The Fire Elf scoffed and headed for the door, the rest of the Roamers following.

"Shall we head for the gates and make for the Ir'Afa Plains?" he asked as they filed out, the witch last.

"Rom and Jolek would be out there, aye," Danira stated, locking her empty shop as they left.

"I certainly hope so" Nihak added as they walked down the street, heads everywhere turning to stare at them.

Danira nodded as she led them back to the city gates. The sun shone down on them as the common peasantry and merchants stared and parted before them. The older folk whispered among themselves, the word "Roamers" falling on the Fire Elves' sharp ears. They couldn't help but grin, glad they hadn't been forgotten.

The Roamers had returned.

CHAPTER 5

King Malder sat at the wide table in his Great Hall, perusing reports of recent attacks on the outskirts of his kingdom. The broad-shouldered man wore only a silvery-threaded dark leather coat, black trousers, and heavy boots. An intricate silver crown sat upon his brow, short dusty golden locks of hair falling to his ears. His squared jaw set in a hard frown, pale blue eyes, still sharp and clear, casting a troubled look upon his company. With the king sat his generals and advisors along the massive table, its polished surface covered with parchments of reports and maps.

"How did these raiding parties sneak through our southern borders?"

Morl Sarm, an older man bearing a graying beard, passed another report to the king. "Sire, this is from our Fortress of Kenlihin on the Long Lake. Our soldiers stationed there found enemy movement, and upon investigation, discovered a hidden path. Those raiding parties must have used that to sneak into the kingdom."

Malder looked it over, rubbing his left temple in disquiet. "Has it been blocked up now?"

"Yes, your Majesty."

"Good. Who made this report? Captain Drade?"

"No, sire. A Sergeant Esilena Tana," Sarm replied.

"Very well. Are there any other avenues into my realm we may have missed?"

The advisors shook their heads, much to the king's relief. "Send messengers to Cendril, Neniri, and Tul'yit. The garrisons there will have to make do with their numbers there and fortify what they can since we cannot send aid to the outer towns."

"Very good, sire," Marn Velten replied, rising to carry out the order. He was a younger man, and would have been a fine soldier, had a sparring accident not crippled his leg. Having a brilliant mind, the king found use for him on his Council.

"Now, to the matter of rebuilding my army," the king continued, leaning back in his oaken chair. "We need to reinstate conscriptions. Every man and lad strong enough to bear arms inducted into the military."

There were quiet murmurs and whispers of discontent among the aged men and grizzled warriors, much to Malder's chagrin. Slamming a callused hand upon the table with a sharp report, the room quieted immediately as all eyes focused on the king.

"This war will be nothing like the last one," he growled, eyeing each man in turn. "I did not start the conflict this time. I regret my younger self's actions in seeking to expand my kingdom and claim more lands. I am content to let Jamiel reign over his lands and prosper, as he should have let us. But now he is seeking more blood and death. Unless any of you have a better idea to increase the size of my army, pray tell."

Silence filled the room, weighing heavy on them all as they came to accept the fact that there was no other way.

"Very well, sire," General Yolbson said at last. "Your standing army right now numbers at 9,000 strong, with another 1,000 guarding each of the three outposts on the southern border."

"Aye. We'll start conscriptions at once. I want training fields established here, in Velntak, and Alzen. No doubt Jamiel will take the winter to prepare his army. The first snows will be upon us in a matter of months, so we must move quickly. Set to it, men."

With that said, the king concluded the meeting. Advisors quickly hurried off to deliver tasks and carry out the king's orders. Horsemen were riding out from Sraztari within the hour, bearing messages to the four corners of the kingdom.

*****

The Roamers stood at the gates of Wyst'hin, surrounded by guards. Once more, Ejen and Nihak had arrows and spears trained on them as they waited for the captain to appear.

"Is this how you were greeted when you first arrived?" Danira asked, eyeing the guards lightly.

"Aye," Nihak answered.

"How did you get through unscathed?"

"Where do you think our weapons are?" Ejen growled, his fingers clenching tightly.

"From my reports," Captain Henlow said, striding towards them from the wall, "you two caused no significant trouble, aside from harassing a night patrol. As loathe as I am to say it, you may have your weapons back and be on your way."

He then signaled to three of the guards, who sheathed their swords and stepped inside a barracks. They emerged a moment later, bearing the Fire Elves' arms. Nihak belted on his knife and longsword,

53

slinging his quiver and bow over his right shoulder. Ejen belted his knife and sickle-sword onto his waist and took his war scythe, holding it close like a long-lost friend.

Nihak glared at the guard holding his falchion; the Human gave a crooked grin as his hand wrapped around the hilt. "I would like that back now."

"Is this the infamous Sudden Death?" the Human asked, pulling the blade halfway out of its sheath.

"Yes, and if you know anything about that sword, you'll hand it over."

"The legend says if you kill the wielder of Sudden Death, the sword belongs to you then."

"It does indeed," Nihak growled. "And if you wish to live past the next minute, you'll hand my sword over."

The other guards bristled at that, weapons raised to strike the elf down. Captain Henlow quickly raised his arms, signaling that they stay their hands.

"Hold! Private Trune, you will give the elf his sword back. I will hear no more about useless legends of weapons."

Grudgingly, Trune slammed the sword back into its sheath and held it out for the Fire Elf. Nihak snatched the weapon from his hands and slung it over his left shoulder, scowling.

"Leave now," the captain ordered.

"Happily," Nihak replied, spitting at Trune's feet before walking past the open gates.

His fellow Roamers quickly followed. Once they were through, the massive doors slammed shut with a resounding *boom*.

*****

Alura stood upon a hill overlooking Wyst'hin, her Left Hand servant beside her. Behind them stood the Huirds, squawking and cawing at each other in their boredom, awaiting further orders. A grin slowly appeared upon her soft lips, watching as the Roamers left the city. The witch could even hear the gates booming shut, despite being leagues away.

"Excellent. Only three more for them to find and then they'll be on their way to get the Sylvan Sword." She turned to glance at her henchman. He in turn met her gaze. "You are to follow them. But keep your distance, dear Sivart. I don't need them finding you out."

The broad-shouldered man nodded, albeit grudgingly, something the witch did not miss.

"Something wrong?" she asked in a sweet tone, her eyes shifting to icy blue, causing the Human to flinch back.

"Nothing is wrong, Mistress," he hurriedly stated, turning his gaze back to the distant Roamers.

He felt her deathly-cold fingers grip the edge of his left ear, followed by the sharp pain of her nails piercing into the sensitive flesh. Giving a cry of pain, his eyes shifted back to meet her cold glare.

"Sivart, if I didn't know any better," she stated, "I would say that you are lying to me."

"Mistress please, I beg you!"

He wanted to slap her hand away, if he didn't mind having his ear ripped off. So the Human stayed his hands, though his arms quivered and his fingers twitched. Hot blood could already be felt dripping down the side of his neck.

"Because you know how much it pains me when my slaves lie to me," Alura went on, ignoring his pathetic cries for mercy. "And you know what happens when slaves lie to me, dear Sivart. Especially my Left Hand."

As she spoke, Alura began to slowly pull down, exerting greater pressure to Sivart's ear. Knowing full well the witch's overwhelming strength, he had no choice but to go to his knees, lest she really did tear his ear off. Alura kept her sharp grip on his ear, watching in amusement as his arms shook and tears streamed down his cheeks. Under her questioning eyes, all Sivart could do was finally nod in defeat. A gasp of pain and relief rushed from his lungs when the witch released her hold on him, letting him fall forward to rest on all fours. He stayed in that position, panting hard as the pain in his ear burned and throbbed. No sooner though had she released him than Alura leaned down, staring intently at the back of his head, knowing he felt her gaze upon him. And he dared not look up into her eyes, lest they were black as stone.

The witch rested a slender hand upon his shoulder, causing her slave to flinch at the light touch. "Do you wish to tell me what the matter is now?"

"It's Danira, Mistress…"

She gave a sigh and straightened to her full height, folding her arms as she did so. Her foot tapping the ground impatiently, Alura commanded, "Get up."

Slowly he climbed to his feet, finally daring to stare into her eyes. To his great relief, they had remained their icy blue color.

"Sivart, poor creature that you are, I do not understand your miserable feelings of love for that woman. But let me make this clear: you are to stay behind them by five leagues at all times." The witch stepped forward until their faces were but centimeters apart. "Do you understand?"

Sivart nodded rapidly. "Yes, Mistress!"

Her eyes softened to dark blue and a sweet smile crossed her pale lips. "Good. Now run along." With that, she turned and walked a few paces away.

"Mistress Alura?"

"Yes?" she asked, turning back to her servant.

"May I ask you something?"

"You may."

"Why must I follow after them? Can't you just send a few Huirds to fly behind them?"

"Oh Sivart, you simple thing."

She grinned and shook her head, coming back to him. The broad Human took a cautionary step back before she reached out and poked a finger against the Black Hand mark on his chest. He cringed at the burning sensation from the simple contact.

"Because I cannot teleport to my Huirds. You are my Gateway, as are all my slaves. With you following the Roamers, I have your eyes and ears on them. And if anything goes awry, I can just come to you. Or would you rather I take on my other form?"

"No Mistress. I understand Mistress."

"Very good. Well, if that's all, then I shall go. The Roamers are on the move and so should you be. Remember Sivart. Five leagues." With that, there came a blinding white flash and the witch was gone.

*****

Golden rays of the sun showered down, bathing the land in warmth as the Roamers walked along a gravelly road heading west. Ejen casually rested his war scythe across his shoulders, letting his scarred arms hang loosely over the shaft.

"I'm amazed that Human sided with you, Nihak," he remarked, glancing at his comrade.

"As am I. That captain was made of tougher stuff," Nihak agreed, then added, almost as an afterthought, "And I wouldn't be surprised if he'd crossed blades with the Roamers during the Great Kings' War."

"He saw enough winters for that to be possible," Aen mused, pulling his pipe out.

As the half-elf filled the bowl and struck a light, Danira skipped along, her pack giving a clattering rattle as she adjusted the straps around her shoulders. "Oh damn," she muttered before looking at the Elvan. "You're having a smoke again?"

"Hm?" he grunted, glancing at her as he exhaled a plume of blue smoke.

"It's only morning, you old fool. Wait until we camp tonight."

Aen paused then took another long drag on his pipe, blowing a stream of smoke into the air. Twirling his staff about, the smoke shaped itself into a hand making a crude gesture. The witch gave an aggravated sigh and rolled her eyes as Myles hopped and skipped around her, giggling.

"Stop being such a child," she huffed.

The Odd Dwarf ignored Danira and instead leapt on the Elvan's back, much to his pained surprise.

"Gah! Myles! Off! Now!" Aen desperately used his gnarled staff for support as he tried to take the energetic dwarf's weight on his aging back.

Nihak and Ejen burst into raucous laughter as Myles wrapped his legs around Aen's waist.

"Carry me?" the Odd Dwarf giggled.

With an annoyed grunt, Aen managed to stand up straight and shoved his staff between his waist and Myles' leg. Straining, he somehow found the strength to pry the dwarf's legs off, followed by his arms.

"Oof!" went Myles, landing unceremoniously on his rump as the others kept walking.

The Fire Elves' laughter eventually subsided as he scurried to his feet and chased after the Roamers. "You two haven't changed in all these years," Nihak remarked, grinning.

"Neither have you two," Danira returned. "Though I see some new scars on both of you."

"Just Fire-Eaters and tremaks," Ejen shrugged, casually twirling his scythe off his shoulders to use as a walking staff like Aen. "Nothing glorious in a hunt. Just simple survival."

"You simple-minded creatures," the witch shook her head. "I still don't understand why you wouldn't let me heal that scar over your eye."

Nihak shrugged. "You never will, Danira."

"Bah!" she waved a hand in dismissal as they walked on.

While the witch grumbled about strange elves, Nihak took their surroundings in, smiling broadly. Clouds drifted lazily overhead, some passing over the sun to cast soft shadows upon them. No wind stirred the grass alongside the road nor shook the paling leaves from the trees.

"Where are we going now?" Myles asked, attempting a cartwheel. The playful dwarf only succeeded in flopping onto his back.

Nihak laughed. "The Ir'Afa Plains. They're just northwest of the city of Strigard."

"Humans aren't wanted out there though," Danira stated.

"Should we leave you in Strigard or...?" Ejen wondered, glancing at her.

"But I am no ordinary Human. And I don't fear the Earth Elves."

"They don't make trade with the city of Strigard?" Aen wondered aloud.

Danira shrugged, giving another bounce to shoulder her hefty pack. "They don't need anything made by Human hands."

"How heavy is that bag?" Aen asked curiously, eyeing the seemingly empty sack.

"Oh, it changes. One minute the pack is as light as a feather and the next it's as heavy as a suit of armor."

"Who taught you your craft?" Myles wondered, scratching his beardless chin.

"Books, books, and endless practice," Aen answered for her.

Danira opened her mouth, but before she could refute that, Nihak stepped in. "And more books."

Without missing a beat, the witch side-kicked the Fire Elf in the shin. He gave a cry of surprised pain as he stumbled. "True, I did much reading on witchcraft, but I learned most of what I know from Lor'Eln. And if you'll recall, Aen, she is the one who gave you your staff and cloak."

"Yes, I remember. I was merely jesting."

"It didn't sound like jesting," she replied.

"That's because Aen's terrible at it," Myles chimed in, hopping over to bat at the Elvan's beard.

Aen promptly slapped the dwarf's hand away, then took up his staff with both hands to grip it near the end. Before Myles could duck out of the swing, the Elvan *thwacked* him hard in the rear. A gust of wind burst from the gnarled oak and sent the Odd Dwarf flying several meters up and away. The unnatural wind ruffled the other Roamers' clothing as they all stopped to observe his flight, hearing the dwarf hoot with laughter as he flew. Danira set her hand against her forehead to better shield her eyes from the glare of the sun. They watched as Myles bounced twice upon the ground, then rolled and tumbled head over heels off the road and into the grassy field.

"That must be at least 21 meters away," she remarked.

"And six meters high," Ejen added, grinning. "That beats the old mark of 17 meters."

Aen merely grunted at the compliment and resumed walking with the other three following after him. They picked Myles up along the way and dusted off the bits of dirt and grass from his face and hair. The bubbly dwarf just grinned that childish grin of his and walked along; showing no signs at all that his landing had injured him.

As the party of wandering warriors moved along, they could make out a forest ahead, the road running straight through it. More clouds began to gather then, much to the Fire Elves' nervousness. Aen took one final puff on his pipe before tapping out the remnants from the bowl and tucked it back inside his robe. Glancing skyward, the Elvan then looked down at his cloak, the heavy fabric flapping gently in the rising wind. Indeed, the enchanted material had turned from a sky blue to a darker hue flecked and spotted with gray.

"It may rain tonight," he mused, glancing skyward again.

"Let us hope it does not," Nihak stated.

"Aye," Ejen agreed, quickening his pace.

"Might we stop for a meal before we enter the woods?" Aen inquired, casting his gaze towards the witch.

Danira stared back at him, then stepped off the road and unshouldered her pack. The other Roamers quickly followed and sat upon the grass as she rummaged through the enchanted pack. Out came a frying pan, a wooden spoon, some plates, and a metal stand.

"If one of you elves could be so kind," she said before opening a different pouch.

Nihak summoned a small flame and tossed it upon the ground, letting it consume the greenery as it grew to a fair size. Once the fire had grown large enough for Danira to cook with, the elf kept the flames under control, ensuring it did not spread over the grasslands. While Nihak was preoccupied with the flames, Ejen set up Danira's three-legged iron stand, placing the frying pan atop it over the cookfire. The witch then pulled out five eggs, a block of cheese, and a loaf of bread. Tossing the loaf to Nihak and the cheese to Myles, Danira expertly cracked the eggs over the pan.

"Boys, put your toothpicks to good use," she said, using the spoon to scramble the yolks.

The Fire Elf shook his head, pulling his knife from his belt. "It's not a toothpick, Danira."

Similarly, Myles pulled his dagger from his baldric and began carving up the cheese into thick slices. "I use mine for picking my teeth," he said, grinning.

"Is that why you're missing a tooth?" Ejen smirked.

The dwarf stuck out his tongue at him but continued slicing cheese.

"Look, a knife is a simple tool. Why do you need such a long blade?" the witch asked, stirring the fried eggs about.

"When all you have between you and a Fire-Eater is a knife, you better hope its long enough to pierce through its scales," the elf replied, handing over ten slices of bread.

The remaining loaf followed, to which Danira tucked away in her pack, along with the block of cheese.

"Thank you, boys." With the eggs done, Danira laid out the bread, laying a slice of cheese on half of them. The fried eggs were divvied up evenly five ways and for the finishing touch, Danira laid the other five pieces of bread on top. "Enjoy," she said, passing the strange food out.

Myles turned the bizarre breaded meal over in his hands before shoving the entire thing in his mouth in one go. The elves did not bother inspecting their food with such curiosity before they wolfed it down. Aen and Danira ate more conservatively, taking smaller bites and actually chewing their food. The Odd Dwarf wiped his chin, smacking his lips loudly as he licked crumbs and bits of egg from his fingers.

"Twenty years and I still couldn't teach him manners when eating," Danira muttered, rolling her eyes.

"I told you it was a lost cause," Aen stated, pulling out his bottle of cider for a drink.

As he took a swig, galloping hooves could be heard in the distance from the forest, carried on the wind.

"Sounds like only one horse, bearing a man travelling light," Nihak surmised, slightly tilting his head to better hear as he took up his bow.

"Is there?" Myles asked, hopping to his feet.

"Perhaps we should get moving again," Danira suggested, hurriedly packing up her cooking tools.

Aen used his staff for support as he rose and returned the bottle to the inside of his robes. When the Roamers all stood, making ready to leave, they turned and watched as the horseman emerged from the forested road, galloping towards them. As he drew near, he pulled on the reins, slowing his panting beast to a trot. The Roamers stayed where they were, looking up at the Human as he passed them. He in turn stared back before halting his mount entirely.

A long silence passed between them before finally the short man wiped his sweaty brow and blinked several times. He opened his mouth, then closed it, then finally he spoke.

"Where are you all headed?"

"Whose business is it for you to know? We might ask you the same thing," Ejen replied, crossing his arms over his war scythe.

"I am riding to Wyst'hin. By decree of King Malder, all able-bodied man and lad in his kingdom are to be conscripted for the coming war."

"Well that's good and all, but we're not citizens of the king. We're heading west," Nihak stated.

"I thought as much. You lot must be the last of the Roamers, are you not?" the messenger asked, his tired beast pawing at the ground nervously.

"There are a few more than what you see before you, but aye, we are the last," Aen nodded.

The Human gulped audibly and urged his horse into a walk. He didn't get far before he stopped and turned to look back at them. "Pray tell you'll stay out of this war?"

"Not a chance," they all called back in unison, then set foot back on the road, leaving the messenger confused and worried as he rode to Wyst'hin's gates.

CHAPTER 6

The hour grew late as the forest loomed before the Roamers. Still they had dying shafts of daylight to see by, so in they went past the first trees. While the foliage above was sparse enough, in the twilight hours the woodland was a gloomy place indeed. An occasional bird flitted by, singing its same old song, but the creatures of the day were readying themselves for sleep, so the forest grew ever more silent. All too soon the city was lost from sight as their wide path began to curve and twist, delving further into the woods. Heading deeper in, the trees soon grew thick together, all but extinguishing any remaining sunlight.

"I will go no further," Ejen stated, war scythe gripped tight.

"Aye, we'll make camp. We'll not see Strigard for another day or two," Nihak agreed, stepping off the road to light a bonfire.

Quick to follow suit, the Elvan stepped off the path to lean against a tree. Slowly, he slid down to sit, laying his staff at his feet while Myles leapt into the air to scurry up the same tree, and quite nimbly so for being a dwarf.

"Myles just took the first watch for the night," Aen stated. "Nihak, you get second watch."

The Fire Elf nodded, coaxing the flames to grow, casting its warmth about them as the Roamers laid out their bedrolls.

"I'm sitting a paltry few meters from the fire and still the chill air bites at me. I hate growing old" Aen grumbled, pulling his cloak tighter about his form. The fabric had turned black with gray cloud-like patches drifting about. "You elves are in luck. No rain tonight."

Ejen blew a sigh of relief and sat, joining Nihak before the flames. With a wave of his hand, it grew larger still, spreading dancing shadows and heat over their small campsite. Danira pulled her bedroll from her pack and laid it out to sit, only to shift about, her face a mask of discomfort.

"Oh damn I've forgotten what it's like to sleep out in the wild."

"Stones under your bedroll?" Ejen laughed.

"Be quiet," she growled, reaching under to remove an egg-sized rock. "Nihak, any chance of fresh meat tonight?"

The Fire Elf cast about before turning back to the witch. "There's no light left for my eyes. Don't you have any meat in your pack?"

"Aye, dried meat. Fresh and bloody is better though."

"Is that the warrior I hear?" Aen asked, closing his eyes.

"My killing days are long over," she replied, fishing out a cloth-wrapped stack of dried meat.

After distributing the meager dinner, the witch laid down, pulling the blanket over herself to sleep.

"Goodnight then," Aen agreed, pocketing his meal.

The Elvan wrapped his cloak about himself and was soon fast asleep. Shrugging, Ejen extended a hand towards the flames and clenched his fist tight. The fire went out instantly, leaving only smoldering earth. Dull smoke wafted from the ground as the Fire Elves turned in too, falling asleep as the moon rose higher into the night sky, leaving Myles alone in his tree. The dwarf did not mind, for as outgoing as he was, he enjoyed time alone every now and then. And what better way to have it than high off the ground with his legs swinging to and fro? Eventually Myles scooted to the trunk, pulling his axe from his back as he did so. This allowed him to lean against the thick trunk in relative comfort while keeping watch, though the dwarf's attention was quickly drawn to the moon through the canopy of pale leaves. The silvery orb and glimmering stars reminded him of the ice within the Glaysher Mountains. It had such a calming effect upon his hyper mind; indeed night was perhaps the only time Myles ever sat still for any length of time. Though the other Roamers would be hard-pressed to believe that; especially Aen, even if he saw him now. Sighing quietly, the Odd Dwarf laid his axe across his lap, tracing the curved and jagged patterns of ice with his finger. Humming quietly, Myles looked around every now and then, but found no dangers to present themselves as the night deepened. Smiling to himself, the dwarf hooked his axe blade over the thick limb he sat upon. With a whispering creak of protest, the bough jounced softly as the Odd Dwarf swung down, wrapping his arms and legs about the shaft to swing lightly about in the brisk night.

When the moon reached her zenith, Myles expertly unhooked his axe to drop down, landing with a dull *thud*. Tip-toeing over to Nihak's sleeping form, the dwarf flipped his axe about to grip it near the broad blade. Leaning as far forward as he could, Myles extended the shaft of his weapon and gently prodded the Fire Elf in the back. He did so with good reason, for Nihak woke instantly, long knife in hand. He calmed visibly when he turned to see the Odd Dwarf's shape in the moonlight.

"A calm night?" he whispered.

Myles nodded and helped him to his feet. "There are no Goblin tribes in Malder's realm anymore. And the beasts of the forest do not attack unless provoked."

"I know. But if we're to journey across Greenearth, we must regain our sharp wits and instincts. Better safe than sorry, eh?"

The dwarf nodded again and smiled, turning back to his tree. Nihak returned the smile and patted him on the shoulder. "Get some sleep."

Myles didn't need telling twice. He climbed back into the boughs and lay sprawled over many of the thick limbs so he would not fall. The Fire Elf merely grinned and shook his head as high-pitched snoring could be heard from above. Odd Dwarves made their dwellings in the mountains, so they had a preference for being as high off the ground as possible. Letting out a long quiet breath Nihak sat, crossing his long legs. Creatures of the night were out and about, filling the night with the occasional birdsong, the hooting of mated owls in concert, and the incessant creaking of singing insects. Myles was right: there was no danger on this road, least in the form of crooked bands of Goblins. Even so, he took up his black longbow to lay across his lap, a comfort more than anything this night, while his quiver of arrows lay within easy reach. Try as he might, Nihak's eyes would not adjust to the dark. Though if he really wanted to see, the elf could just light a fire.

As the night dwindled into predawn, he found himself thinking of the Selveryn Forest and the elves that dwelled within. How he missed that wondrous place! Sighing softly, he rose to his feet as the moon faded and the sun began to crest over the horizon. Padding over to the sleeping Elvan, the Fire Elf leaned down to shake him lightly. Aen's gnarled staff flew up of its own accord, *thwacking* the elf hard in the nose. Suppressing a cry of pain, Nihak recoiled, clamping a hand over his bloody nose. Tiny flames in his blood shone through his fingers as it trickled down his chin.

"Apparently you forgot," came Aen's grumbling voice.

"Son of a bitch!" Nihak spat in a harsh whisper. He sniffled hard, then wiped the blood away. "Aye, I forgot!"

The staff rose to stand up straight on its own for Aen to grip, using it for support as he rose to his feet. "Now why did you wake me? Dawn is only an hour away."

"I'm going to try and catch some breakfast. I decided to wake you because Ejen would have been impossible and I didn't want to risk waking Danira."

"Hmm," Aen muttered, sniffing a little, "fair enough, I suppose."

With that said, Nihak slung his quiver over his shoulder and set out. "I'll be back by sunrise. Hopefully."

"Don't bring back any mushrooms. Remember last time?"

Nihak didn't look back as he walked away. His only response was to hold aloft his fist and extend his first and second fingers together in an Archer's Salute for Aen to see. The Elvan merely scoffed at the silent insult and sat back down, arms folded, his staff resting in the crook of his right arm. Blowing a grumpy sigh, the aging Roamer pulled out his pipe and pouch of weed for a smoke. Danira would scold him were she awake.

Yes, he thought to himself, he did smoke too much. Yes, illu leaves weren't the best for the breath, but damn it all the effects were most relaxing with the altering of the mind. Aen chuckled as he filled the bowl of his pipe and lit it with a strike of his flint. Inhaling deeply, he gave a wide smile as his eyes half-closed, blue plumes billowing from his nose in a contented sigh. Calling upon the lightest whisper of a wind, Aen directed the smoke away from the sleeping Roamers. If Danira caught even a whiff of it she would awake instantly. Coughing quietly, Aen shifted around to move his rear off a thick tree root, grumbling about getting too old for living out on the road. Either that or living in the city for twenty years had softened him. With a grunt, Aen shifted again, his thigh giving a loud *crack*. Wincing his eyes shut, the old Roamer gave a muffled groan of pain.

"No. I'm definitely getting too old."

"Is that why you smoke so much?"

Aen turned his head to stare at the witch, who still lay in her bedroll looking up at him, unblinking. Staring back, Aen stuck his pipe between his lips and inhaled deeply. Danira's right eyebrow slowly rose higher than the other.

As he exhaled, the Elvan gave a grumble under that unrelenting stare. "It soothes my aching bones, you know that."

"Yes, but you know the effects become reduced over time," she said, propping herself up on her elbows. "I just smoke every now and then for the euphoria."

"Sleep well?" he asked, changing the subject.

"Aye, I did, despite not being in a feather bed. Why are you awake and Nihak is gone?"

"He woke me to be on watch while he hunted for breakfast. He said he'd be back by dawn."

"Let us hope so. Else you will all be grumbling and moaning all day over empty stomachs," she said, standing and stretching out the kinks and knots in her back. The witch cringed in pain as her shoulder blades popped back into place.

"Glad to see I'm not the only one," Aen said wryly.

"Ha. I may be old too, but I don't feel it like you do."

Looking around, Danira finished stretching and yawned as she walked over to the Elvan. "Mind if I sit with you?"

Aen merely gestured for her to have a seat as he looked east. As she rested her back against the trunk as well, her eyes followed his gaze, watching the golden glow of the sunrise fill the forest.

"Aye, I may miss a soft bed, but I missed watching the sunrises more. You can't see them from the city walls."

"No, you can't," she smiled. "The beauteous crimson, golden, fiery rosy hues. All merged into a wondrous mosaic. Fit for a king's tapestry."

"Aye. But the king can't have this. The sunrise belongs to us," Aen said, smiling slightly. "Even through the trees it's a sight to behold."

The light grew and grew, slowly spreading through the forest, and with it rosethe chirping choirs of the songbirds. As the two enjoyed the serenity of the forest, it came to an abrupt end as three dead rabbits dropped sharply onto Danira's lap.

"Nihak!" she screamed, looking up at the laughing elf. "May you freeze in the Abyss!"

Myles and Ejen snapped awake at the shrieking curse.

"*Nuraz kyn laik*?!" the Fire Elf demanded, taking up his scythe as he scrambled to his feet.

"Not the bacon!" Myles cried, dropping from his tree, axe in hand.

Unfortunately for the Odd Dwarf, his landing was less than graceful as he planted his face in the dirt. Nihak laughed all the harder as the witch glared up at him. "Nothing wakes the whole camp faster than you, Danira!" he chuckled, gripping the tree limb and swinging down to land solidly on his feet.

"Vuntales, I think I've gone deaf in my right ear now," Aen said, climbing to his feet. "And how did you sneak up like that?"

"I did spend time amongst the Forest Elves. I can move as they can through the trees and underbrush."

Ejen scoffed at that. "A creature of fire moving about in the treetops like some wild animal. Disgraceful."

Nihak ignored him as he summoned a fire in the middle of their campsite. "Fire's ready for the meat, Danira."

A rabbit carcass smacked into the back of his head, nearly shoving the elf headfirst into the flames. "I'll skin you alive if you ever frighten me like that again!" she snarled, taking the dead animals over to her pack.

Nihak merely chuckled, though he knew the threat wasn't an empty one.

"Myles, your dagger please." She held her hand out expectantly to the Odd Dwarf, who in turn pulled the blade from his baldric and tossed it to her. The witch caught it expertly by the handle and set to work skinning the rabbits.

"Not enough meat. I'll have to make a stew," she muttered to herself. "Were there no deer to be had?"

"Aye, if I had more than one hour to hunt."

"Very well," she replied, now gutting them. That done, she set them down and fished out an iron pot, a tripod, and a thin chain. Expertly the witch set up the metal stand and hung the pot over the fire. Next, she delved deep into her pack and pulled forth carrots, onions, potatoes, and wide green leaves.

"You eat, you work," she stated, tossing the various vegetables to Nihak, Myles, and Ejen respectively.

Knives were pulled from belts and the food was quickly chopped, peeled, and diced, though the dwarf seemed sad to see the onions go.

"Myles, could you add ice into the pot? I need water," Danira implored, gathering the ingredients.

Nodding, the teary-eyed dwarf cast his element into the wide maw, the heat of the iron reducing it to boiling water. Once the pot was churning and bubbling, Danira tossed the meat, vegetables, and torn up leaves in to cook. Flour and oil was added quickly after, then stirred to mix it well. As Ejen and Nihak coaxed the flames to burn hotter, it did not take long for the stew to cook. As the witch stirred the pot on occasion, she looked to Aen, who had dozed off.

"Watch the pot," she ordered, sneaking over to the sleeping Elvan.

Danira deftly opened his robes and reached into one of his pockets, fishing out the bottle of cider. As she did so, Aen's staff seemed to come to life again, moving to strike at the thief. The witch merely glanced up, the staff halting mid-strike. It shuddered a moment, then returned to its resting place next to Aen.

"How did you do that?" Nihak wondered, returning his gaze to the bubbling stew.

"Oh, Aen's staff just knew better," she shrugged, returning with her stolen prize.

Danira swiftly uncorked the bottle and emptied half its contents into the stew for more flavor. Ejen and Nihak stared at her, begging with their eyes. When she finally looked up from the stew, the witch tossed the bottle to them, which they eagerly shared. By now, the aroma had filled the campsite, rousing Aen as Danira pulled several wooden bowls from her pack to serve them breakfast.

"Where's my cider?" the Elvan demanded, patting his chest.

Ejen, who was mid-swig of the bottle, paused before hurriedly downing the last of the alcohol.

"You shite-eating cur!" Aen stormed, rising in a flurry with his staff in hand.

While he chased after the nimble elf, Danira passed the filled bowls to Nihak and Myles, who readily accepted them, downing their breakfast with fervor.

"Steal from me?! I'll have your fingers for a necklace!" the aged half-breed bellowed, swinging his staff after the elusive Ejen.

"Aen," Danira called, unable to suppress her grin, "I took it from you. The elves merely begged for it and I gave it to them. I'll buy you a new bottle first chance I get."

"I hate all of you," he huffed, coming back to join the others in their meal.

Ejen hurried over as well, laughing still from their merry chase. Quickly the Roamers downed the stew, thanking Danira for her wondrous skills as always.

"It's my pleasure," she said, nodding appreciatively. "Though I wish you elves wouldn't inhale your food..."

"We grew up in the Volcanoes. If you didn't eat fast, predators or other elves would take it from you," Ejen explained, wiping his mouth.

"Now then, if we're all finished, let us move on."

Bedrolls were packed up and cooking implements cleaned and stowed. Shouldering her clattering pack, the witch took the lead and set foot upon the road. The sun had risen swiftly behind them as they continued their journey, setting a fast pace along the winding road.

"We should make the other side of the woods by tomorrow," she said.

"And Strigard isn't too far from there," Aen added.

So, the Roamers strode on, talking and laughing as they caught up on the past long years.

CHAPTER 7

"The Roamers? They've truly returned?" the king demanded, staring at the messenger.

"Yes, sire. They were seen by Haldrin when he traveled to Wyst'hin. They were heading west."

"They're going to Strigard?"

"It would seem so, your Majesty. Shall I send word to Duke Dalger?"

The king rubbed his whiskered chin, then nodded. As the messenger turned to leave, Malder stopped him. "Wait."

"Sire?"

"I will go to Strigard myself. I wish to speak with the Roamers."

The messenger nodded once more. "Even so, your Majesty, shouldn't I ride ahead so the Duke may prepare for your arrival?"

Once more Malder gave a nod, waving his hand in dismissal. Swiftly, the messenger departed as the king turned to summon Councilman Velten, sending a servant to fetch him. He would not have long to wait, but still the Human king paced before his throne, dozens of thoughts whirling through his head. As he strode about, his eye caught the wavering glint of steel atop the hearth. Above the wildly dancing flames, his great sword Dralon hung for all to see. The long, serrated blade had seen many battles in his hands, and had slain countless enemies. Its edge was still as sharp as the day it was forged, but it had long ago lost its shining luster. The once-polished blade was now faded and worn, bearing dozens of scars from combat. Malder had seen no point in maintaining the sword's sheen, for it was an instrument of war, not decoration to flash about in parades. As he stepped over to admire the blade, the king found himself sad to see his mighty weapon so covered in dust. With a sigh, a lopsided grin appeared as he shook his head, reconsidering that sentiment; better it was covered in dust instead of blood. The aging man gave a dry chuckle as he thought back to the Great Kings' War against King Jamiel. That coward never set foot on the battlefield, while Malder always charged in at the head of his army. Eying the black hilt, the king reached up and grasped the long handle. It felt good like he

69

remembered, with rough leather against rough skin. His muscles straining slightly, the king lifted it off the rack and held the weapon aloft in his right hand. A wide smile graced his scarred face as if greeting an old friend.

Slowly, the broad Human ran his left hand along the edge, gently sliding a finger over the serrated teeth. Malder didn't even flinch as the jagged edge bit into his flesh, despite such a light touch. A trickle of blood dripped down his hand, hardly noticed by the seasoned man. Bringing a finger to rest against the flat of the blade, the king gave it a flick, sending a resonating echo ringing through the wide room; such music to his ears. As the sword vibrated its song, he felt the rough metal of the cross guard, curving up in a wide arc. Next, his callused hand drifted down to rub the ribbed pommel, its surface stained and chipped. Feeling the solid steel, the king found himself reminiscing on the countless helmed skulls he'd crushed under the force of that pommel. As the ringing music faded, he gripped the hilt with both hands, remembering the power in his strong arms. With a grunt, Malder swung the blade in a wide arc, feeling the weight of the sword.

"Sire?"

He turned to see Velten standing at the wide entrance to the throne room. Offering him a smile, the king gestured for the Councilman to enter. "It's heavier than I remember."

"A mighty sword for a mighty king, my liege."

Malder laughed at that and swung the huge sword down, the tip sending sparks shrieking along the stone floor. "I'm not so sure this king is as mighty as his blade anymore. Or perhaps the king is mightier than a mere weapon of war, now that he is older and wiser. What say you, Velten?"

"I say you're a mighty king, sire."

"Oh, come off it, man! That's not what I asked. You're intelligent and quite capable of thinking for yourself. I'd rather you show me honesty than lie to my face in the hopes of pleasing me. You think I'll be offended if you say a piece of crafted metal is mightier than I?"

The young man shifted uncomfortably on his feet, putting more support on his good leg. "Sire, I... Forgive me, your Majesty."

Setting the sword back on its rack, Malder walked over to Velten and laid a strong hand on his shoulder. "Fear not. Sometimes my old anger can still rear its ugly head."

The Councilman nodded. "Now then, sire, what have you summoned me for?"

"I want you and a company of men-at-arms to accompany me to Strigard. Word of the Roamers has reached my ears that they're heading west. I wish to meet with them and I could use a wise man such as you for advice and counsel."

Velten nodded eagerly, smiling broadly. "I would be honored to journey with you, King Malder."

Returning the smile, Malder slapped his hand roughly on Velten's shoulder. "Let us prepare then!"

The friendly blow nearly collapsed the crippled man, much to the king's regret. He held Velten up, apologizing profusely. The Councilman shook his head and brushed off the apologies. "It's quite alright, sire."

"Now let us go," the king stated, walking with him out of the throne room. Soldiers were quickly assigned as their guard and horses were saddled. The king and his company were mounted and galloping southwest for Strigard within the hour.

*****

The wide hill sloped down from the Roamers' feet, standing a mere three meters beyond the edge of the forest. Wind rushed past them, stirring their clothing as they stared out over the vast plains of Ir'Afa. Not twelve leagues from where they stood, the towers of Strigard could be seen; the fortress city dwelt on the borders of Earth Elf lands, unlikely neighbors but peaceful ones. That peace lasted only so long as the Humans stayed out of the grasslands, and the Earth Elves stayed out of the city.

Off in the distance, a herd of meshas stampeded across the uneven ground. Even from this far away, the Roamers could see the glint of their steel-like scales and long horns. A full-grown mesha stood just over two meters at the shoulder and over six in length, from the tip of their meter-long horns to their trunk-like tail.

"I've forgotten how magnificent those creatures are," Danira remarked, cupping a hand over her eyes to better see them.

"Aye, when you're this far away," Aen huffed, pulling his wide hood over his head.

"No need to be so morose," the witch replied, staring at the Elvan.

"Morose?" Myles echoed, tilting his head curiously.

"Dark, lad," Nihak explained. "Glum. Miserable. You know, Aen."

The Odd Dwarf nodded in understanding, his mouth formed in a perfect O, while the Elvan merely growled.

"So Jolek and Rom are out there, Nihak?" the taller Fire Elf asked.

"I can't see them being anywhere else."

"Very well. We'll make straight for the plains. Let's not linger even near the city of men," Ejen stated.

"Agreed," the other Roamers said in unison.

So, saying it, they began to make their way down the steep slope. It didn't take long for Myles to "lose" his footing and go tumbling head over heels down the hill, laughing madly as he rolled.

"How has he not broken his neck yet?" Aen sighed, rolling his eyes.

"You know how Odd Dwarves are. They climb to the peaks of the Glayshers only to tumble all the way to the bottom with naught but rosy cheeks and a smile on their faces," Danira laughed. "Let him have his fun."

"Bah! He's always tumbling and prancing ahead. It drives me mad," the Elvan snorted, using his staff as a third leg to steady his descent. "I'm just thankful we're not going up this hill."

By this time the Odd Dwarf had come to a stop at the bottom of the slope. He hopped to his feet and looked up at the other Roamers, giggling and laughing, Myles bounced up and down, flailing his arms about. Danira waved back to him, her bright smile visible even from that distance.

"Next he'll come rolling back up the hill with no trouble," Nihak chuckled.

As if the Odd Dwarf had heard him, Myles began to tumble uphill. Aen and the others stopped short and watched as the dwarf cartwheeled, rolled and somersaulted towards them as if gravity had no power over him. He came to a halt, sitting perfectly cross-legged before them, his bright eyes closed and mouth agape in such a carefree smile.

"Oh, back you get!" Aen finally said, blowing a mighty gust. With a squeal of joy, Myles went tumbling back down the slope.

Nihak and Ejen laughed too as they walked down the hill, watching Myles come to a stop once more at the bottom. He lay there, panting with glee from the excursion, his eyes unfocused and roving.

"I think twice in quick succession was too much for him," Danira giggled as they reached the bottom and stood over Myles.

Aen tapped the Odd Dwarf's chest. "Nay. He'll be fine in a minute."

True enough, with a shake of his head, his eyes cleared and Myles hopped to his feet and strolled on, whistling a silly tune while he wobbled in his walk. The wind picked up even more as they followed him onto the flat grasslands. So great was the wind that the green blades bent in rippling waves, mesmerizing to Nihak's eyes.

"Let us hope those Earth Elves are not too far away. These grasslands stretch for leagues and leagues," Ejen stated, his visage showing disgust and discomfort.

"If you prefer, there are rocky crevices and canyons some tribes of Earth Elves call home too. But they're far north, and too far out of our way," Danira stated, noticing the look.

A glower was all the witch got in response. Nihak noticed the exchange as well but chose to ignore it. "They'll find us as soon as we get deep enough into their territory. You can never sneak up on an Earth Elf. No matter how far away you are."

"Unless you're a Wind Elf," Aen quipped.

"Aye unless you're a Wind Elf," Nihak agreed.

Once Myles had reoriented himself and regained full control of his legs, the Roamers walked on, still heading west. The wind was a constant, always whipping their cloaks and shirts about. As they strode onward, the Odd Dwarf flung his arms out to his sides and ran while bent at the waist. He circled them many times, laughing and smiling. Aen watched with amusement, his smile showing more and more.

"The dwarf wishes to fly," Ejen remarked, twirling his war scythe about in mock-combat.

"Go on Aen. Give him a short flight," Danira urged, watching the carefree Odd Dwarf.

"Very well," he said, taking up his staff in both hands. Instead of giving a rough swing, the Elvan thrusted his staff forward. He felt the rushing power of the wind, channeling it through his arms and staff. The powerful gust of wind concentrated and blew under the running dwarf, drawing a cry of delight from him. Raising his staff to point skyward, Aen used the wind to lift Myles up high into the air. Whooping and screaming in absolute joy, the short Roamer lay flat in the air, arms still out wide and legs out straight, like a bird in flight. The other Roamers craned their heads to watch as they walked, grinning and shading their eyes from the bright sun.

Controlling the air current, Aen moved his staff in slow circles, keeping Myles airborne. he guided the Odd Dwarf's flight, he gently reduced the power of the wind, bringing him slowly down back to the ground. Soon Myles was back on his feet, his black hair a complete mess from the wind.

"Have fun?" Danira asked, though she knew the answer.

With a vigorous nod of his head, Myles hopped along as they walked. "Oh, and there's something I saw," he added, turning to look back at the witch.

"Oh? Did you see the Earth Elves?"

"No. I saw a company of horsemen riding fast for Strigard. I also saw a large bird just above the trees behind us."

"Horsemen?" Danira and Aen echoed at once.

"Large bird?" Nihak repeated, glancing behind them.

"Did you see who was at the head of the company?" Aen pressed, laying a hand on Myles' shoulder.

"Not entirely. But he had a silver crown on his head, and he was a big Human."

"Malder," they all said in unison.

Aen took up his staff and rammed the end into the ground, propelling himself straight up with a powerful burst of wind. Once high enough, his sky-blue cloak billowed out, slowing his descent. Turning his head northward, he saw in the distance a company of armored men galloping swiftly to the towered city.

"Ugh," he grunted, spinning his staff above his head. The twirling motion propelled him back to the earth quickly. Upon landing, he confirmed what Myles had seen.

"We make for the plains. Once there, they can't follow us," Ejen said, easily spinning his war scythe up to rest on his shoulder.

The Roamers resumed their pace but quickened their steps. Even Myles strode with a purpose and ceased his merry cartwheeling. As they walked, Nihak stopped and looked back to the forest. "Large bird..." he muttered, narrowing his yellow eyes.

"Nihak, hurry along!" Aen called.

Taking one last lingering look, the Fire Elf finally turned and sprinted to catch up with the others.

"What were you looking at?" Danira wondered.

"The forest. That 'large bird' Myles saw. It just seems suspicious."

"Perhaps it was a baral'dar eagle? They possess a mighty wingspan," Aen suggested.

"Aye, but the bird I saw had dark feathers. Baral'dar eagles have golden feathers," Myles stated.

"Dark feathers," Nihak echoed, glancing behind them once again.

*****

Gasping for air, the Huird gave a grating squawk. Sivart glowered down at the creature, his strong hand gripping its feathered throat tightly.

"Stupid bird!" he growled.

The Huird gripped his arm, its talons digging into the Human's flesh. His blood dripped down its dirty claws, but he paid that no mind. Sivart was too infuriated for such trivial pain.

"That bloody dwarf and old half-breed could have seen you!" He bellowed, finally shoving the Huird to the ground.

It lay there, propping itself up on a feathered arm while holding its throat. Already furious at his Mistress' orders, and his ear still throbbing painfully hot, the broad-shouldered Human landed a harsh kick to the Huird's ribs. Giving a pain-filled screech, the humanoid gave a wheezing breath and curled up. The pathetic display very nearly made him feel sorry for the creature. But the feeling of pity quickly passed. The rest of the Huirds stood around them, some shifting on their taloned feet while others preened their wings, uncaring as to what happened to their kin. Other bird-men crouched or sat in the trees above, keeping watch all around.

Growling and grumbling, Sivart stomped over to a wide oak tree and climbed the trunk. The rough bark rubbed hard into his palms and scratched up his muscled arms before he came to a thick limb that would take his weight. A large Huird sat crouched next to him, staring out to the open Ir'Afa Plains. Foliage hid them from view, but it was not so dense that they couldn't see through it. The Roamers were distant specks, heading out to the wide, open grasslands.

"Did they see us?"

Shrugging its shoulders, the Huird gave a grunting caw as it scratched at its chest. Sivart blew an exasperated sigh. "Damn you, filthy creature! Speak!"

Its black empty eyes locked on to the Human and stared deep into his eyes. Sivart was not unused to this staring contest for it was a challenge on his authority. If he blinked, the Huird could so attack him if it chose. Hardening his gaze, Sivart glared back. It was testing him; prying for any signs of weakness. The Human's eye twitched, drawing a slight ruffle of feathers atop the big Huird's head. Finally, though, it blinked ever so slowly. Turning its head back to gaze westward, the grotesque hybrid spoke.

"We cannot be sure if the Wanderers saw us or not. Our eyes cannot see so far. Farther than Mistress' Pet, yes. But not that far." It ran a talon along its chest again, scratching lightly at its downy feathers. "Will we walk? Or will we take to the sky as the Mistress intended?"

Sivart cringed inwardly at the sound of its voice. Its long and wide beak made speech difficult, and its barbed tongue didn't help either. Indeed, it was hard to understand every word the Huird said. There was a constant rasping hiss with each word, low and grating. No matter how many times he heard the Huirds' voices, it sent cold shivers down his spine.

"Very well. And we may well have to fly. Or we go around the plains. The Earth Elves will sense our presence and drive us out."

"Yes, yes," the creature said slowly, tapping a talon to its beak. The sound made Sivart cringe even more. Everything about these creations disgusted him.

"We'll wait a few more hours before we move out."

The Huird merely nodded, blinking slowly again, eyeing Sivart as if he were a meal. With a twitching eye, the Human hurriedly climbed back down to the ground.

"Damn these filthy abominations!" he seethed, walking some ways away from the rest of the creatures. The sooner the Roamers completed their quest, the sooner Sivart could go back to serving his Mistress properly.

*****

With Strigard but a league behind them, the Roamers stood before a long line of black stones, all twice as tall as a man and thrice as wide.

"Barrier rocks. The edge of the Ir'Afa Plains," Aen stated, running a weathered hand over one of the smooth stones.

The rocks all stood four meters apart exactly and every single one was identical to the next. They rose up smoothly not unlike obelisks, but flatter than round, proud and steadfast. While the Roamers stood there, admiring the glassy pillars, they could feel a presence looming over them, the very air seeming to vibrate. It sent shivers up their spines, feeling the weight of the earthen magic bearing down on them. As they stood there, Aen glanced over his shoulder.

"Let us hurry along then," he suggested, turning back to the others, snapping them out of their reverie. "We'll not be alone here for long."

"Eh?" Danira wondered before following the Elvan's pointing finger.

The city gates of Strigard had swung open and a company of men could be seen making a mad dash for them. It didn't take any second guessing on who was at the head of those armored soldiers.

"They must have spotted us from their lookout towers," the witch mused, gazing up at the city's walls.

"And the king wishes to speak with us," Aen surmised.

"Then let us hurry and cross into Earth Elf lands," Ejen said, stepping past the stones.

Aen, Danira, and Myles quickly strode after the Fire Elf, while Nihak turned to face the charging horsemen fully. Ejen noticed and stopped to call his companion along. "Come, Nihak! We should not linger here!"

The younger Fire Elf grinned and turned to follow after them. Once he stood next to his fellow Roamers, he turned once more to face the horsemen. "If the king has any sense about him, he'll not dare cross that line," he stated.

"Do you think this wise?" Ejen asked, taking up his scythe in both hands.

"Aye, I do. Let us hear what Malder has to say, since he seems so eager to speak with us."

The other Roamers said nothing but waited in silence. They didn't have long to wait as the galloping horses slowed to a trot before coming to a halt just beyond the barrier stones. King Malder sat astride his great white horse, staring at them, the band of wandering warriors standing not six meters away from him and his company.

"So, it is true," he called, his voice carried by the wind. "The Roamers have returned and wander once more."

"Aye, it's true," the Fire Elf called back. "I never expected us to be meeting on these terms, as opposed to the last time we met."

Danira rolled her eyes at that and shook her head, grumbling about stupid grudges and old scars.

"Why not come over here so we may discuss the coming war," Malder said, his horse prancing nervously at the thrumming stones.

"I think not," Nihak replied. "My elf-ears can hear you just fine. Speak and then go back to your city."

The king huffed, laying a large hand along his mount's neck to calm the beast. He stared over at the Roamer, looking him up and down; Nihak didn't look a day older since they last fought. Even from this distance though, he could clearly see the elf's eyes and what he saw disturbed him. There should have been only one eye staring at him, and there was something else in that look, but the Human couldn't place it though. Shaking his head slightly, he cleared his throat and spoke, "I'm sure you have heard the news that Jamiel will invade come next spring. My armies are not yet so great as they were last time. I seek your aid in this fight." He bowed his head, flourishing out his free arm.

"Sire, is this wise?" Velten inquired, his own horse neighing nervously. "The Roamers caused such devastation to our ranks in the last war."

"And to the enemies'," Malder was quick to add, glancing at him. "Imagine what they can do for us."

"What do you offer, Malder? Why should we fight for you?"

The company of armed soldiers bristled at the Fire Elf's disrespect of their king. Malder raised a calming hand and their weapons were lowered. "I offer you all amnesty for past offenses against me and my people," he stated. "You have my word, I swear it."

"What say you, Roamers?" Nihak asked, turning to look upon each of his companions. "Do his terms sit well with you?"

"Sounds good and all, but can we trust him?" Myles wondered.

The others nodded in agreement. Turning back to face the king, Nihak called, "Swear it in blood then! Where's that great sword you always carry?"

"You shall see the teeth of Dralon soon enough," Malder called back. "I have no need for that blade right now."

"Barbarians," Danira muttered.

"Swear it in blood, Malder! Else there won't be any peace between us."

"Velten, your knife," the king ordered, holding his hand out to the Councilman.

"Your Majesty?"

"Now!" he growled, turning a sharp eye on the younger man.

"Yes, sire," he said, hurriedly drawing his knife and handing it to the king.

Malder took the offered hilt and held the knife high in his right hand. He bellowed in his deep voice, so all around heard him, "Here is my knife! Let us see yours, Fire Elf!"

Grinning, Nihak pulled his knife from his belt, the long blade flashing brightly in the shining sun. "So swear it, King Malder!"

Malder gripped the blade tightly with his left hand and pulled it sharply from his grasp, leaving a deep cut in the palm of his hand. He held the knife aloft, the blood plain for all to see. "I swear by my blood the Roamers shall have my pardon if they serve to fight alongside my armies in the coming war!"

Nihak followed suit and grasped the blade of his knife. Slicing his palm open, he held the weapon aloft, fiery blood dripping from its edge. "The Roamers swear to fight by King Malder's side in the coming war!"

"Aen, take this pouch and send it to the king," Danira bade, handing the Elvan a small cloth pouch. A small piece of parchment was tied to the drawstring of the bag.

Shrugging, Aen tossed it into the air and waved his staff once. A harsh burst of wind caught it and sent it sailing toward the king. Velten reached out and caught it while Malder wiped the knife clean.

"Now that's done," he muttered, clenching his injured hand into a light fist. He looked up at them and said in a louder voice, "How many Roamers are still left?"

"Just seven," Nihak answered, cleaning his knife before sheathing it. "They dwell here on the plains."

"Very well. Come, we have plans to discuss about the war," Malder bade them, gesturing for them to come with him to Strigard.

"Nay!" the Fire Elf called. "After we find the last two, we will go on to the Duriviel Forest and bring back the Sylvan Sword. It will increase your odds of winning."

"Alura was right," the king muttered, before replying, "Very well! I shall build my armies and prepare. May the gods grant you speed and safety on your quest!"

The Fire Elf merely rolled his eyes at that and turned to leave. While he and the other Roamers moved out, Danira returned the king's wave. "May the goddesses bless you and keep you," she replied, smiling. Then she too turned and followed after the others.

The king sat back in the saddle, watching the Roamers head deeper into Earth Elf territory. "At least she has some manners about her. Not like that wretched Nihak," he stated.

"Sire?" Velten said, holding up the pouch he'd caught.

"Hm? What's that, then?"

The younger man unrolled the parchment and read the message inscribed within. "'Wrap these herbs into your bandages. It will keep the cut clean and hasten its healing. Please forgive my companion's barbarity. Fire Elves can be crude, but they are not without honor. I trust you are not without honor too, O Dire King?'"

Malder took the pouch of dried leaf bits, a slight smirk playing at the corners of his mouth. "Ah, she had to call me that." He gave a self-deprecating laugh and turned his horse about to head back to Strigard. "Come, Velten. We've got a war to prepare for."

With that, he urged his horse to a gallop. His councilman and men-at-arms quickly followed suit, glad to be away from the borders of the Ir'Afa Plains.

CHAPTER 8

The ground rumbled underfoot as the Roamers walked through the grasslands, the city of Strigard far in the distance behind them. Somewhere away in the plains, meshas were on the move, their heavy steps shaking the ground for leagues. Every so often as they moved through the plains, wide paths of churned dirt and dead meadow could be seen, evidence of passing herds. Nihak inhaled deeply through the nose, his head back and eyes closed.

"Ahh, I love it out here," he sighed, smiling happily.

"Glad you're enjoying this wind and the grass," Ejen replied, sarcasm dripping from his voice. The Fire Elf was almost cringing with each brush of the long green blades against his bare legs. His younger counterpart however was almost ecstatic at the touch of grass.

Danira merely rolled her eyes at their exchange while Myles casually chewed on a stalk of grass. It quickly vanished into his mouth, whereby he plucked another from the ground as he walked. Beneath their feet, the rumbling was steadily growing. As they crested a gentle hill, the vibrations in the ground could be felt up to their chests as a herd of armored creatures drew nearer and nearer. The Roamers stopped and watched in awe as a wide body of meshas came charging by, their massive claws digging narrow trenches in the earth. Slamming into each other as they ran together, the horned beasts bellowed and growled, the noise deafening.

"By Vuntales!" Aen exclaimed, leaning hard on his staff.

"Not even an Earth Elf could survive a stampede of those monsters!" Nihak shouted, barely heard over the thunderous noise. As the meshas stormed by, they turned as one and wheeled to the south, leaving a wide swathe of torn and ripped earth. No wonder why as the Roamers came to see, for another group of beasts came thundering over another hill, earth-toned elves astride their backs.

These animals were black and brown in color, with a massive hump along their upper back. They sported six legs and an armored head, with a single horn protruding straight out from above their wide nostrils; the thick keratin curved up at the tip. With a shaggy coat of thick wooly fur and a short-tufted tail, they were rather ugly creatures to behold.

"Ah. Binu'Ulunu. The great mounts of the Earth Elves," Danira said, watching the unsightly creatures charge headlong towards the rampaging meshas.

The Roamers watched as the Earth Elves raised high their thin spears, closing near the back of the herd. As the dark-skinned elves rode alongside the great armored meshas, they singled out the slowest one and worked to separate it from the others by encircling it. Once that was done, they hurled their light missiles, piercing their prey's armored hide. Narrow lances drove deep into the beast's flesh, drawing deafening bellows from its great maw. Spear after spear was thrown, until the mesha bristled with dozens of them in its flanks. After blood loss took its toll, the massive creature stumbled and crashed to the earth, cutting a deep ragged trench in the ground before it skidded to a stop. The rest of the herd quickly left their fallen kin behind as they stampeded away. Whooping and hollering, the Earth Elves reined in their mounts to circle around the wounded beast, though they kept their distance as its mighty tail thrashed the ground. Transfixed, the Roamers watched as one elf dismounted, another strange tool in his hand.

"What is that?" Ejen wondered, squinting his yellow eyes.

"Looks to be some kind of club," Nihak said, shielding his eyes from the hot sun overhead.

Indeed, it was a warclub the Earth Elf carried; it was more than half a meter long, the long handle and widening head oblong. The handle was narrow along the grip but grew wider towards the head of the club. It was not a straight-shafted weapon, the head bent at a wide angle, its edges blunt and thick. From a distance, the Roamers could just make out a short, triangular blade protruding from the elbow of the club head. He stood above the felled mesha and raised his weapon high, gripped in both hands. The club was brought down in a mighty swing upon the beast's armored head, sending a resounding *crunch* through the air. So loud was the blow that it could be heard by the Roamers, who stood less than half a league away from them.

"By Seylivonia," Nihak breathed.

With that one mighty blow, the mesha's life was gone. Kneeling before the massive creature, the hunter bowed his head, gripping its middle horn. The other elves sat silent atop their mounts, heads bowed in joined prayer. After their words of apology and respects were given, the leader rose and held high his strange club. So too the hunters raised high their weapons, giving their cries of triumph and success. Dismounting their ulunu, they pulled wide, short blades from their backs and set to work butchering their kill.

"Come," Nihak said, stepping down the hill. "They might be able to help us."

"Are you sure?" Aen asked, following him nonetheless, the wind whipping his sky-blue cloak about.

"Nihak and I have good relations with the Earth Elves," Danira remarked, patting his back as she walked alongside.

Myles, ever the cheerful one, took the opportunity to cartwheel down the hill, whistling as he went. Ejen merely shook his head and followed his companions.

"I didn't know you were their friend too, Danira," he called after the witch, resting his war scythe on his right shoulder.

"Perhaps not back when we all wandered twenty years ago, but in our two decades of exile, I made several excursions into the Ir'Afa Plains."

"Glad to hear that Danira, because my Earelvish is not so good," Nihak stated.

"Don't worry," she replied, smiling as they drew nearer to the Earth Elves.

The hunters did not look up from their work as the Roamers approached. They began to pile slabs of meat on sleds of bone tied behind several ulunu, while other sleds held the plates of armor. The horns and claws were pulled from the great carcass too and lashed to yet more sleds. Taking as much meat as possible, the elves took the entire ribcage, leg bones, and tail. By the time the Roamers had arrived, all that was left of the great mesha was a husk of under-armor and bones.

Danira stepped closer, raising her right hand in greeting. *"Nawi'eza yu avahune kuakuh neywa sanvguth kaliyaw Tawekdey."*

The Earth Elf with the strange club turned and raised his right hand in greeting as well. *"Ahnka nawi'eza neywa ganta eliem tambah'memhabeh'al."*

Danira smiled and bowed her head, holding her left palm beneath her right fist. The other Roamers watched this exchange as the elf returned the gesture while his kin finished packing up the spoils of their kill. As they mounted their ulunu, the witch continued her conversation in the rough language.

"Nihak, do you understand anything they're saying?" Ejen asked.

"The elf is, if I'm translating correctly, a 'hunter-chief'. He called Danira a 'leaf-caster'…I think. She's asking him how his tribe fares."

"Myaegu lekha'spe soovurtih ahnka okah'Amanahkwi," they heard the hunter-chief say, gesturing over the vast grasslands behind them. *"Neywa ohnikee wosetenee karag'kunur ahyulak ahnka usinahtezi chahaywusik.*

Danira nodded, bowing as she made the hand gesture again. When it was returned, she turned back to the Roamers.

"Well it's settled."

"What is?" Myles asked, staring up at the grinning Earth Elves astride their beasts.

"They know Jolek and Rom's tribe and they'll help us find them," the witch explained.

"That's good news. What tribe are these elves from?"

"Tahniki lekha'spe ohnikee neywa?" Danira inquired, turning back to address the hunter-chief.

The tall elf, stripped to the waist, mounted his ulunu and turned to look at her. *"Yajewihn Luaka."*

"The Luaka of Stone."

"Ah. I remember Jolek mentioning them. Fierce warriors, they are," Nihak said, grinning.

"Akemahn'tay mabikotae sach'alsay. Kasheeoku." the hunter-chief said, gesturing for them to follow.

"He says he'll take us to his camp. He wants us to ride back with him and the hunters," Danira explained.

They walked over to different ulunu, the great beasts standing over two meters high at the hump, snorting and pawing the ground. Once the Roamers were helped onto the backs of the shaggy beasts, the Earth Elves kicked their flanks, urging them forward. With rumbling bellows, the ulunu galloped off, their massive hooves pounding swiftly across the plains, dragging the heavy sleds of meat and scaled armor after them.

Riding atop the six-legged creatures was smoother than the Roamers thought. Despite the ulunu carrying two riders and pulling heavy loads behind, they still made great haste over the rolling grasslands while the sky began to darken. As they rode, the Earth Elves bellowed songs above the thunderous rumbling, using the pounding hoof beats as a kind of rhythm to their revelry. Danira smiled as they sang of living free as the wind and standing strong upon the rocks and dirt. It was a lengthy song, taking up nearly the entire duration of their ride. The sun was near to setting by the time the Luaka camp came into view, setting the blue sky ablaze in purples and brilliant oranges. Great mounds of grassy earth rose up from the land, thin columns of smoke rising from the roofs. Other Earth Elves and ulunu could be seen walking about the wide camp, some small fires lit out in the open.

As they drew near, the riders let loose a volley of whoops and hollers, shouting excitedly in their rough tongues. The elves in the camp shouted back, waving happily as the hunters returned. Bringing their smelly beasts to a stop, the Earth Elves leapt from their mounts into the arms of their loved ones.

"I've missed being out here," Danira said, chuckling as she gently floated down from the back of her ulunu.

Myles took the less-graceful route and merely fell off, landing hard with a grunt.

"You damn fool," Aen muttered, using wind to ease his way off the tall creature. "You control ice. Use it next time."

"And what should we use?" Ejen asked, swinging one leg over the ulunu's back to slide down its hairy flank to the ground. "I'm sure if Nihak and I used fire, it would cause a stampede."

"Aye," the younger Fire Elf agreed, following Ejen's lead on dismounting. "So let Myles do things his own way too. Aside from the Earth Elves, he's probably the toughest of our group."

Picking himself up, the Odd Dwarf dusted his shirt off, smiling broadly. The Luaka Tribe, still chattering and shouting in earnest, unloaded their sleds, while the younger elves ran off to help start a great bonfire.

"Maybe we can help," Ejen suggested, seeing them gather fuel in the center of the camp.

"Nay," his counterpart said, laying a hand on his shoulder. "They've been creating fire without the help of Fire Elves for centuries. They do not need our help."

"Very well. Though I am curious as to what they're using for fuel."

"Mesha and ulunu shite," Danira answered.

"They use what?" came the bewildered question.

"Do you two see any trees out here?" she replied.

"Very well…" Ejen said, eyes still wide.

As they spoke, the great bonfire was lit, sparks flashing in the gathering night. Tongues of fire took hold and soon roaring flames reached high into the starlit sky, spreading its heat and light to the whole camp. The Roamers watched as the entire tribe gathered round that inferno, all smiling and chatting. Their meat was set on great spits to roast while the hunters disappeared into their mound-huts, while other elves brought out massive iron drums, ulunu skins pulled taut over the wide tops.

One small elf child, wearing nothing but an ulunu wool skirt that fell to her ankles, grabbed Danira's hand and urged them all to join them at the fire. Laughing and smiling, the witch quickly went with the girl.

"Well come on. We're invited to share in the feast," she called after the others. They quickly joined the Earth Elves, sitting amongst the tribespeople. As they took their seats, the elves greeted the Roamers, offering their right hand to them. When the Roamers offered their right hand back, the elves grasped them by the wrist and squeezed hard, nearly shattering the bone. Such was their strength, painful despite the friendly gesture.

"Are the Earth Elves always this rough?" Aen demanded, massaging his bruised wrist.

"It is merely how they say hello and welcome," the witch explained, flexing her fingers for circulation. "It is to show the strength of each other and their friendship. The harder they squeeze, the more they like you."

"Glad they didn't break our arms though," Ejen remarked.

"Aye, that happened the first few times to me," Danira said, smiling a little. "They got the idea after that."

Suddenly the talking and laughter of the elves ceased with the single beat of a drum, sending vibrations rippling through the ground. For the Roamers, they felt it go up their legs to their very core, thrumming against their hearts.

The drum was struck again, then again and again, forming a steady rhythm, joined in by another drum. While the first drum was struck once every few seconds, the second drum was struck twice between single beats. They all watched in silence as the music filled the sky and reverberated through the earth like a mighty heartbeat. With this deep resonance, Earth Elves dressed in the wooly hides of ulunu and plated armor of the meshas danced out from their huts and into the middle of the great circle round the fire. The dancers all wore masks of likeness to the great beasts they mimicked. Moving with deliberate steps, the dancers stomped and slammed their bare feet into the earth in time to the beating drums. Others soon joined in, these elves carrying the weapons and tools of hunting. Round and round the fire they danced, raising their spears and heavy clubs high and low. It didn't take long for the Roamers to realize that the dance was a retelling of the hunt they witnessed earlier that day. As the story continued, the drums beat faster and faster, the hunt reaching its climax as the Earth Elves mock-hurled their spears at the mesha-dancers. One such dancer slowed, then gracefully tumbled to the ground, the armored plates clattering and banging together. Their prey having fallen from its wounds, the hunter-chief dancer approached with his club, the drums now merging their rhythm into one massive drumbeat. The hunter-chief elf brought his club high and smashed it down against the earth on the last beat.

All was still and quiet, save the roaring of the flames. Slowly, almost silently, the Earth Elves rose and raised their hands high to the stars, gazing downwards. The hunter-chief raised his club and shouted,

"Hutufaysek Avahune ya Arrute!"

The rest of the tribe shouted in unison, repeating the blessing.

"They're thanking Arrute, the Earth God," Danira explained as the meat was served out for all to enjoy.

As the Roamers accepted their meals, the hunter-chief came over to join them, along with seven elderly Earth Elves. They wore patterned robes of ulunu wool, rigid designs of colored stone and earthen plains decorating their garb. Deep wrinkles and lines could be seen on their faces and hands while their hair was stark gray. They were introduced as the leaders of the Luaka Tribe.

"Danira, ask him when they can take us to Jolek and Rom," Aen said, biting into the tender meat.

The witch relayed the question in near-perfect Earelvish. Smiling, the middle elder nodded and answered, pointing behind them off to the north.

"He says the Tulrok Tribe is camped many leagues away. Could be more. But he says it is an honor to meet the Roamers and he will gladly send his warriors to take us to the Tulrok."

"Please thank them for their tribe's generous hospitality and food, and for helping us," Nihak told Danira. "I'd do it myself but…"

"Yes, I know, silly elf. I'll have Jolek teach you more once we're reunited." With that said, the witch relayed the message to the elders, who smiled warmly in return, offering their right fists over their left palms and bowed their heads. The witch quickly followed suit, bowing back, as did the other Roamers.

"Yu Tawekdey mohaku'yaikma yu taepyoha kahayru neywa ka'weye lekha'spe Tulrok nohinoti yu wuejea keekuatahk."

"He says he will have his people take us in the morning. For now, we shall dance and feast!"

Indeed, the drums had renewed their tempo and a few Earth Elves had begun to stomp and jump to the beat. They gestured for the Roamers to join in.

"But I don't know how to dance," Ejen stated, remaining seated.

"There is no form to their dance, you barbarian," Danira said, grinning as she stood. "Just let the beating drums guide your heart." With that, the witch leapt to the fire and began her dance, far more flowing and graceful than the elves' rough form, but still in time to the beating drums. Myles too was quick to join in, shaking and throwing his limbs every which way, drawing much laughter from the Earth Elves. Aen rose stiffly, tossed his staff aside and, much to the Fire Elves' astonishment, spryly somersaulted in midair to land solidly on his feet by the great fire. Whipping his cloak off, the old half-breed used it as an extension of his arms as he danced, letting the dark fabric flow and dive with him as one.

"This is maddening!" Ejen exclaimed, staring at Nihak.

"This is their way of life," he replied, getting up too.

"Don't leave me here by myself," the older Fire Elf demanded.

"Suit yourself, Ejen."

And like that, Nihak ran to the circle and leapt right through the roaring flames, much to the amazement of the Earth Elves. The Fire Elf gave a cry or two of his own, stomping his bare feet into the trodden dirt, laughing and grinning like mad.

The moon and stars gracefully crossed the skies overhead, passing long into the night before the celebration died down and the camp had gone to sleep in their huts. The elders offered to erect a hut as shelter for the Roamers, but they graciously declined, preferring to sleep under the black sky together.

Unrolling their beds, the Roamers talked quietly among themselves as they prepared for a short sleep.

"I still can't believe you didn't join in, Ejen," Danira scolded, lying down.

"I saw no point in it. And I'm ashamed of you, Nihak."

The younger Fire Elf scoffed as he wrapped his blanket about himself. "Why are you always so angered?" he retorted.

"Because unlike you, I shouldn't have been banished."

"Bah! You chose this life as much as I did," Nihak scoffed, turning onto his side away from Ejen.

"Was he always different from the other Fire Elves?" Myles asked, lying on his belly, propping his head up with his hands.

Without looking up, the younger elf expertly flicked a spark over his shoulder. It landed atop Myles' backside, drawing a sharp yelp from him. Aen quickly clamped a hand over the dwarf's mouth.

"Enough!" he hissed. "Let's not wake the entire tribe. Go to sleep, all of you."

As if on command, Myles was asleep instantly, drooling into the Elvan's hand. He wiped his palm on the dwarf's trousers before rolling over to sleep as well. The other three Roamers quickly followed suit, the bitter atmosphere unpleasant to their thoughts.

When morning finally came, the Roamers were up bright and early, well before the sun peeked its bright face above the grassy horizon. There was still plenty of mesha meat, so they helped themselves to a hearty breakfast. Most of the tribe did not wake until the sun had fully risen. In a matter of moments, the entire camp came alive with activity as the tribe gathered for their morning meal. As they ate and talked, the elders approached the Roamers, smiling wide in greeting.

"Arrute naresak neywae Ayuvosuh yae hilachi'ansipeke."

"And may Arrute's strength be blessed on you," Danira replied in Earelvish, bowing.

They conversed briefly, albeit by Earth Elf standards, as their tongue was a slow and deliberate one. When they finished their talks, Danira gathered the Roamers together to explain what she had discussed with the elders.

"They will send five hunters with us to the Tulrok Tribe. If we leave within the hour, we should make their camp by evening. Ulunu are one of the fastest ground-beasts in all of Greenearth, and their endurance is only matched by meshas and Earth Elves."

"How soon can the elves leave with us?" Aen asked.

"They are calling their ulunu now."

"Then let us be ready," Ejen said, standing up.

"Aye," Danira agreed, rising as well.

They walked to the edge of the camp, where five Earth Elves stood, a short metal flute held to their lips. They gave a single note: a deep, bellowing call. After a few blows from each elf, a fierce rumbling began to shake the ground, rapidly increasing. Five of the shaggy-coated beasts quickly came into view, galloping towards them.

"Do they just let their beasts wander free?" Aen wondered.

"Aye. There's nothing out here that can take down an ulunu. Therefore, there is no danger to them," Danira explained as the five mounts arrived, skidding to a halt. They gave deep, bellowing grunts as dirt was kicked up from their wide hooves.

The Earth Elves grabbed the noisy animals by their curving horn, whispering softly to them, soothing and calming their mounts. Eager to be on the road once more, the Roamers accepted help onto the backs of the ulunu. Once the Earth Elves were mounted, they quickly spurred them into a full gallop. The five wanderers had to hold on tight, for the thunderous charge of the beasts was so sudden they were nearly flung off. As they rode, the Earth Elves struck up another mighty song, this one of racing the wind.

A fine tune for a fine day, Nihak thought as he watched the grassy plains roll past, the blue sky and white clouds rushing by overhead. He and the others couldn't wait to see Jolek and Rom.

CHAPTER 9

Alura laid her head back, letting the boiling water soothe her pale skin. As the witch relaxed, she levitated a bar of soap to her waiting fingers. Turning the yellowed block in her slender hands, she extended a long shapely leg from the water. Purring, she caressed her sleek calf and thigh, spreading lather over her perfect skin. Slowly, her leg slipped back beneath the opaque roiling water. Raising the other leg, she repeated the process, then washed her arms as well, sliding foamy soap from her shoulders to her wrists. Sighing in ecstasy, Alura set the block aside and reached over to a plate near her wide tub. Upon the silvery platter were several chunks of roasted pork, still hot from the fire. Plucking a piece from the plate, the witch brought it to her maw and popped it in, chewing slowly to savor the delicious meat. She smacked her lips as fatty juice dripped out the corner of her mouth and rolled off her chin. The meat was all the more satisfying for the fact that she had been craving pork that day, and as luck would have it, one of her slaves had made one too many mistakes that morning. The cruel witch didn't hesitate to exact punishment on the poor man, and his mangled squeals filled the cold halls of her castle. With a snap of her fingers, other slaves led the animal to the wide kitchen and the pig was butchered and prepared for her meal. Alura giggled to herself before gulping down another piece of meat, letting out a low moan of delight as she closed her eyes.

"Mistress."

Her eye twitched, but she did not open them; rather than answer, she swirled her hands through the scalding water. Curling all but her forefingers to her palms, the witch raised her hands just above the churning surface. Still twirling her fingers ever so gently, the witch began to create twin whirlpools in the frothing bathwater.

"Mistress."

Her concentration faltered and the whirlpools disappeared. Sighing in exasperation, she ignored the call and flicked her right hand up. An orb of blackish water levitated up from the tub, staying intact from the witch's magic as she waggled her fingers before it.

"Mistress!"

The orb of water burst apart, splashing over the edges of the iron tub as her steely gray eyes snapped open, black mist forming on the edges of her irises. Thrashing her arms out wide, sending more water splattering across the polished stone floor, the bubbles ceased frothing as heat was rapidly sapped from the tub. Frost began to form, creaking and crackling around the witch's supple body as she sat up, cold water rolling and dripping off her full breasts. Waving an arm over the glassy ice, an image began to take shape to reveal Sivart and the Huirds. She could see him standing on the border of the Ir'Afa Plains, hand over his heart, while her humanoid soldiers stood in clusters behind him.

"What is it?!" she snarled, seeing Sivart cringe in her makeshift mirror.

"I've pursued the Roamers to the edge of the Ir'Afa Plains but can go no further on foot. The Earth Elves will certainly sense our presence."

Slowly, the witch rubbed her temples, black mists swirling and lashing about in her eyes.

"You disturbed me," she said slowly, inhaling deeply, "to tell me that you simply… cannot continue trailing the Roamers?" she growled, her voice so dangerously soft.

"No Mistress!" Sivart was quick to say. "I merely called you for your guidance."

"Guidance?" was the quiet echo. "Pray tell to Ire'tasmsya, Lord of the Abyss, what guidance you could possibly need in following my very simple orders."

She could see Sivart shaking through her blackened icy mirror, and if she closed her eyes, she could almost smell his fear.

"Mistress, if I continue on foot, the Earth Elves will know we are on their land. But if I go by the sky, the Roamers could well see me with the Huirds. What should I do?"

Alura closed her eyes, the black mists fading away. She pinched the bridge of her nose between her thumb and forefinger while all sorts of punishments whirled around her head. Pulling out his fingernails? Whipping? Or the pear? A slight shudder of joy ran up the witch's spine as she considered that last torture device.

"Mistress?"

Sivart's voice pulled her from her thoughts. Sighing, she opened her eyes again. "What should I do?"

"My patience is running thin, dear, dull Sivart. If you can bear to wait a few moments, I'll be with you shortly."

Before Sivart could reply, Alura shattered the icy mirror with a blink of her eyes. Standing up, shards of blackened frost fell from around her form, tinkling like broken chimes. Slowly she stepped out of the tub, freezing water dripping from her hair and wide hips. As water began to pool around her feet on the black stony floor, the sorceress snapped her fingers, the sharp sound echoing about the wide chamber. A door opened at the far end and a small boy walked in, his footsteps careful and guarded. He had to walk by memory, for he was blind.

"You called, Mistress?"

"Yes, dear Tolm. Bring me a towel and my dress."

The light-haired boy bowed his head, turned to the right, and walked over to the rack where he found the witch's towel. Quickly, he brought it to the sorceress, who dried herself off while her servant retrieved her dress.

"Is everything alright, Mistress? You sound upset, and it is very cold in here."

Indeed, the boy's breath could be seen as white wispy plumes when he exhaled. Slowly Tolm approached her, the white dress draped over his thin arms. The witch gave a slight smile and levitated her clothes into the air and discarded her wet towel in the boy's arms.

"Clever child," she chuckled, tousling his hair.

Unlike most of her slaves, Tolm was treated quite kindly by the witch. He had struck a deal with her two years ago that if she helped his family's crops grow to feed them, he would serve her for ten years. Most Humans who asked the witch for favors often did it out of selfishness. But this boy was different.

"What is the matter, Mistress?"

"Guess."

"Sivart?"

"Correct," she said, sliding her dress on.

Patting his back, she turned him around and directed him out of the washroom. "Wash my clothes, Tolm. I shouldn't be gone long."

He nodded and headed up the spiral stairs to her bedchamber. Watching him go, Alura turned on the spot and raised her arms above her head. White light surrounded her as she focused on Sivart for a brief moment, and then the light dispersed everything away, leaving the witch in a space of infinite blackness. Within seconds, the light returned, bringing new surroundings to her. She now stood upon grasslands, the Earth Elves' land behind her. Sivart stood before her, clutching his chest in pain.

"Hello, Mistress Alura," he grimaced, doing his best to straighten up.

She did not return the greeting; rather, the sorceress merely folded her arms, scowling down at him. Sweat beaded on his forehead as he averted his eyes before she finally walked up to him.

"Rest assured that I will think long and hard on your punishment," she stated, then turned to the sky. Waving her arms in short, sharp motions, she curled her fingers and twisted her wrists about, commanding in the arcane tongue, *"Thaero naskurburen ona esthoruna."* Dark clouds gathered and formed with unnatural speed, stretching out over the vast Ir'Afa Plains.

"There. You have perfect cover and won't be seen by elf or Roamer. Now, the next time you call for me, it had better be for a good reason. Else I will skewer you on a hook, flay you alive, and feed your skin to the Huirds while you watch!"

With that, the witch vanished in a flash of blinding white light. Sivart too was an ashen white, knowing full well the threat was not an idle one. He'd witnessed firsthand that kind of punishment; and he wasn't able to eat for days after. Shaking still, he took a deep breath and exhaled slowly. Calling the Huirds over, he ordered them to take flight. Two of the birdmen lifted him up and above the black clouds they flew.

*****

Aen's cloak had turned unnaturally black. The Elvan looked at the enchanted fabric, then up at the darkened sky, then back down to his cloak once more. Waving at Nihak, then Danira to get their attention, he shouted, "We have a problem!"

He had to shout, for the Roamers were still astride the ulunu as they thundered across the plains. The sun was nearing the horizon and the sky was painted wonderful shades of pink and yellow and red, until those ominous clouds roiled in.

"The sky?" Nihak shouted back.

"Aye! Those clouds are not natural. They were wrought by magic!"

"I only know of two witches who could make a sky like this!" Danira called back, eyeing the black clouds.

"Lor'Eln and Alura," Aen stated, dread clear in his voice.

The Earth Elves too were discussing the sudden change in weather. One of them pointed to a smoke column over the hill.

"Yu lekha'spe Tulrok waygadohk taynche'lohte."

"They say that the Tulrok tribe is just over the hill," Danira translated.

As she said it, they reined in their ulunu. The heavy beasts gave rumbling grunts as they skidded to a halt. With the beasts stopped, the Roamers dismounted, sliding down their shaggy hides.

"Kuwineh'matay nayushari," Danira said, bowing to them.

The Earth Elves nodded, wheeled their mounts about, and galloped off, quickly leaving the Roamers alone.

"Why did they leave us here?"

"They're worried about the sky. It's never a good omen to see clouds like that," the witch said, turning and walking to the crest of the hill.

"You think Alura did it?" Aen asked, following her.

"Of course, she did. But the question is why," Nihak stated, striding along, his eyes nervously glancing upwards.

"Is a storm upon us?" Ejen demanded.

Both Fire Elves turned to the Elvan as they walked, prompting the old half-breed to rub a thumb over his cloak, feeling the rough fabrics. Looking back up at them, he shook his head. "Nay. Black clouds have gathered but there is no thunder, nor lightning. It will not rain."

"Remember that large bird I saw?" Myles asked, barely heard over the elves' sigh of relief.

"Aye!" Nihak said sharply, fire glowing in his eyes for a brief moment.

"Could it have been a Huird?" Danira wondered as they crested the hill.

The Roamers stopped and looked down upon the Tulrok Tribe encampment. Columns of smoke climbed lazily in the wind from the earthen huts and small campfires. It didn't take long for the tribe to see them, and great cries of joy rose as they charged up the hill towards the Roamers. One of the elves was a massive giant, his steps sending shuddering ripples through the ground.

"Oh, here comes Rom!" Aen cried, bracing himself.

Quickly the Earth Elves surrounded them, chattering and shouting all at once. The great ruckus was almost too much for the Fire Elves' sensitive ears. Danira stepped forward, grasping many of their hands, wincing at their strong grip. One Earth Elf approached the Fire Elves, grinning broadly.

"Nihak!" he growled, wrapping his scarred arms about the Fire Elf's torso.

"Not again!" he gasped as all the air was crushed from his lungs. "Jolek you'll break my spine!"

"Bah! You've survived worse!" he howled with laughter, easily lifting the elf off the ground.

Jolek Tulrok'hune stood a meter and a half in height, wearing nothing but ulunu wool pants while his feet were bare, as were his chest and arms. The elf's dark-skinned body, toned with rippling muscle, was as hard as the stones themselves. No wiry hair stood on his head; Jolek having shaved it all off. His eyes were dark and bright, glinting with mirth.

While Nihak's legs flailed in the air, Rom knelt, so he was more on the Roamers' level. Danira approached the giant, smiling warmly.

"Hello Rom."

"My Vuntales, you've grown larger!" Aen exclaimed, walking up to Rom as well.

Rom Tulrok'atu wore ulunu wool pants as well along with an open shaggy vest. But unlike Jolek, he had short, rough black hair on his head and his dark eyes were hard and edged. Another difference was that Rom stood three meters tall and weighed nearly a ton. Not many Earth Elves grew to his size; and those who did were blessed by Arrute.

The great elf gave a broad smile and let loose a single booming laugh that shook the very air as he grabbed the two and held them close to his chest, being careful not to crush them. Even so, Danira and Aen found themselves breathless from the embrace. Rom set them down, then gave a cry of surprise as Myles leapt onto his back. The Odd Dwarf couldn't even wrap his arms and legs around the giant's broad back.

"I missed you and Jolek!" he cried.

"As did I!" he bellowed, laughing more as he tried to get Myles off.

Jolek finally set Nihak down, who fell to the ground, gasping for air. "You got stronger!" he coughed.

"Aye," the Earth Elf chuckled, offering a hand.

The Fire Elf gladly took it and was lifted to his feet. As Nihak steadied himself, Ejen got a crushing hug too. Booming footsteps drew near behind the Fire Elves and Rom stared down at them, Myles sitting comfortably on his shoulder.

"Hello Rom."

"Shut it," was the grating response.

Nihak merely smiled and nodded up at the giant. Jolek grinned too and began to lead them all back to the camp with the rest of the tribe.

"What brings you out to our homeland?" he asked when the Roamers were all seated round a fire.

"Nihak, you can tell him. This whole venture was your idea," Ejen stated.

And so the young Fire Elf told Jolek and Rom about finding the Sylvan Sword and how he had agreed to ally them with King Malder in the coming war. They sat silently through it all before finally Jolek leaned forward, gathering up a handful of dirt.

"A most interesting adventure you've chosen, Nihak," he said, molding the dirt into a stone. "My head tells me Rom and I should not go. Long have we hunted and trekked over these grasslands, and we have prospered and survived. But my heart tells me that the only excitement to be had here comes from the hunt and occasional dispute between tribes. I have missed the open road." With that said, he tossed the round stone into the air

Rom gave a grunt as he caught it, turning the rock around in his huge hands. "Hmm. Stay and be safe? Or roam and fight?" he asked himself, easily crushing the stone back into dirt and tossing it into the flames.

Thin tendrils of smoke wafted up and began to take form in the air. The shape that took hold was that of a sword surrounded by trees. Briefly the image hung there before the smoky trees turned to dancing flames, consuming the sword. The Roamers sat back as the smoke dispersed.

"What does it mean?" Myles wondered, staring into the wavering tongues of fire.

"It means," Rom said, frowning, "that this quest will end badly."

"Is that certain though?" Danira asked.

"Nothing is certain. This we all know," the Giant Earth Elf replied. "But we trust in the stones and the earth and we trust our God. Arrute warns against us taking this journey."

"But will you come with? We're all that's left of the Roamers, old friend," Nihak said, only to be met by silence from the giant.

"Rom, what say you?" Jolek prompted.

The giant rubbed his chin slowly, closing his dark eyes. "We shall go."

Jolek's eyes widened in surprise. "But Arrute doesn't approve of this quest. He warned us of bad omens."

"Yes, but nothing is certain. Not even the Gods can know all. What we know is what Jamiel wants. King Malder may respect our ways and honor the truce, but Jamiel will not stop until we are all slain."

The Roamers sat in silence at the Giant Earth Elf's deep insight.

"Then all the more reason that you come with us," Aen finally said.

"The Roamers are reunited then," Nihak proclaimed, grinning.

"We shall leave on the morrow. For now, let us enjoy this peaceful night," Jolek said as the sun set behind them.

As the night deepened, the Roamers sat around the fire, talking and laughing about times long past and how the years of peace and exile passed.

CHAPTER 10

Sivart scowled at the black clouds pouring past him. The air was frigid up here, small icicles forming on his face and clothes, while the Huirds were more fortunate, their thick feathers insulating them from the cold.

"How long have we been flying?" he demanded, shivering.

"Two days and a night," the Huird on his left croaked.

The burly Human gave a groan of pain and disgust. He hated flying with these creatures.

"Why doesn't Mistress Alura just grant me wings?" he wondered aloud.

The birdmen nearest him all started huffing and grunting. Sivart gave a deep frown as it didn't take much for him to realize that they were laughing at him. Mocking him.

"Shut your beaks!" he growled.

They merely kept laughing while the black clouds roiled beneath them. He could only hope their flight would be over soon and he could set foot on solid ground once more.

Fortunately for the witch's Left Hand, he didn't have much longer to wait. The edge of the unnatural cloud cover could be seen in the distance. Though it only took a few hours, to Sivart it may as well have been another day. He wasn't the only one happy to head back to the earth. As the Huirds began their descent, they squawked and screeched happily. At three meters before landing, the pair of Huirds carrying Sivart dropped him. Screaming, he fell to the ground, landing hard.

"Useless, ugly, horrid creatures!" he growled, spitting blood and dirt out of his mouth.

As the rest of the Huirds touched down, ruffling their wide wings, the black clouds dissipated as unnaturally as they came.

"Where are the Roamers?" he asked, looking around as the sun glared down on him.

The humanoid beasts looked at each other, muttering in their own garbled language before turning back to Sivart. They merely shrugged and whistled softly, uncaring. Some sat down while others spread their wings and preened themselves.

"Useless!" he cried, storming away from the border of the Ir'Afa Plains.

Off in the far distance, down a wide slope lay tiny farming villages and the town of Cendril, though Sivart couldn't see it from here. Scattered about the flatlands, small copses of trees lay in sparse patches.

"We'll take shelter in those trees until the Roamers pass, since I see no sign of their trail here."

The Huirds gave a squawk or two before they all rose up and filed after the sighing Human. As they stomped down the gentle slope, Sivart felt a faint rumbling through his boots. Screeching in alarm, the bird-creatures felt it too, flaring their wings out, feathers ruffled and bristling as the rumbling grew. Off behind them, they could hear faint thundering hoof beats.

Sivart turned back to the northeast, staring out to the horizon. Squinting, small dark forms came galloping over the edge of the earth.

"No."

With the futile denial, the Human shouted, "Run to the trees, you mindless bastards!"

Sivart took off down the hill at a dead run, pumping his arms and legs furiously. The Huirds quickly followed, their long rough legs carrying them easily over the sloping ground. Their long talons dug deeply into the earth, ripping damp grass and mud into the air. Some flapped their wings, giving them an increase in their speed. Sivart soon found himself surrounded by the dirty creatures as they rushed into the nearest copse of trees. Once within the small grove, they hopped and flapped into the branches, quietly cawing and screeching as they settled down to wait.

Panting from the mad rush for cover, Sivart leaned against a thin tree and stared out through the narrow gaps of the woods, only to see the dark forms were growing larger in the distance. If he looked long and hard enough, Sivart could make out the shapes of the hump-backed ulunu beasts. Looking closer still, he could just make out six figures riding atop the ugly mounts. One figure stood out though. Upon closer inspection, Sivart saw the figure wasn't even astride a shaggy-haired beast but running alongside them.

"Rom…" The broad-shouldered Human let out more than a few oaths and curses at the sight of that Earth Elf. He and his horde of abominations would not have long to wait before the Roamers reached the edge of the Ir'Afa Plains.

*****

Nihak slid down from his ulunu, frowning. The other Roamers dismounted in similar fashion, save for Myles who merely fell off, as per usual. Jolek pulled his ulunu horn from his waist and blew a short bellowing note. The beasts pawed the ground, snorting before they turned about and galloped back to their camp.

"Something wrong, Nihak?" Danira asked, stepping over to the Fire Elf.

He stood staring out over the land, almost in the same place as Sivart not a mere hour ago. Behind him and the witch, Aen helped Myles to his feet while Rom stomped over to them as well, gazing out to the horizon.

"Haven't been this far west in a long time," he stated, sitting down with a tremendous *thud*.

"Nihak?" Danira asked again, laying a gentle hand on the elf's shoulder.

"Look at the ground," he prompted.

Ejen and Jolek joined him, while Myles flopped about on the grass like a fish. Aen had given up on trying to help him up and now resorted to poking and whacking the Odd Dwarf with his staff.

"The ground's torn up further down the slope," Ejen noted, frowning as well.

Jolek strode forward with Nihak and crouched down to better examine the earth. Laying a callused hand over the mud, the dark-skinned elf closed his eyes.

"Talons," he stated, glancing over at Nihak, who examined the earth as well.

The Fire Elf stared back at his friend before rising to his full height. "Huirds."

"Now we know for sure that Alura is having us followed. That would be Sivart then," Aen said, finally joining up with the others.

They all looked over at Danira, who merely scowled, folding her arms over her chest. "I've no ties with that man," she growled.

"That's good and all, but it doesn't change the fact that he's very close," Nihak said, staring at the copse of trees where the ripped soil ended.

"Do you wish us to stop him? Jolek inquired. "Rom could rip that forest apart in seconds."

At mention of his name, the giant rose to his full height, shaking the ground. "Aye."

Nihak shook his head and turned to stare at Ejen, sharing a vicious grin.

"Burn them out," the older elf stated.

Before the others could offer protest or suggest a different course of action, the Fire Elves thrusted their arms forward. With fingers splayed wide, angry jets of fire blasted from their open palms. The flames roared angrily as the wide swathe of destruction rolled down the hill, consuming the grass.

"Stop!" Danira shouted over the blaze as Nihak and Ejen fed more fire onto the plains.

Away in the trees, Sivart's eyes widened in shock and anger as he watched the waves of fire come storming down the slope to his hiding place.

"Fly! Fly you damn birds!" he cried, holding his arms out.

Two of the Huirds grabbed him and lifted off with the others. They made a terrible noise of cawing and crowing as they burst from the copse of trees. As they rose into the air, flapping their massive wings with haste, Nihak ceased his flow of fire and unslung his bow.

"Nihak, they have to be near to half a league away," Jolek observed, coming to stand near the archer.

The Fire Elf merely scoffed, drawing an arrow from his quiver and notching it. "Are they now?"

The bow gave a slight creak from the strain as the elf pulled the arrow back, the blood-red fletchings brushing his cheek. Muscles bulging from the weight of the bow, Nihak closed his left eye and inhaled deeply through the nose. Staring down the black shaft, he raised his bow accordingly and exhaled out his mouth. Time seemed to slow as he picked his target, inhaling again, but this time he held his breath, feeling the shot. In an instant, he released and the arrow was sent flying, hissing through the still sky. The *twang* of his bow shook up and down his arm, drawing a smile from the Roamer. As the Huirds flew, one faltered in flight, shrieking in pain as it spiraled back down to the earth.

"Ha!" Nihak howled, the corners of his mouth twitching into a smirk. While he had stood still to take the shot, Ejen had taken off running full out down the slope through the fires. The younger Fire Elf quickly slung his bow over his shoulder and took off after him.

"Ahh, curse the fool!" Danira sighed, giving chase with Myles and Aen on her heels.

Jolek hurried after them as well, Rom lumbering at the rear. As the Earth Elf caught up with the Elvan and Odd Dwarf, he remarked, "I never tire of seeing such skill with the bow."

"Aye, Nihak's a fine archer. One of the best," Aen replied, huffing for breath as he kept pace.

By this time, the Fire Elf was at the edge of the copse of trees alongside Ejen. War scythe and longsword at the ready, they split off as they advanced into the woods, searching for any stragglers. It didn't take much for Nihak to find where the Huird had crashed back to earth, having left a ragged hole in the tree tops and a trail of blood. The creature's rasping screeches made it all the easier for the Fire Elf to find as he came upon its twisted form. It was crawling away, its right leg broken with a wooden branch skewering its tough hide. Nihak's arrow was embedded deep into the base of its right wing, making it useless.

As he approached it from behind, the foul creature turned its head, casting a hate-filled glare upon the Roamer. With a grin Nihak rushed forward, sword raised high. Shrieking in rage, the Huird spun about with surprising agility, its taloned hands spread wide, ready to draw blood. As he drew near, the birdman slashed forward with its right claw, only to be met with the sharp edge of the blade. Scaly fingers fell away, splashes of dark blood following as the Huird screamed in pain. Angrily, it struck at Nihak with its left talon. Weakened by pain and loss of blood, it suddenly found its feathery arm caught in Nihak's strong grip. The Huird could do nothing but screech in agony as its flesh was seared and burnt away until only blackened muscle and charred bone was left.

"Why are you following us?" he demanded, releasing the smoldering limb.

The Huird only screeched and screamed in pain, staring at its wounds. A sharp kick to its gut ceased the violent screaming. "Why are you following us?!" he growled, crouching over the Huird. The elf dropped his sword to the side and drew his knife, holding it to the Huird's throat. Offering only a croaking groan, the wounded beast chittered softly as it stared into the elf's fierce eyes.

"Tell me and I'll make your death swift. If not…" Nihak promised, flames lighting upon the palm of his left hand.

Its black eyes widened in fear at the sight of the dancing fires, the pain of its forearm all too fresh in its simple mind. "I know you can understand me," the Roamer stated, moving the flames closer to the Huird's face. "Tell me or it's a slow death."

It nodded quickly, croaking frantically. As soon as it opened its mouth to speak, a loud *crack* emanated from its feathered chest. Nihak watched as the creature's black eyes drained to a pale white, much like ink being bled from parchment. Though they held no iris or pupil, he could feel its gaze fixate on him as the creature spoke.

"You cruel elf. Torturing one of my poor creations. You will get no information from this creature."

The voice was distorted, echoing, and filled with power. The witch continued speaking through her slave, but now she spoke to it directly.

"I release you."

With that, its eyes returned to their black state. It had only a moment to regain its senses before a white jagged line of light split the skin of its chest over the heart. Shrieking and screaming in pain, it writhed under Nihak as it began to morph back into its Human state.

Nihak did not give it a chance to finish the transformation. He rose to his full height and extended his left arm towards the half-formed man. Despite the pain of forced changes wracking his body, the Human reached up to the elf with bloodied finger stumps, pleading for mercy before he was engulfed in flames.

As Nihak stood over the screaming man, he continued to revert back to human-form, though his features quickly grew unrecognizable. Hearing the others behind him, the elf turned to see his fellow Roamers approaching. They didn't come too close though, for the smell of burnt flesh was quickly filling the air.

"For Suolx's sake, Nihak!" Danira sighed, holding a rag over her mouth and nose. "Put the flames out!"

"Smells nice to me," Ejen remarked, shrugging his shoulders at the woman's glare.

Jolek walked over to Nihak and stared down at the burning corpse. "Did you get any information out of it? Why they are following us?"

"The Huird was about to tell me, but Alura released it from her service."

"The witch was here?!" the Earth Elf demanded, warclub in hand.

"Nay, Jolek. She spoke through the creature," the Fire Elf explained, crouching over the corpse to extract his arrow.

"So, we wasted our time," Danira growled, folding her arms crossly.

"Not necessarily," Aen remarked, gazing up through the leafy canopy. "The rest of the Huirds and Sivart are airborne and they'll think twice about following us now. Let us get to Cendril. We can focus on where to go from there."

"If the witch sent her winged demons, she has purpose. We must be careful," Rom grumbled, his gravelly voice like grating stones.

"She could be after the Sword too," Myles mused, sitting cross-legged on the Giant Earth Elf's foot.

The elf gave no heed to the dwarf as he left the woods, shoving a tree out of his path. As the other Roamers moved to follow Rom's trail, Aen leaned close to Nihak, looking him in the eye.

"Myles isn't wrong, you know. That witch could want the Sword for herself."

"But she would have no means of using it. Only Forest Elves and Humans can wield that blade."

He and Aen resumed walking, taking up the rear of the group as they made for the distant town. The giant had taken the lead, saying nothing while Danira and Myles guessed at the shapes of the clouds to pass the time. Jolek and Ejen hung back closer to Aen and Nihak, listening in on their conversation.

"Aye, only two races can use the Sylvan Sword, but Humans are never in short supply for Alura. And might I ask, of the seven Roamers here, who will carry the Sword?"

"Danira will. She is the only Human with us," Ejen remarked.

"I'll carry it. But I will never use it!" she called back.

"Who then will use the Forest Blade if we cannot?" Jolek asked, staring over at Nihak.

"I'm not sure. We'll find someone we can trust."

Danira rolled her eyes at that, for she knew all too well that Nihak trusted only a handful of Humans. How did he put it all those years ago? The witch thought back to when she and Nihak were just starting the Roamers. Back when she carried swords and not herbs. The memory became clearer the deeper she delved and then his words came back to her now: *"I can count on one hand the number of Humans I trust."*

She laughed aloud at the irony of Nihak's statement, prompting Rom to glance down at her, before plucking Myles off his foot.

"What do you laugh at?"

"Nihak. He said something long ago and I find it amusing now," she explained, looking up at the giant as he set the Odd Dwarf on his own feet.

"He has not thought this quest through. He will fail."

Danira paused as she stared up at Rom. She remembered the Giant Earth Elf to be blunt and indeed, something wasn't right about this journey they were taking.

As the Roamers moved west, they passed through another woodland, welcoming the relieving shade from the hot sun. Aen kept glancing skyward and checking his sky-blue cloak, but he needn't have worried. Patches of white kept floating and drifting across the fabric, not unlike the clouds above. Though it had been hours since they scared off Sivart and his Huirds, the Elvan wasn't about to let them sneak up or make a landing without his knowing about it. While he kept alert of the skies, the other Roamers enjoyed the scenery of the woods. Songbirds flitted past, singing and chirping loudly while a small river rushed by not too far away.

"Bah!" Ejen growled, covering his ears as a pair of birds flew past too close.

As they pushed deeper into the small woods, the other side quickly came into view.

"What will we do in Cendril?" Jolek asked.

"Cendril is a frontier town now. Didn't used to be when Malder's kingdom was bigger. Surrounded by farmlands, it's little more than a supply town. We'll need more food stuffs before we step over the edge into the Wildlands," Danira explained, giving her pack a hefty shrug.

"And beyond the borders of Humans?" the giant wondered.

"The Selveryn Forest, the Farls Swamp, to name a few," Nihak replied.

"I did not ask you, elf!" Rom growled.

"To my ears, you were asking no one," was the retort.

"Bah!" the giant snorted, waving a large hand dismissively, barely suppressing his grin.

"Will we see Goblins or were they wiped out?" Myles chimed in.

"Nay," Aen said, glancing at his cloak again. "The Goblins are like rats. They are a nuisance and easy to kill, but their race, as a whole never dies."

"So, there's a good chance we'll encounter some bands of the crooked wretches." Danira stated more than asked.

"If we do," Ejen said, noticing a falling leaf. He spun his scythe in a single swift motion and the leaf fell to the ground in two, "we will cut them down. Just as we always have."

As the night came on, the Roamers had long since left the forest and did not stop to make camp. They were eager to get to Cendril and keep a steady pace in the hopes of losing Sivart. Upon passing another large copse of trees, the clouds drifted off, leaving a black sky bedazzled by sparkling stars. The night birds struck up their tunes, sharing the sky with flitting bats. For light, Ejen and Nihak lit fires on the palms of their hands, holding the small flames aloft to better see their path. Nihak took up the front of the group, Ejen behind. Danira too added her own source of light: a glowing white orb hovering above her head. As they walked through the grasslands, emberflies flew about the Roamers, blinking their glowing red abdomens at random. Myles, in typical odd fashion, gave chase to the insects, laughing and giggling as he tried to capture one.

"Are there no more Roamers?" the giant elf broke their silent walk.

"None that I can remember," Nihak replied, walking around a prickled-leafy plant.

Rom merely stepped on it, crushing it underneath his foot.

"Does any other Roamer remember?" he asked, ignoring the Fire Elf.

"Nay," came the general answer.

"We were slaughtered in that last battle," Aen reminded him. "You were all running while I was in the air. I saw them all fall to the sword and spear."

The night seemed to loom darker for those solemn words; a harsh reminder of what happened.

"And what's to prevent history from repeating itself, I wonder?" Danira said, glancing at each Roamer as Myles returned, an emberfly in his enclosed hands.

"We fight with Malder this time, not against him."

"What if he betrays us?" was the quick retort to Nihak's statement.

"He won't. For all the cruel things that Human is, he is not without honor," the Fire Elf replied. "Or by the cut on my hand, blood spilled in vows of alliance, I will spill his blood in vengeance!"

The flames on his hand burst upwards, the tongues of fire hissing angrily as they snatched at anything to burn. Danira stepped forward and laid a calming hand on his shoulder, and the flames returned to their normal state.

"Sorry," he said, shadows dancing about them.

"I'm sorry I asked," the witch replied. "That scar still hasn't fully healed, has it?"

Nihak ran a finger over the white line from his forehead through his eye, ending down to his cheek. "No, it hasn't."

With that, he turned and kept walking, ending the conversation. The Roamers let the elf get farther ahead before they too kept walking. They knew he wanted to be alone.

"You fixed his eye," Jolek murmured to her, falling in step beside the witch. "That is powerful skill in medicine."

"I fixed his eye, yes. But the wound it inflicted on his soul, that is something no medicine can ever heal," she sighed.

The Roamers trekked on through the night, the moon gliding overhead as the stars danced alongside. Myles played with his newfound friend the emberfly, blinking its red light in his hands. As the dawn approached, he released it into the air to return to the grassy earth.

"It's too dangerous where we're going," he said as the insect flew off. "He'll be safer in his home."

The Roamers stopped in the blush of dawn, the sky flared with brilliant orange light and violet clouds. Before them, a mere four leagues from where they stood, the small town of Cendril dwelt, surrounded by farms and small houses. The nearest one was but a league away, a decrepit barn and ramshackle house.

"Let us not walk through their fields of food," Jolek suggested.

"Agreed," Aen said, stepping forward into a westerly gust of wind.

With the warm sun rising at their backs, the Roamers made their way to Cendril, walking around the vast acres of corn, wheat, and among other vegetables for eating. As the sun rose higher, the farmers came out to tend to their crops, stopping to stare at the passing band of warriors.

Many of the Humans gave fright and ran back inside while others still mounted their horses and rushed toward the walled town, to give warning no doubt. Still other farmers, the bolder ones perhaps, approached the Roamers, scythes, sickles, axes, and even the occasional sword in hand.

The Roamers didn't draw their weapons as the Humans came up to them, halting them but two leagues from the town-proper. One Human, an older man with a bastard sword in hand, stepped directly in their path. He must have seen at least fifty winters, if not more. His olive-toned skin was wrinkled and cracked, but his brown eyes were sharp and edged. His plain tunic was faded and worn, stitched in many places, and his pants were in no better condition. The old man's hair was graying, but still he stood with a strong back like he was young.

"What business do you have trespassing through our fields?" he demanded as the Roamers came to a stop. The other men formed a thin circle about them, tools and weapons gripped tight, while the old man seemed the only one to have a relaxed grip on his blade.

"We are merely passing through to Cendril. I assure you, our intentions are peaceful and-"

"'Peaceful'? Ha!" the farmer interrupted, cutting Aen off. "You Roamers are anything but peaceful!" He brandished his sword, taking a step forward. "You brought ruin and death to my king and my countrymen. The Great Kings War should have ended swiftly but thanks to you bastards it ended in shame and defeat. And now our enemy has reared his ugly head once more!" The old man took another step forward, his aged muscled arm still holding the sword steady.

"What is your name, old man?"

"I am Nesoln Velzen. I served proudly under the Blazing Falcon in war and slew many in the name of King Malder," he growled, turning his blade to point at the Fire Elf.

"If you and your neighbors wish to die of old age, then you will stand aside and let us pass to Cendril," Nihak stated. The farmers all tensed at the threat, some holding up their weapons, ready for a fight.

The elf glanced about at each Human, weighing their skills, measuring their fear. "Out of all twenty of you, only seven of you know how to fight and only three of you, yourself included," he said, nodding to Nesoln, "served in the war. And you know who we are and what we're capable of. I will ask only once more: please step aside and let us pass."

"Truly, our intentions are peaceful," Danira stated, holding her hands out wide in a gesture of peace. "If you do attack, my fellow

Roamers will defend themselves. I do not wish any blood to be spilled, but if the wrong move is made, I will not be able to stop it."

The witch turned to Nesoln and approached him, her arms still out wide. "Good sir, I know you are angry. You have suffered at our hands and I know your pain. But let us pass. I beg you."

Glowering at her, the old farmer's mouth formed a scowl, but after a moment of staring into her soft eyes, he lowered his weapon. "Very well. I don't trust you, nor your companions, but if you do not wish to fight, then get off our land. I only wish to raise my son and my crops in peace."

"We thank you for your passage and wish you prosperous times," Danira said, bowing with a smile.

"Times will be harsh come next spring, no thanks to the Roamers," he spat, turning and walking back to his house. Likewise, the other farmers spat upon the ground and turned to go back to their own farms.

Their path open, once again, the Roamers continued walking toward Cendril, where alarm bells could be heard ringing. It didn't take long for the wooden gates to swing wide and over half the town's garrison to ride out to meet them.

"How many, do you think?" Ejen wondered, scratching at his chin.

"Eh. A hundred or so," Nihak replied, shrugging.

"Rom, if you please," Aen said, gesturing with his staff.

The giant nodded and stepped to the head of the group and knelt down. Gripping the earth, he twisted his hand to the side, sending a great crack splitting the ground and sending rumbling tremors to the galloping horsemen. Their mounts neighed and bucked at the fierce shaking, knocking several of their riders to the ground. The armored men came to a faltering stop six meters away, reining their beasts in.

"Now that we have your attention," Aen shouted once all the noise died down, "know that we are not here to fight. We only wish to resupply before passing on into the Wildlands. Is that agreeable with you men?"

They could hear murmuring and quiet chatting amongst the garrison. Finally, one man wearing a red tunic walked his horse forward.

"Aye, you may enter Cendril, but only if you leave by nightfall."

"That's all we ask," the Elvan replied.

Rom now laid his mighty hands alongside the wide crack in the dirt and coaxed it to seal shut, murmuring in Earelvish. The men stared wide-eyed as it closed before turning their horses about, trotting back to the town. Rom straightened up, grinning and followed his fellow Roamers towards the open gates.

"If Rom weren't here, what would you have done to stop the Humans?" Jolek asked with a laugh.

"Oh, I'm sure Nihak and I would have given a fiery display," Ejen answered, spinning his war scythe about.

After the soldiers filed through the wooden gates, the Roamers too passed through, drawing the gaze of hundreds of eyes. Men, women, and children alike stood along the streets and peered from the windows of shops, staring in fear at the seven armed wanderers.

"It appears all of Cendril came to greet us," Aen remarked wryly.

The Roamers stopped once through the gates and stared back at the gathered Humans. Neither party made a move as many minutes of uncomfortable silence passed, broken only by the occasional gust of wind. Finally, a barrel-chested man stepped forward, wearing a silver sash across his massive chest.

"He must be the Marquess or some such," Danira surmised, stepping to the head of the group.

"How can she tell?" Myles wondered, looking at the approaching man in confusion.

"His clothes are clean and well-kept," Aen answered, patting the Odd Dwarf's head.

"I am Lord Jedune Reggar," the broad man stated, standing before Danira. "What business does the last ragged remnants of the Roamers have in my town?"

"Lord Reggar, we merely wish to resupply before moving on into the Wildlands."

Reggar stroked his stubbly black beard, frowning deeply at her.

"We have coin," she added, folding her arms. "You wouldn't deny honest business from your townsmen, now would you?"

"And I'm to assume you are the only one who has any coin?"

The witch glanced back at the other Roamers before turning back to Reggar. "Aye, you assume correctly," she sighed.

The Marquess harrumphed loudly before speaking. "Your fellow Roamers will be escorted to the center of town where they will remain under armed guard. You may go about your business of buying whatever supplies you need. Once that is finished, you and the others will leave. Are my terms fair?"

Danira once again glanced back at her comrades. Myles was climbing about Rom while the giant stood still as a statue. Jolek was running his thumb along the edge of the triangular blade of his club, nodding in satisfaction at the sharpness. Nihak and Ejen had resorted to playing with flames upon their hands, the tiny fires jumping and dancing as they juggled. Aen caught her glance and merely shrugged as he stood among the distracted and bored warriors.

"Sir, you may keep them under armed escort if it makes you feel better."

Jedune Reggar's eyes widened a bit at the dry statement. "I have two hundred men ready to fight and kill you Roamers should I give the order!"

Danira merely gave a shrug of her light shoulders. "Then you would be lord of a dead town." With that, she flashed her most disarming smile, turned, and came back to the Roamers. The Marquess stood there, blinking stupidly as she informed them of the plan.

"Sir, should we give up our weapons too? Would that put you at ease?" Nihak called, much to the amusement of the others.

Reggar gave an indignant huff and signaled for his guards to keep them under watch. The Roamers were led to the center of the small town, marked by a large well. Ejen and Nihak would not go near it, preferring to give the cavernous hole a wide berth. Rom sat, sending a small tremor through the ground, much to the protest of the scattered townspeople as they went back to their businesses. Jolek joined him, resting his back against the stony wall, closing his eyes in rest. Aen and Myles sat on the very edge of the well itself, the Elvan resting his eyes while the Odd Dwarf stared down into the black watery depths. All around them stood the Marquess's guards keeping tight grips upon their swords and spears, ready to use at a moment's notice, but the Roamers merely ignored them.

"You all behave yourselves while I get what we need," Danira said, hefting her pack as she walked away. "Please."

"We make no promises," Ejen called, summoning fire to his hand.

The witch merely rolled her eyes as she disappeared down a bend in the street.

"What worlds dwell down in the deep, deep well?" Myles wondered, leaning so very far down. The Odd Dwarf seemed ready to plunge headfirst in but for one thing; without opening his eyes Aen's hand shot out, grabbing hold of the dwarf's trousers.

"I have no plans to fish for an Odd Dwarf and you will not alter those plans," he stated, easily pulling Myles back up to rest his feet on the cobbled ground.

"Blah." The beardless dwarf stuck his tongue at the Elvan before hopping over to sit next to Rom.

Little else was said between the Roamers as they waited for Danira to finish her errands. The townspeople kept to themselves, all the while staring at the odd group of warriors as they passed them by. Growing bored, Nihak stood, drawing his longsword, much to the soldiers' panic.

"Calm yourselves," the elf called, rolling his eyes as he tapped Ejen with his blade. "Up."

Ejen flashed a lopsided grin as he rose to his feet, scythe in hand. "First cut?"

"No need for blood. We'll just spar," Nihak replied, setting his feet, sword gripped in both hands.

"As you wish," the older elf replied, lazily twirling his weapon.

The Fire Elves began to circle each other, bare feet sliding along the cobbled stones. Nihak struck first, lunging forward with a snap-cut. It was quickly knocked aside, their blades clanging loudly, turning more than a few heads. Before Nihak could retort, Ejen pushed on his counter-strike and spun his staffed weapon about, the butt end sailing in for the elf's head. Ducking the blow, the younger elf thrusted for Ejen's midriff, forcing him to backpedal. Nihak pursued, sword leading. Bringing his weapon in close, Ejen pushed the longsword wide and swung from right to left in a diagonal slash, aiming for Nihak's left shoulder. By now a crowd of Humans had joined the guarding soldiers, watching the two Roamers as they danced about. Nihak brought his blade up, blocking the deadly strike. Sparks flew and metal shrieked as he moved his blade to the left until the crossguard slapped into the scythe blade, knocking it wide. Recovering faster than Ejen, he slashed low for his waist. The older elf was quick to let his staffed weapon slide down until the butt struck the ground, effectively stopping Nihak's longsword. A swift kick to the gut had his younger counterpart stumbling back. Now that Ejen had him at a distance, he spun his war scythe about, lowering it to thrust for the heart. As Nihak brought his sword up to parry, a third sword sang through the air, interlocking with his and Ejen's. A gasp of surprise rippled through the gathered crowd at the action.

The Roamers turned to look upon the Human woman standing between them, her auburn hair waving softly in the gentle wind. Sarra McKeer grinned and stepped back, moving to sheathe her falx.

"It's good to see the Roamers again."

"Who are you?" Nihak asked, eyeing her war hammer and sword.

Sarra's brow furrowed in confusion. "Do you not recognize me? I'm a Roamer too."

The Fire Elves exchanged looks before glancing past her at the other Roamers, who were now joining them away from the well.

"Any of you recognize her?" Nihak asked.

The other four shook their heads, looking her over, deep in thought.

"What's your name?" Ejen asked.

"Sarra McKeer," she answered, her smile faltering. "I remember you, Ejen. You and Nihak. The big elf is Rom, is he not?"

"She must have been with us if she remembers our names," Myles surmised.

The Fire Elves had to concede that point, as their names were known to only a few individuals outside the band of Roamers.

"Do you know the others here? We are all that's left," Aen stated, scratching his chin.

She looked about from Rom to Jolek to Myles and back to the Elvan. "I remember the Odd Dwarf, Myles. He was always by your side. I'm sorry to say I do not remember your name or his," she said, nodding to Jolek.

Aen nodded a little, "You were right with the Roamers you've named. Let me see your hands, child," he implored, holding his out.

Sarra laid her pale hands in his weathered ones and he felt them over, running his toughened fingers along her palms.

"You have a warrior's hands. Rough and seasoned. Know how to use a bow?"

"I don't need a bow to fight," she stated. "I kill at close-range."

He chuckled at that and released her hands. "If you are a Roamer, Sarra, I have little recollection of you, though parts of you seem familiar to me. I remember a war hammer wielded by a young and very brash girl who boasted at how many skulls she could split in a fight. And I remember those fierce blue eyes, still so young and spirited, yet hardened by time. You have seen and done things a woman your age should not know. I'd say you did roam with us, those long years ago."

She smiled and nodded her thanks to him.

"Now, Danira, I'm sure she has a finer memory than I. When she gets back, we will ask if you truly walked and fought alongside us. And if you are a Roamer, we would welcome the extra blade," the Elvan stated, leaning upon his staff.

While Aen talked with her, Rom's eyes turned to gaze southeast. He lumbered towards that wall, drawing concerned looks from the soldiers. They lowered their weapons his way, but ultimately moved out of the giant's path rather than be crushed under his feet. The other Roamers immediately followed after the giant as he stared to the distance, the sun at his back.

"Enemies approach," he stated, taking off at a fast pace, each step sending tremors through the ground.

CHAPTER 11

"What enemy?" Myles wondered, hurrying after the Giant Earth Elf.

The other Roamers quickly followed suit and rushed to the walls of the town. As they approached, the alarm bells began ringing in earnest once more. Rom stooped and lifted Jolek up to his shoulder. When he straightened up, the Earth Elf had a perfect view over the high wall, only to watch as farmers and their families from the outer reaches abandon their homes and rush to the fortified town with speed.

"Jolek, what do you see?" Aen called.

The dark-skinned elf turned his gaze back to the southeast. A large mass of men, armed with swords and axes, approached the farmlands on horseback. They were only a league away, but Jolek had sharp eyes and could tell their numbers.

"Companies of armed Humans, 400 strong. They bear the Circled Arrow upon their banner!"

Nihak rushed up the wooden steps, shoving past several soldiers and militiamen, drawing more than a few curses and oaths as he went. The Fire Elf stood near Jolek as he stared out across the plains, watching as the enemy began to set fire to houses and barns, destroying their fields of crops along the way. Soon great blazes had consumed the fields, sending thick columns of black smoke billowing skyward.

"It is the Circled Arrow!" he snarled.

The Circled Arrow was King Jamiel's insignia, a golden arrow passing through a white thin-banded circle of light upon a red banner.

"They must be the platoons raiding up and down the countryside!" the Marquess bellowed, standing a little way down the wall from the Roamers.

"And now they want Cendril," his captain stated.

All the while, the gates were flung wide as families poured through, people carrying what few things they could. Some were farther back however, less than half a league away. Unfortunately for those people, the soldiers of Jamiel rode them down and slaughtered them, staining the wheat red.

"Bastards!" the soldiers growled, watching helplessly as the townspeople and farmers sought shelter within the stores and shops.

"Get every man prepared for battle!" Reggar shouted, hurrying back down the steps of the parapets. He rushed across the cobbled streets to his office, a wide and squat building.

The Fire Elf rolled his eyes as he looked about, watching the Humans rush in a mad dash for arms and armor.

"I know what you're thinking," Ejen said, joining him on the wall. "You're eager for battle. I can see it in your eyes, spark."

The younger elf gave his counterpart a half-friendly shove, resenting the nickname. Ejen merely shrugged it off as the other Roamers joined them.

"So, we stay and fight?" Myles asked, hopping up and down to see over the chest-high battlements.

"Or go where?" Aen said dryly, ever leaning on his staff.

Jolek casually unslung his war club, resting the angled weapon against his shoulder. "Then we do what this town needs us to do."

At that moment, the Marquess reappeared, armored in plated steel with a helm upon his head. A broadsword was gripped tightly in his hand as he stomped over to the wall and hurried up the steps.

"Two lines of men in staggered formation! Archers in front, swords behind! Women and children to the armory and barricade the doors! Seal the gates and stand fast when they try to break through!"

His soldiers and militiamen immediately responded to his orders, hurrying to carry out his commands, the stamp of metal-shod boots ringing through the air. All the while, the Roamers stood by watching as the enemy drew nearer and nearer, now less than a third of a league away. His orders given, Reggar took note of their idleness and pounded over to the ragged warriors.

"Either get out of our way or help us face this threat!"

"We thought you'd never ask," Nihak stated sardonically, unslinging his bow. "Myles, stay close to Aen and Jolek. Rom, the gate. Ejen, where do you think you should be?"

"I'll stay on the wall. Can't use my scythe, but it's better than waiting at the gate while you all have the fun," the Fire Elf said, drawing out his sickle-sword.

"I'll be on the wall as well," Sarra said, drawing her falx with a hiss of steel.

"Nihak, I should think I'll be of more use at the gate with Rom," Aen stated. "My staff would serve better purpose than my sword."

The Fire Elf nodded as he gave his bowstring an experimental tug. The Marquess stared at them in disbelief, left eye twitching erratically as the Roamers began to disperse, moving calmly rather than running and shoving.

"Wait a minute!" he snapped. "This town is mine to defend. I decide what is done and who goes where!"

The Roamers all stopped and stared at him.

"Sir, would you have it any differently?" Aen wondered. "Would you rather our giant stand on these parapets, while the dwarf there does his damnedest to keep the gates shut? Or the archer stands by the gate, waiting to see if the enemy breaks through? We live and breathe combat. If you want to live past today, then I suggest you order your men and trust us to work with you, and not for you, in this fight."

The Marquess stared at the Elvan, flustered and red in the face with anger. "Very well! Carry on!"

With that, he rushed to the center of the east wall. As the last of the families passed through into the town, the gates were slammed shut, barred and bolted. As the last locking bar was secured, the soldiers turned to see Rom lumbering towards them. Prudently, they parted before the Giant Earth Elf, who came to a halt before the wide doors. He turned about, sat with a ground-shaking impact, and leaned his massive back against the gates, the hinges groaning in protest. The Humans stared up at him, concerned, before moving to gather around Rom and brace the gate, with Aen soon joining them. Atop the wall, other soldiers lined in formation with the Roamers taking their respective positions among them.

Reaching over his shoulder, Myles slid his axe from its crude sheath and twirled the shaft about in his hands, scowling. "I wish I could see over this wall!"

Jolek patted the Odd Dwarf's shoulder reassuringly. "I shall be your eyes for you."

Off to their right a few men over, Sarra stood ready, her cloak flapping lightly in the breeze. She cared not for the jeers and remarks thrown her way from the men around her. If her hammer found the skulls of a few allies instead of foes, then so be it.

Nihak stood further down from them alongside the archers and at the ready. As the Fire Elf glanced about, taking in those who stood beside him and behind him, he was surprised to see the old farmer, Nesoln Velzen, standing on the parapets over his right shoulder.

"Shouldn't you be with your family in the barracks?"

The old man glared back at him. "My son is safe with the women and children, though I know he wants to stand by my side. But he's not ready for the hell that is war. And I am ashamed to stand by you in this fight!"

Nihak merely shrugged and nocked an arrow to his bow. "An enemy today may yet be your ally tomorrow. I hope you keep that in mind during this battle and keep your blade out of my back."

Nesoln spat at his feet in reply, growling. The crude response was met with approving murmurs among the other soldiers. Indeed, if Nihak had glanced around further, he'd have noticed that Nesoln was the only seasoned warrior not fully garbed in armor, instead wearing a plain metal helm, mail shirt and bracers. Even more so, if Nihak had taken more time to notice, all the men of the town's militia were dressed in similar fashion, wearing less armor than their fellow soldiers.

By this time, the enemy had come to a halt dozens of meters before their gates, spreading out across the wide wall. Some sat astride mighty warhorses, their riders fully armored. Most of the soldiers were simple footmen, armed with pikes or axes, and some with swords at their hips. Many of those men carried crude siege-ladders upon their shoulders, no doubt having made them during their sweeping march through the countryside. The only other siege instrument carried among the mounted knights was a crude battering ram, once a strong tree, no doubt. As the opposing forces glowered and scowled each other down, one man bearing his king's banner trotted his horse forward.

"Who calls himself lord of this pitiful town?" he shouted, looking up at the ranks of men along the wall.

"I am Marquess Reggar! Who are you, so arrogant to march on Cendril?"

"I am Sir Harin! Surrender and we shall spare your lives, if you kneel down and call Jamiel your king."

"Bend a knee to that runt! Ha! Get you gone from my lands before we butcher you all!" Reggar spat back.

"Then pray for mercy, for we shall-!"

Harin's threat was cut short as a black arrow pierced his throat, sending him tumbling from his horse to drown in his own blood. Behind him, his fellow knights growled and shouted in anger, their banner fallen to the dirt.

The Marquess was just as surprised. "Who shot that arrow?!" he demanded. "I did not order an attack!"

"They came here for bloodshed and death! And they shall have it!" Nihak roared back.

A great cry of fury rose up from the enemy ranks as they charged forward, bearing their long ladders.

"Archers loose! Loose at will!!!!" the Marquess bellowed.

Nihak pulled an arrow from his quiver along with the archers and let their bows sing, sending a deadly rain piercing into the mass of charging men. The soldiers of Jamiel paid little heed to the deadly storm, raising shields as their siege-ladders were hoisted up against the wall. Clattering wood against stone was drowned out by the clamor of arms and armor and the raging war cries as the ladders slapped against the parapets. Soldiers pushed and shoved to clamber up the sturdy rungs, eager for blood and glory.

"Archers back! Swords at ready!" Reggar screamed at the top of his lungs.

The archers hurriedly backed away from the low wall, allowing their fellow swordsmen to step forth as the enemy leapt over the battlements. Cendril's soldiers met them with their ringing steel, swords flashing in the sun as blood spurted from cleaved bodies and stained the parapets a violent red. Eagerly hopping forward, Myles swung his axe, shearing a man's leg in half with a wet crunch. The Odd Dwarf couldn't help but giggle as the unlucky soldier wobbled on the battlements before tumbling backwards, his screams of agony lost in the thunderous noise of battle. Yelling in his babbling tongue, he split another enemy's helm as he emerged atop the ladder. Behind the wild Roamer, other enemies had managed to gain footing upon the parapets, cutting Cendril soldiers down. Myles turned to block an axe cleaving for his neck and sharply kicked his attacker between the legs. Stumbling back from the low blow, the Human wasn't able to bring his weapon to bear as Myles smashed the blunt side of his axe into his enemy's skull. His foe felled, Myles ensured the man would never rise again, bringing his weapon high for a powerful two-handed stroke.

While the Odd Dwarf cleaved and dismembered, Jolek swung his mighty warclub, crushing armor and bones alike. Letting forth his battle cry, the Earth Elf smashed his angled weapon into an enemy's chest, sending the dead man flying off the parapets. Turning, the Earth Elf adjusted his grip, sliding one hand up to the base of his wide-headed club and held it horizontal, blocking an enemy blade. Effortlessly, Jolek swiftly shoved the sword high, then snapped his arms out, ramming the blade of his weapon through the bridge of the man's nose. The solider fell without a sound, gore flowing down his whiskered face. Shifting his grip once more, Jolek took up his warclub and slammed the iron weapon down upon another Human's helmed head, collapsing the soldier's spine. It was almost comical for the elf, seeing a human with his head sunk so low between his shoulders. With a fierce kick, Jolek sent the body sailing back, knocking several enemies off their feet. With a laugh, the Earth Elf leapt atop the battlements and swung down in a mighty arc, his angled weapon knocking a climbing soldier's head clean from his shoulders. The headless corpse tumbled from the ladder, taking more men with it back to the ground.

As the Earth Elf and Odd Dwarf amassed a growing number of bodies strewn about that section of the wall, Sarra held her own position, bloodstained falx flashing in the sun as she decapitated enemy after enemy setting foot on the parapets. Her curved blade allowed her to split heads in half and cleave through armor and flesh with ease. As one enemy gripped the battlements, ready to leap up from the ladder, the Roamer swung her blade down and severed his arm from his shoulder. With nothing to hold on to, the soldier fell back, screaming until he landed atop his comrades below. Around her, soldiers of Cendril held the wall, knocking men from their siege-ladders or slaying them on their feet, staining the stones red. However, even as the men kept the enemy at bay, they too fell to blades and pikes. Cutting down another enemy, her curved sword slicing through the leather armor, Sarra turned to see an ally run through, a spear impaling his chest. Callously, the auburn-haired woman shoved the dying man aside, falx raised high. Singing through the air, she gave a satisfied growl as her blade chopped deep into the pikeman's chest, splitting him from shoulder to sternum. He gave but a gurgling gasp, dying on his knees as his lifeblood spewed forth. About to yank her sword free, flashing steel cleaved down for her arms. Quickly, she let go of the hilt and quick-stepped back, avoiding the attack as she pulled her war hammer from her belt. Glaring at her attacker she rushed forward, turning her hammer to block another strike, the blade clanging against the langets of her hammer. Turning the hammer again, Sarra hooked her enemy's weapon with the spike and yanked it from his grasp. Grinning like a madwoman, she landed a harsh blow to his right shoulder, bones shattering above the din of battle. His screams of pain were cut short as the next blow drove the spike through his skull. Ripping free her weapon, the pierced helm giving a screeching protest, Sarra ran up to another enemy and swung low, the hammerhead coming up between his legs. The man let fall his axe and dropped to his knees, only to take the hammer spike through the side of his neck. Letting the body fall, the auburn-haired woman quickly glanced around before giving a yell of fury, striking a soldier in the jaw, sending him falling off the wall.

As she fought, the allies alongside her began to fall in numbers, allowing the enemy to gain a better foothold upon the wall. In danger of being overrun, Sarra cried for aid, frantically smashing a soldier in the right side of his knee, crippling him. Hearing her call of distress, Aen looked up from the shuddering gate, the enemy outside attempting to ram it down. Leaving Rom and the Cendril soldiers to keep the gate sealed, the Elvan summoned a blast of wind, propelling himself into the air. The aged half-breed landed less than gracefully, stumbling into an enemy, who in turn was sent sprawling right through a crenel of the battlements.

"My thanks!" Aen shouted after him.

Spinning his staff about, the Elvan sent a mighty gust of wind rushing past them, sending more than a few men flying from the wall, their ladders following.

"I owe you one!" Sarra said, knocking aside a thrusting blade and crushing her opponent's chest with her hammer.

"Nay," Aen replied, a broadsword materializing in his right hand. "Roamers always watch each other's backs."

With that said, the aging half-breed turned and slashed an enemy's midriff open, spilling his guts in a gory mess. Frantically the doomed man tried to scoop his entrails back into his body, sobbing and screaming. Mercifully, Aen shoved his blade through his chest next, swiftly ending the soldier's life. With a sharp kick, the Elvan yanked his broadsword free and spun again, swinging his staff to strike another enemy in the throat. As the Human choked on his crushed windpipe, Aen followed up with another swing of his sword, beheading him. Grunting with effort, the Elvan moved to parry a spear thrust, his weapon at an awkward angle. Knocking aside a second thrust with his staff, Aen moved to attack in kind as Sarra brought her hammer down on the spearman's right arm, driving the spike through his forearm. As he dropped his weapon, she turned, yanking him off the parapets to fall to the cobbled street below. Her weapon free, the Roamers stood back to back as they held that section, repelling any who set foot on the parapets.

Farther along to the northern side of the wall, the Fire Elves wreaked havoc upon the enemy. Nihak had long since run out of arrows, sending nineteen more men to a swift death rather than throwing his bow down as the other archers had. Those men had drawn their gladii from their belts and joined the fray, their short blades more maneuverable, thus giving them a keen edge in cramped fighting. When his arrows were spent, the Fire Elf threw down his bow and drew his longsword, rushing forward to stab an enemy through the throat as he crested the battlements. He gagged on his own blood before Nihak ripped his blade free through the side of his neck, nearly decapitating him. Alongside him, Human allies fought to stem the rising tide of Jamiel's soldiers, some falling by the sword or spear. As the hour grew late, Cendril's men began to dwindle in strength and numbers. Nihak ran one soldier through his back before he could cut down an ally. The Roamer was more than a little surprised to find that it was Nesoln, the old man giving him a begrudging nod of thanks. Nihak returned the nod as the seasoned farmer parried an attacking thrust and riposted, stabbing his opponent through the thigh. With his enemy on his knees, Nesoln lopped off his head, grunting with effort. The Fire Elf turned and knocked aside a low thrust and countered with a slash from left to right. The wounded enemy fell to the floor, his lifeblood flowing from a deep gash across his chest. Blocking another sword stroke, Nihak forced his enemy's weapon low and brought the crossguard of his longsword up to pierce the man's throat. As he stumbled back, choking, the elf flipped his blade about to half-swording and swung hard, striking the dying man in the head with the pommel. Feeling someone at his back, Nihak turned, sword raised for attack, only to see it was the old man. He gave the elf a lopsided smirk.

"Thought I was going to stab you in the back, Roamer?"

Before the young Fire Elf could reply, Nesoln's eyes widened and he shoved Nihak out of the way. Quickly turning, time seemed to slow for the elf as he looked upon the aged Human, a spear through his abdomen. Letting out a weak snarl, Nesoln gripped the shaft of the spear and pulled his enemy close and ran him through his chest. As he fell to his knees, the elf rushed to his side, holding him up.

Even with the sounds of battle raging around them, his sharp ears heard Nesoln utter with his last breath, "Nelsh...my son..."

Offering a prayer for the fallen warrior, Nihak ran a bloodstained hand over Nesoln's face, closing his eyes in eternal sleep. Gently laying the Human down, Nihak sprang up, his blade singing through the air with anger burning anew and flames bursting from his hands.

As Nihak laid waste to the enemy, roasting them alive, Ejen wasn't far off, slaying Humans left and right as well. Knife in his left hand and sickle-sword in his right, Ejen's blades sliced and slashed enemies apart, sending blood spurting to paint his face and arms red. Hooking an enemy spear, the Fire Elf forced the weapon low, and stabbed with his knife, ramming the blade through the Human's face. Spinning rapidly, Ejen turned and sliced another enemy's thighs with his curved sword, then kicked him down, stomping on his throat for good measure. A scream of fury brought his attention to a charging enemy, sword raised for a devastating swing. The Fire Elf stepped in close, inside the swing of the blade and spun around his opponent, bringing his sickle-sword up to slice the man's neck. Letting the body fall, Ejen rushed forward to slam into an another enemy; with their bodies colliding together, the elf quickly dropped into a crouch, slipping his knife to the back of the soldier's knee. Swiftly he hamstrung the man and rose to his feet, chopping down with his curved sword. Moving along, Ejen shoved an ally aside to slash an enemy across the eyes, blinding him. A large bellowing soldier slammed his fist into the Fire Elf's jaw, knocking him back. Spitting fiery blood, Ejen recovered quickly, knife and sword double-blocking the broadsword. Using his sickle-sword to keep the blade at bay, Ejen thrust his knife deep into the man's right flank under his arm, piercing his heart. Sensing danger behind, Ejen leapt aside as an axe crashed down where he once stood. The soldier growled and brought his massive weapon up for another swing, aiming for Ejen's chest. Ducking the attack, the Roamer lunged forward, driving his sickle-sword up through the gut to hook the diaphragm. Tearing the weapon free in a shower of blood, Ejen grinned and charged down the parapet, cutting down any who stood in his path, whirling and slashing with abandon.

As swords and axes flashed and clanged above, Rom kept his back against the gates. Outside while men clambered up the ladders, a squad of Jamiel's men had brought the crude battering ram. Yelling with battlelust, they charged forward, slamming the felled tree against the thick gates. The Giant Earth Elf felt it *thudding* against his back but paid little heed, merely folding his massive arms. It was more a nuisance than anything as the battering ram struck the gates again and again. Rom gave a grunt of annoyance as the knocking persisted. He'd much rather help in the field over being used as an immovable object. As the fight raged on through the day, more of Cendril's men fell to the enemy, prompting the giant to glance down at the men standing alongside him.

"Get up there," he rumbled.

They didn't need telling twice. Drawing their swords, they hurried up the stairs to the parapets to reinforce their comrades. The Roamer watched them with a baleful eye before growling in irritation at the ceaseless *thudding* against his back. His ire reaching new heights, Rom gave a mighty roar that caused the battle to take pause. The sudden quiet was immediately broken as he lumbered to his feet and turned to the gates.

"Enough!" he bellowed, kicking the gates open, shattering the bolts and hinges of the doors.

Men fell back in fear and panic as the Giant Earth Elf emerged from the entrance. In their fright, the soldiers had dropped their makeshift battering ram to frantically draw swords. Rom was more than happy to put it to use again. Taking the ram up with both hands, he gave a mighty swing and sent the squad flying back, their bodies broken. At the sight of their comrades' deaths, and the now-open gate, the rest of the soldiers charged en masse, eager for Earth Elf blood. Rom gave a bellowing laugh and swung left to right, then right to left again, sending dozens more soaring through the air like ragdolls. Standing before the smashed gates, Rom crushed and splattered scores of men. It didn't take long for them to realize going up against the giant was suicide and began to make a hasty retreat, more than eager to leave their men still on the wall. Rom adjusted his grip on his club and hurled it after them, one end of the ram driving into the ground like a massive spear before the fleeing soldiers. Deterred from running, they turned to see the Giant Earth Elf stomping towards them. Swords and spears were quickly flung to the dirt in surrender.

Back on the wall, with the rest of the enemy at the mercy of Rom, the soldiers' numbers thinned all too quickly. The way in through the gate was out of the question and no matter how hard they tried, they could not gain a foothold on the parapets. Cendril's forces still stood strong with the Roamers at the tip of the spear. It hadn't taken long for Jamiel's men to realize who was fighting against them during the utter carnage of the battle. With no hope of victory and rather than face death, they began to lay down their weapons, hoping for mercy. A few still fought, one such man clashing blades with Marquess Reggar. Parrying, he stabbed his enemy through the thigh and shoulder-slammed into him. The wounded man tumbled to the floor, his sword flying from his grasp. The Marquess pressed the tip of his sword to the downed soldier's throat and looked about to see the fighting slowly die out.

"Soldiers of Jamiel!" he shouted. "Lay down your arms and your lives will be spared. Men of Cendril, if any enemy still holds a weapon, cut him down!"

The remaining enemy soldiers immediately dropped their blades, holding their arms out in surrender.

For Nihak, the Human standing before him had thrown his sword at the elf's feet. They regarded each other stoically, a smug grin slowly spreading across the Human's face. The Fire Elf's bloodstained longsword tapped against the parapet stones, catching the Human's notice.

"You'd like to kill me, eh? Too bad you can't, Roamer-scum! You're under orders since I threw down my blade," he snickered.

Nihak stabbed him through the chest without a second thought, the dying man gasping as he stared at the elf in disbelief.

"I don't take orders," Nihak stated simply, glaring with hate into the fading light of his victim's eyes. Without another word, the elf callously withdrew his sword, letting the Human fall. Pulling a rag from a small pouch on his belt, the Fire Elf cleaned his weapon while the other soldiers, friend and foe alike, stared at him in fear. Done wiping the blood off, Nihak returned the longsword to his hip and made his way over the bodies to Ejen, who was similarly cleaning his own blades.

"Ahh, the smell of blood and death in the air," he remarked, sheathing his knife and sickle-sword. "How I've missed it. Shame I didn't get a chance to put my fire to use."

"You'll get your chance yet," Nihak said, clapping a hand on Ejen's shoulder. "No new scars?"

"Alas, not this time!" the older elf replied, shaking his head. "Yourself?"

"Nay. This was a mere skirmish. Nothing worth carrying scars over anyway."

Ejen nodded in agreement and cast his gaze about. "Jolek, Myles, Aen, and that new Roamer woman are down that way. Shall we?"

"Aye, lead on," Nihak replied, following his friend.

The Fire Elves stepped over to the other Roamers while the remaining soldiers of Cendril rounded up their captured enemies. As they walked along the red-stained wall, bodies lay littered about, some draped over the edge of the parapets or the battlements. Already the crows had begun to circle the town, cawing and rasping their desire to feed, prompting the warriors to gaze upward.

"The birds of war," Nihak muttered before nearly stumbling over a body. "Damn!"

"I'm surprised we don't have a murder of crows following us wherever we go," Aen remarked with a wry grin.

"Very funny, old man," Ejen replied as he and Nihak stopped before the others.

The Roamers stared at each other, some of their weapons still dirty with blood. Their faces and clothes were soaked with it, but none of them bore any wounds in the fight.

"What do we do now?" Myles wondered, finishing wiping his axe free of blood and bits of bone. "Do we stay here until the morrow or should we move on now?"

"I say we stay and get rest. This town is safe and won't need us for any more fighting."

"Sarra's right," Aen said, wiping his face clean. "And we have to find Danira. If I know that witch, she's healing up the wounded."

"Aye that's where she'll be," Nihak agreed.

As they talked, Marquess Reggar stormed over to them, his left arm bearing a wound before the elbow.

"What were you thinking?!" he snarled, brandishing his dripping blade at Nihak. "I saw what you did. You killed that soldier when he surrendered!"

Ejen's sickle-sword flew up, the outer-edge of the curved blade pressing hard against the surprised Human's throat. "And I will kill you if you continue to irritate us."

"Ejen, stand down," Aen said, laying a calming hand on the Fire Elf's shoulder.

The hot-tempered Roamer made no move to lower his weapon nor did he follow through with his threat.

"Remove your weapon," Reggar ordered, gulping audibly.

"Look around you, my lord," Nihak implored, coating the title with venom, "This town is still yours. You still have at least fifty, maybe a hundred, men left standing and they're all battle-worn. We just helped you stave off an attacking force, and the first thing you do is treat me like one of your common soldiers? If I asked Ejen to cut your throat, he would do so. You can hate us, but do not make the mistake of treating us like you own us. And never underestimate our ability to kill."

With that, Ejen lowered his curved sword and returned it to his belt. Speechless and pale, Reggar could only stagger away.

Aen merely sighed and shook his head as Rom lumbered over to them.

"Ah, there you are, you mountainous heap!" Jolek called, giving the Giant Earth Elf a playful punch to the thigh.

"When do we move?" he wondered aloud, giving Jolek a friendly shove with one hand, sending the laughing elf to the ground.

Aen looked about, surveying the aftermath before them. The soldiers and militiamen of Cendril not wounded had already begun to gather the dead, ally and enemy alike.

"Enough play, lads. Let's make ourselves useful by helping them gather the bodies. Nihak, you and I will go find Danira. The rest of you, get to it."

Ejen gave a groan, rolling his eyes but set about carrying bodies off the wall along with the other Roamers. As they began their gruesome task, the Elvan led the younger Fire Elf away from the wall. The pair walked down the cobbled streets, passing soldiers bearing the wounded and dead, while others rushed past to bring more off the wall. Aen stuck his staff out to halt one such man, his head bandaged to cover his left eye.

"Pardon me, sir, but where is the infirmary?"

"Just down this road and a turn to the left there," the young man said, pointing back the way he came.

"Thank you," the aged half-breed said, moving his staff out of the soldier's way.

They continued on their path, turning the corner and finding themselves in the market square; the stalls and carts had been moved out of the way to make room for the scores of dead, men lain out in orderly rows, their bodies still leaking blood. Beyond the macabre site lay the town church, a steady train of wounded men being carted inside.

Respectfully walking around the square, the Roamers made their way to the doors of the church, stepping inside. While the smell was no better in there than outside, the only real difference was the activity of healers and witches doing their best to patch up the screaming and groaning men; several of them armed with herbs, bandages, and salves were hurriedly running about trying to help as many soldiers as they could. The pews had been shoved aside to make room for makeshift beds, cots, or even piles of blankets; anywhere they could lay a man out so he could be tended to. Sure enough, Danira was at the center of it all, working her magic and skills on men left and right.

"Knew we'd find you here," Aen remarked as they approached her.

She looked up at them briefly before returning to her work: a soldier with a broken spear shaft through his back.

"Where else would I be? I was just finishing up gathering the supplies when I heard the chaos and the coming army. So, I did what I do best."

As she talked, the witch took a small knife and slit the soldier's back open so she could better dislodge the spearhead. Extracting it slowly, she poured a red oil over the wound. The man's ragged breathing turned sharp and pained, but then softened as he passed out into blissful sleep. Danira set to work stitching him up while Nihak and Aen stood by watching.

"Do we leave tonight?" she asked after she was finished.

"That depends on you," Aen replied, shrugging lightly.

Danira paused to look around at the frantic mass of people running about. "I need to stay and help these people. At the very least, we stay the night."

The Elvan nodded in understanding. "Then we stay here the night."

"Now if you'll excuse me," the witch said, shooing them away, "I need to focus on my work."

They nodded and turned to head back. As the Roamers made their way outside, the light was beginning to dim. Through the dusky evening, Nihak and Aen once more began to skirt around the mass of bodies waiting for their final resting place. Along the way, Nihak spotted the body of Nesoln, lain among other militiamen. A boy, perhaps having seen no more than twenty winters, was kneeling next to the slain veteran. His dark hair was short and thick, his body lean and strong from a life of farming. The clothes on his back were just as stitched and worn, nothing more than a ragged grey tunic and black trousers. He bore the look of his father, a strong angular face and dark eyes. Tears wet his cheeks as he cried over his fallen father.

Nihak stopped short at the sight, drawing the Elvan to a halt as well. They stood at a respectful distance, unable to hear what words were passed from son to father.

"Poor lad," Aen muttered.

Nihak said nothing. After a moment of silence amidst the noise, the Fire Elf approached the boy and knelt across from him. The young Human stared up at him, his rich brown eyes still wet with tears.

"Who are you?" he demanded.

"I fought on the wall with your father. I am Nihak, a Roamer, and your father saved my life. He died with more honor than any other man here."

The boy nodded, sniffling a little as he wiped his face clean. "You brought the enemy to our gates. Father always said that wherever the Roamers go, you bring death and destruction in your wake!" Anger flared bright in his eyes.

"Wherever we went, we were attacked by the armies of men. What would you do if you were wandering in peace and were attacked without provocation?"

The boy said nothing, staring in sullen anger at the elf.

"And if we hadn't come to Cendril on this day, Jamiel's soldiers would have still come, and you would either be dead or captured. If you wish to blame someone for your father's death, blame that bastard king Jamiel."

"Father was the only family I had. Now he's gone."

"What's your name, lad?"

"Nelsh," he said, laying his father's hands over his chest.

"Do you wish revenge for your father?"

The young Human paused, staring softly at the ground before nodding. "Yes."

"Are you willing to sever all ties with your home?"

"I have no ties left to my home."

Nihak rose to his full height, looking down at Nelsh. "Then you are welcome to join the Roamers. We leave on the morrow. You have until then to decide, lad."

With that said, the Fire Elf went back to Aen and they made their way back to the wall.

CHAPTER 12

Night had come at last, the moon rising pale with silver light in the black sky. The Roamers had spent the remainder of the day moving the dead and getting the rest of the wounded to the healers. Now they sat together about a cookfire near the shattered gates. Thick slabs of horse meat lay on flat stones, roasting slowly in the blaze. Those men fortunate to survive the battle unscathed patrolled the walls, the aromatic sizzle of meat drawing their gaze to the band of warriors.

"I'm glad we're staying for the night," Myles said, lying down with his hands under his head.

"Aye," Jolek agreed. "You all need the rest for your strength tomorrow."

"Heh...heh...heh," Ejen laughed sarcastically, grabbing his meal so it cooked evenly. "Damn Earth Elves. You never tire, do you?"

"When we stand upon the earth, we are connected to Arrute. His Strength is our Strength," Rom explained, plucking a whole rack of horse ribs off the fire.

"Where do we go from here? What lies in our path to the west?" Sarra inquired, skewering her portion with her knife.

"Our path is to the Duriviel Forest, where lies the Sylvan Sword," Aen explained. "If we're lucky, we can avoid the swamps and marshes out in the Wildlands. Nihak, you seem rather quiet."

Indeed, the young Fire Elf was staring rather intently at the flickering and wavering flames of their cook-fire. He glanced up, yellow eyes unfocused.

"Oi!" Jolek prompted, giving him a rough slap on the back. "Wake up."

Nihak shook his head, "I'm sorry, were you asking me something?"

Ejen's brow furrowed. "What did you see in those flames?"

"Nothing," was the terse reply, much to Ejen's annoyance.

Rolling his eyes, the older Fire Elf took up his roasted meal and bit deeply, oil and meaty juice running down his chin.

"Is Danira still working over the wounded?" Myles wondered, chilling his own meal so he would not burn his hands.

"Yes, she is," Aen answered, sighing a little. "I checked on her earlier. Those men fought valiantly, considering the odds they faced."

"If we had not been here, Cendril would have fallen," Ejen stated through a mouthful of horseflesh.

There was a general nodding and occasional "aye" at that. They fell silent then, the only sound the crackling fire before them, shadows dancing over their forms, eyes shining dully in the chaotic light. They were all anxious to be on the road again and be away from this death-filled place. Indeed, the Roamers were no strangers to death and battle; they were nearly unmatched in combat. But many of their group still felt the need to atone for the lives they had taken.

"Perhaps we should get our rest now," Jolek suggested, breaking the grim silence.

"Aye, that is a good idea," Aen concurred, laying down as he wrapped his cloak about him. "Tomorrow will be a hard day of travel."

The others followed suit and stretched out on their bedrolls, covering themselves with blankets if they had them. Ejen left the fire burning, knowing that it wouldn't go out of control. Sarra was the last to fall asleep while the others dropped off one by one. She couldn't help but reach up and rub her chest a little, scared that she was being watched at that moment. Some small part of her soul warned her, begged her, not to go on this foolhardy quest with the others. Sarra had no idea what Alura was planning, but it could never be good. The other part of her warned against the dangers of defying the powerful witch; and then a third part, the smallest, the one that burned the brightest, told her to journey on the open road once more. Indeed, she had felt cooped up in Cendril, even when she was on wagon-trails protecting the caravans, it was growing quite boring.

Sarra nodded and smiled to herself, lying down. No, it was time to once again feel freedom beneath her feet. Closing her eyes, the Human fell into a deep sleep, awaiting the dawn and the next step in the adventure.

*****

The dawn was greeted by the cawing of protesting crows. Some of the men had gone through the night digging graves for their fallen comrades; while the bodies of Jamiel's soldiers had been set aside for a pyre. Despite working ceaselessly, the men were nowhere near close to finishing their somber task and the birds of war were enjoying their bountiful feast. The Humans did their best to scare them off, but still the black sooty birds pecked and bit at the flesh of the slain to their bellies' content. As the sky turned from flaring orange to soft red, the sun rose over the horizon and began its steady climb.

Nelsh had spent the lonely night knelt alongside his dead father, the restless hours slow to pass. The young Human had thought long and hard on what the Roamer had said to him. Was it really their fault he was fatherless now? He thought back to when he was younger, when his father still smiled, though it was on rare occasion. One night, Nelsh had found his father in the kitchen, a wine bottle in his hand. It had been storming, and the tears on his face were all too clear in the flashes of jagged lightning. Nelsh, in his naïve curiosity, asked him why he was crying. Any other time and his father would have backhanded the boy and sent him away without another word. But that night, the lad remembered, that night his father told him. He told his son about the horrors of war he lived through. The pain of seeing his brothers-in-arms fallen to the swords and spears of the enemy. He was crying because that night he remembered his closest friend and how he wasn't there to save him when he fell in battle. Nelsh had sat on his father's lap, staring up at him in fear and sadness. As a boy, he had reached up and patted the crying Nesoln's face and said in a small voice, "It wasn't your fault, da." In his drunken state, Nesoln nodded, sniffling and wiping his tears away. Nelsh remembered his father hugging him tight after that, another rare occurrence.

Now he stared down at the old man, hurt from the loss. He wasn't the kindest father, and he certainly kept his emotions closed off from the world, but he still loved him. He had been the only family Nelsh had ever known. This pain in his heart now wanted blood spilt; no doubt the men who killed him were slaughtered in the battle, but like the Fire Elf had said: blame King Jamiel. Leaning forward with stiff limbs, Nelsh gazed upon his father's face, his final visage a restful one.

"Sir, I know how much you hate the Roamers, but how will your spirit find peace now? You always told me a soldier unavenged was a lost soldier, damned to wander the mortal plane in search of his killer. I will lay you to rest, sir. But I cannot do it alone. So the Roamers will help us."

Nesoln's bloodstained bastard sword lay by his body, the sheath still on his belt. With shaking hands, Nelsh removed it from his hip and strapped the leather sheath to his waist. Taking up the light blade, the young Human sheathed it and bowed his head.

"I will return your sword when I have avenged you, sir. I promise!"

With that, Nelsh made his way to the east gate where the Roamers had camped. Along the way, he passed a pile of collected weapons and pieces of armor. Thinking quickly, the young man took a pair of greaves and bracers and strapped them to his shins and forearms. He also took leather armor and strapped it over his torso. Lastly, Nelsh took up a black round shield. Admiring his new armor, the boy hurried along to the gate. He found the Roamers up and about, roasting meat on a bonfire. To his amazement, he found the flames were burning on the cobbled stones with no fuel. It didn't take long for them to notice the newcomer.

"State your business, lad," an older Roamer said, his black staff leaning in the crook of his arm as he ate his breakfast.

Nelsh quickly spotted the elf that had spoken to him the other day. Raising a finger, he pointed and said. "That Roamer said I could join your band."

They turned their gaze on the lithe Fire Elf.

"We're taking in strays again, Nihak?" another elf asked, a war scythe held lightly in his hand.

"Bah!" rumbled the huge dark-skinned elf, drawing Nelsh's attention. "He's only a pup!"

"Easy, Rom," his smaller counterpart said, patting the giant's thigh to calm him.

The young Human turned his gaze from the Earth Elves to the other Humans, two women. One he recognized as the healer, who single-handedly mended nearly every wounded soldier from the battle. The other was taller and solidly built, a cloak wrapped about her shoulders and a long, curved blade at her waist. Nelsh stared into their eyes, trying to garner any sympathy from their gazes. The healer merely looked tired whilst the warrior seemed more interested in what her comrades were saying.

"Aen, did he ask the boy to join?" a dwarf-like Roamer asked, tugging on Aen's robe.

"Aye, Nihak did offer it to the lad," the aging Elvan remarked, nodding from Nelsh to the Fire Elf.

"Then you know the rules," the scythe-wielder stated, staring at his kin.

Nihak nodded, rose to his feet, and approached Nelsh. He stopped arms-length away, looking the boy up and down, eyeing the armor and his round shield. Nelsh waited impatiently as the elf's yellow eyes finally stopped at the bastard sword at his hip.

"Do you know how to use that?"

"Of course, I do!" Nelsh snapped. "Anyone can pick up a sword and use it. It's easy!"

Behind the Fire Elf, Aen slowly rolled his eyes, sighing softly. "This will take some work…"

"And why do you wish to join the Roamers?" Nihak asked, carrying on.

"There is nothing left for me here. My father was the only family I had. Now he is gone, and I wish to avenge him!"

"Do you wish to live free? There's more to a Roamer's life than fighting," the elf stated, folding his scarred arms lightly.

Nelsh paused at the question. To live free. He had never given it much thought before. But now that he did, the young man realized that he had lived his entire life under his father's strict rule. It had always been so, so why question it? Was that not how life is, he thought to himself. Nelsh looked from each Roamer before coming back to Nihak, the elf's gaze steadfast and waiting.

Finally, after many minutes of silence, Nelsh nodded. "I do wish to live free. I've never known anything except how to live by my father's rules. And through him, the laws of King Malder."

The elf stared at him longer still before saying, "The Roamers welcome you then." The statement was met with grumbling and raised eyebrows. Nihak turned and sat down next to the giant elf. Nelsh sat opposite him, wary of the Roamers and their skeptical stares.

"If you're going to be one of us, first things first: formalities. The Giant Earth Elf sitting next to me is Rom, and his kin next to him is Jolek," Nihak stated, gesturing to the Earth Elves. They both nodded to the new Roamer with Rom offering a growling grunt.

"Danira I'm sure you know from her aid in healing the wounded." The witch yawned and nodded a little.

"And the other Human is Sarra. She lived in Cendril too, but she walked by our side years before we were exiled. The older man is a half-breed named Aen. Don't cross him lest you want a bolt of lightning up your arse."

The others chuckled at that.

"The dwarf sitting next to him is Myles. It takes a few days to get used to him."

Nelsh glanced over at the two, the Odd Dwarf batting at Aen's short beard, which he merely tolerated as he finished his breakfast.

"The Fire Elf with the scythe is Ejen. Pay him no mind."

Nelsh looked over at the elf, who merely glared at the young Human.

"If we're finished with our meal, let us be away from this town and continue our journey," Aen suggested, slapping Myles, sending the Odd Dwarf tumbling backwards.

The Roamers all stood, the flames of their cook-fires going out in an instant, leaving nothing but scorched stone. They stepped out past the ruined gates and skirted around the town walls. By the time they reached the western side, the sun had fully risen, washing the Wildlands with golden light before them. As they left the town at their backs, the young Human cast one final glance over his shoulder at the world he knew.

"Come Nelsh. We've a long road ahead of us, and you have much to learn before you can have any hope of surviving."

Nodding, the young Roamer followed after Nihak and the others, leaving Cendril forever.

CHAPTER 13

Falling into a rough single-file formation, the Roamers set a swift pace away from the battle-torn town. Ejen took the lead, his war scythe resting easily over one shoulder. The Humans were right behind him, chatting softly about old tales of battles long past. Aen and Myles walked side-by-side in the middle of the line, more often than not the Odd Dwarf trying to gain a perch on the aged half-breed's back. The still morning air was pierced by the Elvan's cursing and swearing, accentuated by the echoing sound of his staff striking Myles' thick-boned head. Nelsh could not help but stare at this strange exchange, he and Nihak bringing up the rear of the line with the Earth Elves.

"You get used to them. Well," the Fire Elf said in afterthought, "you try to."

"Has he always been like that? The dwarf?" Nelsh inquired, finally drawing his gaze away from the energetic Myles.

"Aye," Jolek stated, scratching his chest lightly. "Myles is a strange one, but he's always good for a smile. And don't underestimate him in battle. I've seen that little Ice Dwarf skewer armored soldiers with great spears of ice and he's deadlier still with that axe."

Nelsh nodded quickly in understanding. "I won't forget."

The Earth Elf returned the nod approvingly, grinning a little. As they walked in silence, the young Human glanced about at his fellow Roamers. It was strange that he now noted just how heavily armed they all were. His thoughts turned to the hand-and-a-half sword at his hip, a sense of embarrassment mixed with pride set in the youth's heart.

"I'm not too bad with the sword myself," he said, breaking the silence. It seemed as if they all heard him in that moment. All eyes turned to gaze at their newest member, all questioning, judging, and even mocking.

"Your father taught you how to fight?" Nihak asked. "He was a good man."

Nelsh paused at that. His father's hated enemy, giving him praise. It was a bizarre thing to hear for him.

"Of course," he lied. "Father taught me a bit."

"Excellent. That'll make my job easier," the Fire Elf remarked.

Through the rolling grasslands, a set of hills lay before them in the distance, speckled with rocks and trees. Farther out to the north, leagues into the distance, lay the crumbling remains of a score of huts and a broken wall. Off to the very far south stood the faintly seen peaks of the Pikewall Mountains.

"Your job?" Nelsh asked, taking in the scenery.

"Nihak is the one who took you in," Rom stated. "It is his task to ensure you know how to fight and survive in the Wildlands."

"When we stop for camp, we'll begin sparring. If you already have some skills, then that part of training will go well," Nihak assured him.

Ahead of them in the line, Ejen glanced back at Danira and Sarra. "How much do you want to bet the boy is lying and can't fight at all?" he sneered.

"If he says he can fight, then he can fight," the witch replied coolly. "Why do you care Ejen? He's only just joined and you're already being hostile towards him."

"He's young, weak, and Human," the Fire Elf growled.

"And we aren't?" Sarra demanded, her voice taking on an edge.

"Nihak trusts you two, so I trust you," he replied, not looking back at them. He didn't need to look to know they were glaring daggers at his back.

As the sun continued its climb to its zenith, the Roamers traversed up the rocky-flecked hills. It didn't take long for them to tire of the ups and downs along the grassy knolls, so they stopped for a rest and a meal.

Danira immediately set about the task of cooking up the food, producing carrots, onions, potatoes, and radishes. From a different pouch, the witch pulled a large cast-iron pot and iron stand to hold it aloft above a fire. Nelsh stared in absolute wonderment as he watched the dark-haired woman work. At her prompting, Nihak stepped over and cast a small flame upon the ground. The elf gave it life to swell into a large cook-fire, crackling and snapping in the cool air. Danira set the stand above it and hung the pot up.

"Myles, some ice in there if you please," she said.

The Odd Dwarf hopped to his feet, skipping over to the witch. He smiled and plunked several chunks of ice into the cavernous pot. As the ice melted, so the water level rose, the dwarf continuously adding ice until the pot was nearly full. During this time, the witch was busy cutting, peeling, and dicing the assorted vegetables. All went into the boiling water, cooking quickly. Danira reached deep into her pack, up to her underarm before pulling out a sack of flour. She tossed in several handfuls and pulled out a wooden ladle from yet a different pouch on her voluminous bag. Stirring quickly and effectively, she whistled a soft tune, Sarra joining in nearby.

Quite soon the stew was ready. Eight wooden bowls and a smaller iron pot was pulled from Danira's pack along with spoons and another ladle.

"Enjoy, lads," she said, serving up the soup for the Roamers. The pot and ladle went to Rom, who eagerly dug into his meal. They ate in relative silence, enjoying the delicious food.

"What would we do without you, Danira?" Aen wondered aloud, finishing his stew with a hearty belch.

"You'd be on an all-meat diet thanks to Nihak and his superb hunting skills, equally matched by his lackluster cooking skills," the witch quipped, grinning broadly.

The other Roamers nodded, some giving an "Aye!" in agreement, much to the laughter of Danira and Nihak. Nelsh watched them all quietly, eating his meal slowly. Truly it was delicious and he savored every bite. The wind picked up, sending clouds reeling overhead, casting light shadows over them as the sun winked in and out. As the wind blew over them, a constant reminder that summer was ending, the wanderers sat atop the knoll, the grassy blades waving serenely in the brisk breeze. Off to the lad's right, Nihak was wolfing his soup down hungrily. The young Human didn't think much of it until the elf stood and walked over to him.

"Up," he said, tapping the boy's leg with his dirty foot.

Nelsh stared up at the Fire Elf. "But I'm still eating." He couldn't help but flinch as Nihak drew his longsword, the blade hissing softly as it escaped its leather prison.

"Now."

Nelsh did not need telling twice with the edge in Nihak's tone. Hurriedly the green Roamer downed the rest of his stew and set the bowl aside. He stood quickly, brushing himself off and followed the elf a short distance from the others.

"Draw your sword. Let's see what you're made of."

Nodding, he unslung his round shield, holding it on his left arm. With his right, he pulled forth his father's sword, the blade singing softly in the air. Backing up, the Fire Elf took his stance, setting his feet three meters from the boy. The other Roamers watched intently as their newest member raised his sword at the ready, knees slightly bent in anticipation. Nihak had his left foot forward, his body turned to the side, standing as if at ease. The Fire Elf brought his longsword up over his head in a two-handed grip.

"Ready?"

Before Nelsh could even answer, the seasoned Roamer sprung forward, blade swinging down for a powerful strike from right to left. The Human brought his shield up to block the sudden attack, backpedaling clumsily. The force of Nihak's swing, coupled with Nelsh's poor footwork, sent him stumbling hard to the ground. Ejen's laughter pierced the air as Nelsh fell.

Groaning, the lad tried to figure out what had just happened. His left arm was quickly going numb and his backside stung from the force of impact with the ground. Suddenly the glint of steel flashed in his eyes, making the young Human flinch back in fear and surprise. When no killer-blow came, he slowly opened his eyes to see the tip of Nihak's longsword a few centimeters from his face.

"Were you ready?" the elf asked.

"I would have been if you'd waited," Nelsh managed to say, wincing in pain.

The Fire Elf withdrew his blade and offered a hand down to help the boy up. Nelsh gratefully took it and climbed back to his feet, his left arm and shield nothing more than deadweight. Nearby, the bastard sword lay in the grass where it had fallen. Nihak crouched and scooped it up, holding it out to Nelsh hilt-first, who took it thankfully.

"Your enemies will never ask if you are ready," the Fire Elf explained. "I will not offer you that luxury either."

Nelsh nodded, albeit grudgingly. He cast his eyes down, angry and embarrassed all at once. The elf tilted his head a little, staring at the lad. "I thought you said your father taught you how to fight."

"He didn't. I…lied," Nelsh said, the words tasting bitter on his tongue.

Behind him, Ejen was grinning ear-to-ear while the others made no such judging expressions; they merely ate their stew and watched. Nihak said nothing for many long minutes, studying Nelsh's expression. He took special note in the fire in the boy's eyes, fueled by pride.

"No matter," he finally spoke, drawing the Human's gaze up to meet his own. "I'll teach you how to use your blade yet. But first things first."

Nelsh felt the longsword lightly slap the inside of his knees. "Your footwork was terrible. That's why you fell so easily."

The Fire Elf set his feet like before, instructing Nelsh to do the same. "Less dominant foot out, turn your body so your left flank faces forward, and bend your knees."

Nodding, the new Roamer followed his teacher's words. "In combat, you must always be moving your feet. If you remain rooted in one spot, you leave yourself vulnerable."

Nelsh could only nod again in understanding as the elf moved to stand beside him, sword still drawn. "Do you know the basics?"

As he expected, the boy shook his head.

"Your sword is an extension of your arm in combat. And even though swinging from the shoulder brings more power, swinging from the elbow is swifter," the Fire Elf explained.

So saying it, Nihak shifted his feet and swung his longsword right-to-left across his chest, then reversed the swing. Next, the elf slashed diagonally, from the right shoulder to his left hip, followed with another swing left to right. After demonstrating those angles of attack, Nihak swung up from his right hip to his left shoulder, and again from the left hip up. Lastly, the Fire Elf brought his blade up high and slashed straight down, as if cleaving an enemy from his head to his groin.

Nelsh watched then repeated the angles of attack, feeling the weight of his sword and how it sang through the air. After the young Human completed those basic moves, Nihak lightly tapped his inner thighs with the longsword.

"Bend your knees."

Nelsh jumped a little at the contact, then glanced down to see his stance was indeed wrong. The green Roamer adjusted his footing accordingly, knees bent.

"Only slightly, mind you. You're in a fighting stance, not taking a shite."

"And if my legs are kept straight?" Nelsh asked, trying to find the correct stance.

"A stiff leg is easy to break, and a good way to disable an enemy is taking out a leg. And if you're ever forced onto your back, always remember knees only bend one way. It could save your life."

The lad nodded, committing it all to memory. His teacher gave an approving smile and said, "Set your feet and stand at the ready."

Nelsh did so, hoisting his black shield and sword, ready for another sparring lesson. Much to his disappointment however, Nihak returned his blade to its sheath.

"Practice your sword movements. Slowly."

"We're not sparring again?"

The Fire Elf could only stare at Nelsh in mild disbelief. Ejen, Aen, and Jolek couldn't help but laugh behind them. They had watched in silence while finishing their meal, but the simple question was too much.

"Unless you want to get knocked on your arse again, boy, I suggest you do as Nihak said. Practice your movements and learn the weight of your blade," the Elvan stated.

"Go on, let him spar, Nihak," Ejen laughed. "It's amusing to see the boy flat on his back!"

Nelsh blushed again and turned away, embarrassed.

"Pay him no mind," his teacher said. "Practice your angles of attack. Like Aen said, you need to know the weight of your sword and make it an extension of your arm. Begin."

With that said, the Fire Elf walked back to the Roamers and sat among them. Nelsh took his stance once more, took a deep breath, and began to work through the moves, his attacks deliberate and concentrated.

"What do you think?" Danira asked as he sat next to her.

"The boy has potential. I haven't seen that kind of fire in a Human's eyes, save for yours when we first met."

"And that's no mean feat," Aen remarked, pulling a bottle of cider from his robes.

"I'll have some of that," Myles said, grabbing for the drink as Aen took a swig. The Elvan's staff flipped up into the air of its own accord to sharply slap the back of Myles' hand.

"Yipe!" the Odd Dwarf quickly retracted his hand.

"Aen, may I?" Jolek called from behind.

The Elvan stoppered the bottle and casually tossed it over his shoulder. The slender container flipped end over end, its weighty flight landing solidly in the Earth Elf's hand. Jolek drank gratefully and tossed it back in the same manner. Aen caught it expertly, holding Myles at bay once more with his other hand.

"We should consider moving again," Sarra said, rising to her feet, stretching a little, her back popping in protest.

"Oh, shut it, you're still young," Aen said wryly, using his staff to stand. As he stood, his back emitted several louder pops and cracks.

The younger woman merely smirked and headed off, taking the lead.

"Nelsh, we're moving out," Nihak called. The young warrior sheathed his sword, slung his shield over his back, and quickly fell in line alongside the Fire Elves.

CHAPTER 14

Sivart had watched the Battle of Cendril from a safe distance. Even from half a league away, the witch's Left Hand could see the Roamers slaying men left and right. As the battle had come to a close, Sivart settled into their camp for the night, knowing the Roamers would not set out til first light. With a grunt, the scarred Human settled into his uncomfortable perch, sighing as he wrapped a ragged blanket about himself to combat the nightly chill. It didn't help that he could light no fires either, for fear of someone in Cendril spotting the flickering light. Around him the Huirds settled into their own perches, squawking and cawing softly to one another while others preened or sharpened their talons. With such a constant noise of scraping, calling, and creaking of boughs under shifting weight, Sivart resigned himself to a restless night, or at least until the abhorrent creatures fell silent.

More than once he had to adjust his position so he'd lie more comfortably, sending colored leaves tumbling to the ground. Of course, he could just sleep on the ground, but Sivart had learned the hard way that sleeping under Huirds only ends in shite-covered hair and clothes.

Or worse.

No chorus of nightbirds sang either as the night deepened, not with those foul birdmen about. Sighing again, Sivart carefully rolled onto his side and closed his eyes, praying to any God or Goddess listening to grant him a swift descent into sleep. It quickly became apparent that no one would answer those silent pleas. Cursing his luck and cursing the creatures about him, Sivart shut his eyes and slowly drifted into an agonized sleep.

Indeed, the morning could not come fast enough for Alura's henchman. As soon as the sun's golden rays peeked through the yellowed tree tops, Sivart grunted awake, his body as stiff as the wood he'd slept on. His back gave a particularly harsh *crack* as he sat up, only to be greeted by the growling caws of protesting Huirds, ill-tempered at being woken so suddenly.

"Silence!" he snarled, dropping to the ground. Pain and regret shot up his legs from the impact as he landed. Wincing, Sivart bent over to rub his sore knees before straightening up, while the Huirds continued to squawk and caw at him for the disturbance.

"You rotten curs kept me awake last night, so it's only fair I woke you so early!"

With a harsh wave of his hand, Sivart turned and walked to the edge of the woods to look out past the razed fields of crops to Cendril. The town could be made out in the gathering dawn from this distance and the Roamers could be seen filing out the shattered gates and heading west. As Sivart watched them leave, he squinted, trying to better see their numbers, and if he wasn't mistaken, there were nine of them now.

"A lost Roamer we didn't know about?" he asked no one in particular.

Not wanting to make another mistake with his Mistress, the Human reached up to his chest, pressing lightly over his heart.

"Mistress Alura?" he called, keeping his voice low, as if speaking too loudly would bring her wrath down upon him.

"What is it, Sivart? I do hope this is important," came the telepathic response.

"Mistress, the Roamers are leaving Cendril after the battle. There are nine of them now. Was there a Roamer you weren't aware of? I thought Sarra was the last one to join up with them."

He flinched preemptively, bracing himself for her anger. Instead, she spoke curiously, *"A ninth Roamer? Interesting."*

There was a pause. He could only assume the witch was gazing through her crystalline mirror. Moments later, he felt intense burning blossoming through his chest and Alura appeared beside him in a white flash of light.

"I had to see them for myself," she said, folding her pale arms under her chest. "I had searched all of Greenearth for the last of the Roamers, and only found eight. This ninth one is new. They must have taken the boy on after the battle."

A grin slowly came to the beautiful woman then. "A new Roamer might be useful to me. I'm pleased you brought this to my attention, Sivart. Good dog. Keep following them and report anything else of interest to me."

"Yes Mistress. May I ask a question?"

"Speak."

"What will you do with the new Roamer?"

"Patience, Sivart. I must learn more about him before I can gain any real advantage. But that is not your concern."

With that, she patted her Left Hand on the head, and then turned and teleported away.

*****

The Roamers had entered a broad woodland, wild and pathless, their group now spread about as they walked past the trees along leaf-covered ground. Their feet crunched and scattered the fallen leaves, painting the forest floor a sad tapestry of faded hues of yellow and red. Above them, squirrels and winged rodents scurried and rushed about, hurrying to gather their stores of food for the coming winter. The band of ragged warriors had walked the better part of the day and it was well into evening as they forced their way through a stand of thick thorn bushes. Songbirds chirped and whistled in protest at the disturbance, their chorus adding to the colorful language of the Roamers as they blazed their razor-filled path.

"How much further before we camp?" Nelsh had to ask, his feet worn and blistered from walking so many leagues in a day.

"Aww, the poor lamb is already foot-sore," Ejen mocked, scything his way out of the brush.

"Not all of us have callused feet such as yours," Danira countered, emerging behind him.

As the rest of the Roamers made it past the thorns, the witch dropped her pack with a loud clatter, prompting the others to halt. The healer had chosen their campsite for the night and quickly set about preparing their evening meal. As the Roamers gathered about and unpacked their bedrolls, Danira made room for her cookfire, brushing away the leaf-litter. "Jolek, would you mind terribly?"

The Earth Elf nodded with a grin. "But of course, Danira." He knelt down next to her and scooped a fair bit of soil from the ground as if it was made of snow. The earth-toned elf then began to form the loose dirt into a rough orb, his strong fingers condensing and compressing it until the earthen material had been hardened to stone. Scooping up more dirt, the elf repeated this process several times, crafting earthen stones to make a circle for the fire. While Jolek formed his crude rocks, Danira assigned Sarra, Aen, and Myles to gather twigs and branches for kindling and fuel.

"I'll see if I can't find some dinner," Nihak said, unslinging his bow as he set out away from the camp.

"Should I go with you?" Nelsh asked, standing by Ejen and Rom.

"Nay, lad. You were a farmer, not a hunter. Stay here with the others. I'll be back shortly."

With that said, Nihak drew an arrow and nocked it as he walked off, soon lost from their sight as the sun fell closer to the horizon.

"Come, Nelsh. Sit here," Sarra prompted, sitting down cross-legged. The auburn-haired woman looked up at him, patting the ground next to her.

By now, Jolek had finished making the stones and arranged them accordingly for Danira. As the witch began to pile the kindling in the center, Rom decided to sit down as well, and none too gently as he shook the ground beneath them. Aen nearly toppled over, his staff the only thing keeping him from falling unceremoniously onto his backside. "Rom, you great pile of stones! Mind yourself!" he grumbled, regaining his balance.

The Giant Earth Elf cast an apologetic look the old half-breed's way but said nothing. His visage quickly turned to a mirthful one though, prompting Aen to follow the giant's gaze to the Odd Dwarf. Myles had merely allowed himself to fall over, sprawling eagle-spread with his legs straight in the air. The Elvan couldn't help but chuckle with the others as the dwarf held that pose.

"Fire please," Danira requested, glancing over at Ejen.

The tall elf was seated opposite of Sarra, Nelsh, and Danira. He merely extended his arm and curled his first finger under his thumb. Nelsh watched as Ejen flicked his finger out, a single spark arching through the air to land atop the pile of twigs and bark. From that tiny spark blossomed forth dancing flames, instantly filling the evening air with warmth and light as the darkness deepened.

"That was amazing," Nelsh said, hoping to gain the elf's favor.

Ejen saw through the boy's words and gave him no such satisfaction in becoming friends. He merely stared at the young Human from across the dancing flames, wicked shadows flashing over his yellow eyes. Grinning inwardly, Ejen willed the flames to spark and crackle angrily, startling Nelsh.

"Boy, let me make one thing clear: You've seen too few winters and you're inexperienced with a blade. I don't expect you to live very long, so you'll forgive me if I don't give you a second glance. Just stay out of my way when a fight breaks out, and you might live."

Nelsh bowed his head, frowning. When he looked up again, the Human gave a curt nod and glanced away, trying not to make eye contact with the Fire Elf. Jolek had chosen to sit among the Humans and clapped Nelsh on the shoulder as gently as possible. Even so, the Earth Elf's strength nearly pushed him over.

"Never mind him. He always grows cold around new Roamers. He's seen too many comrades fall in battle."

"We all have," Sarra added. "Ejen just handles it differently. It's to be expected from a Fire Elf."

Ejen ignored her from across the fire. While he pulled his sickle-sword from his belt to sharpen, Danira readied her pouches of spices and jars of oil for their dinner. As the twilight deepened to night, the hour passed slowly. The nightbirds and crickets emerged for their choruses, filling the starlit night with peaceful music as bats flitted by, squeaking in eagerness to catch their meals on the wing. Another sound soon joined in the quiet cacophony; that of grumbling hunger.

"Who's the hungriest?" Jolek laughed, after a particularly loud growl emanated from Rom's gut. It had enough force to send a tremble through the earth, running through the Roamers' feet. The answer was soon given from Myles' stomach that rivaled the giant.

"By the Goddesses!" Danira exclaimed.

The forest had fallen dead silent.

Through the unnatural quiet there came the sound of crackling leaves and fallen branches underfoot, along with low-hanging boughs snapping. Weapons were instantly drawn as the Roamers leapt to their feet, ready to face whatever threat was coming. Stepping from shadows into the flickering firelight, Nihak walked into camp, a dead buck slung over his shoulders.

"Relax, it's just me," he said, dropping the carcass by the fire.

"By Ignicendir's wings, what took you so long?!" Ejen demanded.

"Took a long time to even find a trail. When I did, I had to stalk the damn thing for an hour before I could get a clean shot. By the time I downed the beast and gutted it, the light was almost gone and I had a hard time finding my way back. Hearing Myles' stomach helped though."

"Bless the Odd Dwarf then," Danira muttered as she quickly set about roasting the meat.

Once the majority of deer flesh was skewered and over the fire, the witch added her spices and poured the oils over the meat, sending the flames into angry fits of hissing and spattering. The Roamers said nothing while she worked her magic, waiting eagerly for their meal; and it seemed the meat could not cook fast enough. When their dinner was finally ready, Danira glared at them all, each in turn.

"I'm going to pass the food out. If you all spring upon me at once, I will rip your innards out through your bellies, and you may eat that instead!"

They merely nodded, too hungry to show any fear at the threat. They knew her to be exaggerating, but it wasn't too far a stretch from what the fearsome witch might do. One by one, she passed around haunches of steaming venison. By the time she had given out the eighth piece and taken one for herself, Jolek and Sarra, who had been first in line, had already picked the meat clean from the bone.

"If you want more food, there's dried meat in my pack," Danira stated before eating.

"No thanks, the deer was filling enough," Sarra replied, smiling as she wiped excess grease from her mouth.

As they spoke, the other Roamers finished their meals as well, patting their full bellies and laying back on their bedrolls contentedly.

"So, Nihak," Nelsh said, tossing his bones aside, "will we be sparring more tonight?"

"Good Seylivonia no," the Fire Elf chuckled. "It's too dark for that. Get some sleep and recover your strength. You'll need it for tomorrow."

Nelsh nodded and readied his own bedding.

"Who's on first watch tonight?" Aen asked, wrapping his cloak tighter about himself to stave off the nightly chill.

"I'll stay awake," Rom rumbled, remaining cross-legged.

"Wake me for second watch then," Sarra said, already lying down with her eyes closed.

"And third watch?" the Elvan asked.

"I'll take it," Nihak stated.

The others nodded and murmured their agreement before turning in for bed, more than ready for sleep. They all stayed close to the still-blazing fire, kept strong with fuel. It didn't take long for them all to pass off into their dreams, while the giant stayed silent and vigilant. As the night deepened and the crescent moon rose higher into the now-starless sky, Rom's gaze turned to the sleeping Nelsh. The last thing he expected Nihak to do was take on a Human as a new Roamer. Much less a farmboy with no skill in combat or survival. Still, the Giant Earth Elf did not question the Fire Elf's motives or reasoning. It wouldn't be the first time he had done something that puzzled the giant, but Rom trusted him well enough. Nihak never led him or the others astray, though the giant did have his reservations about this quest, especially with what Arrute had conveyed. Something about Nelsh gave Rom strange premonitions but what they were, he could not say. Sighing as softly as possible so as not to wake anyone, Rom pushed the confusing thoughts from his head. Turning his dark eyes skyward, the giant watched the moon and listened to the soft sighing of wind through painted leaves. Around him, nocturnal creatures leapt, crawled, and scurried about their camp on their nightly quest for food. Strange stripped rodents ambled around the giant, snuffling in the leaf-litter as curious claws dug through the forest floor. He could see their shadowy figures moving in the low light but paid them no mind, for they were common in these forests and no threat to them.

The first few hours of the night passed by without incident, leaving Rom alone with nothing but his thoughts. When it was time for Sarra's turn, the giant tapped the ground once with the palm of his hand. A mild tremor coursed through the earth, narrow and precise. It weaved around the sleeping Roamers and stopped underneath the Human woman. She awoke and sat up swiftly, then calmed when she turned to see Rom slowly laying down where he sat.

"All clear?" she whispered.

In the gloom, she saw the Giant Earth Elf nod once before he drifted off to sleep. Sarra gathered up her cloak about herself and rose on stiff legs, shuddering from the cold. Quietly, she stretched herself out, loosening her muscles and joints. That done, the young woman walked about the camp's outskirts just beyond the ring of firelight. Unlike the others, she saw no need to remain seated in one place for the hours of her watch. By this time, the moon had reached its zenith but clouds had rolled in, sparsely covering the shining sliver in the sky. Faint light, silvery and pale, cast the trees in a grey veil, sending strange shadows among the roots. As Sarra silently patrolled the perimeter of their camp, she heard a noise distantly from where she stood. The Roamer immediately shifted into a fighting stance, setting her feet as she turned her torso. Her callused hand wrapped around the hilt of her falx, the other gripping the sheath, ready to draw at a second's notice.

The softest of footsteps was approaching, making barely a sound. As the moonlight faded, a tall woman clad in a white dress came into view, her figure seeming to glow in the darkness. Sarra's eyes widened and her hands began to shake, her readied-grip loosening in fear.

"A-Alura…" she managed to say as the witch stopped before her.

The forest had grown silent once more. Not an animal stirred. Not a bird sung. The dark-haired woman grinned broadly, slender hands resting on her hips.

"Nice to see you again, Sarra," Alura stated, her clear voice cutting through the air.

Glancing back at the camp, the Roamer was fearful to find not one of her comrades stirred by the sharp voice.

"Oh, don't worry, this meeting will be just between us," she smirked, walking past the terrified Sarra.

"Alura what are you doing here?" she demanded, following the sorceress.

"Sivart brought to my attention that you have taken on a new Roamer."

The witch stepped among the sleeping wanderers, giving Nihak a sharp kick to the ribs. He grunted, but by whatever spell she had laid over the place, he did not wake.

Sarra could do nothing but walk past the Fire Elf, trying not to think about the bruises he'd have in the morning. She halted next to Alura, who stood over the sleeping Nelsh.

"This is the new one?" she asked, though they both knew she knew the answer already.

"Yes. His name is Nelsh. Nihak took him in."

"Of course he did, the pathetic elf."

Alura tilted her head, her black hair hanging down in thick curtains as she stared at the boy. Sarra in turn stared at the witch, shivering. She saw that wicked gleam in the tall woman's pale green eyes. She had seen it before...

"Alura, no!" she managed to say.

The sorceress slowly turned to stare at the Roamer, her eyes crackling to icy blue. "I'm sorry, dear, but did you say the one word I should never hear from your lips?"

The witch's gaze pierced through Sarra, chilling her bones and leaving her limbs numb and useless. She felt herself falling to the ground, her legs splayed awkwardly beneath her as Alura stood over the helpless woman.

"Need I remind you of what happened last time you spoke that word?"

Sarra could only shake her head. "Y-you don't need to remind me, Alura..."

"Good girl. Now, I came here to inspect the new Roamer. Be quiet for a few moments or I'll be happy to remove your speech-cords from your throat."

With a soft whimper, Sarra kept her mouth shut while the witch went back to staring down at the sleeping Nelsh. The Roamer watched as the witch crouched down and laid a gentle hand on the young lad's cheek, then moved up to his thick, short black hair, petting the boy softly.

"He's cute for a farm-boy," she said, rising back to her full height. "I'll be checking in from time to time."

With that, Alura turned and walked away, her pale form soon disappearing past the dark trees. As soon as she was gone, Sarra found strength and feeling returning to her legs. Shakily, she rose to her feet, cold sweat beading her forehead as she gasped to catch her breath, her heart pounding furiously in her chest. Glancing up at the sky, the moon had shifted greatly from the last time she'd checked. Sarra's eyes widened as she realized how much time had passed; the witch had been in their camp for nearly three hours! It had to have been the spell she'd cast before appearing, no other explanation made sense for the speedy passage of time. Taking a few deep breaths to calm herself, Sarra padded over to Nihak and shook him lightly. She found a knife held to her throat, fierce yellow eyes glaring up at her. They quickly softened and the knife was removed when he saw who had woken him.

"Are you alright?" he whispered, before wincing.

"I'm fine. What about you?"

"I feel like Rom stepped on my chest..." Nihak gasped softly, sitting up slowly. Even in the dark with little moonlight, Sarra could see the bruising through the Fire Elf's ragged shirt. "How did that happen?" he wondered aloud.

"No idea," she replied, turning and biting her lip.

"No matter. Danira can fix me up in the morning. You get some sleep, Sarra."

She nodded and went back to her bedroll, laying down with her back to the elf. She wanted to tell him, but her fear of the witch far outweighed the loyalty she felt for the Roamers.

Nihak stood up and climbed into a tree, settling into position in the boughs. He laid his longbow across his lap, his quiver within easy reach. As the hours began to pass by, he remained steady and relaxed, despite the pain in his chest. Soon the songbirds struck up their morning chorus, the light ever so slowly turning into dawn. Behind him, the rising sun painted the sky pink, drawing the Fire Elf's gaze.

"Such a shame we can only gaze upon the sunsets on this journey," he whispered to himself, dropping down to the ground.

As the other Roamers began to stir, some nearly ready to wake, Nihak padded over to the still-sleeping Nelsh. Deftly, the Fire Elf plucked a twig from the ground with his toes and passed it up to his hand. With two fingers, he snapped the dead wood in half, the sound loud enough to wake every Roamer in the camp. Some startled awake, weapons drawn, demanding what was wrong. Others merely sat up or opened their eyes.

"What's the meaning of waking us all at this hour?!" Ejen demanded, sliding his sickle-sword back into its sheath.

"Teaching Nelsh a lesson. And I'd rather you were all awake, lest I have seven angry Roamers drawing their weapons on me."

"Too late," Aen muttered, rubbing his temples as Myles flopped into his lap, axe in hand.

Nihak merely shrugged and drew his longsword as Nelsh stirred at his feet but did not wake. The still morning air was split by the Fire Elf's war cry, sending birds scattering from the trees, crying in protest at the outburst.

The young Human snapped awake, only to find the tip of Nihak's sword pressing into his throat. He slowly gazed up at the elf, uncertain on what to do.

"You're dead," the seasoned warrior merely said, returning his blade to its sheath.

"What...?"

"You heard me boy. Had this been a real attack and you had mere seconds to react, you would be dead."

With that said, he turned and stepped away to sit cross-legged amongst the other Roamers, while Danira rekindled the cookfire for an early breakfast.

"Get off!" Aen growled, slapping the back of Myles' head.

The sleepy Odd Dwarf merely stuck his tongue out and rolled off the old Elvan's lap.

Nelsh managed to get to his feet, stripped to the waist, and joined the others in the circle around the fire. As he approached, Sarra made room for the green Roamer so he could sit next to his teacher, while Danira fried several eggs, sizzling and popping in the frying pan.

"Why did you wake me like that?"

Nihak's eyes slowly turned to stare at the Human. "You grew up on a farm," he stated more than asked.

Nelsh nodded anyway. "Aye, I did."

"And farmers wake up to the crowing of a rooster, no?"

Again, the boy nodded. "What does this have to do with your war cry and sword in my face?"

"You are used to waking at the sound of a loud bird," the elf paused and picked up another twig, holding it between his thumb and two fingers, "we are used to waking at the slightest sound."

He snapped it in two, the brittle wood making a small *crack*. "If you wish to survive out here, you must sharpen your senses to the point where you wake if you even feel someone approaching you in your sleep."

Nelsh groaned inwardly, something the Fire Elf did not miss. "I never told you this life would be easy. It's not for everyone, and not everyone who has joined lived very long."

The young Human nodded. "I understand."

"Good. I'll be waking you up with sword in hand until you can fight me off at a second's notice."

Despite his determination, Nelsh blanched at the thought of the Fire Elf "killing" him every morning. He felt a comforting hand on his shoulder and turned to see it belonged to Sarra.

"It's alright lad. Some of us have been through that training too."

"Some?" Nelsh echoed as a breakfast of spiced eggs was passed around for everyone.

"Myself, Danira, Aen, and Myles. We all went through this training to snap awake, ready to fight, if need be."

"What about the others?"

"The elves are gifted with higher senses. Jolek and Rom are connected with the very earth. The saying, 'You can't sneak up on an Earth Elf,' is a true one. It's impossible in fact. As for the Fire Elves, well..." she paused, taking time to shovel a few mouthfuls of egg down her gullet.

"What Nihak and Ejen have been through is their business," Danira interrupted, overhearing Sarra. "If they wish to tell the boy, they will in their own time."

Sarra nodded and ate the rest of her meal in silence, as did the others. When they finished, the Roamers rose to their feet, ready for another long day of travel. Aen took the lead this time, setting a leisure pace.

"We should make the Aer'lune River by nightfall," he remarked, his sky-blue cloak billowing lightly in the cool wind, the sun climbing above the tree line.

The Fire Elves muttered oaths in their native tongues.

"Will there be Water Elves? We've not been near that river for years," Myles inquired, using his axe to mimic Aen's staff as a walking stick.

"With good reason!" Nihak and Ejen snapped in unison.

"Aye there'll be Water Elves," Sarra stated, grinning. "Beautiful creatures they are. Well, to some."

The Roamers could not help but chuckle at the string of curses spewing from the Fire Elves' mouths. They kept at it well into the afternoon as they passed through the woods. Only the occasional deer and wolf saw them on their way, paying them no heed in their daily struggle to survive the day. Leaving the elves to their muttering, the other Roamers joked and laughed as they walked along the forest floor, accentuated by Myles' energetic acrobatics. It was well into evening by the time they left the woods and came to a domed mountain, jutting with rocks and tough evergreens finding purchase on the jagged surfaces.

The sound of a river rushing by could be heard, bringing Nihak and Ejen to promptly sit down near the edge of the trees.

"Come now boys, we still have a few hours of daylight left. We should at least try to-"

"No!" they both cut Danira off in unison.

The witch rolled her eyes and sat as well, unpacking her cooking gear for an early dinner, the rest of the Roamers joining her.

"Why can't we go up that mountain yet?"

"The river runs along the base of it, and we're not going anywhere near it unless it's daylight," Ejen growled, tossing small fires between his hands in agitation.

Shaking his head, Nihak stood up and walked off, the sinking sun to his back.

"Where are you going?" Danira demanded, looking up from her preparations.

"Nowhere," was the reply.

147

After the elf had gone off back into the woods, Nelsh turned to Sarra. "So, are there any other creatures living out here?"

Before the woman could answer, they all heard Nihak's fierce battle cry and reached for their weapons.

CHAPTER 15

Longsword in hand, the Fire Elf came charging back from the woods.

"Nihak, what is it!?" Rom demanded, his voice shaking the air.

No answer came forth as the Fire Elf shouted again, running straight for Nelsh.

"Oh," Danira merely shrugged when she realized the elf's intent. So too did the other Roamers, and they stayed their hands as they returned to their seats.

Nelsh on the other hand was not so quick to catch on. As he started to ask what was happening, casting about in confusion, Nihak was upon him. His foot slammed hard into the boy's chest, knocking him back several meters. Angrily, Nelsh scrambled to his feet and drew his bastard sword, growling.

"What in the Abyss?!" he bellowed, ducking a high swing from the Fire Elf.

The Human retaliated with a low thrust, aiming for the elf's belly, but the nimble Roamer merely sidestepped the attack. Bringing his longsword up, Nihak swung down, slamming his blade against Nelsh's.

"Come on, boy!" the elf snarled, kicking at him again.

Nelsh leapt back, avoiding the attack. Taking up his bastard sword in both hands, he gave a yell and struck for the elf's neck. The longsword was there to stop the strike, their blades clanging loudly in the dusky evening. Growling, Nelsh bared his teeth and swung again from left-to-right, but the attack was parried just as easily. Now the Fire Elf took to the offensive, snap-cutting at Nelsh's left shoulder. As the blow landed, Nihak deftly turned his sword so the flat of the blade struck instead of the edge. Groaning in pain, Nelsh stepped back and lost his grip with his left hand. In came the longsword, singing through the air, aiming for Nelsh's left flank again. The young Human quickly turned his body to better parry the attack but this left his right flank wide open for a harsh kick to the ribs. The breath knocked from his lungs, Nelsh desperately tried to inhale but only succeeded in coughing instead. He felt his teacher's foot hook behind his right ankle and then he was palm-shoved to the ground. Nihak leapt atop him and stabbed his sword down.

Nelsh turned his head to stare at the blade, not two finger widths from his face.

"Tell me what you learned from all that."

Nihak pulled his blade from the dirt and offered a hand down to the boy. Nelsh gratefully accepted it, coughing and wheezing still as he was hauled to his feet. They both walked back to camp-proper, Ejen having started a fire as the sun began to set. Taking a ragged cloth from his belt, the teacher cleaned his blade of dirt and mud, moving to sit beside Jolek, while Nelsh sat opposite him.

"Well?" the elf prompted, sheathing his sword.

Nelsh mirrored his actions, coughing more.

"Danira, you may wish to look the boy over. Nihak was rough with him," Aen pointed out, pulling his long-stemmed pipe from his robes.

"Yes, I noticed," the witch remarked, shuffling over to the young Roamer.

"I need to be on guard and alert at all times," Nelsh finally said as Danira felt his body over, whispering her healing spells.

Nihak nodded in approval. "Very good. What else?"

"I didn't have my shield…" he stated, albeit hesitantly.

Another nod. "Aye. You need to learn how to fight without it. I would have been impressed though if you'd thought to grab it as I came charging. Better yet, if you managed to circle back to camp and grab it while I was attacking you. Never underestimate the usefulness of a shield. But don't depend on one either."

"Why is that? None of you use shields."

The other Roamers chuckled at that. "Most of us come from cultures that do not use shields or even know what they are. Those who do simply chose not to make use of them," Nihak explained.

"I used to carry one," Danira remarked, feeling over Nelsh's ribcage. The boy gasped and winced as her light fingers brushed over his right side.

"Anything else you took away from this lesson?"

"I left myself open to attack. Ow!" there came a loud snapping.

"Sorry. Just popping your ribs back into place," the witch explained, going back to making supper. "You broke four of his ribs with that kick. His collarbone was fractured as well," she said, looking over at the Fire Elf.

"Shall I use a padded stick?"

Danira merely rolled her eyes at the retort but said nothing else.

"Now," Nihak said, turning back to Nelsh. "You left yourself open to attack, aye. What could you have done differently?"

The young man paused, thinking. "Blocked your kick?"

"How?"

"I don't know," Nelsh replied, looking down at the crackling fire. "All I could have done, now that I think of it, is to have leapt back out of range."

"Aye. If you leave yourself open and know it, your enemy will know it too and aim for that opening. If they don't, then count yourself lucky."

The boy nodded as Danira passed out their meal for the night, a plate of roasted sausages and boiled carrots. They ate silently, the Fire Elves glancing in the direction of the river every so often.

"Who will be on watch tonight?" Jolek inquired, setting his empty dish down once they'd finished their dinner.

"Ejen, Danira, and you," Aen replied, sending a smoke ring drifting lazily into the air.

The older Fire Elf gave a huff accompanied by a Firelvish oath but nodded.

"In the morning, you two stay your weapons and hold your tongues," the Elvan continued. "Let us do the talking. The Water Elves are more likely to listen to Humans and half-breeds."

"And Ice Dwarves!" Myles reminded, picking his teeth with an icicle.

"And Earth Elves, old man?" Rom added.

"Aye. Anyone who is not a Fire Elf for that matter," Aen consented as an afterthought, settling into his bedroll with a groan.

By now, the only light for the Roamers was the stars above and the crackling fire among them. The others quickly crawled into their bedrolls as well, leaving Ejen up for the first watch. Rising up, the Fire Elf strode over to sit directly in the flames of their campfire, his gaze set directly west towards the river. It was going to be a long vigil.

Fortunately for the Roamers, nothing occurred that night. The sunrise came swiftly, admired only by Jolek, the Earth Elf gazing with longing back east to his homeland. While he enjoyed the freedoms of the outside world, Jolek would always return to the Ir'Afa Plains and his tribe. Truly, he thought to himself, once this quest was over, he would journey home with Rom and spend the rest of his days among his people. Blowing a soft sigh, he set about rousing the rest of the Roamers.

Nelsh awoke to the sound of fierce yelling and then all he could see was the tip of a longsword in his face. Sighing in exasperation, he merely stared up at his teacher, bracing for his berating.

"Always be on alert," was all Nihak said, sheathing his weapon and helping the lad to his feet.

Nelsh merely nodded and packed up his bedroll and belted on his sword. "Do we cross the river today?"

"Hopefully, and without incident," Ejen growled from across the camp.

Nodding their agreement, the others finished packing up and moved out. Jolek and Danira took the lead with the Fire Elves taking up the rear, and gratefully so. The river itself was no more than a league away, and for those two, the short time it took to journey to the rushing waters seemed to last an eternity. As the rapid blue waters appeared with the Roamers drawing nearer, tall lithe creatures could be seen leaping out of the churning surface while others sat upon the rocks along the shore.

The Water Elves were slender creatures, sleek and smooth-skinned. Their hair ranged in length from their shoulders to their lower backs, and their colors varied from pearly-silver to seaweed-green to ocean-blue. Their faces were narrow and angular with eyes of deep sparkling sapphire. As the Roamers drew closer, they could see webbing between the fingers of their slender hands and if they looked close enough, fleshy lines under their jawbones. They wore no clothing; nothing to cover their tanned bodies, male or female.

It didn't take long for them to notice the approach of the strange warriors and rose to their webbed feet, all standing over two meters tall. The ones in the river climbed out to stand upon the rocky shore as well when the Roamers drew even nearer. One Water Elf, her long wavy hair reaching to her waist and shining blue in the morning sun, stepped forward and held up a hand, webbed-fingers splayed.

"Arelai," she ordered.

"Sounded like 'stop'," Nihak whispered, as if speaking too loudly would give away his heritage.

Rom, who stood before the Fire Elves, stomped his foot once, drawing the others' attention. "Stop," he stated, folding massive arms over his chest.

The Roamers followed suit and stayed their feet, standing a mere fifteen meters from the Water Elves. Tilting her head, the she-elf eyed them, perplexed yet intrigued at such an odd mix of peoples before her river. After several minutes of a curious inspection, she spoke.

"Otuawesqui'naekgans-eralighimi'ea'ehlequa-voerku-nairehae?" Her words flowed together, almost impossible to distinguish where one word ended, and another began.

Standing alongside Nihak, Ejen and Nelsh looked to the Fire Elf expectantly.

"What did she say?" the new Roamer asked, genuinely curious.

"Aye, what did she say?" Ejen demanded in a hushed tone. "You understood her telling us to stop, so translate!"

"I don't speak Watelvish!" Nihak growled in a harsh whisper. "Forelvish is similar but different!"

"Then speak tree or something!" Ejen snapped. "Maybe they'll know that language."

Nihak rolled his eyes but spoke nonetheless. "We are the last of the Roamers. We wish to cross your river, if we may," his Forelvish was nearly flawless, stumbling over but a few words.

The Water Elf's eyes narrowed, her brow furrowing.

"Taoln'kouela'eshte'maern. Otuawesqui?" She demanded, striding towards them.

"Tawschei," Nihak swore, then spoke in Common Tongue, "She said my Forelvish sounded strange and demands to know who I am. Let her through."

Jolek and Danira grudgingly parted before the Water Elf. Aen stepped aside, but Myles did not move. The she-elf skirted around the Odd Dwarf, casting him a cautious glance before moving past Sarra and finally Rom. She stopped dead upon seeing the Fire Elves, her blue eyes widening dramatically.

"Kalkelhi!!!! Kalkelhi!!!!" she shrieked at the top of her lungs.

The Water Elves reacted instantaneously, nearer elves dropping into fighting stances with their arms turning to waving tendrils of water, ready to strike. Those standing on the banks of the river turned and lifted great orbs of liquid from the rushing waters. The she-elf too changed her limbs, drawing her right arm back like a whip to strike the hated Fire Elves.

"Stay your hands!" Nihak shouted in Forelvish, throwing his arms out wide in a desperate show of peace. "We only wish to cross your river! We do not want to fight!"

The she-elf paused, the water of her arms hanging dangerously in midair, still ready to strike.

"Ceompefaineh-Kalkelhi'inkenatre'lae-kouela-desr-lae-akareleu?" she asked quizzically.

"I am friend and kin to the Forest Elves. Seylivonia Herself spoke with Queen Ayewndre on this matter. That is why I can speak their language. Now, will you let us pass peacefully?"

The she-elf turned back to her kith and kin and conversed with them, their words flying so rapidly that, to the Roamers, they all said nothing but one long continuous word. Finally, the elves relaxed their stances and their limbs returned to a solid state.

"Hiavukeleeveparas'siamak'varei-panierke-alru," she said, gesturing for them to proceed.

"What did she say?" Aen asked as the Roamers stepped forward, the Water Elves parting before them; many spitting and hissing at the Fire Elves.

"She said we may pass, but they will not help us across," Nihak answered, flinching away from a stream of water aimed at his feet.

"No problem," Rom stated, picking him and Ejen off the ground and lifting them high into the air.

"Rom!" they both shouted in unison.

The Giant Earth Elf stepped into the rushing waters, the strong current splashing high around his thick torso. As powerful as the water was, it could not move the giant. He waded across, the water flowing up to his chest. Much to the relief of the Fire Elves, they stayed relatively dry during the ordeal, though they were still quite shaken when Rom set them down on the other side. They glared across the way to the Water Elves, who stood by laughing and pointing.

"Rom, would you mind terribly making another crossing?" Sarra called.

"No," the giant merely said, shrugging.

They all stood staring at each other as they waited for Rom to make another crossing, but it soon became evident that the Giant Earth Elf was not coming back. Sighing, Jolek stepped forward. "Rom, catch." With that, he grabbed Danira by the back of her shirt and the belt of her trousers and tossed her across the river. Screaming profanities of every kind, she flew over the rushing waters only to be caught in the arms of Rom. The Water Elves joined in as he and Jolek shared a boisterous laugh as the witch was set down.

"Jolek, when you get over here, I will turn your legs into mud!" Danira shrieked, visibly shaking from the rush of adrenaline.

The Earth Elf merely laughed and grabbed Sarra.

"Don't you dare!" she exclaimed, but her words quickly turned into screams of fear mixed with exhilaration. Rom caught her too and set her down.

"Nelsh, you're next," Jolek chuckled, gesturing for the young Roamer to step forward.

Shrugging, the boy walked up to the elf and relaxed his body. Jolek picked him up and tossed him effortlessly across the wide river. Nelsh gave a whoop of joy as he sailed through the air. Rom ensured he landed safely and set him down, ready for the next victim. The Earth Elf turned to Aen, but before he could even reach for him, the Elvan's staff jabbed him in the eye, forcing the elf to stagger back.

"I'm too old for that and you know it," the Elvan huffed, bringing his staff up in both hands. Slamming the black oak into the ground, the force created a tremendous gust of wind that propelled him high into the air.

Aen's flight was short-lived and he quickly began to descend, turning his staff parallel to the ground and began to gyrate. This created enough of an air current to slow the Elvan's descent, allowing him to drift slowly across to the other side. While Aen's takeoff into the air was impeccable, his landing was less than pristine; dizzy from spinning, he landed, stumbled, and then fell face-first into the rocky ground.

"By all means, don't catch him," Nihak said dryly, staying well back from the water's edge.

"Oh, be quiet," Danira growled, helping the Elvan to his feet.

Jolek couldn't help but grin at Aen's crossing, then turned to Myles. "And you, little Odd Dwarf? Shall I toss you or will you cross on your own?"

"Hmm," Myles murmured, tapping his foot as he thought. "Ah!"

He snapped his fingers with a wide grin and hopped over to the water's edge. Kneeling down, the dwarf placed his hands in the water, much to the distress of the Water Elves. Indeed, their agitation grew ten-fold as Myles formed ice on the water's surface, their panicked chattering incomprehensible. But they needn't fret, for the hyper dwarf merely created a wide disc of ice, large enough for him to sprawl across. Jolek's eyebrows rose quizzically as Myles lifted the wide sheet of frozen glass, laid it on the ground and flopped atop it, arms and legs eagle-spread.

"Now you may toss me."

"You wish me to throw you, or would you like to skip across?" the Earth Elf laughed, grinning wide yet again.

"Skip, skip, skip!" Myles giggled.

"Very well," Jolek replied, picking up the icy disc and spinning about. With a grunt, he released his hold on it, sending Myles spinning rapidly through the air. He fell to the surface of the river and bounced back up, only to fall again, skipping across. The other Roamers quickly parted out of the way, so as not to get maimed by the spinning missile. Myles skipped along the land a few times before his wild ride shattered and he skidded to a halt, laughing and giggling like mad.

"How will you get across?" Danira shouted over the rushing waters.

The earth-toned elf merely shrugged and stepped into the river, quickly disappearing from sight, as the frothing water engulfed him. They didn't have long to wait as Jolek reemerged a few short minutes later, having walked across along the riverbed.

With that obstacle crossed, the Roamers continued on their quest, making their way rapidly up the sloping rocky mountain. Upon reaching the top of the wide ridge, they could see for leagues upon leagues around them. Off in the far distance to the north, a vast forest spread over the landscape. West of those ever-green woods, a grotesque swamp ran like a pustulating scar from north to south for hundreds of leagues, leaving but a tiny passage of grassland between the northern tip and the greenwood. Farther west lay hills and a valley, another wide river cutting through the vale, spotted with copses of trees, rocky outcroppings, and more ruins of long-abandoned Human settlements.

"The Selveryn Forest," Nihak noted, with a small smile.

"Our path does not lead there," Ejen quickly stated, scowling.

"What about that darker tree-line?" Nelsh inquired, pointing off towards the far west.

"Farls Swamp," Sarra said, her heart sinking. "And our path does lead there."

"Farls Swamp?" the young Human echoed.

"It's filled with trolls, goblin tribes, and all manner of creatures that will rip, tear, and maim you," Jolek added, folding his arms.

"You forgot 'devour you alive,'" Myles stated, not smiling for once.

"Why can't we just go around it? Through that narrow passage of grassland between the forest and swamp?" Nelsh inquired.

"Because it would take us at least seven days, if not more, just to get to the northern tip," Aen explained, sweeping his staff in a wide arch, as if to encompass the sheer length of the swamp.

"Aye, while going through is only about two days at most," Danira added, shouldering her pack and heading down the mountain.

"Are we in such a hurry?"

"Have you not noticed the summer air growing colder? The leaves on the trees now painted?" the Elvan asked, glancing back at Nelsh as they began their descent down the rocky slope. "Autumn is upon us, and if we wish to get to the sword before the first snow falls, then time is of the essence."

"Hurry along," Rom urged, giving Nelsh a light nudge with his foot.

Nihak caught the stumbling Human before he careened out of control down the path. "Rom, must you?"

"Aen said to hurry," the giant shrugged, lumbering down after them.

CHAPTER 16

For the better part of the day, the wandering warriors spent negotiating their descent. The mountain was not a treacherous one, but one misstep could easily send the luckless person tumbling all the way down. Sending more than a few loose rocks clattering down the steep slope, the Roamers eventually made it safely onto level ground once more, the sun near to setting. With little daylight left, the wayward band made camp, the evening and night passing peacefully and without incident. Waking in the shadow of the stunted block of a mountain, the Roamers wasted no time in setting off for Farls Swamp. Nearly a week would pass them by just to reach the edge of the foreboding place. As they traveled, the wanderers shared their tales and adventures with the curious Nelsh, regaling him with stories on how Rom toppled a siege tower, or Danira slayed a legion of Jamiel's soldiers single-handedly. As their journey progressed, so too did the young Roamer in his training under Nihak's teachings, who continued to wake him at the point of a sword or knife, and to attack him when the young man least expected it. Nelsh's body was growing stronger and his reflexes faster. Despite his growth as a warrior, the boy still had a long way to go before having any hopes of besting his teacher with a blade. When they finally arrived at the edge of the foul swamp, none were too eager to even set foot near the rotted roots of the tree line.

Fortunately for them, no Goblin band or other wretched creature attacked when they made camp on the borders of Farls Swamp, though there was no shortage of old tracks left by Goblin tribes. Even so the Roamers remained on full alert as they prepared, ready to fend off any attack at the slightest sign of danger; easier said than done as putrid gas wafted up from the muck among the trees, making it difficult to see past that toxic veil.

"Three warriors each watch at night, every night," Aen stated as the Fire Elves wrapped thick cloth about their feet and calves.

"Weapons at the ready at all times, either in your hand, or ready to be drawn," Sarra added, pulling a strip of thick fabric over her mouth and nose.

Nelsh watched the other Roamers make their own preparations; Danira and Aen too were covering their mouths and noses, while Myles and the elves didn't bother. As Nihak and Ejen finished wrapping their feet, Nelsh had to ask, "What's all this for?"

"Do you not smell that?" Danira asked, her voice softly muffled.

The lad inhaled and a powerful whiff of rotting meat and rancid eggs assaulted his senses. "By the Abyss!" he cried, his eyes watering.

Quickly the young Human covered his nose and backed away from the gaseous tree line. Danira tapped him on the shoulder and handed him some cloth to protect his face. "It's not much," she said, "but it'll keep you from passing out."

Nelsh took it gratefully and tied it over his face, leaving only his eyes and hair visible. "What's in there?"

"Death," the Roamers all replied in unison, some testing the edge of their weapons.

"And the fastest way is straight through?" the young Roamer asked again.

"Aye," was the general answer.

"Let's not waste any more time," Nihak said, dousing his wrappings in oil.

Reluctantly, the Roamers turned and stepped past the first decayed tree, the stench immediately overwhelming their senses. As they headed farther in, Nelsh looked about the ghastly place, his hands shaking as he gripped the hilt of his sword, while his shield was held aloft for protection. It was as if all the sunlight had been blocked out by the dense foliage, casting them in grey shadows, dim and desolate. The trees grew in disturbing angles, bent and hobbled as if the very soil was killing them. Beneath their feet, the ground was squelching and sickly, hissing and gurgling bubbling protested the Roamers' passing as they trudged through. In short, everything in the cursed swamp seemed to be in a perpetual state of dying.

Entering Farls Swamp brought another problem to the Roamers and only grew worse the farther in they went. Winged insects emerged, ready to ravage the newcomers and steal their blood with needle mouth-parts. As the air filled with the incessant droning of translucent wings and whining flies, the Humans began swatting and slapping their bodies at any place that was exposed. The elves and dwarf however were not so bothered by them in the slightest. This drew the young Nelsh to inspect his comrades closer, confusion stamped across his face. Myles paid the stinging flies no mind, for when they landed on his flesh to feed, they froze solid and fell to the ground. Indeed, it gave the Odd Dwarf a rather strange and sickly appearance of "shedding" icy shards. Grimacing, the boy then turned to look at Nihak and Ejen, only to see tiny bursts of fire flickering over their bodies. As for Jolek and Rom, the insects could find no purchase on their tough skin and were unable to pierce their stony flesh.

"Danira, pray tell you have something in that bottomless pack of yours that wards off these wretched bloodsuckers!" Aen demanded, inhaling deeply and sending a fierce gust to clear the air for a blissful moment.

"I searched in vain for the paste before we entered this forsaken place," the witch replied. "But maybe I can find it this time. My pack is deeper than you realize."

"I can imagine!" Aen growled, slapping his cheek.

Jolek offered to hold Danira's pack while she dug through the contents so they did not linger in one place for too long. Pushing ever deeper in, Ejen and Sarra, who led in front, had begun to crouch and examine the ground while taking in their surroundings more thoroughly.

"What is it?" Nelsh whispered, looking to Nihak.

The Fire Elf merely nodded to the leading Roamers, who were busily looking over the trees along their path, patches of rotted bark having been shorn off.

"Goblins have been through here," Ejen stated, looking back at them, his scythe at the ready.

"Looks to be a tribe of thirty strong too," Sarra added, rising from her crouch, her falx seeming to appear in her hand of its own volition.

"How do you know?" Nelsh asked, curious and worried all at once.

They stopped and allowed the young Roamer to move ahead to the front of the group. Ejen merely gestured to the mucky ground with the butt of his scythe.

"The ground is trodden and worn down, showing that many beings passed through here." The tall Fire Elf pointed to a certain footprint, more distinct than the others. It was in the shape of a cloven hoof, nearly the length of Nelsh's boot and twice as wide!

"What could have made such a trail...?" he wondered aloud, staring at the heavy tracks.

Tentatively, the lad extended his foot down to rest in the hoofprint and nearly stumbled forward! The hoofprints were sunken in far deeper than the other tracks.

"Duradur boar," Jolek answered, still holding Danira's pack. The witch was nearly inside up to her waist digging around inside for the insect paste.

"A boar? It must be huge!" Nelsh exclaimed, looking up at the other Roamers in bewilderment.

"Oh, they are. As tall as a man and twice as thick. They're half the weight of Rom and their tusks are damn near the length of broadswords," Sarra explained, cautiously moving forward, Ejen right beside her.

"The Goblins use them for mounts and pack-animals," Nihak added, his longsword in hand. "Humans used to live further out beyond Cendril."

Nelsh glanced at his teacher, wondering about the odd statement. "What does that have to do with Goblins and their mounts?"

"Goblin tribes razed those settlements to the ground decades ago, lad," Aen answered. "Ever wonder why Cendril was always fortified? Humans finally got smart about defending their towns. These days the Goblins rarely leave the swamp."

"Why is that?" the young man inquired.

"Goblins and other creatures of this swamp don't care for sunlight too much. Had you been around when they raided Human villages, you would have seen them wearing ragged cloaks and hoods to protect their ugly hides."

"I've got it!" Danira exclaimed, popping out of her pack, a small jar held triumphantly in her hand. The Roamers stayed on alert while the Humans spread the thick paste about their exposed skin, finally achieving relief from the insects.

"What do we do about the tribe of Goblins?" Nelsh asked, reddish-black repellant covering his face.

"Not follow their tracks," Ejen stated, setting off again, making his pathway as west as possible.

"But if the Goblins are evil, shouldn't we stop them?" Nelsh, ever the inquisitive one, continued to ask as he hurried after the other Roamers.

"That's not our purpose, boy," Nihak replied. "The Roamers do not destroy evil. We survive. We just kill anything that gets in our way."

"And the shorter our stay in this wretched place, the better," Jolek added, stomping with a resounding *crunch* on a massive centipede crawling near his feet.

Onward the Roamers trudged, muck and filth soon covering their feet, boots, and clothing. No danger, be it Goblin or feral creature, presented itself to the Roamers, but even still, the seasoned warriors remained on edge. The calls and echoes of insects and other, larger beasts, sounded through the dense wetland. It didn't help that the bent trees distorted the noises, sounding closer than they were, or farther than they seemed. After what seemed like endless hours of pushing and hacking through thick undergrowth, dense brambles and tough vines, and taking arduous detours around stagnant pools and scummy bogs, they came to a stop on relatively dry ground with a few sparse trees crookedly growing in a wide clearing.

"This will have to do for camp…" Ejen said resignedly.

Nelsh sat down with a tired sigh, dropping his shield next to him.

"I'm starving," Myles stated, belly-flopping onto the soft soil.

Danira set her pack down and rummaged about within, producing a handful of dried meat and passed it around.

"No fires," she stated shortly, pulling out a large piece for Rom.

As they ate in silence, Sarra glanced skyward. "Damned foliage… I can't tell if it's dark or not."

"It's close to nightfall," Aen remarked, holding out one of the sleeves of his robe.

In the dim light, they could see the fabric had faded from a dull blue to near-black.

"At least it's a clear night," Myles remarked, finishing his portion of meat. "No rains this time."

"Shut your mouth," Ejen and Nihak warned in unison. "We don't need any reminder of how much worse it could be," Ejen continued while his younger counterpart went back to eating.

Jolek finished his meal first, coughing once as he wiped his hands upon his wooly trousers and asked, "Who gets first watch this night?"

"Nelsh and I will stay up," Nihak said.

"I shall as well," Sarra added, coming over to them.

"Very well," Aen said, rolling out his bedroll. "Four hours and you'll wake me, Myles, and Danira."

"Aye," the Fire Elf agreed, lighting a small flame on his palm.

He curled his fingers over the tiny light, muffling its gleam. The rest of the Roamers settled down to sleep, all laying within arm's reach of each other on their bedrolls. Sarra, Nihak, and Nelsh sat in the center of their camp, all with their backs to each other so they could see outward at all angles. Sarra slid her war hammer from her belt, laying it across her lap in preparation. Nelsh followed suit and laid his bastard sword across his lap, whilst his shield sat on its edge, leaning against his flank. The Fire Elf had unslung his longbow and laid it next to him and rested his longsword against his shoulder.

The only sounds that filled the night now were those of the ever-present insects and tiny creatures, all shrieking their horrid choirs into the gloomy night. Every so often, a deeper sound, such as a tree crashing to the ground, or a reverberating growl could be heard but, fortunately, it wasn't close enough to be a threat. All three Roamers could feel every little movement the other made and it didn't take long for Nihak and Sarra to feel a constant shivering from their newest and youngest companion.

"Are you afraid, boy?" Nihak whispered, keeping his tiny flame to his chest.

"No, I'm not," Nelsh whispered back.

There was a loud *snap* near the clearing, sharply drawing their gazes to the source. Nelsh's trembling had not relented, if anything, it only increased. Another *snap* of wood sounded but this was closer, yet from a different area of their surroundings.

Nihak slowly stood up, extinguishing his light as Nelsh and Sarra followed suit, weapons at the ready. The Fire Elf slung his bow over his right shoulder and glanced at Nelsh.

"Then you're a fool."

With that, he lowered into a crouch and made his slow and cautious way to the trees bordering their campsite. Sarra and Nelsh watched his form fade into the blackness as the elf slipped out of the clearing.

"I am no fool!" Nelsh growled in a hushed tone, gripping his sword tightly.

"Nelsh," the auburn-haired woman said quietly, "I'm scared right now. So is Nihak, as well as the others. There is no shame in admitting your fears. Bravery isn't denying you're scared. It's rising up to face it."

"Nihak is just getting ready to spring out and attack me now," Nelsh muttered, still angry over his punctured pride.

Before Sarra could reply, several arrows hissed through the air. Yelling in surprise, Nelsh hurriedly threw his shield up for protection, feeling four of the projectiles slam into his defense, forcing him back a step. Sarra dropped to the ground, avoiding the rest of the missiles. Before the Roamers came the shrill keening of Goblins as three trees exploded in a ball of fire, casting the area in chaotic light. The rest of the Roamers were up in seconds as a tribe of Goblins swarmed their camp. Ejen sent more fire blazing into the trees, spreading the roaring flames about the clearing, followed by a mighty explosion as a gaseous emission reacted with the fire. Broken swords and notched axes clashed as the Goblins leapt upon the Roamers, screaming in bloodlust. Nelsh held his shield high and his sword at the ready as three Goblins rushed him, their slender gangling legs carrying them with speed. In the raging light of the flames, the Human had little time to take in the sheer ugliness of the foul creatures.

They towered over him with unnaturally long arms and legs. Their tough hides ranged from mottled red hues to striped greyish skin. Between pointed chins and hooked noses sat narrow mouths, lined with needle-like teeth. With dancing shadows lunging everywhere, the Goblins' eyes shone with bluish veins, their pupils slanted like a beast.

A jagged falchion swung for the boy's neck, stopped only by his shield. Crying in pain from the shock of the blow, Nelsh shoved his attacker back and stabbed it through the abdomen, black blood coating his blade. Shrieking in pain the Goblin fell away, its rusted weapon falling from its spindly grasp. The remaining two attacked at once, armed with a spear and short-hafted axe. Frantically, Nelsh sidestepped a spear thrust and blocked the axe with his shield, the serrated edge biting through the wood. His arm wounded from the blow, Nelsh ripped the stuck-weapon from the Goblin's grasp, leaving it open for a slash to the neck. He had no time to watch its head hit the ground as the final Goblin thrusted its spear again. The green Roamer batted it away with his blade and riposted, his weapon stabbing through the Goblin's leather jerkin. Arms going limp, the creature slumped over the boy, dead. Struggling to hold the carcass up with his shield, Nelsh growled with effort and yanked his weapon free, letting his slain foe fall.

With no time for rest, Nelsh moved to fend off another Goblin, his bastard sword clanging against a jagged blade. Around him the other Roamers held their own; Jolek swung his warclub, the force of the blow knocking a Goblin's head clean off. Before its body hit the ground, the Earth Elf dove into a roll, avoiding an axe swing, and came up in a crouch behind his attacker, striking the monster in the back of its knees. Its bones shattered, the Goblin gave a horrid shriek of pain as it fell. Jolek silenced the creature as he brought his weapon high and slammed the broad blade of his club through the beast's spine. Rom kicked and stomped, sending guts and squelching muck flying every which way. The giant even ripped hobbled trees from the soft earth and crushed several Goblins at once, leaving their broken bodies sunk into the ground. Myles ran about the battlefield, sending frost crackling from his hands. The Odd Dwarf didn't bother freezing their foes, rather, he strategically laid ice over the earth to send the Goblins slipping and sliding out of control. Or in other cases, to lend himself greater speed and maneuverability. Falling to his knees, Myles slid along a narrow path of ice, his broad axe cleaving through Goblin legs like saplings. The dwarf's ice did not last long as Ejen and Nihak sent jets of fire into the midst of the attacking tribe, lighting them ablaze, their cries of agony ripping through the night air. With volatile gasses emitting from the ground and flailing Goblins rushing about panicked and aflame, a wildfire was quickly beginning to rage, consuming all in the area. One such Goblin ran at Sarra, its body ablaze. Snarling, she sliced the creature in half at the waist with one swing of her falx, then turned to parry a strike for her chest. Twirling her curved blade through the air, she forced her enemy's broken sword wide and cut deeply into the Goblin's chest. Callously freeing her blade as it fell to its knees, she slammed her head into its crooked nose for good measure. In the roaring light of the fires about them,

Nelsh could make out Aen running a Goblin through and thwacking another in the throat with his staff. While that one choked on its crushed windpipe, Aen jabbed his staff into the chest of the impaled creature and a fierce blast of wind blew forth, sending the dying Goblin off his sword. The Elvan had taken careful aim too, cleverly using the body as a crude missile to ram into other Goblins, the sound of crunching bones heard over the din of battle and flame.

Nelsh grinned at that, then barely knocked aside another attack, replying in turn with his own slash from right to left. His enemy was quick enough to parry the strike and kicked the young Roamer in the gut, knocking the wind from his lungs. Backpedaling and gasping desperately for air, Nelsh was hard-pressed as his enemy pushed the advantage. The Human's shield halted another slash, then a second one before he found firm footing. Side-stepping a thrust, Nelsh batted the blade away and stepped in close, his right foot slamming into the Goblin's knee. With a sickening *crack* the joint inverted, dropping the Goblin, keening in pain. Growling, Nelsh raised his shield high and slammed the edge down on its throat, silencing the wounded creature forever. As the Roamer straightened up, he didn't react in time as sharp pain lanced into his lower back. Groaning, he stumbled forward, turning to see another Goblin leering at him with black moldy teeth, its broadsword dripping with fresh blood. As it moved to strike a killing blow, Nihak leapt in, his longsword singing through the air. Aiming low, the Fire Elf sliced cleanly through the Goblin's calves. With his weapon angled down on his left, Nihak turned his torso and pommel-smashed the wounded Goblin's back, sending it flying to land face-first in the muck. Before it could raise its head, Nihak reversed the grip on his sword and stabbed into the downed enemy's back. Twisting the blade, the Fire Elf yanked his weapon free and looked to Nelsh.

"Are you alright, lad?"

He managed a nod, panting. "I'm fine, Nihak."

As the Goblins' ranks began to thin out, rumbling could be felt through the ground. Roamer and Goblin alike paused in combat, all heads turning to the growing ruckus. Trees creaked and groaned as they were smashed and uprooted, the sounds heard over the spreading wildfire. Accompanying the ripping of trees was heavy pounding footsteps and quickly approaching. Through the blaze about them, a massive form shoved aside a crooked tree, toppling it with a crash.

A Farl Troll stood before them, attracted by the noise of the battle. At four and a half meters in height, it dwarfed even Rom. In the crackling light, its skin tones appeared a grayish green, mottled by patches of mud and moss. The great beast's hide was rough and ragged, crusts of dried blood and scabbed skin covering its torso and claws. Terrifyingly enough, the behemoth's head was more mouth than anything, wide and angled, filled with rows upon rows of serrated teeth. Four bulbous, sinister eyes were spread along the sides and set near the top of its head. Atop the head sprouted a single curved horn, the tip angling forward, perfect for impaling head strikes. Thick veins and muscle rippled through its trunk-like arms and legs; seven clawed fingers adorned each hand. The massive creature opened its disgusting maw wide and let loose a bellowing roar, shaking the air about them.

Rom's fist slammed with thunderous force into the troll's wide jaw, sending it stumbling. "Be silent!" he roared back, tackling the monster before it could fully recover.

As the two behemoths did battle, more rumbling could be felt through the ground.

"Now what?" Danira shouted, her form reappearing beside Sarra and Aen.

"Where were you?" Ejen demanded.

"Staying out of the fray," the witch replied coolly, the rumbling growing louder.

The remaining Goblins gave shrieks of terror and turned tail, fleeing the clearing as fast as they could. But they weren't fast enough as another tribe of Goblins arrived, astride charging Duradur boars.

The mighty creatures gave squealing roars of rage as they trampled through the clearing, their long tusks impaling anyone in their path. Nihak tackled Nelsh, throwing the young man out of danger as a boar barreled towards them. The other Roamers similarly scattered, yelling in confusion and anger.

Now the site of a tribal war and littered with dozens of Goblins corpses surrounded by a raging wildfire, the clearing was no longer safe. Dragging Nelsh with one arm, Nihak half-crawled, half-crouched away from the battlefield into the darkness around. The boars stamped and snorted, sending ever more trees toppling to the ground as the newcomers slaughtered the dwindling tribe that had first attacked the Roamers. Fortunately, the boars' destruction of the area began to muffle and extinguish much of the wildfire, leaving the two Roamers in near-darkness. Still Nihak moved on, forcing Nelsh to keep up with him. As the sounds of battle faded, the Fire Elf stopped and looked about. They were completely alone.

CHAPTER 17

Only blackened trees could be seen in the flickering flames, held aloft by the Fire Elf's palm. Fortunately for them, nothing else presented itself in the meager light. However, faint crashing and roaring could be heard, but it was muffled and gave Nihak no sense of direction. In their mad rush to get away from the boars and Goblins, the pair had lost all sense of where they were.

Panting hard, Nelsh rose to his feet, looking around as well. "Where's everyone else?"

"I don't know, lad."

"Can't we just retrace our steps?"

"If I knew where our trail was, yes," Nihak replied, trying to cast a bigger light. "But I can hardly see anything in this gloom. And anything could be drawn to the flames if I make them too big."

As the elf cast about, searching desperately for their tracks, Nelsh dropped his sword, slowly falling to his knees. Noticing his student, Nihak hurried over, crouching beside the young Human.

"Nelsh? Are you alright?"

"My back is on fire," was all Nelsh managed to say, his body trembling as he broke out in a feverish sweat.

Nihak moved to his back and lifted his shirt up. Holding flames near Nelsh's flesh, the harm he sustained became clear as day. Black veins had begun to spread from the stab wound, turning the skin a sickly gray.

"Oh Seylivonia…" he muttered upon seeing it. "DANIRA!!!!" Nihak bellowed, hoping against hope the witch would hear him.

Nothing but dull echoes and silence met his desperate call. The elf waited a few moments then called to the healer again, screaming at the top of his lungs. Still nothing.

"Damn it all to the Abyss!" he cursed, rising to his feet.

Rustling brush nearby, accompanied by heavy footsteps, drew his attention. His longsword at the ready, Nihak cautiously stepped towards the noise. Pushing past thick bushes and shoving aside a rotten tree, he sighted a single Goblin astride a lone boar passing through. Thinking quickly, the Fire Elf adjusted his grip on the blade, holding it like a spear. The Goblin caught the dull glint of steel in the corner of its veiny eye, turning its head in time to see the vague shape of a sword hurtling through the air. The blade impaled the unsuspecting Goblin through the chest, the body slumping over in the wide leather saddle. Hurrying up to the giant hog, Nihak grabbed the corpse's leg and yanked it from atop the boar's back, messily twisting his weapon free. The great mount seemed not to care for the loss of its master, or the presence of the frantic elf as it began to root through the ground, snorting as its tusks dug deep trenches in the mud. While the animal was preoccupied, the Fire Elf rushed back to Nelsh, grabbing his fallen sword, and helped him to his feet.

"Come, boy. You're not dead yet!"

"Where are we going?" Nelsh asked tiredly, his shield hanging limply on his wounded arm.

"We can't waste time searching for the others. But I know someone else that can treat wounds like yours," the seasoned warrior replied.

Half-dragging, half-carrying the lad to the massive creature, Nihak helped the boy up onto its broad back. "Stay awake."

Without waiting for the Human to respond, Nihak nimbly climbed a curled tree, making his way to the dying canopy of crusted leaves. Managing to find a perch strong enough to hold his weight, the Fire Elf stuck his head above the tree line and was rewarded with a gust of fresh air, filling his lungs with a cool breeze. The night sky was fading to light, the stars slowly winking out as dawn approached. A faint orange glow was off to Nihak's left, showing him the way east. Finally having his bearings, the elf leapt back to the ground, coughing from inhaling the stagnant air once again.

"We're going to see the Forest Elves," he stated, mounting the boar with Nelsh sitting behind him.

Taking up the reins, Nihak guided the boar to turn and face east, then gave its flanks a sharp kick with his heels. The great beast gave a roaring squeal and charged forward, smashing down trees and brush alike, clearing a solid path in their wake. Nelsh hung onto Nihak as much as he could, keeping his head down to avoid flying debris from the boar's charging. What took the Roamers a full day of walking to achieve, the boar covered in a mere two hours. Bursting from Farls Swamp with an angry grunt, the boar stopped as the sun rose over the horizon.

"Fresh air…" Nelsh murmured, the poison spreading further along his back.

"Aye lad. Fresh air. I'm going to get you help."

With that said, the Fire Elf snapped his heels into the boar's flanks again, pulling hard to the left on the reins so the beast's snout was pointed northward. Squealing in anger, the great creature thundered off, making straight for the Selveryn Forest.

*****

Rom slammed into the ground, the Farl Troll stomping hard on his chest, its claws digging into his flesh. The air forced from his lungs, the Giant Earth Elf gave a harsh gasp of pain before shoving the monster off of him. As it stumbled back, he climbed to his feet, growling as rivulets of blood ran down the grooves of his muscles. Roaring, the troll charged forward, head lowered to impale Rom upon its curved horn. The giant braced himself, catching the creature by the head and torso. Arms bulging with popping veins, Rom slid back several meters, his feet digging shallow trenches in the mucky earth. Snarling, rancid drool flying from its wide maw, the troll reared up and slashed at Rom, its long claws raking the Roamer's abdomen. Weakened by the decaying soil of the swamp, the elf could not draw strength from the earth. Blood poured from his stomach as the troll brought its arm up for another strike. Growling with fury, Rom caught the monster's arm and slammed his fist into its gut, grunting in satisfaction at the sound of ribs shattering.

The Farl Troll gave a gargling groan and lunged its head forward, its horn stabbing forth again. More than ready for it, Rom brought his leg up, catching the troll in the face with a hard kick. Triangular teeth flew from its mouth as it recoiled, snarling in pain. Pressing his advantage, Rom stepped forward and wrapped his massive arms about the monster's torso in a fierce crushing grip. As he did so, he brought his knee up to slam into the creature's loins. Howling in pain, the troll wrapped its bulky trunk-like arms about Rom's torso, claws digging deep into the giant's back. Fighting through the pain, Rom brought his knee up again and again, all but obliterating the troll's genitals. Yelling with the effort, Rom set his left foot behind and leaned backwards, lifting the monster into the air. Letting gravity take over, he smashed the troll's head into the ground, toppling after it. Fully stunned, the creature rolled over, its breathing labored. Quicker to recover, the huge Roamer climbed to his feet and delivered a harsh kick to its side, snapping more ribs. Rearing back for another kick, the Farl troll's arm lunged out and grabbed his leg, flipping Rom easily onto the ground with tremendous force. Slowly the monster staggered to its feet and brought a foot up to crash down upon Rom's chest. The Giant Earth Elf rolled out of the way, sending more trees crashing to the ground. Not fast enough to pursue the elf, the troll hurriedly lumbered after him. With dozens of trees flattened, the giants did not notice fetid, murky water nearby, its surface crusted over with bile-colored weeds. Rom kept rolling to gain ground, the splashing of mucky water echoing about the area. Little did the Roamer know what lurked beneath the foul surface.

The splashing mud shocking the giant from his retreat, he had little time to react as another massive creature erupted from the shallows. Ferocious hissing splitting the air, the pointed head of a blade-beaked ridgeback turtle snapped and waved about, barbed tongue flailing in its incisor-like mouth. Behind Rom, the troll quickly backed off, not daring go near this creature. The giant was not so fortunate as he found himself staring into the glassy amber eyes of the turtle before frantically moving atop its wide, pointed shell. Clanging its toothless maw in anger, the mud-dwelling beast easily stood up and clambered onto shore, carrying the Roamer with it. Once on land, Rom finally got a full idea on just how large this monster was. From the tip of its beak to the end of its scaly tail, the turtle was over three and a half meters in length, with its angled, sharp-edged shell nearly as wide. Standing on thick, half meter-long claws and powerful legs, the beast stood over two meters tall.

With a deep gurgling snarl, the armored ridgeback began stalking towards the now-panicking troll, who turned and began to make as quick a retreat as possible.

"Oh no," Rom stated, rolling off the turtle to fall behind it, ignoring the pain of its jagged shell.

Rising to his feet, the Giant Earth Elf bent down and grasped the turtle's thick tail, drawing another hissing growl from it.

"We are not finished yet!" he bellowed, lifting the furious creature into the air with a spin, whirling about for momentum.

His grip released, Rom sent the hissing, blade-beaked creature hurtling through the air to collide with the troll's back. Howling in surprise and pain, both creatures tumbled hard to the ground. To the Roamer's satisfaction, the turtle quickly climbed to its feet and hurriedly shambled away, whimpering growls emanating from its throat. Lying where it fell, the troll was not so lucky as Rom stomped towards it. The behemoth's left arm was nearly severed at the shoulder, hanging by a few thick strands of shredded muscle and tendon. Offering weak snarls of fear, the troll managed to climb to its feet, clawing for Rom's face. The giant easily caught the troll's thick wrist with his left hand, then snapped his right arm up to connect with the monster's elbow. With a sickening *snap* the troll's trunk-like arm was violently inverted, a roar of agony ripping through the air. Now desperate, it moved to headbutt the Giant Earth Elf, but Rom merely shoved his enemy out of range. Before it could wind up for another attack, he grabbed it by the horn and yanked the troll's head down. As the creature was forced to bend forward, Rom's knee smashed into its face. The force of the blow was enough to snap the horn off as the troll staggered back, now delirious from pain and blood loss. Yowling in terror the monster turned to flee but the Roamer wasn't about to let the troll go.

Gripping it by the back of its neck, Rom forced the monster to bend backwards as he drove the broken horn through the base of its spine. The troll didn't even get a chance to howl as the giant let loose a fierce growl and rammed the monster onto its back. Straddling the dying monster, Rom bellowed a mighty roar and began to pummel the troll's head with punch after punch, raining down an endless storm of blows. Bone crunched and shattered, while flesh squelched and spurted as Rom reduced the troll's skull to bloody pulp, staining the ground and his massive fists. When there was nothing left but a bloodied stump atop the troll's shoulders did the Giant Earth Elf stop. Panting hard, he rose to his feet and shouted in victory, pounding his chest twice.

"Rom?"

The giant turned at the voice to see Jolek pushing his way through a stand of brambles.

"By Arrute's Heart!" he exclaimed, gazing upon the remains of the troll.

"Claws sharp enough to cut stone!" Rom growled in pain.

"Come my brother. Danira and the others are near."

He followed his kin back the way they had come, the gloom beginning to vanish as the dawn came. The rest of the Roamers were gathered about a small campfire, sitting or standing around, while the witch was treating a cut to Ejen's head when the Earth Elves walked in.

"That sounded like quite a fight," Aen remarked, leaning tiredly on his staff.

"You should have seen the beast," Jolek stated. "Rom turned its head into nothing but a stain!"

Finished tending to Ejen's injury, Danira straightened up and looked over at the Giant Earth Elf.

"By the Goddesses!" she shrieked, seeing Rom's chest.

"You should have seen the troll though," Jolek repeated, eyes still wide in surprise.

The witch hurried over to the giant, who eased down to a sitting position so she could better treat his wounds. Muttering to herself, she felt the deep gashes over, cringing at their depth.

"These won't heal quickly, even with my magic," she stated, looking up at him.

"I need pure earth," he merely replied, unmoved by Danira's concern.

"I have a mud-like salve," she remarked, going to her pack, hands wet with blood.

"That will do," the elf rumbled.

As Danira rummaged about in her pack, Sarra walked into their camp, her falx dripping red with blood.

"Are we all here?" she asked.

The other Roamers looked over at her. Ejen shook his head, grimacing as he rose to his feet.

"Nay. Nihak and the boy are still out there. When the boars charged through, they went off in the other direction."

"And there's no way we can try and find them in this damned place," Aen added, sighing.

"What do we do then?" Sarra asked, wiping her curved blade clean before sheathing it.

"As long as Nelsh is with Nihak, they'll both find their way back to us. Our first concern right now is getting out of Farls Swamp. We head west and wait for them once we're on the other side," the healer said, her voice muffled from within her pack.

The Roamers looked to Danira as she emerged, straightening to her full height with a jar of mud.

"Should we not wait for them here?" Myles inquired as the witch strode back to Rom.

"In this hellish place?" Aen asked, gazing at the Odd Dwarf with concern.

The wet sounds of muck slapping flesh filled their camp as the witch smeared the medicine over Rom's chest and stomach, causing the giant to wince every so often.

"We get out of the swamp and wait then. That's all we can do," he said as Danira tended his wounds.

The others nodded in agreement. Once the healer had finished her work, Ejen snuffed out the fire and hefted his bloodied scythe over his shoulder. "Then let us make haste for the west," he said.

Quickly they made their way through the thick forested wetland, dreading facing another night in the swamp. They could only hope Nihak and Nelsh found their way out too with all speed.

*****

Slowly the sun rose to the east, casting a warm glow upon the grasslands and blackened trees of Farls Swamp. Nihak felt the warmth of the fiery orb but had no time to appreciate the feeling. Onward his stolen mount galloped, ripping the earth asunder with its mighty hooves. Nelsh leaned against him, barely holding on as the duradur boar thundered over the land, eating up the leagues in no time at all. The green woodland could be seen in the distance, drawing nearer by the hour, but not fast enough for the Fire Elf. Still, the Roamer counted his blessings they were astride a huge boar, making the journey in less than half the time on foot.

Nihak and Nelsh had been riding hard nonstop since yesterday's sunrise and only now the war pig was beginning to show signs of tiring. Blood was dripping from its wide snout and its breathing was starting to come in ragged gasps. Even so, Nihak pushed the creature on, uncaring of its condition, but by midday, the animal was slowing to a trot, giving great coughing heaves that shook its riders to the core.

"Are we stopping…?" Nelsh asked tiredly, looking around.

The Fire Elf stood in the saddle, gazing ahead. Gauging the distance, they were still at least two days away.

"No, we're not!" he stated, pulling his knife from his belt.

Sitting back down, he drove the nine-inch blade to the hilt into the boar's flank, invoking squeals of pain and anger. The beast gave a loud snort, spraying bloody mist into the air before it leapt back to a full gallop again, running all the harder when Nihak stuck it twice, then thrice again, urging it ever onward.

Once more, the leagues began to fade away under the pounding hooves of the boar. With the wind blowing fiercely in their faces, the riders were forced to lean low in the saddle; this was no problem for the fading Human. Nihak wanted to check Nelsh's wound, but there was no time to stop. Instead, all the elf could do was hope they made it to the forest and sought medicine for the poison coursing in Nelsh's veins. As they rode on, the Fire Elf glanced westward, noting that the blackened trees of the Farls Swamp had long since ceased following them. Now there was nothing but open grassland onward to distant peaks. The Roamer took it as a good sign and took comfort that they were nearly to the ever-green woods.

As the sun sank to the horizon that day, the boar gave a pained squeal and collapsed beneath their feet, throwing both Roamers from the saddle.

"Aaagh!" Nelsh cried out, landing hard and laying where he fell.

Nihak on the other hand, nimbly rolled forward upon landing, his momentum carrying him back to his feet. Wasting no time, he hurried over to Nelsh and lifted his shirt up to see the boy's skin had turned grayish-black, the wound oozing blackened blood. The poison had spread to the Human's entire lower back and was creeping around his sides to his stomach.

"Hold on, lad!" the elf growled as he rose to his feet, striding over to their fallen mount.

The duradur boar lay on its side, massive flanks slowly rising and falling with labored breath. Looking the creature over, the Fire Elf saw the cracked hooves and broken leg. Sighing, he knelt by the great beast and drew his knife.

"Seylivonia, please forgive my cruelty to this creature. I commend you, boar, for your great strength and endurance. You served me well in my purpose, and may the Goddess watch over your spirit as you wander Her Eternal Forest. Farewell, and thank you!" The elf finished his Forelvish prayer and plunged the blade deep into the boar's throat, ending its life swiftly and painlessly.

Pulling the weapon free in a gush of hot blood, Nihak quickly cleaned his weapon and returned it to his belt. With that done, he quick-stepped back to Nelsh and hoisted him up onto his back, grunting with the effort.

"Right! Just a little longer, Nelsh!"

With that said, Nihak took off at a dead-run for the forest, now only half a day from where he stood. In the dying light, he could just make out individual trees; and as the sun set, Nihak was forced to run blindly in the dark, but still he did not stop.

*****

Sivart crouched down, collecting soft dirt into his palm. Before him lay the Farls Swamp, many trees splintered and shattered. The ground had been torn up, a wide swathed trail of ripped earth heading north from his right. The Human slowly stood, sniffing the dirt. It reeked of pig-flesh and foul sweat.

"A Goblin-ridden boar…" he muttered to himself. "But why leave the wretched swamp?"

A great burning in his chest coursed through his skin, catching Sivart off-guard as he doubled over in agony. The Huirds behind him stepped forward, talons flashing in the bright sunlight and their beaks dripping with eager saliva. A bright flash of white light gave them pause, then they immediately cowered as their Mistress stood before them.

"Stay back, my pets," she ordered, her voice calm.

The Huirds nodded, squawking in quiet nervousness.

With the birdmen cowed, Alura turned to Sivart, who had since recovered from the sudden pain.

"Mistress, this is most unexpected."

"Indeed," she replied, eyeing the ground. "No doubt, you are lost as to what has happened here."

"I must admit Mistress, I don't entirely know. The Goblins rarely venture from the swamp anymore, and a lone boar galloping off to the north makes no sense at all."

"That is because a Goblin did not leave the swamp. I was watching through my mirror. The new Roamer, Nelsh, was poisoned by a Goblin-blade, so foolish Nihak stole a boar and rode it to the Forest Elves, since they were separated from the other Roamers."

"Who do I follow then? The rest of the Roamers, or should I now pursue only the Fire Elf and his pet?"

"Sivart, if you set one foot past the first tree of the Selveryn Forest, those elves would descend upon you and tear you apart."

He stood there, a look of confusion still stamped upon his face. Alura gave a sigh of exasperation, rubbing the bridge of her nose.

"Must I explain everything for you?"

'Forgive me, Mistress…'" was all he could say, kneeling and bowing his head.

"Oh, stand up, you fool. No need to grovel."

Her slave quickly rose to his feet, mumbling another apology. Shaking her head, the witch's eyes turned steely grey.

"Since you are incapable of thinking for yourself, listen. The main group of Roamers will wait on the other side of the swamp for Nihak and Nelsh to return. No doubt the Fire Elf will get the boy the help he needs. Once they emerge and rejoin with the others, then you may continue in their wake. They've not much further to go before they reach their destination. Can you remember all that?"

Sivart did his damnedest to keep from trembling under that fierce gaze. Somehow, he succeeded.

"I do understand, Mistress," he managed to say, lowering his gaze to the ground.

"Good. Make camp here and wait. I shall let you know when you should be on your way again. Try not to attract too much attention from the creatures dwelling within the swamp."

"If the Huirds weren't so unruly, it wouldn't be a problem," Sivart muttered.

"I beg your pardon?" the witch said, her voice but a soft whisper.

The Human dared glance up to see her eyes narrowed dangerously.

"My creations respond to authority and strength. If you cannot control them, perhaps I should seek a new Left Hand to do my bidding!"

Sivart recoiled at her stinging words. Being the witch's favorite did come with benefits, despite the dangers and higher risk of punishment should he fail.

"Forgive me Mistress! I will keep the Huirds in line!" he stated, his voice faltering but a little.

Alura's right eyebrow slowly rose higher than the other, her pale arms folded across her ample chest. She stared at her slave for a while longer, letting him stew in his own sweat before she finally spoke again.

"Best you do. My patience has grown thin of late with your incompetence and surly attitude, Sivart. Cross me once more and you'll find my Huird ranks increased by one and I'll have a new favorite before long."

With that promise, the witch turned on the spot and teleported away.

*****

Ejen's sickle-sword hacked and chopped through the dense underbrush of the Farls Swamp, clearing a path for their company as they neared the western edge of the forested wetland. Beside the Fire Elf came Jolek, his warclub knocking aside shrubs and trees with brute force.

"I think I see the end of the swamp," Aen said, looking past the two warriors, cupping a hand over his eyes against the light of the setting sun.

Indeed, the muck and the trees seemed not so scary and gloomy now that golden sunlight was streaming in from the horizon. Picking up their pace, the Roamers hurried for the last few trees. All of them were filthy, worn and wearied from the harsh days of tension and constant edged alertness. When finally they stepped past the last tree, they all gave a sigh of relief, but still the Roamers did not stop. Now free of the Farls Swamp, they took off at a tired jog, putting as much distance between themselves and the wretched place as they could. When the sun set before them, the ragged band of warriors halted, many collapsing where they stood.

"If I never set foot in that damned swamp again, it won't be soon enough!" Ejen spat, ripping his soiled foot-wrappings off and throwing them away. While the protections he had taken to keep his feet dry succeeded, some moisture had still formed on his arms, the cursed wetness leaving burn-like markings on his flesh.

Danira, Aen, and Sarra pulled their face-covers from their mouths, breathing in fresh air at long last. While the healer tended to Ejen's water-burns, Rom ripped the earth open, making a great rift in the soil. Easily tearing off his bandages, the Giant Earth Elf stepped down into the wide hole and leaned back, letting the cool dirt speed up the injuries to his torso. He gave a great sigh, the wind from his nose was enough force to knock Myles off his tired feet.

For once, the Odd Dwarf had run out of energy and he fell asleep where he fell, snoring contentedly.

"If it weren't such a pain to go through the Farls Swamp, I'd take the little shite there more often if it meant a peaceful night's sleep for him, and more importantly, for me," Aen remarked wryly, pulling out his long-stemmed pipe to clean.

Danira was too busy with Ejen to notice the Elvan getting ready for a much-needed smoke, as she set a small pot of oil on an enchanted heating stone, quickly setting the oil to boil through her magic. When it was ready, she handed the pot to the Fire Elf.

"Rub this on your wounds and they'll be healed within a few days," she instructed.

Ejen nodded his thanks and began applying it to his arms, dipping his hand freely into the bubbling liquid. As he did so, Danira sniffed the air.

"Aen," she sighed, looking over at the Elvan.

The aging half-breed was smoking hastily on his pipe, blue smoke rising in erratic puffs from his mouth, while a steady wisp of smoke drifted lazily into the chill night air.

"Damn it, woman, leave me be! This calms my nerves and you know it!" he growled, his weathered hands shaking.

"Aye…" she consented, lighting a small orb of light upon her palm to better see. "Just take your time with it. I could use some illu leaves myself…"

"Take some then," he grumbled, clearly agitated before tossing her his pouch of weed. As she caught it, Aen took one final, long drag on his pipe before tapping out the smoldering contents.

Danira gave another soft sigh, filling her ivory pipe before tossing the pouch back to the Elvan. Lighting a small spark, she closed her eyes, inhaling slowly, savoring the euphoric effect. She muttered an incoherent spell, letting her light hover in midair while she laid out her bedroll.

"Someone take watch, I don't care who. It won't be me right now," Aen huffed, wrapping himself in his cloak and lying down next to Myles.

"I will," Sarra offered, sitting down in the middle of their makeshift camp, facing back to the east lest anything follow them from the foul place.

"Wake Ejen when the moon reaches her zenith," Danira added before dropping off to a quick and deep sleep.

"My war scythe will tear you open if you wake me before the sun rises," Ejen stated, rolling onto his side so his back was to them.

"I'll take my chances," Sarra retorted with a tired half-grin.

The Fire Elf gave a grunting laugh and slipped off to sleep, the night deepening. As the other Roamers slept, Sarra stayed vigilant, her body weary and exhausted, yet no sleep came to the woman. Sighing softly, she felt the chill breeze bite crisply at her nose, sending a shudder up her spine. Off to the east, a white flash lit up the night, causing the red-haired woman to flinch hard, wincing as the light faded. Slowly, she stood and walked through the camp towards the approaching witch. Sarra padded quietly through the short grass, walking half a league before Alura stood before her, their hair and clothing flowing and flapping; carried by the strong autumn winds.

"I must admit, I'm surprised," the witch finally spoke, her eyes the color of a sea storm. "I didn't even have to call you forth to me."

"What do you want, Alura?" Sarra asked after a span of silence, her skin cold and crawling under that gaze.

It was all the more haunting as the moon, now full, gave such little light. It almost made the witch's eyes glow pale and ghostly, sending goosebumps all over Sarra's back and shoulders, while cold chills ran up her spine like an icy centipede; each leg piercing her skin and bone with agonizing precision. As if sensing this, Alura gave a cold smile, almost akin to a smirk.

"Where is the boy?"

They both knew that Alura knew. They also knew it would be wise for Sarra to merely answer instead of questioning the witch on why she would ask in the first place.

"Nelsh and Nihak got separated from us in the Farls Swamp," she answered, pulling her fluttering cloak tightly to her form to stave off the unnatural cold in her bones. It did nothing to bring her warmth.

"Ahh. Do you know where they are now?"

Sarra merely shook her head, drawing a harsh grin from Alura.

"Of course, you don't. Nihak is taking Nelsh to see the Forest Elves. The poor boy got stabbed by a poisoned blade and is in danger of dying."

A gasp escaped Sarra's lips before she could suppress it. The witch stared at her, an amused expression stamped on her face, one eyebrow higher than the other.

"So, you care that much for Nelsh. I see," she muttered, chuckling softly. "That will make this next part all the more delicious."

The pale sorceress stepped forward, approaching Sarra with easy, silent strides. She began to circle around the Human, her long dark hair brushing against Sarra's pale cheeks in the harsh wind.

"When Nelsh and Nihak return and you all resume your quest to retrieve the Sylvan Sword, I shall call upon you again, dear Sarra. When I do, this is what I expect of you. Wake Nelsh and bring him away from the camp. I will be waiting to speak with the boy."

When nothing more was forthcoming, Sarra dared ask, "Is that all?"

"Aye that is all, girl. No doubt you know what's coming."

It was a statement more than a question and Sarra dreaded it. Grimacing, she very nearly bit her lip to keep from speaking against the white-clad witch. Alura could see it in her eyes and from the blood beginning to drip from the corner of her mouth, it made the witch grin all the wider, more than amused and very pleased.

"Good. I shall see you and the boy again soon. Now get back to your precious comrades. What kind of Roamer leaves her brothers-in-arms unguarded in the middle of the night in the Wildlands? Such misguided trust they put in you."

The words stinging far more than any wounds she had ever suffered in her years of combat, Sarra turned and all but ran back to the camp, tears streaking down her cheeks as the unrelenting wind bit at her back. As she ran, she could swear she heard Alura cackling in the night, the harsh laughter ringing in her ears long after the witch teleported away, briefly illuminating the black night.

CHAPTER 18

Slowly the dawn came, rich golden rays barely piercing through the thick foliage of the Selveryn Forest. Despite the dim lighting, it was just enough for even Nihak, with his poor nightly vision, to find his way. He and Nelsh had entered the vast woodland some time ago in the blackness and it had been a hellish struggle for the Fire Elf to keep his feet under him. As a result, his face, torso, and feet bore multiple scratches and scrapes, with crusted blood clinging to his dirtied limbs. On his back, the young Human was barely conscious, uttering but a moan or mumbled word every so often.

All around them the trees grew tall and broad, towering far above them as silent sentinels, seeming almost to leer down upon the intruders. Anyone else stumbling through the pre-dawn forest would have been intimidated, but the Fire Elf took comfort in the feeling. Especially with a wounded young Human on his back; and the sooner the Forest Elves found them, the better.

Pausing to adjust his grip on the boy, the Roamer grunted with effort and kept moving as quickly as he could. Running efficiently was no longer an option as the underbrush formed too many obstacles and the trees' roots grew too thick and numerous for firm footing without tripping or twisting ankles. With no other choice, the elf trudged on as fast a pace as he could muster. As the rosy dawn turned to day, so too the rays of the sun steadily filled the woodland, bringing warmth through the greenery above. Brightly colored birds began to sing and chirp, invisible on their high perches while the occasional gliding tree-rat or rabbit bounded by, paying little heed to the strangers, unless they ventured too close.

"If only you were awake to see this, lad," Nihak breathed, looking straight ahead. "What a sight to behold, and you're the first Human to enter this forest in ages."

He knew Nelsh wouldn't answer. But he talked to the boy all the same in hopes of getting a mumble or groan; anything to tell him Nelsh was still alive. Another reason for his chatter was so they would be found out faster. As the Fire Elf went along, a herd of deer stood nearby, grazing on short grass in a clearing. These were no ordinary creatures though as the magic of the woodland affected all its inhabitants, making some quicker, stealthier, or in the case of the deer, bigger. One grazing stag easily dwarfed a normal whitetail, standing higher and thicker in the flanks. Bark-like growth covered patches of their hides and mossy green antlers adorned their narrow heads. Spotting the herd, Nihak paused for but a moment and blew a shrill whistling sound. Every animal's head shot up, dark eyes trained on the potential threat.

"Send word to the elves! An old friend has come!" Nihak called to them in Forelvish.

Without waiting for a response, onward he loped. The Fire Elf didn't see it, but one stag peeled off from the herd and swiftly bound away, far outpacing the slower elf and his companion.

By now the sun was high enough in the sky for the forest to be truly filled with deep sunlight. A soft breath of wind moved the treetops, sighing with a rustle of bright green leaves. The Fire Elf allowed a small smile at the sight above him.

"By the Goddess, I've been away too long," he muttered.

For the better part of the day, Nihak strode on, even managing to sprint a few distances when they entered the occasional glade. Brooks and creeks presented themselves too, but fortunately for the elf, they were small enough to clear with a good jump. More than a few times though, he landed near mucky ground, the moisture in the soil searing his feet. Grunting in pain, the Fire Elf shrugged it off and kept moving, ignoring the burning in his legs.

Near dusk, the Roamer was beginning to feel the effects of carrying Nelsh and coupled with moving at such a harsh pace with no food or rest, they were taking their toll on the elf.

"Nelsh," he said, nearly tripping on an upraised root, cutting his shin wide open, "if you die here, I'll find a way to bring you back to life and I'll make you carry me for a week!"

Groaning, he gently set the boy down and tended to the gash in his leg. Fiery blood was pouring steadily down his foot and onto the ground, the splatters forming flickering blazes, spreading from his injury. Kicking dirt over the spots of flames, Nihak quickly extinguished them and steadied himself, bracing for the pain to come as he scooped damp earth into his palm, scalding it. With a sharp inhale, he pressed the soil to his gash, cauterizing the wound. It sizzled and hissed softly, sputtering angrily as the wound sealed itself. Breathing hard through gritted teeth, Nihak let fall the burnt soil and slowly stood, taking Nelsh up on his back again.

Resuming his unrelenting pace, the Fire Elf pushed deeper and deeper into the forest as twilight began to creep upon him. The animals of the day had all but disappeared as the sun sank below the horizon. Nightbirds emerged, giving their own chorus, while bats and other creatures began their hunting and courtship under the pale shafts of rising moonlight. Nihak ignored them all, focused only on getting Nelsh to the Forest Elves. When it grew too dark, he shifted his grip to hold both of Nelsh's arms with one hand. The other hand free, Nihak held it before him and called forth a substantial ball of fire upon his palm. Refusing to stumble and fall on his treacherous path this night, he made the flames strong enough to alight ten meters around, giving him ample sight to pick out his path in the darkness.

Traversing any forest at night was dangerous, and this one was no exception. Not to mention the fact that Nihak's light was all but a beacon for nightly predators. More than once, the snapping of twigs and soft growling could be heard behind him but the elf had no time for delays, so he merely shouted in Forelvish, hoping his words would stave off whatever beasts were trailing after him. Bears and wolves, among other creatures, stalked the night in this forest and even its elves never wandered far from the safety of their hovels. Throughout the dark hours, one massive creature stalked the pair of Roamers, drawing nearer and nearer despite Nihak's admonishing. Finally, the elf could stand it no longer and turned about, standing face to face with a kul'an bear. The brute of a beast stood seven meters high at the shoulder, its body covered in thick, pine needle-like fur. Its claws were long and curved, made for ripping and tearing apart flesh and vegetation alike. A wet, wide nose rested on its short snout, flabby lips curled back in a harsh snarl to reveal rows of long yellowed teeth. Short round ears laid back flat on its head as the beast let out a fierce growl that would shake anyone to their core.

Nihak merely sighed, staring into its glinting black eyes.

"I've been telling you all night to leave me and the boy alone. He's been poisoned, so his flesh would taste foul to you. I am of fire, so you would burn your tongue with my blood. But clearly you cannot listen. Leave now and I will not harm you."

The Forelvish words seemed to have no effect on the feral monster as it merely reared up on its hind legs, roaring down at the elf with a hungered look. Silvery saliva dripped from its maw as it raised a massive paw to strike.

Nihak snorted loudly, then let fly a thick wad of flaming spit, accurately nailing the bear in the eye. It gave a pained roar, stumbling back as it rubbed at the smoldering wound. The sound of Nihak snorting loudly again drew its attention rather quickly. Dropping to all fours, the bear turned about and ran for it, but not fast enough for the Fire Elf. A ball of fire struck it on the rear, burning its green-furred hide. The creature gave a grunting whimper and ran all the faster.

"Next time, listen!" Nihak shouted after it, swallowing his spit as he resumed his hard pace through the night.

Oddly enough, no other creatures bothered the Roamers for the rest of the night, and so the hours carried on without incident before dawn arose once more. By now, the days and nights of running nonstop had all but drained the Fire Elf of his energy. Still he pushed on, his breath coming in ragged panting now, his pace little more than a hurried walk. If the Forest Elves didn't find him soon, Nelsh could very well die.

Sighing in frustration and exhaustion, all Nihak could do was keeping moving forward. The trees had thinned out in a few areas, giving him more space to make a few last-ditch attempts to run. Leaving one such clearing, Nihak looked about before spotting a lone deer standing some distance away from him. An angry rumbling in his gut was loud enough to scare the animal off, much to his chagrin.

Step after weary step, Nihak continued on, until suddenly a green arrow hissed through the air, slamming into the tree before him. Due to his dulled senses and exhaustion, Nihak fell backwards in surprise, looking up at the quivering missile stuck in the trunk. Nelsh lay sprawled out behind him, his breathing faint and weak.

"Hands away from your weapons!" a feminine voice called out. Nihak was unable to tell where the elf was.

Even in his sleep-deprived state, he held his arms out slowly, keeping them far from his sword and bow. Before him, three Forest Elves emerged from the brush, arrows notched and drawn. Their green hoods were lowered over their faces, the cowls leaving their features in shadow. Behind Nihak, four more elves appeared from the underbrush, making not a sound more than the wind against the trees. The Fire Elf glanced behind him to see them, adrenaline giving him a small boost of awareness and alertness. Above him, five more elves made themselves known in the treetops, their legs giving them steady purchase on thick boughs or the very trunks themselves. Those elves held their positions, arrows trained on the Roamers.

The middle elf of the three standing before Nihak stepped closer, her bow still drawn back and ready to loose. It was she who had spoken.

"State your name and business in our forest or, on my word, we'll shoot you dead where you lay!"

Nihak sighed a little, lowering his tired arms. Bowstrings tightened further at the unwarranted movement. "On any other day, I might find this little game mildly funny, but now is not the time for this, Zethe," he replied.

The Forest Elf stood still a moment longer before sighing and easing tension on her bow. Swiftly, the arrow was returned to her hip-quiver and she lowered her hood. An angular face stared down at him, her eyes a fierce blue. Pale golden hair hung in straight curtains down to her shoulders as her pale lips pulled up into a slight grin.

"No, I suppose not, Nihak. Lower your bows, ladies," she ordered.

As the other Forest Elves eased off on their bows and returned their arrows to their quivers, Zethe offered the Fire Elf a hand. Though it was delicate and smooth, her grip was strong and firm and easily hauled the Roamer to his exhausted feet.

"In all seriousness though, why do you come running into our forest, disturbing the wildlife, and telling deer to take us messages?"

Nihak looked down at Nelsh, "This young Human was stabbed by a poisoned blade in the Farls Swamp. The other Roamers and I were traveling through and we got separated. I didn't know who else to come to, so I came here as fast as possible."

At Zethe's gesture, one of the other elves came forward and began to examine the unconscious Human.

"Where was he stabbed?" she asked, looking at the Fire Elf from under her cowl.

"The back," he replied, leaning against a tree for support.

The elf gently rolled Nelsh over and pulled his shirt up. Nearly his whole back had become blackened and grayish skin, as were his sides with the infection ever-creeping closer to his chest. It had also begun to spread up his neck and along his shoulders too. The wound itself was constantly oozing black blood.

"By Seylivonia!" she exclaimed, flinching back from the wound. "Ortsu poisoning! It's a wonder this boy is still alive!"

"Get him medicine quickly!" Zethe ordered.

The rest of the elves scattered while she and the other Forest Elf remained. Nihak and Zethe watched as she cut away the blood-soaked fabric and began to make small incisions along Nelsh's back. Every time she did so, she pressed down firmly around the spot, causing more black blood to flow out. She kept at it, muttering prayers to her Goddess. The more blood she drained, the grayer Nelsh's skin became, slowly losing its blackened hue. It wasn't long before the other elves returned with different plants in hand ranging from brightly colored flowers to gnarled roots. They added them together into a small bowl and ground it up into a fine powder. With that done, one of the Forest Elves went off to collect water. She swiftly returned with another bowl full of shimmering clear liquid. The powder was added to the water and stirred thoroughly.

"Tilt his head back and open his mouth," the healer ordered, taking the medicine in hand.

One elf easily held the boy up in a half-sitting position while another gently coaxed his mouth open with a soft squeeze of his cheeks. The medicine was poured slowly into his mouth and down his throat. Murmuring more prayers, they gently laid him back down and rolled him over onto his belly. The black blood had finished pouring out, leaving gray skin where it had dwelt. Producing a bone-needle and fibrous thread, the healer quickly stitched up the incisions, closing up the stab wound last.

"There. We have done all we can," she said, rising to her feet and pulling her hood back.

This one had shorter, brown hair hanging just past her pointed ears with a silken sheen. Her face was not as angular as Zethe's, nor were her eyes as intense, but they possessed a soft, gentle warmth.

"Thank you, Leha," Zethe said, giving the healer a soft pat on the back.

They both turned to Nihak, who had slumped down to the forest floor, his back against a sturdy ash tree.

"You look terrible," they said in unison, Leha crouching next to the Fire Elf.

Nihak allowed her to run her small, delicate hands over his face and arms, finding the multiple cuts and scrapes from his mad dash through the dense forest.

"How soon will Nelsh be well enough for travel?" he managed to ask; his eyes half-closed.

The Forest Elves exchanged a look, communicating with their eyes. Leha turned back to the seasoned Roamer and said, "If he is strong, a few days. The poison was in him for a long time, and it could have done lasting damage."

Zethe stepped over and crouched down on the other side of Nihak while the rest of the Forest Elves stood about silently, awaiting further orders.

"We'll take the boy to our nearest village. You need the rest too, Nihak. We'll call the elk and they will help carry Nelsh. You as well."

"I can walk. Get the lad there first. He'll be fine without me for a day or two."

"Very well, stubborn one. You haven't changed at all I see," Zethe muttered, shaking her head.

Unceremoniously, she hauled the Fire Elf to his feet and forced one of his arms over her shoulder. "If you must walk, you will do so with my help."

The Fire Elf didn't bother arguing that point. He allowed it while Zethe spoke more orders. Working as one, the elves surrounded Nelsh, bent down and carefully lifted him up, keeping his body level with the ground. A lone elf gave a whistling call and waited but a few minutes before three colossal elk trotted out to them, their broad antlers trembling with ash leaves. Two elves each mounted one, the mighty beasts having to kneel down, while Leha mounted the third. Gently and carefully, the rest of the Forest Elves set Nelsh sitting upright on the elk's back in front of Leha. She wrapped her arm about his frame, holding him softly but firmly.

"We'll see you in two days in Su'elneu," she said before sounding a soft whistle.

The three animals easily stood on vine-enwrapped legs and took off, quickly disappearing into the ever-green woodland in but a single bound.

"Come along," Zethe said, taking most of the Fire Elf's weight.

Slowly they followed the elks' path, the rest of the elves forming a half-circle about them, lest any hostile creatures presented themselves.

It was going to be a long walk indeed.

CHAPTER 19

Sunlight filled the small room, bringing relaxing warmth to the sleeping Human. Nelsh gave a quiet groan as he rolled onto his side, kicking off the pelt blanket in the process. All around him, soft voices filled the air, talking and chattering in hushed tones, many a giggle accompanying their words.

The young Roamer had been taken to a priestess' hovel; a simple, elegant structure comprised of living trees. Through the Forest Elves' magic and song, the trunks had grown and woven together, bending and twisting to form a soft, dome-like structure with a roof of vibrant leaves and boughs. Each hovel served as a home for every elf in the village, some housing mated pairs and their children.

In his slumber, Nelsh felt a presence hover over him. Reflexes triggered in his mind, his arm jolting around to reach for a weapon that wasn't there. Panicking, he awoke with a sharp gasp of breath. Sitting up too quickly, pain shot through his back. A strong hand grasped his wrist, a soothing voice calming him.

"Nelsh corsal'ocem oreneh. Pagas tarie'bavade."

The young Human found himself staring into gentle eyes of luminescent green. Her face was smooth-skinned, the curves of her cheeks more round than angular. Dark brown hair tumbled down to her shoulders in luxuriant waves. Her pale pink lips lifted in a reassuring smile as Nelsh attempted to catch his breath, pain still throbbing in his back. His eyes wandered over her, taking in her slender frame, covered by a forest-green tunic; the delicate fabric ending at her wide hips. Birch-patterned leggings adorned her shapely legs, ending at the ankles. Deerskin boots covered her small feet, going up to her shins. Lastly, the boy found his eyes lingering on her ample chest.

"Jea'anu miolsi," she said, releasing his wrist and gently pushing him back to rest upon the mat. *"Tae'sutu surabhal anescei."*

"Wh-who are you...?" he finally said, his voice scratchy and dry.

She shushed him, placing a finger over his lips.

"Jios soezi erdov mialsf."

"I don't-" her finger cut him off again, more insistent this time, but just as gentle.

186

Resigning himself to the elf's care, Nelsh closed his mouth, his eyes soon following; the pain was still very fresh in his back. She spoke again, shaking him ever so gently by the arm. He opened his eyes to see her holding a polished wooden bowl filled with water. Reaching around, she gently lifted Nelsh's head while bringing the bowl to his lips to drink. Grateful, he sipped slowly, coughing a little. She waited patiently for the fit to end, then brought the bowl back to his mouth. With the water finished, the elf set the bowl down and let his head rest back on the mat. The Human gave a soft sigh, smiling a little as she placed the blanket back over his body. Next, she reached up and placed two fingers over his eyes, forcing him to close them.

"Laordirim," was all she said, which Nelsh could only guess meant sleep or rest.

When she removed her hand, he opened his eyes again, ready to speak, but she merely repeated the action and forced his eyes shut, reiterating the simple order. Her hand removed once again, Nelsh kept his eyes closed, sensing her form still sitting over his tired body. He thought of looking around once she left him, but this elf was a patient one. Before he knew it, the boy had drifted off to sleep again, his breathing light and even. With practiced stealth, the Forest Elf rose to her feet and padded from the small room of her hovel. Stepping into the main room, a circular space carpeted by lush grass, she turned and made for the narrow passage to her front door. Waving a hand before the entrance, a portal of twisted and knotted roots of living trees, all woven intricately together through magic; it spiraled open with but the slightest creaking noise. Stepping out into the village, Hylaie took a moment to bask in the rays of the sun, shining brightly through the spread treetops. Behind her, the door sealed shut of its own accord, while before her stood a pack of she-elves, all trying to peer through the small windows of her home.

"Be gone," she chided, shooing them away.

"But Hylaie," one of them whined, "he's such a handsome boy and we've not seen a Human for nearly hundreds of years!"

"You'll see him soon enough when he's well-rested and healed, Ell'chim," she replied, sighing. "Don't you have Dre'ke to bother with your chatter?"

Ell'chim, a short, golden long-haired elf, huffed and pouted before muttering, "Yes."

"Well, then take your mouth to his ear and leave our guest to sleep in peace," Hylaie remarked, folding her arms.

As the other elves dispersed among the neighboring hovels and clearings, Leha approached her.

"How fares he?"

"As well as he can," was Hylaie's reply, unfolding her arms. "Let us walk."

"While the others are so hungry?" Leha asked, her brows raised incredulously.

"Nay, the door to my hovel is sealed. Only I may enter. No one else would be able to get in unless they had the Lady's permission Herself."

"Very well," the other priestess consented, walking with Hylaie to a grove of maple trees, just on the outskirts of their village. "So, he is recovering well from the wound?"

"You did your work well with the plants on hand, Leha. Most impressive," Hylaie said, a wide smile on her lips. "For a Human, having been poisoned for as long as he was and for it to have spread so far, he is healing faster than I would have expected."

"Humans could have changed in the past few hundred years though," Leha pondered, rubbing her chin in thought.

"Possibly, though from what I remember, they seem the same in body as this one."

"Perhaps," Leha agreed, hopping nimbly into the boughs of a strong maple.

Hylaie smiled again and followed her, both elves picking spots to rest and relax among the branches. A contented sigh drew Leha's attention down to her friend, a serene look of bliss stamped on her face.

"I've heard that sigh before," she grinned. "What's on your mind, girl?"

"This boy Nelsh reminds me of when Nihak first came to our forest," Hylaie murmured, her bright green eyes closed.

"Oh yes, such a romantic time. We thought him a threat, we nearly killed him, you somehow taught him our tongue, and the Queen allowed him to dwell here for a time. Yes, Nelsh is going through so much like Nihak did."

Hylaie opened her eyes, huffing in mock-indignation. As Leha gave a clear laugh, she flicked her finger, a thin twig bending unnaturally to flick her friend in the forehead.

"Hey!" she giggled, returning the gesture in kind.

The pair shared a good-hearted laugh. Around them, gliding tree-rats raced about in the higher branches, nimbly leaping from tree to tree. A red and black streaked songbird landed near them, chirping rapidly. Both turned their heads to the noise, listening intently. When the bird finished, it fell silent, awaiting their response. Leha turned to look at Hylaie, whose face had flushed a light red. Giggling, she turned back to the bird and gave a rapid, short-note whistling call in answer. The songbird gave a slight nod of the head and fluttered off, singing on the wing.

"You are blushing," she stated, grinning broadly.

"I am not!" Hylaie squealed, her cheeks flushing brighter still.

"Nihak's only a few hours away and you're blushing!" Leha cackled, falling from her perch. The agile elf caught herself as she tumbled down and landed nimbly on her feet.

"Be silent!" Hylaie shrieked, leaping from the trees, giving chase after the laughing Leha around the grove.

Their mirth and fun could be heard back at the village, making many an elf turn their head in curiosity at the reason for their levity. It wasn't long though before Hylaie had to go back to her hovel to check in on Nelsh. Leha left her at the entrance, sharing a quick kiss on the cheek before heading off to attend other matters. Hylaie spoke her password to gain entry and stepped past the threshold as the roots spiraled out. She could only roll her eyes as she-elves flocked back around her home in hopes of seeing the Human. As she entered the room, Nelsh stirred, blinking awake.

"Where's Nihak?" he asked hoarsely.

Hylaie did not bother to answer that question. She merely knelt beside him and poured more water for him to drink. He allowed her to hold his head up while he sipped slowly from the bowl. That done, he laid back of his own accord, eyes roving about the room. On the far side of the small space leaned his sword and shield against the curved wall. Hylaie watched him intently, studying his every move. Her eyebrows rose in surprise when he reached out for the weapon, then they rose higher still in alarm as he tried to get up.

"Rastaerz!" she cried urgently, grabbing his arms and legs gently, forcing him to lay back down.

"B-but I must g-go," Nelsh tried to argue, coughing hard as more pain lanced through his body.

Hylaie sighed and continued to hold him down, the boy's strength nowhere near enough to force her off. Even if he had been at full strength, Nelsh would have still been hard-pressed to get out from under the elf's hold. When he finally stopped struggling, the Forest Elf released him, looking him over in concern. The boy's breathing had grown ragged and shallow again.

Muttering to herself about foolish Humans overexerting themselves, she quickly got up and rushed to another room, this one filled with ingredients and mortar and pestles. Skillfully grabbing the right amounts of different herbs and ground-roots, Hylaie mixed together more medicine and brought it back to the Human. Dissolving it in water, she helped him drink. Once it was swallowed, he laid back once more, his eyes fluttering shut. To her great relief, his breathing returned to normal and he was asleep once more.

"Get here soon, Nihak," she murmured, sitting back with a sigh.

*****

Once more voices filled the room, but this time it was just a male and female. They spoke in the language of the trees, their words soft and flowing, soothing to the ear. Nelsh slowly cracked an eye open, his blanket strewn half over his legs while the rest had spilled onto the soft floor. Looking to his left, he saw through blurred eyes Hylaie talking with another elf, this one dressed in ragged black clothes.

"Nihak!" he called; his voice dry again.

The Fire Elf paused conversing with his friend, turning tiredly to look upon the boy. A small grin played at the corners of his mouth.

"Good to see you in fair health, lad," he said in Forelvish, leaning back against the curved wall.

"Sihaen'ruliaesm tae'behzti faensin," Hylaie said, patting Nihak's knee gently, before rising from her seat.

"Mirqur'osnuaex ixes saifeldea," the Roamer replied tiredly with a smirk, closing his eyes in exhaustion.

Hylaie cast the battered elf a mixed look of pain and dismay before tending to the young Human. As Nelsh's vision cleared, he could see how terrible his companion looked. The Fire Elf's arms and legs were covered in dried cuts, one leg sporting a burn-like mark. His face and hands were smeared with dirt and flecks of bark and leaves.

"What happened to you...?" he asked as Hylaie knelt over him, helping him drink more water.

"After you got stabbed in the Farls Swamp, we got separated from the others. I rushed you here, the journey taking many days and nights. A squad of patrolling scouts found us and gave you aid before rushing you here where you could receive better care. I followed at my own pace."

"Aye, and it took you two agonizingly long days to walk here. Zethe even carried you at one point," Hylaie remarked, petting Nelsh softly.

"What did she say?" the boy asked, smiling a little at her gentle caressing.

"Nothing," Nihak said, chuckling roughly.

"Siel tiasochesi cosal'nilumde," the Forest Elf said, looking back at Nihak.

"She said you need more sleep, lad," he relayed to Nelsh.

"But I'm not tired," the young Human protested.

Nihak shook his head, though it looked as if the simple motion pained him. "No. She's the priestess. If she says you sleep, then do so."

"But-"

Hylaie's finger once again sealed his lips with the lightest touch. He looked up at her, only to be greeted with that disarming smile. Sighing, the boy consented, shifting his weight so pressure was relieved from his back. It didn't take long for him to drift off to sleep again.

"How long until he is ready to travel?"

Hylaie laid the blankets over Nelsh and turned to the Fire Elf. "Not for a few more days. Though he really should rest for at least a week. Journeying will put strain on his body."

"We can't wait a week, Hylaie."

"Why this urgency, Nihak? I knew you to be eager for the road, but never this much. Is there somewhere you are going with purpose?"

"I will not tell you, Hylaie."

"Oh?" she huffed a little. "Very well. You don't have to tell me. But word of your presence has reached the Queen, and she is coming to have audience with you and Nelsh. You cannot refuse her, Nihak. To do so would be to refuse Seylivonia Herself."

"I am well aware," he sighed, closing his eyes once more.

The Forest Elf padded over to him, crouching down so they were at eye-level. "Can I get you anything?"

"Some food and drink," was all the Roamer said, eyes still closed.

"Food will be easy. Drink on the other hand…" she replied, biting her lip in thought.

"The fat from a deer will do if I can melt it down," Nihak said, slowly getting up, wincing in pain.

Hylaie quickly stood with him and helped the elf to another bed, this one in a different room. With practiced hands, the priestess pulled Nihak's torn shirt off and guided him onto the feather-stuffed mat, pulling another pelt blanket over his lithe form.

"I'll get your food and drink. For now, sleep gently. Know that Queen Ayewndre will be in this village on the morrow."

Nihak gave a short nod before passing out, his breathing coming rhythmically and evenly. Satisfied, Hylaie left her hovel in search of food, leaving the Roamers to their much-needed rest.

CHAPTER 20

The sunrise blossomed swiftly, alighting the sky in fiery orange hues, tinted with pink clouds drifting lazily over the misty-veiled woodland. With the dawning of a new day, the Forest Elves awoke and emerged from their hovels, ready to greet the coming sun and its nourishing rays of light. Together their pure voices joined in song and rose through the air, filling the forest with warmth and joy. Nihak had risen early with the elves and ventured outside to join them, though he sat quiet and respectful as the Forest Elves sang. The light strengthened as the orb of fire cleared the horizon, invigorating the elves to dance as they gave their thanks to Seylivonia for such a beautiful day.

Nelsh woke to the soothing comfort of their music. With effort, he managed to rise to his feet and slowly made his way out of the hovel, groaning softly as he sank into a sitting position beside Nihak.

"You're up," the Fire Elf noted, surprise evident in his tone.

"Their singing drew me outside," Nelsh replied, his voice stronger today.

"I'm glad you're recovering, lad. We can't stay here much longer."

"But it's so beautiful in these woods," the young Human protested, looking about as the elves slowly ceased their song and began to go about their day.

"Aye, it is, but we've a task to finish, and a war to fight in," Nihak stated as Hylaie approached.

The Forest Elf stood before them, hands on her hips with a look of soft annoyance stamped upon her fair face. *"Betlisu'tae dehaux marhse'dalon cerquth?"*

Nelsh could only look up at her in confusion and mild fear. She didn't look happy at all that they were out of their beds.

"Canemb'banh toerv Chamhnoar," Nihak replied, slowly getting to his feet. "Nelsh, let's get back inside. Hylaie's orders."

"Why-" he began to say but was silenced with a shake of Nihak's head.

Grumbling under his breath while wincing as he stood, Nelsh followed his teacher back into the hovel, sitting upon a grassy pad in the center of the main room. The Fire Elf joined him, flicking a grain of sleep from his eye. As they eased themselves down, Hylaie padded over to a small room across from the Roamers, its purpose for preparing meals and medicines.

"She'll make us some breakfast before the Queen arrives," Nihak explained as Hylaie busied herself mixing fruits and leaves together.

"The Queen?"

"Aye, boy," Nihak nodded, snapping his head to the right, a sharp crackle emitting from his neck as a reward. "We've gained an audience with the holiest Forest Elf in the Selveryn woods."

"Is that good or bad?" Nelsh wondered, watching Hylaie, his rich eyes traveling up and down the elf's slender form.

The staring didn't go unnoticed by the Fire Elf. So fixated on the Forest Elf's backside, Nelsh did not see his companion reach over and flick him sharply on the ear.

"Ow!" the young Roamer protested, rubbing his left ear as it went numb.

Hylaie glanced sharply back at them.

"Seompare'oune Jea faervahd sahdor'luariltoerv!"

"Jea'anu nioheamhtace," Nihak merely stated, shrugging.

Hylaie stared at them a moment longer before going back to preparing their meals. Nelsh glowered at his teacher as soon as her eyes left them.

"What was that for?!" he demanded in a hushed tone.

"Guard your gaze better next time," was all Nihak said, staring the boy down.

They broke off their staring contest when Hylaie approached, bearing two bowls of food. In her left hand was a dish filled with cut-up fruit and leafy greens for Nelsh. She smiled as he took it from her and he offered a smile of thanks in return. The bowl in her right hand contained a slab of raw meat which was dropped unceremoniously in Nihak's lap with a disapproving scoff.

"You shouldn't be so cruel," she stated, folding her arms as he picked up the meat to roast in his hands.

"He was staring at your rear," was the reply, the aroma of cooking flesh filling the room.

"Like you used to?" Hylaie asked, her cheeks reddening.

"Still do," Nihak smirked, biting into his breakfast.

Before the she-elf could retort, there came a knock on her door. Flashing the Fire Elf one final glare, albeit a blushing one, she hurried down a narrow corridor to the entrance. At her command, the wooden portal spiraled open, revealing Leha and Zethe on the other side, greeting her with warm smiles.

"Bright morning to you both," Hylaie said, returning the smile and inviting them in.

"And golden sun upon you," Zethe replied in kind, hugging the priestess once the door sealed shut.

"What brings you two here?" Hylaie asked after her embrace with Zethe.

"Queen Ayewndre is coming and will arrive within the hour," was the reply.

Hylaie nodded, biting her lip.

"Are you well?" Leha inquired.

Hylaie nodded again. "Yes, I am. I'm just concerned how she will receive them."

"I think the Queen will take to the boy with curiosity. This is the first Human after all that we have allowed into our homeland," Zethe replied, patting her shoulder reassuringly.

"Yes, but Nihak on the other hand...I think he's hiding something," Hylaie stated, rubbing her arms a little.

"That may be, but it is Lady Ayewndre's business, not ours," Leha replied, pulling her friend into a gentle embrace.

Zethe nodded in agreement and they walked back into the main room as Nelsh and Nihak finished their food. Looking up at the three elves, they offered nods of greeting.

"Good to see you again, child," the taller she-elf remarked.

Nihak translated Zethe's words to Nelsh, taking their bowls to a low table, the furniture set against the wall. Hylaie would wash the dirtied dishes in a nearby creek later.

"Thank you, fair lady," Nelsh replied, which the Fire Elf translated.

That drew a giggle from the three Forest Elves.

"Are all Humans this polite?" Zethe asked, looking to Nihak as he sat back down.

A dark shadow passed through his eyes as he looked up at her, and only shook his head. "This one is different. I trust Nelsh, and that is something I do not say lightly," he said after a pause, his tone solemn and serious.

The three nodded, frowning slightly.

"Something wrong?" Nelsh wondered, looking from one to the other, his gaze finally resting on his companion.

"No, lad. Zethe just wanted to know if all Humans were as polite as you." The Fire Elf gave him a reassuring smile, breaking the somber mood. "You've got better manners than King Malder."

The young Human laughed at that, his mirth infectious enough to make the she-elves smile. As they talked and laughed more, the elves grew curious to know about Nelsh's wanderings and adventures with the

Roamers. The Human regaled them with tales of his training and moments of peril on the wild roads. Nihak also told them of the war that had torn the land apart and how the Roamers went into exile. As he finished, a clear horn sang through the air.

"The Queen has arrived," Hylaie stated, hurrying to the door and commanded it open.

Nihak stayed back with Nelsh as the other elves hurried outside, eager to greet their ruler.

"What will happen now?"

"Queen Ayewndre will speak with me alone first," Nihak stated. "She may wish to speak with you alone as well."

"But I don't speak Forelvish."

"Aye, but she's their direct line to Seylivonia. And it is not beyond a Goddess to break the barriers of language. If she speaks with you alone, show your utmost respect. Queen Ayewndre is not one to take arrogance or disdain lightly and will not hesitate to show you your place beneath her."

"The Queen sounds rather arr-"

Nihak cut the boy off by clapping a hand over his mouth. "I'd guard my tongue on that if I were you, Nelsh."

The young Human gave a slight nod before the Fire Elf released him. As he did so, Hylaie came back in.

"Nihak, milady wishes to speak with you first."

The Roamer turned to his companion and gave a knowing look before nodding to the Forest Elf and leaving the hovel. Zethe was outside waiting for him and she led him down a wide pathway, passing by many other hovels. The way before them lay deserted, for the rest of the Forest Elves had all flocked to a great willow tree. The mighty tree stood hundreds of meters high, its whip-like vines hanging in thick curtains down to the very ground, shrouding its mighty creaking limbs and boughs. Every Forest Elf in the village had gathered around the curtains, talking excitedly amongst themselves, for their great Queen had graced them with her presence. As Nihak and Zethe approached the throng, she called out sharply, demanding they make way for them. Quickly the crowd of elves parted, leaving a wide berth for Nihak to pass through with Zethe by his side. So wide was their path that two more elves could have easily walked abreast with them and their shoulders still would not have touched the crowd.

The Fire Elf glanced left and right, seeing the elves whisper and talk softly with each other in guarded tones. Before he knew it, Nihak found himself standing before the vast wall of leafy vines. Craning his neck all the way back, the Fire Elf found he could just make out the top of the veritable wall of branches.

"Mavaisochirsei," Zethe commanded, and the vines of the willow parted before Nihak, allowing him access.

"I can go no further," she explained, patting him comfortingly on the shoulder. "She requested only you."

The Fire Elf gave a half-hearted smile before steeling himself and stepped through. As soon as the curtain of leaves sealed behind him, all sounds of the forest ceased, leaving the willow eerily silent. The twisted trunk was massive, its roots delving deep into the soil, making the ground uneven and knotted with tendrils of wood. As Nihak stepped closer, the great sentinel gave a deep groan, its branches up top shaking and stirring, almost as if the tree itself was alive. A few meters away stood an arched doorway, sealed shut in the trunk. Slowly, almost cautiously, the Roamer approached the closed portal, uneager to go through. But at last, he stood before it and laid a hand on the uneven bark, biding it open for him.

"I am Nihak of the Roamers, summoned to Her temple, for the Queen has demanded my presence," he spoke in Forelvish, the words echoing strangely in this hallowed circle of willow leaves.

Unlike the hovel doors, where their portals spiraled open, these doors merely parted before him, much like traditional doorways. Taking a steadying breath, Nihak stepped over the threshold and the doors silently closed behind him. The interior was no less as magnificent as it was outside. Floors were carpeted in lush moss and the walls were smoothed and carved, prayers of strength and life in Forelvish adorning the curved surfaces. White glowing orbs hung from the walls and high twisted ceiling, giving perfect light for its occupants to see as clear as day. Across the way, sat the Queen on a raised dais.

Ayewndre wore a silky robe of green and brown tones, the patterning that of swirling crooked tree boughs and leafy patterns of varied leaves lining the hems of her voluminous sleeves. In her right hand, she held a staff of intertwined willow vines and ash roots. Upon the tip was a single ash leaf, its simple pattern glowing with unnatural brilliance. Her feet were bare as were her shapely legs, their pale slender length revealed through a slit in her royal robes. The Queen's face was flawless, but there was no warmth to be had in that cold stare of her glinting emerald eyes. No crown sat upon her fair head, though her thick wavy locks of dark green hair were adorned with leaves of willow, ash, and maple; along with the clear wings of dragonflies and beauteous patterned butterfly wings tied into her hair. The decorated tresses tumbled down to her slender shoulders, serving its purpose of announcing her rank in place of a crown.

Nihak stared upon the Queen before bending his knee to her, head bowed in respect.

"It has been too long, Nihak," she remarked, her voice rich and powerful.

"Should I have returned sooner?" the Fire Elf replied, head still bowed.

"Look upon me when you speak."

Slowly, the Fire Elf brought his yellow eyes up, her beauty and power filling his gaze.

Ayewndre allowed the slightest of smiles to appear on her full lips, knowing the effect she had on the elf. She remained silent, letting him bask in her radiant glamor, but soon enough, the Queen spoke.

"You were made welcome amongst us and will always have a place here, should you come wandering back. And so, you finally have, with a young Human in tow no less!" she exclaimed at the last statement, her tone growing edged.

"Were Humans forbidden from entering the Selveryn Forest?" Nihak inquired, tensing lightly under her surfaced ire.

"As a general rule, yes. Humans are lowly creatures that have no other instincts but to breed, slaughter, and enslave."

"Perhaps Humans have changed since the last time you defended these borders?"

Hmm," she mused, drumming her slender fingers along the length of her staff. "Perhaps, if this one proves so. But he does not represent the entire race. And from what I learned of them; they are not creatures of change."

"I shall not argue that point, my Queen. Now, why have you summoned me? I know it was more than to discuss what few qualities Humans possess."

"Indeed, my Fire Elf. As you know, I am connected with Her Ladyship Seylivonia, and She speaks to me on many matters. Of late, She has told me of your quest with the last of the Roamers."

Nihak looked away, feeling her piercing gaze boring into his very soul.

"Look at me when I speak!" she ordered; her tone was light, but that whispering wind carried such venom.

The Roamer found himself staring up into her eyes again, the Queen's green orbs shimmering with rage.

"Did you think She wouldn't know about your little plan to take the Sylvan Sword, my people's holiest relic? Seylivonia's own Sword, a Goddess' weapon, and you, a mere little Fire Elf, will take it? How can you even know where it is? The blade's location is known only to me!"

"My Queen," Nihak began, pausing under her harsh glare. "Please do not mistake my intentions."

"Very well. I am listening," she replied, folding her arms expectantly.

"I don't remember how I know the hidden place of the Sylvan Sword. It came to me in a dream. I only wish to use this weapon to save Greenearth."

"Pray tell, why Seylivonia's Blade will save this land? Are the Fire Elves marching again? I have not heard word of such a thing." The sarcasm in her voice stung him, though he knew she had good reason for such disdain to his words.

"My Queen, the Humans will march again. I know you care not for their petty wars, but understand that if King Jamiel defeats King Malder, he will sweep over all the land in a path of destruction and death. Even your homeland will not be safe."

"So, you reason the Sylvan Sword will aid King Malder in this war? How do you know he will not follow the same path as King Jamiel?"

The Forest Queen was still skeptical, her emerald orbs hardening by the minute. Nihak wouldn't put it past her to throw him in the dungeons again at this rate.

"He would have done so already. He keeps to his kingdom and has no desire to expand. To do so would be war with the Earth Elves and your people."

Queen Ayewndre gave a long sigh, holding a delicate hand to the bridge of her nose. Her eyes closed softly, as good a sign as any to the Roamer. Nihak waited patiently as she sat there in tired silence, but soon though, he heard her muttering softly. Straining his sensitive ears, he could barely discern her words but it didn't take much for Nihak to realize that she was communing with her Goddess. So the Fire Elf remained kneeling, patiently but fearfully. After many long minutes passed, Queen Ayewndre opened her eyes and spoke.

"Seylivonia did not impart the Sword's location to you. Even She is concerned how you know it. However, She has seen reason in your quest and will allow it. She trusts you to do the right thing with Her weapon."

"Thank you, my Queen. I shall pray to Seylivonia tonight and thank Her as well."

The Forest Queen raised a soft hand, instantly silencing the Fire Elf. She stood and padded towards him, walking in a slow circle with her staff tapping the ground, making not a sound. "But understand this, Nihak. A Goddess has put Her trust in you. That is something She does not do lightly. Fail in this quest; let Her Blade fall into the wrong hands; and that trust will be lost and nigh impossible to gain back."

"I understand, my Queen. After this war is over, the Blade shall be returned."

The tall Forest Elf nodded. "Good. Now leave me. I will speak with the boy. On the morrow you shall both be on your way."

"Yes, my Queen."

With that said, Nihak rose to his full height, bowed his head to her, and left the temple. The doorways opened of their own accord to allow the Fire Elf to leave. Walking past the curtain of leafy vines, the chattering and shuffling of the crowd before him struck the Roamer like a force of wind. It was so unnaturally quiet inside that he had forgotten about the gathering. As he walked through the throng, they plied him with questions of what the Queen wanted and what they spoke of. Zethe quickly stepped to his side and warded the curious elves off.

"What Nihak has discussed with Queen Ayewndre is their business alone. If her Majesty wishes to speak to us all about it, she will do so. Now make way."

The Forest Elves quickly parted before them as they made their way back to Hylaie's hovel. Once there, Zethe knocked lightly upon the door. It quickly spiraled open, Hylaie inviting them in with a smile. They stepped over the threshold, passing down the short corridor. Entering the main room, Nihak stopped short, seeing Nelsh wearing a finely woven dress of leaves and silk.

"Hylaie, why?"

The Forest Elf giggled as she inspected her work. Nelsh was blushing fiercely, unsure of what to do.

"Help me..." was all he could say.

"I thought it would look cute on him," was all the priestess said with an innocent smile.

"Like it was with me?" Nihak asked quizzically, folding his arms.

"Oh, come now, you wore it fine."

The Fire Elf ignored that and told Nelsh he could take it off. Gratefully and eagerly the lad did so, handing the garment back to Hylaie. Nihak raised an eyebrow upon seeing Nelsh stripped to the waist.

"You took his shirt off? Really now, Hylaie? Don't you have suitors clamoring after you like mewling pups?"

"None of them interest me," she replied off-handedly, folding the dress neatly. "And is it a crime to examine such a fine specimen?"

"Lad," Nihak said, catching Nelsh's attention while he searched for his shirt.

The Fire Elf translated what Hylaie had said, causing the boy to blush fiercer still.

"Aww, did you tell him what I said?" the healer giggled.

"Aye. Now kindly give Nelsh his clothes back. The Queen wishes to see him, and I doubt she'll be pleased that he is naked above the waist."

"You never know, Nihak. Queen Ayewndre may appear stern and rigid outwardly, but she is just as female as the rest of us, and like us, she can have desires too," Zethe remarked, picking up Nelsh's shirt and handing it to him.

"What are they saying now?" he wondered, looking to his fellow Roamer.

"Uh…" the Fire Elf paused, glancing between Nelsh and the she-elves. "Just keep your pants on when you see the Queen…"

"What???" Nelsh exclaimed, looking in bewilderment between the three elves.

"Never mind that. Queen Ayewndre has summoned you, so off you go. Remember to kneel before her and speak only when bidden. Show her respect and you will be fine," Nihak said, urging Nelsh to the door.

"Aren't you coming with?"

"Nay. She requested you alone. Now go."

Zethe took Nelsh by the hand, gave him a reassuring smile, and gently led him outside. Nihak sighed and leaned against the curved wall of the hovel, slowly sinking to the soft ground. He could tell when they had reached the gathered elves by the temple. The Fire Elf could hear the squealing and clamoring of the she-elves even from where he sat.

"Are the males really so dull around here?" he asked tiredly, looking over to Hylaie.

"Oh no, there are plenty of fine males in this woodland. Leha is being courted by one such elf now. Many of those ladies out there are bonded for life to a male. You must remember there are ones looking for love, and everyone is curious to see the young Human. He is such a strange creature to us, yet they are so similar to elf-kind. Don't you agree?"

"Similar in body, but not even that. Otherwise there is nothing we elves have in common with Humans."

"Are you sure? Fire Elves seem to share the Humans' destructive and war-like nature."

Nihak stared at her for a moment before looking away, the statement cutting deeper than any wound he had ever sustained in his lifetime of battle. Hylaie hurried over to him and wrapped a comforting arm round his shoulders.

"Forgive me, Nihak… That was a cruel thing to say. I am sorry."

"I forgive you," he murmured, fighting back tears of fire. "I had thought Fire Elves were the most evil, bloodthirsty race to ever exist. That's why I left home. And then I encountered Humans and suddenly I felt right at home again…"

"May I ask you something, Nihak?"

The Roamer merely nodded; his eyes closed tight.

200

"Why Nelsh? He is Human. Why take him under your wing? Why nearly kill yourself to save his life?"

"Because I see something in him that I've not seen in a long time. That boy gives me hope. Hope for the future, come what may. Nelsh carries a fire in him unlike any I've seen in other Humans. I saw it in him the moment I met him. I trust Nelsh with my life, Hylaie. You know I don't do that lightly."

She could only nod in understanding, offering a gentle smile. The two elves stayed there, sitting in each other's embrace as the time passed, minutes fading into hours. The sunlight was low in the sky when Zethe finally returned with Nelsh, and the boy looked worn and out of breath.

"Had a long talk with the Queen?" Nihak asked, looking him up and down, an eyebrow raised in skepticism.

"Aye, I did," Nelsh nodded, sinking into a sitting position.

"All you did was talk?" the Fire Elf pried.

"Yes!" the lad said, now agitated.

"Fainarai lan'Bainen sadesilde tae mulmes'lunithtem?" Hylaie added, her own skepticism mirroring Nihak's.

Zethe's eyes widened at that. "Hylaie!" she gasped, trying in vain to stifle a laugh.

"What did she say?"

The Fire Elf looked from the elves to Nelsh. "Hylaie merely asked if 'the Queen rode you like a beast'."

"Wh-what...!" he stammered, unable to retort to such a statement. "I, n-no, I did not!"

Zethe smiled and explained that indeed, Nelsh did have a long talk with the Queen, but when he reemerged outside, some of the she-elves could not contain themselves and pursued him, eager for "companionship". Zethe led him on a long, arduous path in an attempt to lose the lonely elves.

"Very well," the Fire Elf said at last, clearly not convinced.

Even so, he let the matter drop. Zethe and Hylaie shared another giggle at the thought but ceased teasing the flustered boy. He was so red in the face he could pass for a ripe tomato.

"So, what happens now?" he finally managed to ask, when no more jokes were forthcoming.

"Are you fit to travel again, lad?"

The Human gave a nod as Hylaie went about to prepare a meal for them. Zethe sat next to them in the main room, crossing her long legs.

"Nihak, if Nelsh is fit, we can provide you with mounts," she said.

The Fire Elf gave his thanks and translated for Nelsh. The Human gave his thanks, which was passed in Forelvish to Zethe.

"Horses will serve us well if we are to be on our way again," the boy stated as Hylaie came over, bearing bowls of leafy greens, covered in a milky cream.

Nihak gave a laugh and relayed that to the she-elves, who shared in the laughter.

"There are no horses in this forest, Nelsh," Nihak said after, pulling some dried meat from his pack. "We'll ride elk. They are swifter and more agile."

"When do you leave?" Hylaie asked, taking a few bites of her meal.

"Queen Ayewndre said on the morrow. Though I wish we could stay longer; we must be on the road."

The priestess frowned at that. "You're sure you cannot stay longer?"

"We must get back to the other Roamers. And the Queen made it clear we leave tomorrow. I don't wish to upset her any more than I already have."

Nelsh sat in silence as Nihak and the Forest Elves talked. He ate slowly, thinking about the coming days of their quest, and the Queen's words of caution when confronted with the Sylvan Sword. It wasn't long before Zethe bade them goodnight and departed. At Nihak's suggestion, they retired for the night. It would be the last night's sleep they'd have in complete comfort and safety for a very long time.

CHAPTER 21

Alas, the swift sunrise blossomed much too soon for Nelsh. He awoke with a start, reaching for his blade only to find none there. Again.

"At least your reflexes have been honed," Nihak remarked, dropping the Human's bastard sword on his chest.

Nelsh gave a grunt of protest as he sat up, rubbing the sleep from his eyes. "Is it morning?"

"Aye it is. Get dressed and get armed."

Nelsh pulled his shirt on and belted on his sword, glad to feel the familiar weight. His round shield was leaning next to his bed, which the young Roamer hefted and slung over his back as he followed Nihak to the main room. Hylaie was there, waiting for them. She had specially prepared a breakfast of rabbit stew in a deep stone bowl; serving it with haste to the Roamers, who ate heartily and quickly.

"Thank you Hylaie," the Fire Elf said, hugging her close. "I'll come back someday."

"You promise?"

"Jea faervahd resavir aui'tae," he promised, offering a small smile to the Forest Elf.

She nodded, satisfied, and then hugged Nelsh close to her bosom. "You must come back someday too."

Nihak translated her words and clapped a hand on the boy's shoulder. "Come."

The priestess gave her final farewells and waved from her door as they set out from the village. Before they were out of sight, the pair turned and gave one final wave goodbye before heading back into the dense woodland.

"Zethe said she'd have mounts for us," Nelsh stated, yawning lightly as they walked, the village quickly fading from sight, lost among the thick trees.

"Aye, further down the path. Elk don't usually wander into the Forest Elves' dwellings. They keep to the forest."

Sure enough, it wasn't long before they came upon a small clearing. In the middle stood Zethe and Leha, both petting and

203

feeding two of the giant creatures, singing softly in their elvish tongue. Nihak greeted them quietly, slowing his pace so as not to startle the beasts.

"How far away are the other Roamers? Do you know?" she asked, rubbing the animal's muzzle.

"If they got out of the Farls Swamp, they'll be waiting nearby. If not…" Nihak let the unfinished thought linger.

Zethe whispered in the elk's twitching ear, the beast's head lowered just to hear the elf as she patted its wide flank. "They'll carry you to the tip of Farls Swamp. You'll have to walk from there."

"That will be more than enough. We are grateful for your hospitality, and deeply appreciate your help. Thank you, Zethe and Leha."

They smiled in thanks and embraced the Roamers before steadying the creatures so they could mount up. Sounding their shrieking cries, the beasts knelt so the Roamers could better reach their high backs.

"It may be uncomfortable but stay astride them. If you dismount, they may think their task is complete and would return here."

"We understand," Nihak said.

Speaking in the tongue of trees, the elves bade the elk carry the Roamers with all haste. The creatures shook their antlered-heads and rose to their full height, ready to be on their way. Gently, the Forest Elves reached up and gave a tap to their rear flanks, prompting the moss-covered creatures to prance forward. They waved goodbye until the Roamers were gone from their sight.

"This is easily one of the strangest things I've done in my life," Nelsh stated as he adjusted to his mount's nimble stride, lightly bouncing along the uneven forest floor.

"I can't say the same," Nihak chuckled, grinning as he watched the trees and brush pass by.

It was a fine change of pace to enjoy their surroundings for once. The Fire Elf gave a sigh of contentment as he took the view in, admiring the beauty the woodland held for him. Nelsh on the other hand was more preoccupied with keeping his seat on the elk's wide back.

"Once we reach the edge of the forest, we'll be able to move at a swifter pace. And trust me lad, these beasts are more comfortable than a boar. More pleasant on the nose too."

"Why a boar?" Nelsh wondered, finally adjusting his seat enough to ride comfortably.

Nihak glanced over at his companion and grinned. "While you were sick, I dragged you along on a ride from the Abyss."

And he told Nelsh of all that happened when the young Human was stabbed and how he got him to the Forest Elves. After he finished, the boy sat quietly on his mount.

"Nihak, I may not be able to repay this debt," he said slowly, looking over at his friend.

"Bah! Live through this war and you'll have repaid me," the Fire Elf stated with a wave of his hand.

Glancing skyward to glimpse the sun through the canopy, Nihak gave a slight sigh. "I think a little more speed could be coaxed from these walking flanks of meat!"

He gave his beast a slap on the rear, sending the elk into a bounding run, pounding along past pines and oaks alike. Nelsh's mount followed suit, nearly throwing the Human off as it leapt forward.

"Warn me next time!" he bellowed as he leaned low against the animal's back, his arms wrapped tightly about its mighty neck.

*****

Ejen stood some ways from the other Roamers and their camp, swinging his scythe about. The fine blade seemed to slice the very air, singing sharply as the Fire Elf mowed down invisible enemies. His visage was a snarl of bloodlust and battle rage, yellow eyes narrowed in frustration.

By their campfire, Danira turned sides of meat over, cooking it steadily and evenly. "They'll be back soon, Ejen."

"When they do, I'll punch him in the mouth!" he growled in response, breathing hard from his "fight".

"Which one?" Jolek inquired, resting casually on Rom's chest while the giant dozed.

"Whichever bastard comes in range first!"

Sighing and shaking her head, Danira rose to her feet, passing their meals around. Aen ate quietly, Myles alongside him. The Odd Dwarf finished first and curiously leaned close to the Elvan's plate, still hungry. Leaning away from him, Aen extended his arms out to the left, further distancing his meal from the greedy dwarf. Just as quickly, Myles scurried around, now trying to actively snatch the food from Aen's plate.

"Get off!" he snapped, planting his boot on Myles' face in a vain attempt to keep him at bay. "I'm too old for this!"

Sarra could not help but laugh at the display, despite the heavy burden on her shoulders. The auburn-haired woman did her best not to think of what Alura had charged her with, and deep down, she hoped Nihak and Nelsh did not return. Wincing inwardly, she regretted that wish. The only way they would not find their way back is if they had perished.

"You alright, Sarra?" Danira asked, sitting next to her, eating slowly. "You look ill. Did I not cook your portions correctly?"

"Hm? Oh, no dear I'm fine," she quickly stated, shaking her head a little.

"You should eat up then, before Myles tries to take your food as well," the witch chuckled, playfully nudging the woman.

Sarra managed a small smile and resumed eating, watching as Aen, now on his feet, spryly ducked and dodged the flying Odd Dwarf.

"Myles, I will embed your axe in your arse if you don't stop!" he stated, ducking as the dwarf flew over his head, hands scrabbling for meat. As he landed, something caught Myles' eye in the distance. Hurrying to his feet, he ran over to the sleeping giant and leapt onto Rom's face, who grunted and lazily swatted his arm about. Avoiding the trunk-like arm, the Odd Dwarf then jumped first onto Jolek's shoulder, then stepped up to balance atop his head.

"Really!" the Earth Elf exclaimed, glancing up at him.

"Myles what on Greenearth are you doing?" Sarra demanded, rising to her feet.

Aen took the opportunity to quickly finish his meal, lest the Odd Dwarf lose interest in whatever had caught his gaze. The energetic Roamer pointed northward.

"Look!" he cried, bouncing eagerly atop Jolek.

"Myles, off!" he said, grabbing the Odd Dwarf by the legs as he stood, easily tossing him away.

They watched the dwarf tumble through the air before landing hard, bouncing on his side, then his rear before skidding to a halt in a sitting position. He stayed where he landed, still pointing northward, which was now at his back. Following the Odd Dwarf's unerring finger, the Roamers looked to see two figures coming towards them at a light run.

"Nihak!" Ejen cried, rushing forward to meet them.

"Ejen!" his counterpart called back, waving as they drew nearer.

"Oh no," Danira muttered.

Indeed, the two Fire Elves slowed to a stop as they approached each other. Nihak had but a second's warning before Ejen's fist flew up to deck him in the chin. Aen winced at the blow, while Sarra and Danira merely shook their heads. The younger Fire Elf stumbled back, then toppled hard with a grunt.

"That's for taking so long!" Ejen growled, then stalked back to camp, leaving a very stunned Nelsh to help Nihak back to his feet.

"Indeed!" the younger elf replied, spitting blood.

They followed the surly Fire Elf back to camp, the Roamers eager to hear of their adventures.

"What happened after the Goblin attack?" Jolek prompted, grabbing Nelsh and Nihak in a tight embrace, nearly cracking their spines.

"Let go and I'll tell you!" Nihak gasped, his breath forced from his lungs.

The Earth Elf gave a hearty laugh and dropped them both. Stumbling about before they could regain their breath, the pair sat with their companions and told them of all that had occurred in the past few days. Nihak told most of it, with Nelsh adding in his own views on the tale. He kept his conversation with Queen Ayewndre to himself though.

"It still amazes me that you're on good terms with the Forest Elves," Aen muttered when they had finished their story.

"Aye, the first time we met they had such a way with words. I recall they were along the lines of 'Draw and release!'" Nihak remarked, giving the Elvan a crooked grin.

"Ha…ha…ha," the half-breed said, returning the odd smile.

"Well, glad you got Nelsh there safe. Now," Danira said, "back to the matter at hand."

"Aye, our little quest," Rom added, rolling over with the sound of stones cracking in two.

"Everything is little to you, you heap of rock," Aen retorted, drawing a laugh from everyone.

"We've still many leagues to cover from here to the Duriviel Forest," the witch pointed out. "Not to mention going past *her* castle…"

Nelsh looked about in confusion as the other Roamers solemnly nodded at that last statement.

"Her?" he echoed. "Who is 'her'?"

"You'll find out soon enough," Sarra said, the other Roamers nodding again.

"Aye, best we not talk about that creature now," Nihak added, eying the sun. "The hour's growing late. We'll set out at first light."

"And what will we do in the meantime?" Myles asked, hopping about the camp.

"Well, I can think of a few things," the Fire Elf said, rising to his feet. "Nelsh, come."

The young Human rose with his teacher. "Another lesson in swordplay?" he asked, hefting his shield.

"Aye, but I will not be your opponent."

"Who then?"

"Aen, today's your lucky day."

All eyes turned to the aged half-elf, who stood up slowly, grumbling, "I'll kill you, Nihak."

"Many have tried, all have failed. I'll let you off with a bleeding arse if you wish to cross blades with me," the Fire Elf replied without missing a beat. "Besides. Nelsh will be more fun."

The young Human drew his bastard sword and hoisted his shield up, standing at the ready. Aen approached him and leaned upon his sturdy staff a few paces across from the boy.

"Where's your sword, old man?"

"Old man?" Aen echoed, cocking an eyebrow.

A few chuckles could be heard from the others as the Elvan shifted his weight, but subtly enough that the young Human didn't notice.

"I'll not attack until you're armed," Nelsh said, followed by a cry of pain.

With uncanny agility, Aen had swung his staff up in a wide arch to smack Nelsh atop his head.

"Ow…" he whined, wincing from the throbbing sting.

"Call me 'old man', again and it's your nose next, boy," Aen promised, emphasizing the last word.

Now angered, Nelsh swung hard with his blade, the weapon singing through the air from right to left. To his great surprise, steel clanged against steel, the harsh sound ringing out in the evening air. The Elvan's broadsword had materialized in his hand just in time to block the attack. Aen smirked at Nelsh's shock and easily twisted his sword around, redirecting the boy's blade out and wide, leaving him open for attack. Twisting at the waist, Nelsh threw his shield up to deflect Aen's swing, his sword bouncing off the wooden barrier. However, his back was left defenseless, something Aen took full advantage of in the form of his staff, the black wood flying in and striking the lad harshly on his rear, drawing another cry of pain from him.

"Hey!" he yelled, ramming his shield into the oaken rod, knocking it wide.

Nelsh retaliated with a thrust, but the Elvan merely knocked it aside with his broadsword. Bringing his weapon up with amazing strength, Aen made a snap cut at Nelsh, the swift strike too quick for the boy to stop. The tip of Aen's sword gashed deep into Nelsh's right shoulder down to his chest, drawing a loud scream of pain. A swing of the staff, whacking Nelsh cleanly on the right temple saw him flat on the ground, his sword fallen from his grip.

"Danira, you're needed," Aen remarked, his weapon dematerializing into thin air.

Sighing, the witch rose and hurried over to the whimpering Human. Kneeling over him, she gently rolled him onto his back so she could better do her work on his wounds.

"What did you learn, boy?" the Elvan asked, tapping Nelsh with his staff.

"Leave him alone, old bat," Danira growled, swatting his gnarled walking stick away.

"You're faster and stronger than you look..." the young Roamer muttered, holding his throbbing head.

"Aye. Never underestimate an enemy. Now if you will excuse me," Aen said, chuckling a little, "this old bat needs his sleep."

As Danira healed up Nelsh's gash and his pounding headache, the rest of the Roamers made ready to turn in for the night as the sun began to set.

"Myles, you're on first watch," Ejen stated, rolling onto his side, hugging his war scythe close.

The Odd Dwarf stuck his tongue at the elf but moved to sit in the middle of their camp, axe laid across his lap. As they all laid down in their bedrolls, Danira finished her work on Nelsh, the wound on his chest sealed and his head treated.

"He nearly cracked your skull," she stated, helping him up. "And as harsh as Aen was, he is right. You mustn't judge an opponent by their age or appearance."

"Aye, a hard-learned lesson, but I will remember," Nelsh promised, sheathing his sword and tossing his shield to his bed.

"Good. You have second watch after Myles," the witch said, patting his back before going to bed herself.

As the young Human laid down, Sarra caught his eye. The auburn-haired woman was staring at him, silent and perturbed. He met her gaze but said nothing at first, confusion and worry stamped on his face. When finally Nelsh opened his mouth to speak, Sarra rolled over onto her side, showing her back to him. Slowly the boy closed his mouth and laid his head down, unsure whether he should ask her what was wrong or just keep quiet and go to sleep. Exhaustion quickly made the decision for him. As the moon rose, so Nelsh closed his eyes, the comforting arms of sleep taking hold.

The peaceful rest did not last, however.

Nelsh's eyes snapped open. He sat up quickly, glancing around in a panic. When no immediate danger presented itself, the young Roamer calmed down, breathing deep in the cool night air. Something had woken him up. As he began to think of what could have caused such a sudden awakening, soft music drifted through the air. It was almost intangible, but Nelsh could hear it. A haunting, eerie flute playing a slow and somber song.

CHAPTER 22

Slowly, Nelsh rose to his feet, the moon's pale glow giving him enough light to see. Glancing skyward, he noticed it was not yet midnight.

"Myles?" he asked in a hushed whisper.

Turning to where the Odd Dwarf was supposed to be on watch, he found the bizarre Roamer tipped onto his side, fast asleep.

"Anybody?" Nelsh raised his voice a little, nudging Danira, then Nihak with his boot.

Neither of them so much as stirred. The song increased in volume, louder in his ears now, playing faster as if with a sense of urgency. Or beckoning. Now that he thought of it, Nelsh felt the growing desire to seek out the source of that music. As he looked about their camp again, realizing that all the Roamers were sound asleep, he saw Sarra stir. She sat up just as quickly and suddenly as he had. Looking around, her eyes finally alighted on Nelsh, her bright orbs widening in surprise, then softening to sadness.

"You hear it too?" he asked, helping her to her feet.

As he spoke, the boy noticed that the tune had shifted, if only slightly. Some minor variation in the notes, but still it called to him.

"Sarra, is the music calling to you as well?"

She nodded slowly, pulling her cloak tightly about her form. "We'd best not ignore it..."

"What do you mean?" he wondered, tilting his head curiously.

"Whoever is playing the flute wishes us to go to them. Come," she beckoned, heading off into the bleak night.

Nelsh hurried after her, not bothering to belt on his sword. He couldn't explain it, but the music made him feel safe; as if he knew there wouldn't be any danger when they met the flutist. So he followed Sarra, feeling a chill breeze whipping up. Despite the wind's mournful howling, the somber song rose up, carrying over the gusting cry. It grew louder and louder as they drew further and further from their camp.

"Sarra, where are we going? Do you know who is playing the flute?"

She didn't answer for many minutes as they walked, passing into a nearby copse of trees, the other Roamers now long gone from their sight. Finally, when Nelsh thought he'd have to ask again, Sarra came to a stop.

"I wish I didn't, Nelsh. Please forgive me," she whispered, the darkness hiding her silent tears.

The young Human stepped around to stand beside her, staring at her quizzically. How could she sound so upset when the music was so comforting? So calming.

So alluring.

When Sarra didn't move, Nelsh looked ahead, freezing in place. There before them in a clearing, no more than a few meters away, sat a woman of surpassing beauty. Her midnight hair flowed down her back like a starless waterfall, her dress almost glowing white in the night. Her pale skin too seemed to shine softly as she played her entangling melody. The mysterious woman's eyes were closed, but Nelsh could sense she knew they had arrived.

And then, the lady opened her frozen blue eyes, piercing through Nelsh's soul as he stood rooted to the spot. Her soft lips moved away from the simple instrument, and yet it continued to play, her fingers no longer dancing over the many holes. The song took on an eerie echo, as if displaced from the very air itself. Now the mysterious sorceress released her hold on the flute, leaving it hanging in midair. She rose from her stony seat and approached the two Roamers in a slow, confident gait.

"Child," she greeted, sighing softly with a gentle smile.

"Who are you?" Nelsh had to ask, transfixed on her flawless form.

"Oh, they haven't told you?" she grinned, standing before the young lad, leering down at him with a cruel grin.

Nelsh and Alura glanced at Sarra, who averted her gaze, shame written in her eyes. A soft hand cupped Nelsh's chin and he found himself gazing into the witch's enchanting orbs, the unforgiving blue shade sending endless chills down his spine.

"I am Alura," she stated, lowering her hand.

Alura. The name sounded vaguely familiar. Surrounded in a web of enthralling music and held by the magic of the powerful witch, any memories he had of the tales encircling her name, and her evil deeds committed over the centuries was lost to him. The witch smiled again, appearing soft and warm but her eyes on the other hand, they spoke of darker intentions.

"I'm rather surprised Nihak and the others have not told you who I am," she said, clicking her tongue in disappointment. "One would think because of Nihak's past experiences with me, and you as well Sarra, that you would have been well-warned, dear child."

Nelsh once again looked back at the weeping Roamer, her tears now shining in the faint moonlight.

"What is she talking about?" he asked, unable to go to Sarra.

"If you had known, you might have had a chance of escaping their fate," Alura stated, drawing the boy's attention back to her.

Before Nelsh could ask what she meant, the witch held a finger to his lips, silencing him. Slowly, almost teasingly, her hand moved from his face down to his chest.

"Alura!" Sarra cried, giving the witch pause.

"Pray tell what troubles you," her words dripped with venom, yet she never took her gaze off him.

Nelsh paused, still unable to move from where he stood. Had Alura's eyes just changed from icy blue to stony grey? He looked over to Sarra, who took a step towards them. Alura waved her hand, uttering *"Thaero murgar enia'frimgai."* Nelsh could swear he heard a cracking sound not unlike glass threatening to break. Sarra stumbled back from the magical barrier and stayed her feet.

"You already have me! You don't need Nelsh!" she begged.

"You're quite right," Alura agreed.

And she pressed her right hand into the center of Nelsh's chest. He gasped in shock as he felt intense heat spreading through his heart. It grew and grew, blossoming into a white fire that burned hotter than the sun.

"But I want Nelsh! And I want Nihak to know that he has completely and utterly failed! That no matter what he or any of you do, your actions will be futile and in vain! That your suffering and misery will know no end so long as my cold heart beats!"

Sarra fell to her knees, staring in defeat as Alura held Nelsh fast, her palm still against his chest. Nelsh's screams of pain ripped through the black night and no one came to his aid.

*****

"Nelsh?"

The voice was faint and familiar. A strong hand shook him, albeit gently.

"Nelsh?" the voice was louder and more insistent.

Opening bleary eyes, the young Human slowly woke, groaning as the sun's rays stabbed into his hazy vision.

"Are you alright, lad?" Danira asked, rolling up her cooking supplies.

Nelsh glanced over at her before turning back to stare up at Nihak. The Fire Elf was crouched over him, concern etched into his face.

"What time is it?" he mumbled, moving sore limbs to rub his eyes clear.

"Mid-morning," Ejen answered as he walked past. "You were passed out as if you'd gotten into Aen's drink."

"That was you!" the Elvan bellowed, hurling an empty bottle at the Fire Elf's head.

Ejen easily ducked the crude missile and shrugged. "Don't blame me. Myles found the right pocket and was happy to share this fine morning."

Nelsh blinked in confusion as Nihak helped him to his unsteady feet.

"You look terrible," he stated, still holding onto the wavering Human.

"I do?"

"Aye, lad. You've got dark circles under your eyes and it took forever to wake you. I'd have thought you dead had Danira not checked your heartbeat. Did you not sleep well?" his mentor raised a worried eyebrow.

"I had…" Nelsh tried to recall last night's events. He remembered falling asleep, only to be awoken by an eerie flute song. A walk through a haunting night and getting caught in a pale spideress' web… Alura! "Nightmares," he finished, unwilling to bring up what had happened.

Across the way he caught a quick, ashamed glance from Sarra, who also remained quiet of what had transpired last night. Danira stepped over to Nelsh and handed him a steaming bowl of porridge.

"Here. We've already eaten. I infused this with enchanted herbs that will help you regain your strength faster. Eat up."

Gratefully, the young Roamer wolfed it down, uncaring that it burned his mouth. Once finished, the witch took the bowl back and stuffed it in her pack.

"If you're quite finished," Jolek said, slinging his warclub over his shoulder, "let us be off. We've a valley to cross, and then a lake to walk around and we should get there within a few days if we make haste."

"Lead on then," Nihak called back.

The Earth Elf nodded and turned west, taking off at a light jog. As the other Roamers followed suit, Nihak and Nelsh took up the rear, Sarra trailing behind them.

"Are you sure you're alright?" he asked, patting the boy on the back.

"Yes, Nihak," he replied, the enchanted porridge fueling his limbs back to full strength. "I just had a horrible night's sleep."

Sarra bit her lip enough to draw blood. She so wanted to tell Nihak what had happened, but her fear of Alura was so much more potent. Cursing herself, the woman remained silent yet again.

"Sarra, are you alright as well?"

Nihak's voice snapped the woman from her dark brooding. Visibly starting, she gasped a little and shook her head.

"Hm? Oh, I'm fine, Nihak."

"Truth be told, you don't look much better than the boy," he observed.

"You had nightmares too?" Nelsh asked, giving Sarra a mixed look of questioning and pleading.

"Y-yes," was all she managed to say, unable to bear that gaze.

Descending into the narrow valley-proper, the journey downhill was an easy one with sure footing and soft grass. Rabbits dotted the landscape among the shrubs and lone trees, watching the ragged band of warriors pass by. The only thing those creatures had to worry about was the overactive Odd Dwarf giving them chase. Nelsh watched in amazement as Myles not only kept up with the fleeing long-eared creatures, but that he followed their paths perfectly, leaping and hopping from side to side with as much agility and grace as the rabbits. Once to the floor of the vale, the Roamers set a hard pace for a wide river, crumbling ruins of old settlements in their path.

"Did Humans once live here?" the young Human inquired, staring at the remnants of old cottages and farms in wonderment.

"Aye, before they realized that Goblins lived nearby, and thanks to the war and the inhabitants of the Wildlands, no one dwells here now," Danira answered, adjusting her hefty pack.

As they passed through the moss-covered crumbling walls, they neared the whispering river, its waters brown and murky. Fortunately for the Fire Elves, this river had a wide bridge, albeit a decrepit one. Fragments and sections had fallen away, giving it a rotting appearance.

"Why are there no Water Elves here?" the inquisitive lad wondered, looking about for those slender elves of flowing grace.

"Look at the waters," Ejen prompted, he and Nihak stepping onto the bridge with all caution. "It used to be clear as glass but too much blood turned it dark and stained. Least, that's how the stories go."

As he finished, the Fire Elves swiftly crossed over, only a few stray stones tumbling into the depths below. One by one, the Roamers crossed the old bridge, the Earth Elves passing last. Praying to Arrute, Rom went last, the stones underfoot cracking and grinding in protest beneath his massive weight. Fortunately for the giant, the bridge remarkably stayed firm, allowing them to continue and head up out of the valley. With only half the day passing them by, the Roamers made the steady climb out of the empty vale, leaving it as quickly as they came.

Now as they walked on, the land slowly began to change. Flat grasslands scattered with copses of trees fell away to uneven hills and crags, the ground becoming rocky. As the Roamers traversed the harsh terrain, they began to pick their steps with care. Even so, treading with such caution was not always enough.

"Oof!" Nelsh grunted.

The stones beneath him gave way in a light rockslide, sending the young Human tumbling and half-sliding down the steep slope.

His skin scraped and bruised, Nelsh came to a halt, coughing from the dust.

"You alright?" Rom had stopped where he'd landed.

"Aye, I'm fine," the boy managed to say, struggling to his feet.

"Watch your footing," Aen reminded as he walked further ahead, his staff coming in very handy as a third leg.

"Why is the land changing now?" Nelsh asked as Rom leaned over and lifted him to his feet.

"We're on the outskirts of the Barren Plains," Nihak answered, sliding down the slope after him, maintaining his balance.

"The Barren Plains?" Nelsh echoed, looking back at his teacher.

"Aye, but they weren't always known by that name," Sarra stated, joining them.

"What were they called then?"

Nihak, Sarra, and Rom all shared a look before they turned back to Nelsh.

"No one remembers," the woman answered, shaking her head.

"Come," the Fire Elf laid a comforting hand on Nelsh's shoulder. "Let us not linger here too long. Best to keep moving."

The Roamers continued walking, picking their paths carefully as they became more spread out. While they struggled to stay atop loose stony ground, the only one who seemed unaffected despite the damned place was Myles. Indeed, the wild Ice Dwarf made good use of the sloping hills and even the crevices, making a game out of how many times he could hop over a crack in the ground, or how fast he could roll down a stony hill. It was a welcome relief to the Roamers. The brightly shining sun and clear sky helped to ease the tension they all felt. Despite the uneven and rough ground, the band of warriors made good time in their travels that day, discussing the war to come and the possibilities victory or defeat would bring.

Soon though, as the sun drew nearer to the horizon before them, they grew somber again. Nelsh soon found out why as they crested a particularly massive hill and came to a stop. Before them, they could see the vast landscape, filled with nothing but cracked and jagged earth, covered in a blanket of stones and boulders. A wide lake could be seen many leagues away, but that was not what drew their gaze.

As the young Human surveyed the land, a far distant structure caught his eye. Straining his sight, Nelsh could just make out a blackened castle against the angry red sunset.

He pointed out as much to the others.

"Aye, lad," Nihak replied, a gust of wind blowing from the east. It sighed past them, ruffling their clothes and hair. "That's her castle."

"The witch Alura," Sarra added before Nelsh could ask.

"And we're much too close for comfort," Aen remarked, pulling another bottle of cider from within his robes to drink.

Nelsh looked over at the Elvan, incredulity stamped on his face. "Much too close?" he echoed. "Aen, it's no more than a speck to our eyes, and you say we're too close???"

"Boy, if you've heard even one tale of Alura, then you would know full well why we fear her!" the old half-breed retorted.

"And that if you can see her castle at all, then you are too close," Nihak added.

"Which is why we'll make for the lake's edge, and then skirt south and give the witch's dwelling as wide a berth as possible," Ejen stated, pointing out a general path with his war scythe.

With that said, the Roamers began to make their slow descent down the steep hill, choosing their footing carefully as ever.

"Taking a southerly path will add on to the time it takes us to reach the Duriviel Forest," Nelsh said, following in Nihak's footsteps.

"Aye but it's worth it if we don't have to pass right next to that dreaded castle," Danira countered, patting him gently on the shoulder.

"No doubt she's watching us now," Myles piped up, choosing the quick path by sliding down the hill on his rump.

"Let us hope not," Jolek replied, following suit on his back.

As stones clattered and clacked against each other in their descent from the Roamers' passing, they kept their gazes on her castle, as if expecting her to emerge forth and cast black sorcery upon them.

*****

Sivart stopped at the edge of the Barren Plains, the grass growing sparse among loose pebbles. The flight over the swamp had been an easy, if not tense one. Just flying over the godforsaken place gave the Human the chills. It didn't help that the Huirds, in their infinite sense of humor, found it funny to pretend to drop him, or better yet, actually drop him only to catch him again. The inhabitants of the swamp no doubt ate well from the half-digested contents of Sivart's stomach that day.

Glad to once again be on the ground, he made the Huirds walk the rest of the way, their bitter and angry crowing music to his ears. Now that he was on the edge of his Mistress' land, he never thought he'd be so happy to return home. While he admired the view, the telltale burning erupted in his chest and Alura appeared before him, bringing light to the darkening day for a brief moment.

"Ahh, Mistress," he greeted, immediately falling to one knee, bowing his head.

Alura said nothing. She let her servant bask in her presence for a few long minutes. Finally, she spoke.

"Sivart, dear, there is something of great importance that I must tell you."

"Yes, milady?" he asked, daring to look up and meet her gaze.

To his great relief, her eyes were a soft green and unchanging, for the moment. Her light frown however was a little disconcerting, but when Sivart thought about it, she didn't smile that often; and when she did, it never boded well. Even so, he did not let his guard down.

"You may stand," she said, folding her delicate arms over her chest.

He obediently rose to his feet, silently grateful. Sivart remained in place as Alura began to circle him, her arms shifting to holding her hands behind her back as she walked. Behind her Left Hand, the witch stopped and locked eyes with the biggest and strongest Huird. It blinked its hollow orbs and began to screech and rasp in guttural tones. Sivart visibly shuddered at hearing such noises. What really stabbed into his spine like an icy knife though was when Alura began to respond in similar tones. For the span of many minutes, the witch screeched and cawed in a rasping voice in perverted speech with the abominable creation. Finally, she finished and resumed pacing around Sivart, her soft feet padding over the dry grass and loose stones.

"You have served me for many, many long years, Sivart," she stated.

"Yes Mistress, and gladly so," he replied with a grin. "There's nothing more I love than to serve and obey you."

"In the first years of your servitude you were ruthless, vicious, and quite the willing slave," she agreed. "But as time went on, your loyalty to me became rotten and festered into a sick obsession for Danira."

Sivart blanched at that. "Mistress, whatever desire has beset my heart, it still ultimately belongs to you as the rightful owner."

"That may be, and wisely spoken," she consented, nodding a little. "However, I cannot ignore your lack of competence over these past months."

"Mistress, I assure you-"

"Be silent!" she ordered, turning to face him.

Prudently, Sivart closed his mouth and waited, daring not to even breathe loudly. Alura's eyes had not changed color; a good sign for him, but the Human wasn't about to hope for the best. The witch resumed her pacing about her servant, continuing on.

"I have given you a simple task. That was to follow the Roamers with an escort of Huirds. Not only have you failed to grasp the simplicity; you have mistreated my pets."

"I carried out your orders, Mistress," he stated, neglecting to bite his tongue.

An invisible force gripped him by the throat, painfully constricting his vocal cords and windpipe as he was lifted into the air. Alura had stopped behind Sivart, her back to him.

"Be quiet," she said, her voice dangerously soft.

The powerful sorceress stood there, listening to the pained grunting and desperate gasps for breath. She didn't need to turn around to know that his legs danced futilely in the air, searching for any purchase of firm footing. She smiled as she knew he was clawing at his neck, as if to pry her magical grip from his flesh. Finally, she spoke again.

"I have come to a decision, Sivart."

To her admitted surprise, she heard his pathetic struggling cease. In fear, no doubt. Taking her time, Alura turned and padded around to stand before her slave once more. She saw surprise in his eyes as well. Indeed, the witch's eyes had not changed color this entire time, despite his insolent interruptions.

Snapping her fingers, Sivart dropped to the ground, his legs crumpling underneath him as he took rapid gasps of air, his lungs on fire. She watched him hold his bruised throat, resting on all fours like an animal. Rather fitting, she thought with a smirk. When he finally managed to stand on his feet again, his broad body still shuddered from the ordeal.

"I'm releasing you from my service," she said, so very calmly and casually.

The Human blinked.

"Mistress..." he began, his voice faltering.

"There's really no need for you to call me that anymore, Sivart. You are free of your enslavement. Be gone with you."

"But I am your Left Hand! You always have one!" he protested, uncaring of the consequences now.

"I have found another," she stated simply, shrugging.

"But Mistress!" he pleaded.

"If you wish to keep serving me, I shall make you into a Huird. Though I doubt they'll let you live very long. They're not as stupid as you make them out to be."

"I don't want to be a disgusting birdman!"

"Then get out of my sight. Those are your choices."

Sivart stood there, stunned and in shock as Alura gave a shrill whistle. The flock of Huirds leapt into the air, eager to return to their roost and be away from the foul man. He watched them soar into the clear sky, leaving him behind until there was only the witch.

"Farewell, Sivart. I do hope you can make a life for yourself without me. And my protection," she said, ready to turn, but then paused and looked back at him. "One more thing. Should I find you anywhere near my castle or my lands, I will not be so welcoming. Goodbye."

And with that said, the witch turned on the spot and teleported away in a white flash of light. Sivart stood there still, before doubling over in pain as a fire took hold on his flesh. He grasped his chest as tears streamed down his face, weighing his heart down like a stone. After what felt like an eternity of pain, he finally managed to straighten up. Pulling his shirt open, Sivart looked down at the mark of Alura's Black Hand. It had become faded, turning from dark pitch to soft ash in color with a white jagged line lancing through it. Truly, Sivart was no longer a servant of the witch Alura.

CHAPTER 23

The dark waters of Mune Lake lapped at the crusted black stones of the shoreline. Jagged and fragmented towers and spires of salty rock rose up from the murky depths, leaving eerie shadows upon the gray waves. The Roamers had stopped and made camp a safe distance from the water's edge as the sun began to set before them. While Nihak and Ejen went about making fires and Danira began her daily task of feeding nine ever-hungry mouths, Nelsh began to approach the edge of the lake. Seemingly before his eyes, as the sky darkened and silver glimmering stars began to gleam in the twilight, the surface of the wide water began to mist over. Ghostly structures of stone quickly vanished into the smothering veil of fog. As the uneven pillars of salt disappeared, the young Human swore he could see figures in the fog. Squinting, he could just make out shriveled, gaunt people, their long wispy hair rustling in the shroud as they walked about the surface of the haunting lake.

Behind Nelsh, Nihak stepped carefully, the water lapping no more than a mere few paces from where they stood.

"What's that stench?" Nelsh wondered, crinkling his nose as the sun winked out. "And what are those things...?"

He could see them reaching out to him, empty eyes glowing through the haze.

"It's salt," the Fire Elf replied, laying a trembling hand on the boy's shoulder. "Come. It's best to keep your distance from this lake. Old legends say these waters are haunted, and any who set foot in the lake are never seen again."

The young Human didn't argue as he was hurriedly led back to their camp. When he turned back to gaze upon the lake, the brackish waters were clear with not a sign of fog or ghostly figures anywhere.

"What is this place?" Nelsh wondered in dreading curiosity.

"The Mist of Mune," Aen stated, leaning against a rough boulder.

Sarra patted the ground next to her, inviting him to sit. As the other Roamers gathered round, Ejen made their fire bigger for light and to aid Danira in her meal preparation.

"You see the witch's castle," the auburn-haired woman stated, shadows dancing across her pale face.

Nelsh craned his neck to see over the other Roamers' heads and looked west. Even in the deepening night, Alura's castle could still be seen, despite no moon casting pale shafts of light.

"Do you really think a castle was built in the middle of a wasteland?" Aen asked, as if reading the boy's thoughts. "With a brine lake where no life thrives?"

"Some kingdom that would be, eh? Queen of muted rock and stone," Jolek scoffed, accepting a bowl of stew from Danira, who handed out dinner for all.

As the Roamers ate in silence, Nelsh had to ask, "Is Alura a queen?"

Aen swallowed a lump of meat wrong and began hacking and choking. Myles immediately leapt on his shoulders and began hammering his fist into the aged half-breed's back. The gravy Nihak was slurping up went down the wrong pipe and he began to cough and spit fiery stew from his mouth. While those two struggled to breathe, Ejen, Jolek, and Rom threw their heads back in laughter. Sarra could only stare at the spectacle before her while Danira tried desperately to pry Myles off of Aen.

"Rom! Jolek! One of you hard-headed elves help me!" she bellowed.

As Jolek got up and grabbed hold of the Odd Dwarf, Nihak had more or less cleared his airway, taking a ragged breath.

"No lad, she is not a queen," he managed to say, coughing as he finished speaking.

They looked over as Aen collapsed, his face turning blue. Jolek and Rom were now both trying to get Myles off as the energetic dwarf kept hammering away at Aen's back to force the stuck food from his throat. Finally, persistence seemed to win as Myles gave him a particularly hard slap and the meat was dislodged with violent force. Ejen quickly ducked the half-chewed food as it shot away into the darkness.

"Ha!" Myles exclaimed, leaping off the Elvan's back.

Aen merely laid there, gasping for air. Rom bent over to help him up, but the old Roamer rasped, "I'll kill the next one to touch me!"

The Giant Earth Elf wisely let him be and sat down as slowly and gently as possible. With the spectacle passed, they resumed their meal, urging Nelsh to withhold any more questions until after they'd finished eating. By the time they were done, Aen was well enough to sit up and eat his own bowl of stew. He kept casting baleful glares at Nelsh and Myles though, finally handing his empty bowl back to Danira.

"Now, what on Ath're made you ask such a silly question?" Sarra inquired, turning to Nelsh.

"Jolek said she was a queen," he replied hesitantly.

"Nay lad. I was mocking her. There is nothing out here. Only death and waste. Even the very rocks are absent of life."

"A king or a queen must have a kingdom. And a kingdom must have subjects. Otherwise their title is meaningless," Sarra added.

"Besides," Nihak stated, laying out his bedroll, "the witch would not have such petty ambitions."

"How do you know?" Nelsh asked, following suit along with the others.

"Alura and I have crossed paths in the past. And it is a past I do not wish to remember or recount."

With that, Nihak laid down, rolling over so his back was to the Human. Sarra merely shook her head and turned to the Giant Earth Elf.

"Rom, you take first watch. Ejen and Danira, take the next two during the night," she said, lying down as well.

They nodded in response and settled in for a long night's sleep. Before Nelsh fell into slumber, Danira came over to his bedroll. The healer crouched down and laid a gentle hand on his shoulder.

"A word of caution. Do not stray too near the water at night. People have ventured into the mist-shrouded waters before. None have ever returned."

He nodded his understanding, pulling his blanket tight over his form to ward off the cold as the night deepened.

Fortunately for the wandering warriors, the night passed swiftly, much to their relief. Danira roused them with the aroma of frying bacon and ham, along with the hiss and crackle of eggs. Quickly the rest of them woke and gathered round, sitting tiredly while they rubbed sleep from their eyes.

"Did anyone else hear shrill screaming last night?" Nelsh asked, dark circles under his eyes.

"No. But I heard the creaking of broken boats and the crack of forming stone," Danira replied, divvying even portions of their morning meal for them.

"I heard a woman's cackle," Nihak remarked, shuddering.

"Did any of us even sleep?" Aen wondered, giving Myles a harsh kick to the side. "Except this one?"

The Odd Dwarf let out a surprised squeal and remained lying on his side, legs still crossed in a sitting position.

"Must you be so violent towards him?" Ejen wondered.

"I'm still sore from yesterday's beating, thank you very much. And I'm not as spry as I used to be."

"If we did sleep, it was restless and damn near impossible," Sarra yawned, drawing the Elvan's attention. "How do you know Myles slept well?"

The half-elf gave a dry chuckle. "When you've got a dwarf clinging to your back, snoring in your ear, you know just how well he slept."

The Roamers looked over at Myles, still lying in the position he fell, happily munching on his bacon.

"Bless him for his boundless levity," Nihak chuckled, raising Aen's bottle of cider in toast, then took a deep swig.

"How do you people keep stealing my drink?!" the Elvan demanded.

"We know which pockets you keep them in," the Fire Elf shrugged, taking another drink before tossing it to Ejen.

Aen stuttered and babbled in angry half-words before it was finally returned to him. The others shared in the laughter at the old man's expense as they finished their meal. Once Danira had everything packed away, they rose to their feet more than eager to move on.

"Come. We swing southwest and put as much distance between ourselves and this lake, and the witch's castle," Ejen stated, tucking his war scythe into a crude sheath on his back.

"Aye. And we run," Jolek added, tilting his head, a loud crack emitting from his neck.

"We run?" Nelsh asked, looking among the Roamers.

"Yea. For all day, and the better part of the night as well," Rom answered.

"I can't possibly run for that long," the young Human protested.

"Boy, you've been walking with us for months now. I should think your endurance and stamina have built up, "Aen replied, grinning. "If you can't keep up with an aged man like me, then you're weak."

"I'm not weak!"

"Then prove the old bat wrong!" Nihak laughed, falling into line with the rest as they began a slow jog. It didn't take long though for the Roamers to fall into a dead run, moving side by side instead of single file. Nelsh marveled at his companions, specifically the Earth Elves. Jolek kept a hard pace, his muscular arms pumping rhythmically as his chest heaved evenly with each breath. Rom seemed not to be running, but loping, his long strides carrying him over the land with heavy speed. With each footfall, Nelsh felt the ground shake beneath him as he and the others ran. For every three steps they took, Rom took one, his trunk-like arms swinging lightly as he moved.

As the day wore on, they began to spread out while still keeping their formation. Myles, Jolek, and Rom had remained ahead, with the Odd Dwarf keeping far ahead of the dark-skinned elves. Behind them, Nihak, Ejen, and Aen kept a steady pace, the Fire Elves remaining neck-and-neck ahead of the Elvan. Taking up the rear was Sarra, Danira, and lastly Nelsh who was starting to lag behind. Long after midday had passed, the Roamers slowed to a jog but did not stop to rest. Slowly, they resumed their formation side-by-side, keeping close together. While the Humans panted, sweat pouring down their brows, the elves and dwarf weren't even winded.

"Doing alright, Nelsh?" Nihak asked, patting him gently while they rushed along over the uneven stony ground.

"I'm fine," he managed to say, wiping his forehead.

"Here," Danira called, tossing him a heavy waterskin.

The young Human caught it, stumbling a little from the weight and drank deeply from the oblong pouch. "Does anyone else need water?"

Nelsh looked left, then right and tossed it to Sarra. She too drank deeply and passed the waterskin along to other Roamers parched of thirst.

"Aen, how about some cider?" Ejen asked, grinning broadly.

"Keep your hands off," the Elvan growled, his staff laid over his shoulders to support his arms.

"I've got dried meat," Danira announced, expertly digging through her impossibly deep pack.

"Aye we could all use a meal," Jolek replied.

The witch rapidly tossed the food to each Roamer, all of them gratefully devouring the meat hungrily.

"Has anyone ever considered just buying horses?" Nelsh wondered, his mouth full.

"Say again, lad?" Aen said, cocking his head a little.

"He said we should buy horses," Myles chimed in, grinning.

"How in the Abyss did you understand that?" the Elvan demanded.

The Odd Dwarf opened his mouth, which was stuffed with chewed meat, and started to speak. Before he could, Aen quickly waved his hand in dismissal. "Never mind, don't answer!" he cried.

"Look at me," Rom prompted.

Every Roamer turned their heads up to look at the Giant Earth Elf. "Not all of you. Just Nelsh," he corrected, his chuckle rippling through the air.

Indeed, the young Human kept his attention fixed on his massive companion as they jogged.

"Could a horse bear my weight?"

"No, Rom."

"Not even the great ulunu can carry a Giant Earth Elf," he continued.

"A six-legged shaggy beast twice as big again as your horses," Jolek quickly explained, noticing Nelsh's look of puzzlement.

"So why should we ride while Rom walks?" Sarra asked, directing the question solely at the young Roamer.

"Aye," he replied in understanding. "That does make sense."

"And even if our giant could ride, why should we? The destination is never the point of the journey. The road is," Danira added, smiling as evening set in.

Nelsh nodded again in understanding, a smile slowly raising up his cheeks. "I like that."

With their meals finished, they began to run again. To the boy's great surprise, it felt good to move at that pace once more, like his legs had grown accustomed to the feeling and it hurt when they had slowed to eat and drink. The others nodded and chuckled knowingly at his expression of relief as they flew over the Barren Plains, keeping Alura's castle leagues away to their right. Soon enough, the sun set and still they ran swiftly, loose stones kicked up under their feet.

A sliver of moonlight shed little illumination on the wayward warriors, so they made their own light. Nihak and Ejen held aloft fires blazing upon their open palms while Danira cast orbs of flickering golden light that winked in and out in the dark. The Roamers spoke little now, saving their words so they could breathe easier and faster as they ran. By the time the moon had reached her zenith, they slowed to a gentle halt.

"Rest hard and fast," Aen advised, tossing his staff to the ground, his body quickly following.

Nelsh watched as the Elvan slowed his fall with a gust of wind so his landing was as soft as a feather touching down. He chuckled a little as he picked the softest patch of stony soil he could find, uncaring to the discomfort or lack of bedding.

"We rise at dawn and run for the entire day and some of the night," Sarra added, wrapping her cloak tightly about her form and quickly passing into sleep.

One by one, right after the other, the Roamers passed into deep slumber, not bothering to set a watch. There was nothing out there to be a threat, save Alura, and if the witch wanted to kill or capture them in the night, there was nothing they could really do about it. But they all knew the witch wouldn't bother, not when they stayed on her borders. That woman always had other devious plans to conjure or carry out, so for that night and many more to come, there would be no point in setting a watch to guard the others.

Much too soon for the Roamers, the night ended and dawn woke them with gentle rays of light, warming the chill air. Despite having traveled at such a grueling pace, they were up and moving within the hour, having consumed a light breakfast from Danira. As the day before, so they hurtled swiftly over the ravined ground, leaping and hopping crevices or sliding and rolling down treacherous slopes. Going up steeps hills was hellish on their legs, but still the Roamers pushed on, their eagerness to be away from this desert outweighing any physical pain they felt. By nightfall, exhausted though they were, onward they ran. Once the moon was highest in the sky, only then did they stop and sleep fast.

Thus it was day after day for the wandering warriors. And every day, they drew nearer to the western borders of the Barren Plains. As they swung to the northwest, Alura's castle was soon at their backs, much to their great relief. And soon enough too, as they crested a particularly large hill, they could see a wide horizon of green trees in the near distance.

"Only a few more leagues now," Ejen panted, grinning.

"Try twenty-four," Danira sighed, clapping her hands with forced enthusiasm.

The Roamers set off down the wide slope, not even bothering to stay on their feet. They just followed Myles' example and slid on their bellies or arses, sending a landslide of pebbles and stones cascading down with them. Nelsh beat them all to the bottom, having cleverly ridden on his shield, much to the general cry of "Cheat!" from the others. As quickly as their fading stamina would allow, they set to it, their running speed now reduced to a trotting pace. Even the elves were now slowing down, tired from the distance they had covered in such a short time. The only one who seemed unaffected after days upon days of sprinting and hurtling over the land was Myles. They would have been worried if that was not the case.

Indeed, by the time the Roamers came within five leagues of the Duriviel Forest, they all but collapsed into the dirt, their sides heaving from the ordeal.

"I think we'll make camp here for a day or two just to regain our strength!" Danira panted, dropping her pack with a tremendous clatter!

"Aye," Nihak agreed, falling hard into a sitting position. "Boy."

Nelsh half-stumbled, half fell to his teacher, failing to keep his balance in the end. "Yes, Nihak?"

"Tomorrow your training resumes," the Fire Elf stated, patting his back.

"Am I to be sparring with you, or the old bat?"

Aen, who sat across from them, deftly flicked a pebble Nelsh's way, accurately nailing the boy between his eyes. Groaning in pain, he rubbed the stinging wound, blood trickling down his nose. "Ow!" he growled.

"Nay," Nihak couldn't help but chuckle. "You'll be facing Rom and Ejen."

"What?!" they both demanded in unison.

"Not at once, you fools," the Fire Elf replied, huffing a little. "Rom will be first."

"How am I supposed to fight a giant???" Nelsh asked, disbelief stamped on his face.

"Well you'll find out then, won't you?" his teacher grinned.

"And what of me?" Ejen inquired, propping himself up on his elbows.

"Facing an opponent armed with a war scythe means fighting someone unpredictable. If you can hold your own against someone with skills like that, then no man will stand before you."

Ejen gave a nod of approval and laid his head back down on the ground, letting sleep take him. Nihak grinned and looked to Nelsh. "Get some sleep. We'll be here for a few days."

The young Human nodded and rolled onto his side, sleep taking hold over him instantly. Danira on the other hand found enough energy to dig through her pack, pulling a few parcels of meat from within.

"Is anyone hungry?"

Her query was met with the sound of snoring and deep, steady breath. "More for me then," the witch chuckled softly.

CHAPTER 24

"Move your feet, boy!" Nihak called, sitting alongside Jolek and Ejen.

Nelsh frantically backpedaled as Rom lurched towards him, deliberately stomping his feet to shake the ground.

The Roamers had slept sounder than the dead the previous night, now that their mad rush through the Barren Plains was done. Indeed, most of them did not awake until midday was nearing overhead. Refreshed and sore, Danira took her time preparing a veritable feast of bacon, eggs, fried potatoes, and even honeyed biscuits. After devouring the delicious meal, they took more time for much-needed rest and recovery, joking and laughing as they lazed about. Aen and Danira even drew out their pipes and shared in a hearty smoke of weed, blowing smoke rings to fill the air. Some of the others quickly turned it into a game of accuracy and speed as the Fire and Earth Elves, along with Myles, shot missiles of flame, stone, and ice through the wavering wreaths. As evening drew near though, Nihak turned to Nelsh, directing him to continue his training.

Today's opponent was the Giant Earth Elf, and Nelsh was struggling. The young Roamer had initially struck for Rom's chiseled abdomen, but his sword merely glanced off Rom's stony skin. Grinning, the earth-toned giant gave a booming laugh and sent the boy flying backwards with a light kick. Despite such a gentle blow, Nelsh easily covered seven meters through the air before landing hard. Coughing, the wind gone from his lungs, Nelsh charged forward only to barely avoid a swing of Rom's arm. His method of attack was so terrible that his teacher began calling out to him, giving him help and advice.

However, Nihak's bellowing words of encouragement did little to improve Nelsh's performance in this match. Rom bared his teeth in a wide grin, the giant suddenly charging forward. His speed threw the young Roamer off as the behemoth lunged towards him, his feet leaving dents in the earth as he kicked up stones in his wake. Thinking quickly, Nelsh leapt aside just in time as Rom thundered by. As he tumbled and rolled, his shield came loose, left behind in the dirt.

"Not bad with the evasive jump, but now you have no defense!" Nihak called as Nelsh scrambled to his feet.

"He could break my shield with a single blow!" the boy retorted as Rom gave chase, laughing deeply.

"True, but it's a comfort to have!" the Fire Elf replied, not missing a beat.

"Come on, lad! Think!" Aen shouted, bluish smoke pluming from his mouth. "Where's a giant's weak spots?"

"It's hard to think while being chased by one!" he cried, desperately rolling out of Rom's path once again.

"Learn!" the Elvan shouted back, sticking his pipe between his teeth.

The others shared another laugh as Nelsh came back to his feet and stood his ground as Rom turned about, ready to charge again. Taking a moment, the young Human looked the giant over, muttering to himself. As Rom lunged forward once again, the boy stood his ground, gripping his sword tight in both hands. Just before Rom was upon him, Nelsh stepped to his right, spinning to strike the giant in the back of the knee. To his great surprise, Rom faltered to a stop and fell to one knee, groaning.

"Well go on! Finish him off!" Ejen called, waving Nelsh on.

With a war cry, he ran up behind the giant and swung for the huge elf's thick neck. Rom caught the blade easily with his right hand.

"What?!" Nelsh bellowed as his sword was yanked from his grasp.

Rom rose to his feet and turned to the boy, nodding approvingly. "Well done."

Unsure how to react, Nelsh hesitantly took his sword back, looking about in confusion.

"What did you learn?" Nihak inquired, stepping over to him.

"I'm not entirely sure."

"Look at Rom. What is he?" the Fire Elf prompted.

Nelsh gazed up at the hulking mountainous elf before him. "He's far bigger and stronger than I am."

"So?"

"That means he's tougher and can easily kill me with one or two hits."

"And?" Nihak prodded, nodding.

"I have to be quick and clever in fighting beings much larger than I am."

"Not only that," Jolek interjected. "Indeed, you are on the right path. But there is still more you have learned today."

The young Human racked his brain for the hidden lesson behind their sparring. "I had to bring him down to my level to deal an effective blow."

"Yes!" Jolek cried jubilantly.

Nihak laid a hand on his student's shoulder, offering a smile. "When fighting giants, hitting them in the legs or groin is the best way to bring them down. Then you kill them with a stroke to the head or neck."

"Granted, that'll work for trolls. Not too sure about Earth Elves," Ejen laughed, nudging Jolek in the ribs.

The elves shared in the mirth, Jolek playfully punching Ejen along the shoulder. Though it was light, it still caused the Fire Elf to wince in pain.

"Why is that?" Nelsh had to ask.

"You struck Rom with all your might on the back of his knee," Nihak pointed out, directing the boy's gaze to the giant's leg. "Do you see any blood?"

"Nay," Nelsh replied, shaking his head.

"That's because Earth Elves have notoriously thick flesh. It's almost as hard as stone."

"What do I do if I get in a fight with a Giant Earth Elf?"

"Don't," Aen replied with a smirk.

"He speaks the truth!" Rom boomed, his laughter shaking the very air.

"But if you ever do something that stupid," Sarra called from across the camp, "use a hammer or mace."

So, saying it, the red-haired warrior held aloft her war hammer, grinning wide. Jolek and Rom snorted in unison, waving a hand in dismissal.

"Bah, that is but a toy to us!" Jolek stated, his grin betraying his serious tone.

Giving a mock huff of indignation, Sarra rose from her seat and strode to the elves.

"Shall we put that to the test then?" she asked, brandishing her hammer under Jolek's nose.

The Earth Elf chuckled and unslung his angled warclub from his back, tapping the heavy iron weapon against Sarra's hammer. "Of course."

"Oh goddesses," Danira muttered, giving a lopsided grin as the other Roamers quickly backed away, giving them room to spar.

"You're in for a show, lad," Nihak said, sitting cross-legged next to Nelsh.

"How come I never see any of you spar?"

"No need," Ejen answered. "We already know how to fight and fend for ourselves."

"But on occasion, we do cross blades. Usually over something stupid," Aen added, chuckling as Jolek and Sarra began to circle each other.

Suddenly she leapt forward, hammer sailing in for a strike at the elf's head. Jolek easily parried it, turning his body to the left for a stronger defense. Before she could retract her weapon, he shoved her back with an elbow. Backpedaling to stay on her feet, Sarra steadied herself and ducked Jolek's wide swing, the iron weapon whooshing over her head. After the heavy weapon passed, Sarra rose quickly, swinging her weapon up. The square head collided hard with the elf's chin, snapping his head back violently. Groaning, he rubbed his chin and spat blood from his bitten tongue.

"Ooh Sarra," he muttered, wincing as his jaw emitted a loud crack. "So soft?"

She growled at the jest and aimed for his flank next, the strike blocked by his club. With a yell, he retaliated, gripping his weapon with both hands. Over his head it rose, and down it came with devastating force. Sarra quickly sidestepped it, letting the angled head rend the ground apart. Jolek recovered faster than she anticipated though and was hard-pressed to keep her feet as he slipped his club round her ankle and tripped her up. The Human toppled onto her back, staring up at the Earth Elf as he held the short blade to her neck.

"Only a toy," he chuckled.

"Then why do you look worried?" she grinned, tapping the pike-end between his legs.

"Indeed," he replied, removing his weapon from her neck.

They held their serious stare a moment longer before bursting into laughter. Jolek offered a hand down to her and easily hauled the woman to her feet.

"Next time though, I ask you swing a little softer," he said, rubbing his jaw. "That did hurt a bit."

"Oh, I'm sorry!" she said, genuine concern in her eyes. "I thought you could take it."

"You weren't wrong in saying a hammer is effective."

At that, Danira rose to her feet, striding over to them. "Apparently I'm needed."

"As always," the Earth Elf nodded, letting the witch fix his jaw and heal his tongue.

"Notice anything about their sparring?" Nihak asked, looking to Nelsh.

The boy shook his head. "Seemed he was intent on hitting her as hard as she was hitting him."

"If he did, he would have killed Sarra," came the reply. "Jolek was holding back. Such is the cost of great strength. It takes a great amount of control."

Nelsh gave a nod in understanding. "I'll keep that in mind."

"Good lad," the Fire Elf said. "Now, let us get some food and rest, and we'll continue at our normal pace tomorrow. When we stop for camp, Ejen shall train with you."

The young Roamer glanced over at the taller Fire Elf, who flashed a devious smirk his way.

"I have a feeling Ejen shall enjoy it more than I," he remarked.

"I don't doubt it," Nihak replied as they waited for Danira to prepare their meal.

Once the witch was done working on Jolek's jaw, she set to it, skillfully preparing a pot of roast duck dripping with oil and covered in herbs and spices. The Roamers eagerly and voraciously ripped into the meat, grease messily coating their fingers and mouths.

"Where did you get the duck from?" Aen wondered, licking his hands when he finished.

"I've been holding onto that meat for months now."

"Was it still fresh…?" the Elvan dared ask, rubbing his stomach.

"Of course it was, old bat. I am a witch after all. It doesn't take much to preserve meat with a little magic. Or I can just have Myles hold it for an hour, but I've found that method costs the meat its flavor and tenderness."

"What would we do without you, Danira?" Sarra asked, giving a hearty belch.

"Damned to a life of tasteless, tough meat," she chuckled.

"Was that intended for me?" Nihak wondered, throwing Danira an archer's salute.

"If I still had my swords, I'd be happy to fight you," she stuck her tongue at the Fire Elf.

Chuckling, Nihak laid out his bedroll, the others following suit. Indeed, the sun was quickly setting beyond the trees of the Duriviel Forest, casting the land in a deep orange glow.

"No watches tonight. We're still recovering from that run."

"You all are. That run was child's play to me," Myles piped up with a boyish grin.

"My dear Odd Dwarf, you are a child," Aen stated, tousling his messy hair.

"Am not!"

"Are too," the Elvan muttered before nodding off in his bedding.

All too soon the rest of the Roamers were fast asleep, having had a full day of rest and mirth in the coming dark days. When the sun rose swiftly far to the east, they were up and ready, their bodies invigorated for the final leg of their journey. Danira outdid herself yet again on their morning meal, serving a wide platter of fried potato-cakes, flattened and crispy.

"Do you have an entire farm in that pack?" Nelsh wondered in awe.

"Sorry dear, but a witch has her ways and more than a few secrets," she chuckled.

Nelsh merely stared at her pack, scratching his head in amazement. Noticing the look in his eyes, Aen walked past the boy and whispered, "Don't bother reaching into that cavernous bag. I tried once. Found nothing but a rat trap. It took a lot of convincing for her to heal my fingers."

Blanching at that, Nelsh gave a quick nod and slung his shield over his shoulder.

"If we're all ready, let us move on," Sarra prompted, tightening her sword-belt and heading off for the forest.

The green borders were still a few leagues away, easily within a day's walk for the seasoned Roamers. With the skies clear of clouds and a brisk breeze blowing from the north, they set an easy pace, walking steadily with long strides across the edge of the Barren Plain. Now the rocky terrain was becoming less and less, interspersed with patches of ragged grass and even crumbly dirt instead of dust and rock underfoot. To their great relief as they descended a large hill, they could no longer see Alura's castle at their backs. No doubt the witch knew they'd crossed her lands, but the ragged warriors weren't about to question their luck that she had done nothing to impede their progress.

"What shall we do once we have the Sylvan Sword?" Nelsh asked as they walked, the sun making its way down into evening.

"We'll make our way back east to Sraztari and speak with King Malder. The war won't start until the thaw of spring, so we'll have all winter to prepare."

"Aye but we'll spend a few months trekking through deep snow, not to mention having to stay warm and getting bogged down by harsh storms," Ejen reminded his kin. "And I don't fancy losing my feet to the ice."

"You and I have dealt with the cold before," Nihak replied. "This winter will be no different."

They walked on in silence for a while longer, drawing nearer and nearer to their destination. As they came before the wide trees of the Duriviel Forest, Nelsh asked another question.

"Who will carry the Sword?"

The others stopped and looked at the young Human, their silence leaving him confused and worried. When they said nothing, he asked again. Slowly the Roamers made camp, while Nihak gestured for Nelsh to follow him some ways from the group. They walked silently, Nelsh's heart thumping rapidly in his chest. "Nihak, why-?"

"I will explain. Be silent."

The young Roamer hesitantly closed his mouth at the curt reply. When they stood far enough away, where the Roamers could not hear them, the Fire Elf turned to his student.

"Do you know what the Sylvan Sword is?"

"A powerful weapon crafted by the Forest Goddess, Seylivonia."

Nihak gave a slight nod. "Of course, Ayewndre told you. What else did the Queen say in your talk?"

"That I should take great caution and be warned that removing the Blade will awaken ancient evils," Nelsh replied, shaking a little.

"Then do you know how many species on Greenearth possess the strength to wield such a powerful Sword?" the elf prodded.

Nelsh nodded a little, running his tongue over his dry lips. He swallowed once, feeling a lump in his throat and spoke. "Just two. Forest Elves... and Humans..."

"Aye," Nihak nodded, folding his scarred arms. "And who among our group do you think would be most likely to take such a mantle of power?"

"Just Danira, Sarra, and I."

"Danira gave up the way of the sword long ago. She uses magic and heals wounds and disease."

"Sarra then," Nelsh said, feeling where the conversation was headed.

And he didn't like it.

Nihak slowly shook his head, eyeing the young man who stood before him. "I've talked this over with the others. And in great length, I might add. Originally, when we set out from Cendril, we all agreed that Sarra would be the one to carry it. But when you showed us all what kind of man you've become, well," Nihak paused, allowing a small smile to rise to his lips. "Nelsh, I can think of no one who would wield the Sylvan Sword with more honor and strength than you. I've taught you how to fight and how to survive. You've shown me, shown us, that you are a great warrior. We believe you should be the one to carry the Sylvan Sword."

Nelsh stood in silence when the Fire Elf finished speaking. He? Wield the Sword of the Forest? He looked at Nihak, his mouth gaping open but no words coming forth. His teacher leaned forward and clapped a firm hand on his shoulder.

"Your father would be proud," he said, bringing Nelsh to his senses.

"Aye... he would," he managed to say, smiling a little.

"Come," Nihak gestured back to camp. "You've sparring with Ejen this night. Show us your skills, Nelsh."

As they walked back, Nelsh took note of where each Roamer sat or stood, milling about as they jested among themselves. Danira sat by the fire, preparing their dinner as always. Ejen however, was nowhere to be seen at their camp. Furrowing his brow, eyes narrowing, Nelsh slowly unslung his shield to sit ready on his left arm. As they drew nearer, Nelsh kept a close eye on Rom, the giant sitting cross-legged with Jolek near the fire. Once in the camp-proper, Nihak sat by Sarra while Nelsh kept walking. As he began to turn away from the Roamers and gaze upon the tree line, the hairs on the back of his neck stood out and he spun, shield raised high. Ejen's war scythe bit deeply into his round shield with force, sending Nelsh to his knees.

"Hiding behind Rom," Nelsh stated more than asked, grunting as he tried to stand.

Moving his right hand under his left on the shaft of his scythe, Ejen spun his weapon to the left, violently tearing Nelsh's shield from his arm, nearly breaking the boy's limb in the process. With a cry of pain, the young Human was flung to his right, stumbling as he desperately tried to keep his feet under him. While Nelsh was preoccupied with his balance, the Fire Elf dropped the head of his scythe to the ground and slammed his foot on the shield to dislodge his weapon. The hiss of drawn steel drew his attention back to see Nelsh charging at him, bastard sword gripped in both hands. With a creaking and splintering of wood, accompanied by a shriek of metal, Ejen's scythe popped free. Rapidly spinning the weapon in his skilled hands, the seasoned elf moved forward, the curved blade humming through the air. Wisely the boy pulled up short as the ever-moving scythe blade whooshed in at neck-level. Barely having enough time to react, Nelsh dropped to the ground. Just as quickly, he had to roll aside to evade the wicked blade from ripping through his gut. As Nelsh came to his knees, ready to spring to his feet, Ejen's scythe flashed in from the right at the boy's neck. Just as fast, it halted, the cold edge biting lightly into his flesh. Nelsh grimaced as he felt a few ruby droplets trickle down his throat.

"Dead," Ejen declared, removing the weapon.

"What did you do wrong?" Nihak called from his seat, a safe distance away from the two.

"I dropped and made myself vulnerable on the ground," the boy replied, rising to his feet.

As he walked over to his shield, Ejen's scythe once more flashed before his eyes and stopped at his neck, halting his walk.

"You lost the right to use your shield in this fight. Face me like a Fire Elf!" he demanded.

Nelsh slowly turned to stare at Ejen, his sword gripped knuckle-white in his hand.

"No armor! No shield! Just your weapon and your wits!" the Fire Elf snarled, spinning his staffed blade through the air at the ready.

"Very well," Nelsh replied, setting his feet and raising his blade high over his head.

Ejen took a few paces back, "Ready?"

Nelsh allowed a smirk to dance across his visage. "No."

Lunging forward, the Fire Elf's war scythe sliced through the air before him. The young Human's eyes followed the blade, his bright orbs flitting every which way. As the curved blade came hissing towards Nelsh's left flank, he shifted his feet accordingly, moving out of range. Just as quickly, Ejen brought his staffed blade to bear, swinging in from his left now. Adjusting his left hand to grip the blade while his right stayed on the hilt, Nelsh stepped inside the swing of the scythe, turning to his right as he did so. His sword stopped Ejen's weapon dead, their blades locked. His arms shaken from the strength of the impact, Nelsh tightened his grip, drawing blood down his left palm as he shifted more to his right, his back to the Fire Elf. Before his opponent could react, Nelsh lifted his right leg up, his boot striking Ejen squarely in the ribs.

With a grunt, the Fire Elf stumbled back, his grip on the shaft broken. Grinning in triumph, the young Human turned to face the seasoned warrior. His grin quickly disappeared as Ejen recovered, far quicker than he expected. Growling, his pride wounded more than his chest, the Fire Elf drew his knife and sickle-sword and attacked with a vengeance. Nelsh was quick to change his grip to have both hands on the blade, moving his sword more like a staff to stave off several slashes from various angles, all the while backpedaling. Ejen did not let up, growling as he hooked Nelsh's sword at the hilt. Sharply pulling to his right, the Fire Elf brought his knife up, held in a reverse-grip, and stopped short of slitting the boy's throat.

"Dead."

Panting, Nelsh dropped his sword. He glanced over at the others as Nihak rose, striding over to them and picking up Ejen's fallen scythe as he went.

"Well done!" he cried, clapping a hand on Nelsh's shoulder.

"But I lost twice," the boy said as Ejen returned his weapons to his belt.

"Doesn't matter," the Fire Elf replied, grinning. "You did something countless warriors before you could not: you disarmed Ejen of his scythe."

"Bah! I went easy on him!" his older counterpart snapped, taking his scythe back.

As he stalked to camp, and his bedroll, he glanced back at Nelsh. "You've got a warrior's spirit though, lad. And I respect that."

Nihak knelt and took up Nelsh's bastard sword, handing it to his student. "Ejen is a prideful elf and has never known defeat. Truly, you've come a long way, Nelsh."

The Fire Elf led his young friend back to camp where he received a hot bowl of stew along with the others. They ate in silence, savoring the delicious meal as always. Afterwards, the young Human rose to his feet and retrieved his shield, examining it with quiet irritation.

"Look at this notch…" he muttered.

"It's still perfectly functional and bears the mark of battle," Ejen stated, lying upon his bedroll. "Bear it proudly in the coming war."

"I suppose," Nelsh replied, following suit, resting his round shield under his crude pillow.

"Get your rest," Nihak said, still sitting upright as the fire's shadows danced across the lying forms of the Roamers. "Tomorrow we delve to the very heart of Duriviel. Your training is over for now."

Nelsh fell asleep to those words, thinking back on all he'd been through since that fateful day he joined the Roamers. The young warrior chuckled in his sleep as he dreamt of his first fight with his teacher. It was a restful night's sleep for the wandering band until the dawn came, the sky blushing crimson on the final days of their long quest.

CHAPTER 25

Nelsh craned his head back, gazing to the tops of the trees as the wind rattled and rustled their grey limbs. A shudder coursed up his spine, whether from the cold blustery air or from some unexplainable feeling of dread, he couldn't say. The sun shone fiercely at his back, yet the shafts of hued light did nothing to warm his being. Before him yawned the deepening maw of the Duriviel woods. Behind him, his companions finished packing up camp while Ejen clenched his fist to extinguish the campfire. Slowly, the Roamers stepped up to the tree line, standing alongside Nelsh as they gazed into the seemingly abyssal woodland.

"Does 'Duriviel' mean anything in Forelvish?" Nelsh had to ask, Nihak standing upon his right.

"It used to. Now it just means 'Empty'," Nihak answered, glancing left and right at his fellow Roamers.

They needed no signal, no words. None of them needed to tell the others to move forward, to set foot in such an untouched place. As a band of different races, bonded through battle and bloodshed, enduring countless terrors and hardships in all their wanderings, the nine Roamers stepped past the first tree as one in soul and steel.

The very air seemed to shift before them, feeling as though they had stepped through a viscous wall of tree sap. Their hearing muffled for but a moment, most of them did not pause as they continued to walk past the first few towering sentinels of the woods. Nelsh halted and looked about, seemingly engulfed by the flora of the forest, the canopy rising higher and higher into the sky. His breath catching in his throat, the young Human felt as if he was choking. About to clutch at his neck, Danira grabbed his hands, squeezing them tightly.

"Nelsh!"

With a rushing whoosh, as if he was bursting to the surface of a raging sea, sound returned to his senses. Frantically, he tried to pull away as the shock of flooding sensations assaulted his ears, but the witch held him fast.

"Nelsh!" she called again, staring him in the eyes. He stared back, his breathing slowly returning to normal. "You have to keep your wits about you in this place."

"Aye, else you'll lose your senses, be it one or all of them. Soon enough you'll become lost within this labyrinth and eventually die," Aen stated, walking past them, his staff tapping the ground lightly.

"How do we find our way…?" the young man asked slowly, looking about to see the Roamers spread around in a loose circle.

A sharp clatter of stone could be heard, and all heads turned to gaze upon Myles, who had been using his axe in similar fashion to Aen.

"There are stone-lined paths spread throughout these woods," Nihak explained as Aen swung his staff, sending debris and leaf-litter scattering to the wind, revealing a wide pathway lined with black stones.

The path itself was trodden dirt, packed down from hundreds of marching feet. Quickly gathering to this lonely road, the Roamers followed it with their eyes, seeing it twist and curve among the trees, quickly disappearing into the depths of the darkening place.

"If we stay on this path, we'll get to the sword soon enough."

With that said, Aen took the lead, using his staff to keep their path cleared of fallen leaves and twigs. The rest of the Roamers fell in relative line behind the Elvan, Nelsh and Nihak staying in the center. Myles stayed close to his older companion, for even the Odd Dwarf was reserved and quiet in the foreboding forest. Danira took up the rear with Jolek while Ejen stayed near the front. Rom and Sarra kept pace behind Nelsh, all eyes shifting and staring about them, keeping their surroundings in check.

"Why do the Forest Elves call this place the Empty Forest?" Nelsh wondered, his right hand subconsciously gripping the hilt of his sword.

"No. Just 'Empty'. As to why, listen," Nihak prompted, gesturing about them as they walked.

The young man did just that, his footfalls making only the slightest noise as his boots scrapped against the packed earth. Aside from the sounds of their movement, the young Roamer could hear nothing. Not a single bird called, nor a single animal moved in the gaze of the corner of his eye. For that matter, now that Nelsh thought of it, he hadn't even seen a single creature upon their entering these woods. As he strained his ears, almost desperate to pick out a sound in the ever-deafening roar of the forest's silence, one noise did seem to come through.

Creaking.

The harder he tried to listen, the louder the creaking grew. High above them the tree tops shivered and shook, moved by unseen winds. As the foliage swayed to and fro, the creaking of their wooden limbs and trunks grew louder and louder until Nelsh could bear it no more, slapping his hands over his ears. He gritted his teeth as the deafening sounds quieted, until all he could hear again was silence.

"It's best not to focus on what you can hear," the Fire Elf explained, his voice too loud in the Human's ears. "Remember, this place will play tricks on you, be it on the mind or the senses."

"Why did the elves abandon this woodland?" the curious Nelsh had to ask.

"When the gods and goddesses of the elements gave each race their Sword, the bloodshed became insurmountable. So, they forced our ancestors to call a truce and hide the Blades away, never to be disturbed. From what the legends say, each weapon had a different effect upon their particular region," Ejen explained, surprising both his kin and the young man.

"And this Sword?"

"This was the result," Nihak answered his student, sweeping his arm about them. "A suffocating blanket of dread and hopelessness. Would you want to live in such an everlasting state of despair?"

The young Roamer quickly shook his head.

"Nor did the ancestors of the Forest Elves."

"But I thought this was a weapon of Good," Nelsh said, puzzled by Nihak's statement. "Why would it create such a terrible feeling?"

"Why indeed," Sarra replied, pulling her hood over her head.

"No one knows, lad," Aen answered for the Fire Elves. "My father's people have their own tales of the Ventys Sword, how it howls loudly atop its lonely peak, so much that no one can stand to hear it lest they are driven mad."

"Which is odd because the Ignis Sword gives off feelings of comfort and bliss," Ejen remarked, smiling a little.

"I felt no such warmth in that Sword's presence," Nihak stated, venom in his voice.

"Bah! You never did appreciate the gift your clan gave you for being born in that holy mountain," Ejen spat, glaring sidelong at his kin.

"Peace, please I beg," Danira said, stepping between them as they moved along the winding path.

"She's right," Nihak sighed. "We shouldn't be at each other's throats, least of all in this wretched place."

Ejen gave a scornful laugh. "Never thought I'd hear you say 'wretched' in a forest. I take it as a sign of humor from Ignicendir and leave it at that!"

Nihak left it as well, loathe though he was to retort again. Danira shot him a warning glare that cowed his anger and he remained silent. Nelsh looked between the two elves, questions written in his eyes.

Noticing the look, Danira shook her head again, halting his questions on his tongue. Wisely, the young Human stayed his words and kept silent on the matter.

As the Roamers continued on, stepping through beams of gray light shafting down through the thick canopy above, Nelsh began to notice strange roots protruding from the bases of the trees. As he paused to better examine one, he noticed that though the root was gnarled and twisted, it maintained a relatively straight shape, bent only once near the middle. At the end of the upraised tendril, were five knobbed and bent branches. Nelsh's eyes widened in horror at what it resembled and quickly backed away from it, drawing the other Roamers' attention.

"What is it, boy?" Ejen demanded, moving to grip his scythe in both hands.

"Those roots! They... they look like..." Nelsh dared not finish the sentence, lest saying it somehow made it true.

Nihak approached one of the eerie sprouts sticking from the dry ground. "It's just the forest playing more tricks on you, Nelsh."

"Nay, they seem quite real," the young man retorted, his voice shaky.

"Pay it no mind," Aen said, waving his hand dismissively.

Nelsh managed a nod and fell in line with them along the path again, all too eager to leave the foreboding tree roots behind. He found little relief though as the further into the forest they delved, the more he and the others spied twisted sprouts appearing in greater and greater numbers upon the woodland floor. Dead, dry leaves fluttered amongst the upraised roots, rustling along the creaking and cracked wood as a fierce wind rose up, howling about them. With a cry of surprise, the band of warriors huddled together, Rom moving to the front of the group to bear the brunt of the gale. A wave of leaves roared past them, hitting them with enough force to sting their flesh.

"What sorcery is this?!" Sarra demanded, shielding her face with her arms.

"We could be drawing near to the center!" Nihak shouted to be heard.

"How?" Nelsh cried, tucking his shield close to his face and chest. "We've only been in these woods for half a day!"

Just as suddenly, the winds stopped and the leaves settled into a blanket of gray and brown, completely carpeting the ground. Aen was quick to swing his staff about, sending powerful gusts of wind to clear their path.

"Time has no meaning in this forest," the Elvan stated once he was done. He pointed up at the trees, directing Nelsh's gaze. Not a single green leaf lay upon the twigs and branches.

"How...?" he wondered, looking among his fellow comrades, confusion stamped on his face.

"This is one of the oldest forests in the land. It carries ancient magic that none of us could ever hope to understand. Time holds no power here. We could have only been gone a few hours to the outside world. Or we could have already spent a week in here. We won't know until we get out again," Nihak explained.

"How do you know all this?"

"Queen Ayewndre told me as much as she could of the stories surrounding this woodland. Even she doesn't know which stories are true, and which are legend. The absence of time was one of the few truths she warned me of."

"Any others I should know of?" Nelsh asked, following Aen as he continued clearing their way.

The Fire Elves fell in step beside him, the rest of the Roamers following.

"She told me there may be fell creatures in these woods. So far it seems she was wrong."

"And we're glad for it!" Jolek exclaimed, his warclub gripped tight in his hand. "I do not wish to be in this cursed forest any longer than we have to. It is evil... Rom and I can feel it in the earth beneath our feet!"

"There is no life in the soil?" Myles inquired, scratching his chin lightly.

"I did not say that," Jolek replied, kneeling to scoop a handful of dirt into his hand. "I said it is evil. Something lays beneath us and we should not linger to find out what it is."

So saying it, he flung the gray soil from his hand in disgust, shaking it in the air to rid himself of any remnants of the foul stuff. At the Earth Elf's prompting, Aen picked up the pace, leading them further and further in. Despite the canopy being devoid of greenery, they could not see the sun. It was as if the great fiery orb in the sky had been shrouded eternally in misty clouds. However, the skies did begin to darken soon enough, but no moon shone, nor any stars winked in the blackening night. There was just enough gray light though for the Roamers to barely make their way through the trees on the winding path. Even when the Fire Elves and the witch created light, their flames and magic were reduced and muffled, giving very little illumination. Still the Roamers pressed on in the silence, not knowing what would happen if they stopped.

Fortunately for them, almost as swiftly as darkness fell, light returned in what felt like only a mere few hours. Grateful for that, they hurried on, now more eager than ever to find the Sword and get out. Every so often, Danira passed around waterskins and dried food, though not a single Roamer had felt the pangs of hunger or the parched scratch of dry throats. Still, the witch insisted they all keep their strength up, even if they didn't feel weak.

As the light began to fade, despite only five hours passing for a day this time, the path began to change. Indeed, the road had begun to grow wider and wider, so broad that it could accommodate all the Roamers if they walked abreast. The stones lining the path soon joined up with other paths as well, until they found themselves in a wide clearing. In the center stood a massive willow tree, its green-leafed vines swaying gently in a non-existent breeze, the trunk and thick boughs creaking softly. Approaching with caution, the Roamers gazed transfixed upon the sight before them. They barely noticed the patches of grass and soft spread of moss beneath their feet as they looked past the veil of vines.

Stuck in the tree was a broadsword of unsurpassable glory. Its pommel was an emerald orb, glinting with unnatural light from within that swirled and shimmered in a mesmerizing sheen. The crossguard were that of ash leaves, vibrant and lifelike while the hilt was patterned to the likeness of tree bark, yet smooth as glass. The blade itself was the shade of deep forest green, shining brightly despite the dim light of the woods. As the Roamers gathered about the Goddess' Sword, the iridescent pommel began to pulsate with life.

CHAPTER 26

"Can you feel it?" Nihak said, his voice but a half-whisper.

"Are all the Elemental Swords like this?" Nelsh wondered, staring in awe at the Blade.

"Aye, they give off quite an aura," Ejen breathed, for even he was struck by the intensity of energy radiating from the godly weapon.

"Take it, Nelsh," Danira prompted, urging the Roamer with a slight push.

Slowly the young man stepped forward. As he did so, he felt an invisible force beginning to pull him towards the Sword. Was it the Blade itself calling to him? He recalled his conversation with Ayewndre, but she had said nothing about this. A mere few paces had been taken and suddenly Nelsh found himself standing before the hilt. His soft eyes filled with shimmering green light as he stared into the depths of the pommel. Peering deeper into the orb, he could almost make out a woman's face, Her hair falling in thick tresses of wavy green, adorned by leaves and willow vines.

"Seylivonia...?" he murmured, his right hand reaching out to grasp the hilt.

Slowly his fingers curled about the handle, the Sword's aura jolting through his arm and spreading throughout his body. Still he held fast and began to pull.

The Blade did not budge.

Tugging harder, Nelsh found the Goddess' weapon remained stuck firmly in the trunk of the willow. Giving a short huff of breath and steeling himself, Nelsh wrapped his other hand about the hilt and braced his boot against the base of the tree. He began to pull again, slowly at first, but building in strength and resolve. His muscles bulging, tendons straining, a growl of determination and effort formed on the young man's face as he put everything he had into freeing the Sylvan Sword. Time seemed to halt as he let out a silent scream as the Blade came loose, sending a massive crack jagging up the willow's core.

The Roamers stood silent as Nelsh held the Sword aloft in both hands, his eyes running up and down the length of the magnificent weapon. It was warm to the touch, as if something were living within it. As his eyes once again fell to the emerald pommel, Nelsh could feel the singular power, the energy, of all growing things radiating from its glimmering depths.

"Who are you that has freed me?"

Nelsh jumped in surprise at the voice. He looked about him, as if the speaker would be among them. But the only people around him were his fellow Roamers.

"You alright, lad?" Aen asked.

Nelsh managed a nod, then turned his eyes back to the Sword as the voice prodded again for an answer.

"I am Nelsh Velzen. I am a Roamer and we have journeyed far to find you." He thought, keeping the conversation between him and the Sword.

"My Lady wishes me to be used in war again? This is most strange."

"No…well yes."

The Sword gave pause, as if contemplating Nelsh's strange answer. As he stood by, the crack from the willow expanded loudly, the tree giving a mighty groan of protest. To the Roamers' surprise and worry, the widening maw lanced down into the earth, splitting the green soil. The growing fissure jagged away into the crowded trees of the woodland, causing low rumbling underfoot.

"Nelsh, what just happened?" Jolek cried, staring out into the forest, his brow furrowing with concern.

"Sword???"

He felt indignation all but spewing from the weapon as it shook a little in his hands.

"I beg your pardon?! 'Sword'? I have a name! Or should I just call you 'Human'?"

If Nelsh had ever stuttered in his mind, he did so now, fumbling for an answer as the emerald sphere began to glow brightly, a soft humming could be heard accompanying it as the light grew in intensity.

"I meant no offense. What are you called? And what are you doing…?"

"I am Servant of the Forest Goddess, Giver of Life. I was not meant to be drawn until my Lady deemed it necessary. Did you not feel the warnings and not see the signs to turn you back? I must now give my Final Defense. I shall tell you my name if you live through this."

With that said, the Sylvan Sword went silent and a wave of deep green energy pulsed from the pommel, rushing over the Roamers and spreading through the forest in an ever-widening circle of light. It dispersed almost as quickly as it was created, leaving the band of warriors in a deathly silence.

The oppressing stillness, smothering them like a leaden weight did not last long. Beyond the clearing, the sound of snapping wood and violent creaking rose in a disjointed chorus, echoing among the trees.

"Come! Let us leave while we may!" Danira cried, rushing from the clearing, the others quickly on her heels.

As the Roamers stepped back onto the path they had followed in, they halted in confusion as a veil of mist began to cloud their way, making sight difficult a mere ten meters away. What they could make out struck terror in even their stout hearts.

The peculiar "roots" Nelsh had been so terrified of, were moving. The five crooked appendages curled and cracked as fingers and the bent section moved as an elbow. Grotesque arms were slapping the ground as cracks split the earth about them and horrid creatures hauled themselves from the earth, bent and hobbled. Steel hissed loudly as the Roamers drew their weapons, staring into empty socketed eyes of ghoulish monsters with bark-like skin and creaking limbs.

"By the Goddess…" Nihak breathed, his left-hand alighting in fire.

"I don't give a damn if this is a forest, my flames shall bite their flesh and obliterate their bones to ash!" Ejen snarled, gripping his war scythe tightly.

"With my blessings," his kin replied.

"What are they?" Nelsh demanded, clenching the Sylvan Sword tightly in his sweating hands.

"You tell me," his teacher replied, eyes flitting about them as more and more of the strange zombie-like creatures drew near. "What does the Blade tell you?"

"She isn't talking. She said she would if I live through this…"

"Countless times before, we have been outnumbered and outflanked. We cut down anyone in our path. We will do so again!" Jolek bellowed, his war cry rivaled only by Rom's booming roar.

The Giant Earth Elf raised his thick leg and brought it down hard, the force of the blow jolting the ground before them, jagging and cracking the earth in stony shards. The ruptured land sent dozens of the wooded ghouls flying off their feet, clearing a temporary path for the Roamers.

Forward they charged, pounding feet stampeding forward in bursts of fire and blasts of icy missiles, rock and stone ripped from the earth to sail into the hordes of monsters. Aen stayed at the head of the charge, staff lowered in a constant whirling storm of wind. That concentrated cyclone of shrieking air was strong enough to knock most of the creatures off their feet. Jolek and Rom stayed near the aged Elvan, the Earth Elf's mighty club shattering the skeletal monsters with ease. Rom ripped the ground asunder, be it for clearing swarms of the beasts or using shards of stone as crude missiles to splinter their bodies apart.

Behind the Earth Elves, Sarra and Nelsh closed ranks with Danira and Myles. Falx and Sylvan Sword raised high and cut down anything that came too close to their flanks. Long spindly arms swung and struck, twisted claws seeking to sink deeply into warm flesh. Sarra's curved blade severed arms and heads, even cleaving through tough torsos, her hair wild about her screaming visage. Nelsh parried and blocked, their arms crackling against the enchanted steel. He sliced a ghoul in half, the torso opening wide its splintered maw and gave a gut-wrenching growl, reaching out for his legs before Myles split its head in two with his axe. As the warriors cut their enemies down, blackened sap-like blood spurted from their wounds, coating the Roamers' faces and weapons in the foul-smelling muck. While the Humans were busy, Myles watched Danira's back as the witch cast orbs of light, sending them streaking through the air to flash or burst. Some emitted white-hot sparks to light ghouls afire, while others sent bolts of crackling lightning to cinder holes through their wood-carapaced hides. The Odd Dwarf hacked apart ghoul after ghoul, splitting their bodies with ease. When no targets presented themselves within axe-range, he created sharpened shards of ice and sent them flying into the monsters' faces, dropping them instantly.

Bringing up the rear was Ejen and Nihak. The Fire Elves staved off the great host as the creaking monstrosities shambled and stalked after the Roamers. Longsword flashed in the dim light and cold scythe blurred through the air, mowing down dozens of ghouls seemingly all at once. While one used his steel to keep the enemy at bay, the other laid down a wide swathe of fire behind their ranks, consuming everything in its blazing path.

The forest burned bright as the light faded, destruction spreading ever farther through the forsaken woodland. Still the band of warriors did not stop, jets of flame and bolts of silvery lightning lit the night, eerie shadows splashed on the trees as the ground ran thick with dirtied stale blood. Ceasing his fiery blasts, Nihak took up his blade in both hands and severed limbs and ran ghouls through by the dozens, snarling in Forelvish at the cursed creatures. Ejen stopped his gyrating weapon and held aloft his right hand to pulse balls of fire into the midst of their foes. Wherever the volatile missiles struck, be it the ground, a tree, or a ghoul, they exploded in a violent burst of flames, engulfing everything within meters of the blasts.

Legs pumping hard and feet pounding, the Roamers noted with dismay what light they had from above turned to grey dusty night, making it nearly impossible to see the ghouls around them. The creaking of their limbs and snapping rattles of their joints neared to deafening noise in the pitch-black forest. Hardened claws tore and ripped in the gloom as the warriors hurried on. Indeed they were making good headway against the endless swarm, that is until the monsters began to drop down on them from above. Danira gave a shriek of surprise and pain as one wooded ghoul leapt upon her back, tearing into her shoulders. Myles' axe bit deeply, chopping the creature nearly in half below the arms, dousing the wounded witch in foul blood. Sarra then skewered the still-moving ghoul on her falx and finished it off. The other Roamers stopped, Rom and Jolek quickly erecting barricades of earthy rock to prevent further attacks. Just as quick, the Odd Dwarf created a roof of ice over their makeshift shelter, giving them all a momentary respite.

In the darkness, the Fire Elves lit tiny orbs of flame to light their cramped space. Outside, they could hear claws and teeth scraping and shrieking as the monsters feverishly tried to break in.

"How bad is it?" Danira asked, unslinging her pack to relieve her wounds.

"They're deep but you'll live," Aen said, examining the gashes in the flickering light.

Sighing, she dug through her bag until she produced a jar filled with blackish-green mud.

"One of you needs to smear this into my wounds, and don't be gentle about it. Stick your fingers in and spread that sludge well. I don't need any infections or diseases taking hold."

Sarra took the jar from her and dipped her slender fingers in, wincing at the squelching it made as she scooped it out. Turning her head away a little, the auburn-haired warrior began spreading the mud in thick layers over Danira's wounds. The witch flinched as Sarra dug her slick fingers into the deep claw marks. Once she was done, Danira pulled bandages from her pack and wrapped them about her shoulders with Aen's help. Sarra quickly wiped her hands clean of the slippery paste and sat down with a sigh, her bloodied falx laying across her lap.

The others sat or knelt, all panting hard from their mad rush through the forest; their adrenaline was all but spent. Rummaging through her pack, the witch produced several waterskins and square-packed food wrapped in paper.

"Everyone eat these and drink if you can. We'll need every bit of our strength if we wish to make it out of this alive," she stated.

Nelsh did his best to ignore the sheer noise of creaky growling and scratching as the monsters incessantly tried to break in. He took a waterskin and drank deeply, not realizing how parched he was. The food he unwrapped noisily, the dry paper crinkling in his hands. Within lay a neat little block of what looked like bread and meat and herbs. The young man found it to be delightfully chewy with a sharp kick of flavor, changing from garlic to beef. With the reduction of his hunger, Nelsh found his strength returning, and rapidly so.

"We can't possibly fight them all off," Jolek sighed, massaging his right arm. "Even with our abilities."

"Nay, we need to be smart about this. If we can somehow just punch through their ranks like a battering ram, we just might make it," Aen stated, leaning back, his breathing labored.

"But we must protect our heads from attacks above," Myles pointed out, scratching his chest.

As he spoke, a hole was punched through their icy roof, an elongated claw wildly grabbing at anything it could. The Odd Dwarf leapt up and shot his hand forth, sending a short burst of ice to seal the hole up, leaving the ghoul atop stuck by the arm. Just for spite, Ejen stood and deftly swung his scythe, shearing the limb in two, drawing an angered snarl from above.

"Tough bastards..." he muttered.

"Rom, Jolek," Nelsh said, leaning forward in the dim light. "I've an idea."

"Let's have it," the Earth Elf said, leaning forward as well.

"It will require great strength on both your parts. If Rom could rip a slab of stone from the earth and carry it over his head as a shield, while you make a wedge from two smaller slabs of stone as well, like a ram. You two could put them together and we make one final rush."

"What of our flanks?" Nihak asked, grinning a little.

"I have enough strength left in my fingers to create a barrier of light. Nihak, you and Ejen, Myles and Aen, you will all be our guard. Sarra and Nelsh, you will defend our rear and cut down any ghoul that comes at us from behind."

They all slowly nodded, the plan coming together.

"If any one of us falters, it could be our doom," Ejen stated, knowing they were all thinking it.

"Then may each of you make peace with your God or Goddess. But I have no plans in letting any of you fall, nor any of you letting me fall," Nihak replied, standing up, longsword in hand. "There are many fine days to die. But not today."

So, saying it, the Roamers rose to their feet, tired but resolved.

"We'll need something to buy Rom and Jolek some time to make our ram," the Elvan said, summoning his broadsword to his hand.

"Leave that to me. On my signal, drop the walls," Danira replied, then began to speak in Archaic, runes of golden light beginning to swirl about her hands. *"Chasidir mieh ona Suolxes nesia asikrusen ona brisnekotadi ~ Chasidir mieh ona Suolxes nesia asikrusen ona brisnekotadi ~ Chasidir mieh ona Suolxes nesia asikrusen ona brisnekotadi."*

The others braced themselves, ready for whatever fate awaited them. With the magical field of golden light surrounding the witch growing more and more intense, humming fiercely, she bellowed, "Now!"

Myles waved his arms wide, the icy roof exploding outward in a blast of glacial shards, blowing ghouls off their shelter with many impaled by flying blades of frozen glass. Rom and Jolek leveled their earthy barriers and for a split second, time stood still as the hordes of ghouls stared at them, ready to pounce and tear the intruders to bloody pieces. Danira spread wide her arms, shouting the last words of her spell and a sphere of pure light burst forth from her hands, quickly growing to envelop everything in the forest. The force of energy passed over the Roamers and struck the ghouls hard, sending them flying off their feet.

Rom wasted no time slamming his hands into the ground. Growling with effort, he began to lift, the earth cracking loudly in protest.

"Arrute forgive me!" he cried, ripping a long slab of stone from the crusted soil.

Grunting with effort, the Giant Earth Elf held it above his head, the stone four meters in length and two across in width, giving the Roamers enough space to move while staying close together.

While Rom did that, Jolek struck the ground hard twice with his warclub, splitting the earth with wide cracks. Driving his free left hand into one, Jolek gripped the stone and pulled aloft a thinner slab, just over three meters in height and two in length. Once it was free of the ground, Jolek slung his club over his back and ripped a similar stone from the other crack. Gritting his teeth, the dark-skinned elf lifted both flat stones up and snapped them together, forming a crude wedge. Gripping it tight, Jolek moved before Rom, the giant resting the tip of his stone roof atop the head of their makeshift battering ram. Quickly the Roamers moved under the shelter of the Earth Elves' creation, while Danira waved her arms slowly through the air, chanting, *"Faesi mieh murgar frimgail."* Dappled golden light sparked from her fingertips as magical barriers covered their exposed flanks. The rest of the Roamers took their positions in front and behind Rom, weapons at the ready.

"Charge!" Jolek roared, hefting the stones and ran forward, Rom moving in step with him.

The rest of the warriors kept pace as well, fire, ice, and wind blasting forth through the barriers of light. Recovered from the magical blast, the hordes of monsters gave a scream of defiance and rushed the band of Roamers, their bodies being crushed and smashed from the force of the ram. Similarly, no tree could stand in the way of the onslaught either, the Earth Elves felling dozens of them on their blind rush. Wood-carapaced bodies flew in every direction from the wedged head, while many others tried in vain to gain purchase atop the stone shield. Golden light flared with every strike from the ghouls upon Danira's barriers, causing the woman to grunt with effort each time.

"You need to keep them off the light. It costs me more energy to sustain the barriers if they hit them!"

Nihak, Ejen, Myles, and Aen nodded and increased the vigor of their attacks. Powerful jets of fire and flashing sword and scythe kept the monsters at bay. Ice froze and impaled, patches growing on the forest floor to send the ghouls sliding chaotically out of control into each other. Cyclones of wind shot forth to knock ghouls off their feet, some gusts powerful enough to tear limbs and torsos apart the closer the ghouls came.

At the rear, Nelsh and Sarra cut down any creatures trailing after them in the wake of their carnage. The barrier still protected them, but their swords sailed through with ease, running the ghouls through, or hacking their heads from their shoulders. The pair of Humans took it in turns, one covering the rear flanks while the other spun to attack directly behind their sheltered ram. As they kept up their mad charge, the numbers of fallen ghouls began to increase dramatically.

"We must be close if they're putting up such resistance!" Jolek growled, hefting the stone ram.

"Onward then!" Rom bellowed, matching his kin's increasing pace.

Indeed, the ghouls had gathered en-masse and were doing everything in their power to stop the Roamers' makeshift battering ram. Their bodies began to pile up against the stone wedge, frantically trying to halt the relentless charge. The wood-fleshed monsters began to leap atop it, piling on in an attempt to weigh the ram down. Growling under the added weight, Rom kept it aloft, refusing to drop the growing bulk on his shoulders. The Earth Elves let out screams of defiance as they rushed past the last line of trees, sending multiple ghouls flying from the forest's borders, and sending more than a few trees to slam into the ground. As debris and bodies flew wide, Nelsh felt the Sylvan Sword vibrate once in his hands and the pommel emitted another arching pulse of magic.

He watched as the wave of energy struck the ghouls beyond the forest borders and they immediately disintegrated to dust. Glancing back at the tree line of the Duriviel Forest, the young Roamer stared as a barrier of green light shone among the trees and into the sky, and then vanished.

Roaring with finality, Rom hefted the stone slab high and heaved it aside, the heavy mass of rock sailing slowly through the air before it crashed into the ground many meters away. Similarly, Jolek gave a cry of exertion and flipped the massive stone wedge away from them, the two slabs cracking and crumbling apart as they slammed into the earth. Finally, the Roamers came to a stop, all dropping to their knees, unable to even stand any longer. All heaved for breath, their energy and strength utterly spent from their desperate flight.

"We've done it!!!" Nihak cried, his jubilance undiminished despite the fact his body shook from exhaustion.

Nelsh had collapsed to lay on his back, holding the coveted holy Sword up just enough to stare into the swirling jeweled orb.

"You may call me Seyva."

"Was that your Final Defense?"

"Indeed. The Heem'lokru were cursed to keep me from leaving the Duriviel Forest should anyone deemed unworthy lay hands on me. However, since you have all survived their onslaught, you are certainly worthy."

"Good to know. What happens now?"

"For now, rest. You are all battle-worn and weary. I am rightfully yours now, Nelsh Velzen. I shall teach you my powers and how to use your own with time. But sleep now."

Indeed, before he could ask any more questions, the young man felt soothing waves of energy wash over him from the enchanted Blade, rocking him gently to sleep in a cradle of leafy boughs. Eyelids already heavy with fatigue, Nelsh quickly found himself slipping into deep slumber, his last sight that of a dark gray sky filled with darker clouds.

*****

Hours passed for the Roamers. Some slept. Others merely took their rest on their knees or sat. For Nelsh, the young Human was rudely awoken with burning pain stabbing through his chest. He snapped awake and found himself staring into a pair of cold, icy blue eyes.

"Hello, Nelsh," Alura smirked.

The Roamers leapt to their feet, weapons in hand, weary though they were.

"Alura!" Nihak snarled, his blade leveled at her back. "You've no business here! Be gone!"

"Oh please," the witch laughed, straightening to her full height.

She turned about slowly, eyeing each warrior coolly, smiling into their violent faces, chuckling at the pathetic weapons pointed her way. Sluggishly the Roamers moved to encircle her, while Nelsh stayed upon the ground, some unknown force locking his limbs.

"None of you even have the strength to fight. Lower your weapons and I may consider mercy," Alura gloated, grinning wide.

"You've lied in the past!" the Fire Elf growled, lowering his longsword.

It was not because he believed her. Far from it. The witch's stinging words were painfully true: none of them had any strength left. A few paltry hours were not nearly enough time to allow them all to regain even half their energy. The others slowly followed suit, keeping their arms in hand, but lowered in weakened grips.

"Oh, and I do have business here, dear Nihak," she chuckled, stepping up to the Fire Elf.

They locked eyes, their faces a mere handspan from each other. Alura casually reached up and laid a soft hand upon his chest, smirking as she taunted him, daring the elf to lash back at her. Wisely, Nihak made no such move, but still his eyes smoldered with hatred and fiery anger.

"So defiant, even in defeat," she said, her voice low and gentle. "You had so much potential."

"Enough with your mocking!" he spat. "If you are not here to fight, then state why you came and be done with it!"

"Oh, very well," the witch sighed, turning away from him back towards Nelsh.

The young man looked up at her, terror evident in his gaze as he attempted to move, but still something held him down. Alura stopped as she came to stand over him, her eyes piercing through his very being. He stared back into those hollow orbs of ill-intent, catching only a glimpse of what evil lay within her soulless body.

"I will take what is rightfully mine," she stated, the words scouring over Nelsh's flesh like shards of ice peeling his skin.

"There is nothing here that is yours!" Danira snapped.

"Isn't there?!" Alura retorted, whirling to face her fellow witch. "For one so gifted in our Craft as you, you know so little. Be silent, mewling child. When I wish to have a nail fixed, I will come to you."

"Alura, you-"

"Did I give you permission to speak?" she demanded, cutting Sarra off mid-sentence. Her voice was quiet and calm, but they all knew what dangers lurked behind that deceiving tone.

"Enough of this!" Nihak growled. "What makes you think anything here is yours? You cannot take the Sylvan Sword. You can't even lay a hand upon it, so be gone!"

The white-clad witch turned once more to face the Fire Elf, her frown turning into a devilish smirk. "You know, that never occurred to me. Damn my arrogance," she said in mock-defeat, dramatically sweeping her arm through the air. "But then I thought, 'If I can't take the Sword, then I'll simply take the warrior who wields it.'"

With that, she brought her right hand up, fingers curling into her palm. Nelsh found himself lifted into the air by the witch's magical hold, levitating with his feet off the ground. Similarly, the Sylvan Sword was brought up as well, hanging in suspension next to the entrapped Roamer.

"Go on, Nelsh. Show them."

His arms free to move on their own, the Human brought his hands to his shirt and lifted it up, revealing the Black Hand of Alura branded into his chest.

Nihak's longsword clattered to the ground with a mournful clang.

"No..."

The futile denial fell to the cold winds as the Fire Elf fell to his knees. He looked up at the witch as she let out a triumphant laugh.

"Oh, you foolish little elf!" she cackled, the other Roamers staring in defeat at their youngest companion. "You didn't think I gave you the location of the Sylvan Sword just to use in the coming war, did you?" Alura continued her gloating mirth. "I wanted the Goddess' Sword for myself, of course! I was going to take Sarra, since she was the obvious choice for wielding it and I already own her too, but then you picked up this lost little orphan. How could I resist corrupting such a perfectly naïve creature?"

As Alura snickered and giggled, the Roamers' gazes turned to the auburn-haired woman. Her falx too fell to the ground, the blade droning a sad echo as it settled in the dirt.

"Sarra...?" Aen asked, his voice trembling as he stepped towards her. "What is she talking about?"

Fighting back tears, she pulled the front of her shirt down to reveal the top section of Alura's mark, the fingers of the Black Hand plain to see against her pale flesh.

"She branded me her slave years ago... when we were in retreat from the Massacre of the Roamers... She made me watch as she took Nelsh and commanded I say nothing... And I obeyed because I'm weak..." she sobbed, falling to her knees, callused hands covering her face.

Aen hurried over to her, kneeling beside the crying woman, her shoulders bobbing hard. Danira rushed to Sarra as well, going down on her knees to embrace her, rocking the weeping warrior gently.

"You could have told us you were marked by the witch," Jolek stated, sighing as he tiredly sat, crossing his legs. "But you are not weak, Sarra. I know weakness when I see it."

"Yes, this is all so very touching. But I'll be taking my new Left Hand servant and the Sylvan Sword. You may all do what you will with that whimpering mess over there," Alura remarked, her tone bored.

She waved a hand in dismissal towards Sarra and turned to Nelsh, grinning once again. "Any last words to your dear companions?"

"Nihak... please don't let her take me!" the young Roamer cried, reaching for his friend.

"I'm sorry, Nelsh," the Fire Elf whispered, looking up at him. "Truly I am. But there is nothing I can do... Nothing any of us can do. Alura has branded you with her magic. You belong to her now. And through you, the Sylvan Sword. When next we see each other again, it will be on the battlefield, and we will cross blades for blood. I offer you these words: even entangled within her grip, twisting your mind to her will, your spirit is still your own and yours alone. Remember that."

"Nihak..." Nelsh pleaded, tears threatening to rise.

"He's quite right, dear," Alura stated. "You are mine. Now if you will all excuse me, I really must be going. I've other business elsewhere with King Jamiel, and I've got my new slave to break in. Good day, Roamers."

And with that, Alura pulled Nelsh and the Sylvan Sword to her form. White light consumed them, and then the blinding brilliance dispersed. Where the witch had stood with her prize, now there was nothing.

Nelsh was gone.

EPILOGUE

"I'm sorry."

The words hung in the air among the Roamers, a harsh cold wind whipping into their faces. Sarra's cloak flapped wildly as her apology seemed to go unanswered, her face still wet with tears. She had said it to them all, but mainly it had been directed towards Nihak. Their eyes were on him now as he knelt in the dirt, arms limp at his sides.

"I bear you no hate or anger, Sarra. Nor do you deserve blame for Alura's actions. The witch has control over you and she used you. That is all there is to it."

The Human took heed of the Fire Elf's words, nodding a little in understanding. Though she still frowned at how easily the evil sorceress had taken Nelsh from them.

"The quest has been in vain then," Aen stated more than asked. "We journeyed across Greenearth only to fail."

Nihak's hand slowly clenched into a tight fist before he reached down and grasped the hilt of his longsword. "No."

The Roamers turned to look upon the Fire Elf as he slowly rose to his feet. Just as slowly, the tip of his blade lifted up from the soil and was held high once more.

"We failed to keep the Sylvan Sword. As we have failed Nelsh too, but I will not abandon him to his fate. Nor will I sit by idly when this war begins."

"Nihak," Ejen said, laying a hand on his kin's shoulder. "We're at the far end of the country with winter bearing down upon us. Even if we somehow made it through the snows back to Sraztari, we've no Elemental Sword to aid our fight against King Jamiel."

"We've traveled in the deep snows before," the younger Fire Elf replied, sheathing his longsword.

"This isn't the same!" Ejen exclaimed.

"Jolek, Rom," Nihak called, quickstepping to the Earth Elves.

They waited silently for their companion to speak, knowing full well what he was going to suggest.

"I need you both to go back to the Ir'Afa Plains and see if your tribe and any others will stand by Malder's side."

257

"It will not be easy," Jolek replied, sharing a look with his giant counterpart.

"Nor will our elders be likely to offer such an alliance," Rom added, effortlessly lifting Jolek to his feet.

"But we will try," the Earth Elf said. "Even if our tribe alone helps, we will ride through the enemy's ranks like a blade cleaving meat."

"Aye. Aen, I need you and Myles to go the Selveryn Forest and ask Queen Ayewndre if she can lend any Forest Elves to our aid."

The Elvan and Odd Dwarf stared at Nihak, one frowning immensely while the other appeared mildly eager, respectively.

"First of all," Aen huffed, "neither of us speak Forelvish. And secondly, you should be the one on your knees before the Queen begging forgiveness for losing their Sword. I highly doubt she'll be so eager to send her elves to a war of men."

"I cannot face her, nor the elves in my shame," the Fire Elf admitted. "But I will make things right. Tell her I swear on my life I will undo what has been done. Will you tell her that for me?"

"You seem quite confident Myles and I will-"

"We'll do it for you, Nihak," the Odd Dwarf chimed in, patting Aen's back.

"I hate you," the old half-breed growled, his eyes narrowing as he glanced down at his short companion.

"Aen, we cannot leave the fate of this land to King Jamiel. Victory will not be an easy feat without allies, and the Forest Elves will want to help."

"If you say so," he sighed, shoving Myles into a sitting position.

Nihak gave a nod and turned to Sarra and Danira.

"And what task do you have appointed for us?" the witch demanded, venom seeping through her words.

"Go to Sraztari and tell the king we failed but we are not out of the fight. We will honor the alliance."

"An alliance you agreed to! Not us!" she snarled. "We became the Roamers to live free out here! Away from the laws of men and kings! Now suddenly you think we should pick a side in a war? A war unfinished because of us!"

"Malder is weak now! He is not the murderous king he once was! You saw him as well as I. A mangy beast with his younger years long gone. Jamiel's forces will run over this green country and turn it red with blood and decay!" Nihak shouted back, the two now staring each other down.

"So, you'd have the women act the part of messenger," she snorted in derision.

"If you can think of any other alliances, we can make on the way to Sraztari, I'd love to hear them! Or you can go to the Selveryn Forest while Aen and Myles can deliver the message."

"Bah!" she huffed, waving a hand as she turned away from him. "Sarra and I will go to Sraztari. I've grown tired of being in the company of elves."

Nihak ignored that stinging remark as Ejen approached him from behind.

"And what are we doing as this conflict looms?" he asked, folding his arms expectantly.

"We're going back to the homeland."

"The Ignis Sword? Nihak, there's no way we'll get that Blade from the Holy Mountain of Fire!" Ejen declared, pointing back east.

"We have to try. Only that Sword could match the Forest Blade now. It's our best chance at defeating King Jamiel and stopping Nelsh."

Ejen merely shook his head, sighing as he spun his scythe about before resting the butt of the shaft in the dirt.

"I knew you were mad before, but this is beyond madness. If we somehow get our Elemental Sword, I should be the one to wield it. My faith is stronger than yours."

The younger Fire Elf did not confirm nor deny that Ejen would indeed be the one to wield the Ignis Sword once they'd acquired it. If they even got that far.

"It's decided then," Jolek stated, slinging his warclub over his shoulder. "We'll journey back and go our separate ways when the time is right. We should all meet back at Sraztari, and may the Gods allow it before the spring thaw."

"Aye, we'll make it. We always do," Nihak said, starting to walk.

With that said, the Roamers gathered their arms and began their journey anew. With the cold rays of the sun now at their backs, they made their way east as snow began to drift down, dappling the land with pale frost. Howling winds rose up behind them, urging them onward to make haste back to the kingdoms of Humans. With their hearts resolved to their awaiting fate, the Roamers wandered ever forward, stepping through stinging ice and frozen stone to an unfinished fight twenty years ago. As the sun set behind them, the dark sky above was cast into angry flames, awash with glowing red embers; a sign of the blood to be shed and the all-consuming fires of war to come in the long days ahead.

ACKNOWLEDGEMENTS

Before I thank the countless others involved, one way or the other with this story, I must first thank A. Gabanski, who skillfully and masterfully created my cover art. Love you darling.

Now, of all my friends and family, two people have stuck with me through the years. With all our ups and downs, we came to be family. Thank you, Harry and Rob for enduring endless excerpt-readings and giving me endless amounts of much-needed feedback. You two are the siblings I never had.

My deepest thanks goes to Tina, Josh, and Devin for being the family I needed in my life. The saying "You can choose your friends, but you can't choose your family" has nothing on us. And Greg, I didn't go through three years of living with you in college just to forget your name in these acknowledgements. Thanks for everything, brother.

For my inspiration, three people come to mind that need my endless thanks. Nothing influenced my writing more than J.R.R. Tolkien and R.A. Salvatore with their wondrous tales. Enya, whose music carried me away to my own worlds of Fantasy and set my mind aglow with imagination. Thank you all for inspiring me to create what I saw in my mind's eye to share with the world. I would also like to thank my English Professors at Luther College. Your teachings guided me and helped me hone my writing in so many ways.

Thank you to my mother, who supported and encouraged me to pursue my dreams. To the rest of my blood-family, many thanks goes to my uncle Glenn, and my aunt Lori, the wisest woman I'll ever know.

And thank you to the countless peoples, both friend and stranger, who have given me words of encouragement, inspired me, helped me, or given me ideas for this novel. Everyone I have ever met has helped shape me and my writings in one way or another. I used to wear a shirt back in high school that said, "Careful, or you'll end up in my novel." I can't think of truer words to sum up this novel, so to that end, thank you everyone.

N. Gabanski

Special thanks goes to Kristi and the wonderful team at Dreaming Big Publications. You truly are an amazing woman, Kristi, and I couldn't have done this without you. Thank you again.

Made in the USA
Coppell, TX
09 October 2020